# Praise for *Darkside: Horror for the Next Millennium*

"A solid roster of horror writers and . . . more than 450 pages of original horror fiction, much of it powerful."

*—Omni*

"The contributor list reads like a Who's Who of Contemporary Horror Writers."

*—Lip Dink*

"Serves up one smart, biting story after another."

—Amazon.com (official review)

# THE DARKER SIDE

## GENERATIONS OF HORROR

Edited by John Pelan

A ROC BOOK

ROC
Published by New American Library, a division of
Penguin Putnam Inc., 375 Hudson Street,
New York, New York 10014, U.S.A.
Penguin Books Ltd, 80 Strand,
London WC2R 0RL, England
Penguin Books Australia Ltd, Ringwood,
Victoria, Australia
Penguin Books Canada Ltd, 10 Alcorn Avenue,
Toronto, Ontario, Canada M4V 3B2
Penguin Books (N.Z.) Ltd, 182–190 Wairau Road,
Auckland 10, New Zealand

Penguin Books Ltd, Registered Offices:
Harmondsworth, Middlesex, England

First published by Roc, an imprint of New American Library,
a division of Penguin Putnam Inc.

First Printing, May 2002
10   9   8   7   6   5   4   3   2   1

Copyright © John Pelan, 2002
All rights reserved

*Authors' copyrights for individual stories can be found on p. 387.*

Cover design by Ray Lundgren

RoC REGISTERED TRADEMARK—MARCA REGISTRADA

Printed in the United States of America

PUBLISHER'S NOTE
These are works of fiction. Names, characters, places, and incidents either are the product of the authors' imagination or are used fictitiously, and any resemblance to actual persons, living or dead, business establishments, events, or locales is entirely coincidental.

# CONTENTS

# DO YOU SEE WHAT
# I FEAR?

## *Edo van Belkom*

Things changed after they'd removed the tumor.

It had been about the size of a golf ball, sitting low in the back of her cerebrum near the cerebellum in the area of the brain that controls sight. She had complained of blurred vision and headaches for months before a CAT scan revealed that there was an abnormal growth between the hemispheres.

Although the problem had been identified, it took another month of tests and scans to determine that the tumor could be removed surgically. By that time it had grown to resemble a Titleist and had compressed the surrounding brain tissue together, pressing it down into the base of her skull. She blacked out often, saw double all the time, and spent the last few days before the surgery confined to her bed.

Then the tumor was removed and she was fine.

That was the word the doctor had used. *Fine*. Other doctors liked to use words like *full recovery*, *survival*, even *normal*. The reassuring words were supposed to make her grateful for what they'd done, but she didn't feel grateful. The tumor had been removed, the blackouts had stopped, and the blurred vision was gone, but she didn't feel much better.

She certainly didn't feel *normal*. Or even *fine*.

For one thing she could see more now. Not farther, or in the dark, or small things she couldn't make out before, but *more*. There were more colors in the world, areas of blue and green and orange floating on the air as if other realities had been laid

down on top of our own. She could see other people, too.
Faceless humanlike forms of gray and black moving silently
as shadows between the crowds at the mall, riding in the back-
seats of cars, and lingering out on the street in front of her
house.

That's where she saw the first one.

She'd been looking out her living room window late one
night and noticed several dark figures moving about on the
street in front of the house. They looked to be dressed in some
sort of formfitting black bodysuits that covered them like a
second skin. Their faces were obscured as well, but the eyes of
each were clearly visible, not so much as part of a face, but as
a pair of eyes set well back in the darkness.

There were four of the figures out on the street, moving
from curb to curb, seemingly pacing out distances, and pointing in different directions. They appeared to be concentrating
most of their attention on the tree across the street. It was an
ancient oak, with a gnarled trunk that had to be at least four
feet around. The tree's branches reached up to the sky and
towered over the surrounding houses like a mother's arms, but
the four dark figures seemed only interested in the trunk. They
measured up the trunk to about five feet, pointed to the base of
the tree, then moved their arms as if they had just witnessed a
traffic accident and were reenacting the collision, using their
hands to represent the vehicles involved.

She'd assumed they were some sort of special police unit
that investigated accidents or designed systems to help improve traffic flow. But, there hadn't been any recent accidents
on the street—and in fact, she couldn't remember an accident
ever occurring in front of her house. And if they were working
to improve traffic, why were they dressed in black? Road
workers wore bright colors and carried lights so they wouldn't
be run over by the traffic they were supposed to help keep
moving.

"Bill," she called, "can you come here a minute?"

Her husband got up from the living room couch and came
up behind her, putting a hand on her shoulder.

"What do you think they're doing?"

"Who?" asked Bill.

"Those men in black on the street," she said, as if she were pointing out the nose on his face.

"There's no one out there," he said. There was hesitation in his voice.

"Four men. Dressed in black. They're measuring things. That oak over there, and the curb."

Bill was silent a few moments. Then he gave her shoulder a gentle squeeze and said, "It's getting late, hon. Maybe we should get to bed."

"I'll be there in a minute," she said, twisting her shoulder away from Bill's grasp. "I want to see what they do."

Bill sighed, said, "Okay," and headed off to bed.

She remained at the window, watching the dark figures out on the street. When a city bus drove by, she instinctively shouted, "Look out!" only to see one of the figures get run over by the bus. She closed her eyes a moment, not wanting to see what had become of the man, but when she finally did open her eyes, the figure was still standing there in the middle of the street, looking as unconcerned about the passing cars as he had been about the bus.

"Good night, dear," called Bill from the bedroom.

She turned away from the window. "Good night." When she turned back around, the figures were gone, the street empty. Where did they go? she wondered. Or were they ever there?

She closed the curtains and headed off to bed, haunted by the image of the man seemingly run over by the bus, and chilled by her husband's inability to see what she could.

As she lay in bed, Bill snoring loudly by her side, she wondered if it had anything to do with the tumor. How could it not? The tumor had aged her, she thought. Stolen away the few good years she had left. She was a lot older now than she'd been at the start of her ordeal, and maybe, just maybe, she'd grown a bit more foolish, too. That thought seemed to allow her mind some peace and she managed to sleep well until morning.

\* \* \*

She was awakened abruptly by the sound of screeching rubber, twisting metal, and breaking glass. She ran from the bedroom to see what had happened and felt her body go numb the moment she reached the window.

There had been an accident on the street in front of the house. A green coupe traveling eastbound had struck a minivan traveling westbound, sending it careening to the right and directly into the oak tree across the street. There was steam coming from under the car's smashed hood and the woman driving the van was hanging limply out the open window, a pool of blood forming directly under her lacerated arm.

But that wasn't the worst of it.

The back door of the minivan had popped open on impact and a small child lay facedown in the middle of the street. There was a growing pool of blood beneath the child as well.

The next-door neighbor's dog was out inspecting the scene, sniffing at the child. It was about to begin lapping at the blood when a passing motorist stopped and jumped out of his car and scared it off. The man had a cell phone to his ear.

She hoped he had called 911.

She would have done it herself, but she didn't trust her trembling fingers to get the numbers right.

The position of the coupe and the minivan, the route they'd taken, and the trajectories they'd followed had all been carefully measured by the dark figures the night before. They had *mapped out* the crash scene *before* it had happened.

And she had seen them do it.

Bill came up from the basement then, still dressed in his bathrobe. "What happened?" he said before he got to the window. He pulled aside the curtain and gasped. "Oh my God, there's been an accident."

She shook her head. "It was no accident."

"Hello," said the police officer, tipping his hat politely as he stepped into the living room.

"Hello," she said.

"Your husband said you know something about the accident."

She hesitated a moment, then said, "It wasn't an accident."

The policeman's eyes got wider and his eyebrows arched slightly as if he were suddenly more interested in what she had to say. "Can you tell me about it?"

She nodded, then sighed. "Last night I came to the window here to have a look outside and I saw these figures moving about in front of the house. They were measuring things on the street in relation to the oak tree. This morning when I heard the crash and came to the window again, I saw the cars had crashed just like they had measured it out."

The police officer made notes in his book. "Do you remember what time this was?"

"Just after ten. My husband had a look out the window before he went to bed. He didn't see anything."

"How many men were there?"

"There were four of them, but I don't know if they were men or not. It was dark out and they were all dressed in black."

"Can you describe them?"

"They were dressed in black. All black, in skintight suits that covered their bodies, including their heads."

The policeman hesitated and his forehead wrinkled in confusion. "All black?"

"That's right."

"Anything else about them you remember? Any noticeable limps, distinctive facial features?"

"They had no faces."

"I don't understand."

"Their heads were all black, including their faces. All I could see were their eyes. But they were just like two lighter points on their faces. Nothing distinct about them at all."

At that point she noticed Bill standing at the edge of the living room, his arms crossed and his eyes inspecting the floor. How long he'd been there, she couldn't be sure.

"Anything else?" asked the policeman, the tone of his voice suggesting he had lost interest and was simply going through the motions.

"Yes," she said. "When a bus came by, it ran right over one

of them, but he didn't seem to notice. It was like . . . like the bus drove right *through* him."

The policeman sighed.

"My wife's recovering from an operation," said Bill. "They removed a tumor from her brain."

The policeman's face lit up again, but not like before. This time there was a look of pity on his face. "Well, thank you for your help, Mrs. Clarke."

She had to ask the question, even though she wasn't sure she wanted to know the answer. "You do believe me, don't you?"

The policeman smiled. "We'll be following up on all the leads we get today. Have a good day." He tipped his hat again, and was gone.

"Breakfast?" asked Bill.

She hadn't had another "vision" since the night before the crash and with each passing day, she was more able to dismiss the episode as simply a strange occurrence. Perhaps, as her husband had suggested, she'd been in desperate need of sleep, or she'd let her imagination run wild at the sight of a few oddly shaped shadows out on the street.

Whatever the reason, she was fine now. *Fine.* That was a word her husband, Bill, used a lot these days. "You'll be fine, dear," he'd say if she complained about a headache. Or, "Everything will be just fine after a nap," if she felt weak in the middle of the day. It was almost as if he thought the more he said the word, the more it would be true.

For the most part, it had worked. She'd all but forgotten the crash and had managed to convince Bill she was well enough to go shopping. She didn't need anything, and she doubted she'd even buy anything, but after being cooped up in the house, getting more rest than she knew what to do with, a trip to the mall seemed like just the thing to bring some cheer back into her life.

Bill seemed as eager as she was to get out of the house. He'd spend his time in the bookstore, flipping through picture books of old warbirds, and then they'd have coffee together while they sat on a bench and watched the world go by.

But that's not how it turned out.

She was coming out of Watch World, where she'd picked up a new band for Bill, when she noticed a young mother pushing a stroller down the concourse. The baby was dressed in pink and sucked on a bottle filled with juice. There were balloons tethered to the stroller that bounced and bobbed on the air a few feet behind them.

And a few feet behind the balloons was a figure dressed in black.

She immediately recognized it as one of the shadow men who'd been outside her home the night before the crash. She stopped where she stood and placed a hand over her open mouth in an attempt to stifle her scream, but to no avail. Her cry was sharp and shrill and people all around her, even those several stores away, all stopped to look at her.

The mother stopped, too, and as she looked around for the source of the scream, the shadow man began measuring the child in the stroller. He seemed to pick her up for a moment as if gauging her weight, and then he measured a spot on her throat.

She wanted to cry out again, chase the shadow man away from the child, warn the mother about what was going on, but she didn't. Couldn't. She was paralyzed with fear, as much for herself as for the child. What did this mean? Was it a gift, or a curse? Or had they removed part of her mind along with the tumor?

She looked again at the mother and child. The shadow man was gone now and they had resumed their walk down the concourse. Still, her knees felt weak, her hands trembled, and she needed to sit down. There was a bench ahead and to the right, next to the escalator. She hurried over to it, sat down, and began to cry.

People passed her slowly, looking at her with a mixture of curiosity and pity, but no one dared approach her.

At last there was a hand on her arm.

"What happened?" asked Bill.

She looked up at Bill. He looked more angry and disappointed than worried. She considered telling him about what she saw, about the shadow man and the little baby that was doomed, but she knew he wouldn't understand.

"Are you all right?" he asked, sliding onto the bench beside her.

"I'm fine," she said. "I just . . ." She paused, wondering, just what? She took a deep breath. "I just got sad for a moment, that's all. I'll be fine."

Bill smiled. He liked the sound of that word, *fine*. "Good," he said, giving her a wink. "Let's get some coffee."

They got up from the bench and headed for Starbucks.

It was two days later when she read about it in the paper. A child on the other side of town had been in her baby carrier out in the backyard while her mother hung out the laundry. The family dog had also been in the backyard. The dog was usually on a leash, but the mother had just been playing with it, so it was still running loose.

While the mother's back was turned, the dog got too close to the baby carrier. A neighbor, who had been digging in his garden and had witnessed the attack, said the dog had been sniffing the baby when the child's body jerked suddenly and a finger poked the dog in the eye. This appeared to enrage the dog, which grabbed the child by the neck and thrashed back and forth until the neck was broken and the child was dead.

She closed the newspaper, slid into bed, and wept for days.

The psychiatrist was Bill's idea.

He sat in his chair, legs crossed and a notebook on his knee. He looked at her through a pair of bifocals that sat low on his nose, giving her the impression that he thought her problems were beneath him.

She didn't have to lie down on the couch, but it made her feel better to do so. The couch itself was cold and uncomfortable, but when she lay all the way back, she couldn't see him looking down at her, and that more than made up for the slight discomfort.

He asked her all sorts of questions and she gave him all sorts of answers. Mostly she tried to explain the changes she'd experienced since the operation . . . her improved sight and all the new colors she was aware of. And of course, she told him about the shadows.

He seemed interested when she first began to explain what she had seen. He asked questions that at least suggested he believed her and she felt that he really wanted to know more about this strange phenomenon.

And then things went wrong.

"Is there any history of dementia in your family?"

"What?" she asked.

"Any dementia in your family? A relative, perhaps on your mother's side, or anyone in the extended family?"

"No." She shook her head.

"Did you have any imaginary playmates when you were a child?"

"No!" she said, trying to state the word firmly, but her trembling voice betrayed her. The faint hope that he might be able to help her was fading fast, leaking from her body like blood from a mortal wound, the empty space in her heart taken over by anguish and despair.

She tried not to cry, but she could not hold back the tears.

"Perhaps that's enough for today," he said, as if he fully expected her to return for another session.

"Thank you, Doctor," she said, almost out of breath.

"Get some rest," he said, patting her shoulder gently as if she were a child. "And I'll see you next time."

She told the secretary that in order to book another appointment she'd have to check her schedule when she got home. She never called the doctor's office when she got home, or ever. Bill knew enough not to mention doctors again.

She did her best to ignore the shadow figures after that, but the more she ventured out of the house to live at least a semblance of a normal life, the more chances she had to see *them* in action.

Like the police officer she'd come upon while out for a

morning walk. He was parked in his car, watching motorists stop at an intersection, and while he watched the cars go by, a shadow loomed over him. The black figure reached through the open window of his patrol car and prodded at his chest, first with an open hand, then with the stub of a finger. Dissatisfied by what it found over his chest, it began poking at the policeman's forehead, settling on a spot just above and between the eyes.

She knew what would happen to the young officer, and although her heart was breaking for him and his family, she did her best to look away and ignore what she was seeing. She also tried to avoid any news reports over the next few days, but she still heard about the policeman, who chanced upon a drug deal being conducted in the stairwell of an apartment building. The officer had been shot three times by the dealer, twice in the chest and once, fatally, in the head.

After that, she never went anywhere without Bill by her side. If he couldn't accompany her, then she didn't go out, which suited her fine because venturing out of the house seemed only to dare the shadow figures to cross her path. She would much rather stay home and watch television.

But soon even that provided little respite. She was watching a gardening show, when the host was suddenly surrounded by a group of shadow figures. The woman continued yammering about her roses while her skull and arms were being measured—most likely in advance of some grisly automobile accident, or the bludgeoning by a heavy object.

She turned off the television and cradled her head in her trembling hands.

"Are you all right?" asked Bill when he came into the room.

"I'm fine," she said. She said the word a lot these days, after learning it was just what Bill wanted to hear.

"Want to go to the park?"

The park, she thought. It sounded so peaceful. "Yes. That might be nice."

"I'll get your coat."

\*　　\*　　\*

It was a beautiful summer day. Families were out together and young couples walked hand in hand. For a while she was able to forget what she had seen, forget about it all.

But *they* wouldn't let her forget for long.

A young girl, no more than three years old, ran after a ball her mother had thrown to her and she had missed. The young girl caught up to the ball, tripped on it, and gently fell to the ground.

As she lay on the grass, a shadow figure emerged from behind a tree. It seemed to be interested in the girl's genitals, poking at them with black fingers, then working at that part of the child's body as if trying to pry her open.

"No!" she screamed, rising from the park bench and running toward the girl. "Leave her alone!"

The shadow figure continued to inspect the child for a moment, but then it looked up. . . .

Looked at her.

And for a moment, she knew that the gap had been bridged and a connection had been made between her world and theirs.

"Get away from her!" she cried, still running toward the child as fast as her aged legs would carry her. "Leave her alone!"

The shadow figure remained where it was, staring at her as if it wondered if this was really happening, or if it was merely coincidence.

When she reached the child's side, she began striking out at the shadow figure. Kicking and punching at it, even though her blows went right through its darkness.

At last the shadow figure rose, looked deeply in her eyes, and slowly faded from view.

She was left standing over the child, breathless. Bill and the child's mother were rushing toward where she stood. The world seemed to spin around her as if she were in the eye of a storm.

She heard Bill say, "I'm so sorry. . . . She's had a tumor and—"

And then everything went black.

\* \* \*

She awoke in a pale blue room. The sun was shining in through the window and the scent of antiseptic hung on the air like a pall.

Bill was asleep in a chair next to her, his breathing loud and regular.

There was no one else in the room.

But that soon changed.

The first one appeared at the window. The next came out from under the bed. The others all seemed to prefer the door.

They looked at her as if wondering what to do with her; then one of them stepped forward and reached for her. Its arms moved about her neck, then in an up-and-down motion, as if she might—

"Yes," she said, smiling broadly.

Of course, she would hang herself. How else would it end, this madness?

"Yes," she said, laughing. "Thank you."

Her laughter was loud and vibrant. She would be relieved of her burden. For the first time in weeks, she felt happy.

"What's wrong?" asked Bill, looking her over as if he might be able to do something to help.

"Nothing's wrong," she laughed. "I'm going to be *fine*."

# DEMON ME

## *Simon Clark*

When Jackie Vorliss saw the horse head that was as dark as death itself rise up behind her daughter, she wanted to cry out to Caitlin to run for her life.

Jackie held the mike in her hand, her thumb on the TALK button, watching her daughter on the closed-circuit TV screen. All around the teenager the deserted supermarket formed a gloomy cavern that swarmed with half-seen shadows, while air-conditioning fans sent unmouthed whispers murmuring and sighing across canyons of dead aisles to haunt those distant corners. Slowly, Caitlin moved along the aisle of a thousand grinning cereal packets toward cardboard cutouts that had become shadowy humped figures laced with menace.

Jackie tried again, but the scream couldn't force its way through her throat. Her vocal cords had knotted tight. She stopped breathing; her heart thudded with a doom-laden rhythm to slam inside her skull. *Run, Caitlin!* The words blazed inside her brain, but she could no more speak them than dig her hands into that cold grave soil and raise her husband from the dead.

On screen three, her daughter was in close-up. Her long hair was tied back in a neat pony; her eyes, catching what little light there was, looked as if they'd caught fire.

Screen six. The overhead cam high in the supermarket roof looked down as if through the eyes of a hovering vulture. There was Caitlin walking slowly. Behind her a pulpy shadow,

closing all the time. A dark horse's head rising above the tile
supermarket floor, something submarine breaking the surface
from whatever depths it called its lair.

Closer, closer

*Run, Caitlin!*

Formed from an uncanny postmortem darkness, that horse's
head bobbed eerily along the aisle . . . faster now, homing in
on the seventeen-year-old girl.

Close-up on camera two: head height. Caitlin, still unaware
of what stalked her, shivered as if cold fingers fumbled down
her spine. She folded her arms across her breasts.

*Caitlin, run!*

The horse's head rose higher, the neck arching, now suggesting something more cobra than mammal. Even the mane
looked more membrane than hair. Once more Jackie tried to
force the warning scream from her mouth, her eyes locked on
the dark shape that bore down on her daughter. Instead her
breath hissed though her lips:

*"I remember you. Good God, I remember you."*

"What's that you said, Jackie?" Ben looked round, speaking
through the pencil gripped between his teeth. "Has number
eighteen gone down again?"

"No, it's . . . nothing."

"Uh?" He glanced up from the technical manual to check
the screens, his broad forehead gleaming under a wispy fringe.
"Camera eighteen's the lemon if we've got one. I'll go down
and check it."

*"No, not yet!"*

He looked stung by her razor voice. "Okay. You're the boss,
Jackie."

She no longer heard him. Thumbing the mike button, she
said, "Caitlin. You might as well come back to the pod. We've
got glitches."

On six TV screens Jackie saw the blond head nod. Quickly
now, the pretty seventeen-year-old jogged along the aisle toward the office. Jackie immediately hit monitor keys firing up
cameras in her wake.

*Where are you? Where are you?* She searched the aisle behind Caitlin, hunting for the horse's head that moved with that churning motion. At the same time she listened for her daughter's feet on the stairwell, willing her to get through the pod door so they could shut—

*Shut it, be damned. Lock it tight. We'll barricade the door. We won't let that monster in. We'll—*

"Hey, Jackie." Ben whistled. "What the hell's that in aisle three?"

"Hurry it up, Caitlin." Jackie snapped the words into the mike and they rolled across the canyoned face of the supermarket like the word of God. On three monitors, one in distorted close-up, Caitlin glared up at the camera. *Yes, Mother dear. Any more orders, Mother dear?* The girl's scowl said it all.

Jackie shot a look back over her shoulder. "Ben? Where are you going?"

"Didn't you hear? I told you I was going to check out what's on aisle three." He watched her strangely now. "Do you feel okay, Jackie?"

She whipped her face back to the screens, scanning each one that Caitlin passed through either in dwarfish miniature or bloated giant.

"Jackie?"

Jackie glared at aisle after empty aisle. The horse's head shadow had vanished. Behind her the door opened. Caitlin entered with a flash of rebellion in her eye. "It's like an oven down there. I'm not going out again until I've had a Coke."

A melting sense of relief poured through Jackie. Taking a steadying breath, she said, "Ben, you said you saw something in aisle three. Where exactly?"

"Screen five. It's a ceiling cam. I can't make it out."

"Where? I don't see it?"

Jackie noticed Ben raise an eyebrow at Caitlin that as much said, *Why's your mother playing the super bitch today?* Then he added, "At the top near the intersection. It looks like someone lying on the floor."

Rolling the tennis-ball-sized camera remote, she zoomed in

on the thing that lay like a fallen corpse, its swollen head at the foot of a cereal stack.

"Aw, he gone and fallen over." Ben grinned.

"What is it?" Jackie's voice was brittle.

Ben's grin broadened. "Don't you see?"

"Would I ask you if I could?"

"It's only the Honey Bear cutout. I must have knocked it as I passed." Caitlin shook her head. "Jeez, Mom, what are you so uptight about?"

"Nothing. I'm all right."

Ben said, "Look, Jackie, you've been burning the midnight oil on this job for too long. Why don't we—"

"I'm fine."

"Take a look in the mirror, Jackie. Those bags under your eyes . . . we could carry groceries home in them."

Jackie knew Ben was trying to lighten the atmosphere with a joke. And maybe that was it. Maybe she was overtired. But this was the biggest contract yet. Everything must work; everything must be one hundred and one percent before the supermarket reopened.

Ben realized he'd penetrated her shell. "Let's call it a day. I'll fix us all a big cold salad while you unwind with a gin and tonic. Sound good to you?"

Jackie sighed. "It does sound good to me. In fact it sounds damn wonderful. Call security and get them to open the door." She touched icons on the computer screen that would activate the automatic system. Now any intruders (and any guards tempted to light finger a bottle of Scotch) would be caught on video. "Done," she announced. "Let's get some fresh air."

The pod exited directly into the supermarket parking lot. All part of the new thinking in security. To avoid "contamination" by supermarket employees, CCTV operatives sealed themselves in their sterile pod at the start of their shift and exited by a separate door at the end of it. No fraternization, no social intercourse, no colluding.

Jackie's business machine was fuelled by hi-octane paranoia—supermarket owners don't trust customers; supermarket managers don't trust their pilfering staff; and security guards on the day shift don't trust those on nights: So Jackie Vorliss wins a heiress's ransom to stanch that dollar bleed out.

Sun scoured the parking lot. Its new blacktop filled the air with tarry fumes so thick you could cut slices with a knife. Jackie's white BMW sat out there as lonely as a skull on a desert plain.

Ben and Caitlin flinched before the onslaught of summer heat. But at that moment Jackie felt a freezing sensation run up through her bones to the back of her neck. Suddenly she was no longer in the parking lot with her daughter and boyfriend. She was thirteen years old. Standing in the warehouse back in a cold northern town where winter gales from the lake cut like a blade. That was when she'd seen that sinister horse head before. It had risen from the floor, a mass of veined black with monstrous eyes. Seconds later Melody Tranter had burst against the warehouse wall. Coroner photographs record the rare butterfly pattern left there in luscious crimson daubs.

Yes, I remember you. . . . Jackie Vorliss walked in her own envelope of midwinter air on that blazing August day. She raised the image in her mind: the horse's head of shadows, Bible black, all veined, and somehow engorged with sinister promise. *Yes, I remember you.*

That evening Caitlin and Ben treated her like an invalid. Dressed in her bathrobe, Jackie was made to sit in the cool of the air-conditioned lounge while she sipped a gin and tonic over boulders of ice. She could smell the garlic they crushed for the salad dressing floating from the kitchen. Their voices came ghosting into the lounge, too.

Ben said: "I haven't seen her like this before."

Caitlin replied: "It's that supermarket job. It's gotten too big for her."

"She hasn't been sleeping well either."

"I'm worried, Ben. It's like she's not really here."

"If she's not any better in the morning, I'll get her to see a doctor."

"You mean you'll try. She's a walking, talking definition of stubborn."

Although Jackie heard them, it seemed it didn't relate to her and they were talking about a stranger. Meanwhile, her past had begun to exert its own gravitational pull, tugging her from the four-bedroom house with its serene pool lying in the grove of orange trees. In a strange, dislocated way she seemed to look down through the eyes of a hovering bird of prey. She saw the distinctive tiles that were the color of ripe cherries and the pink stucco walls. Good God, she was fiercely proud of that house. Once in a red heat of fury she'd chased a would-be housebreaker two blocks in her bathrobe. The police officer said it was a good thing she hadn't caught the intruder. She'd interpreted that as the thief might have harmed her, but Caitlin and Ben agreed it would have been the thief who was the one in real danger. They said it jokingly . . . well, half jokingly over breakfast the next day. The police did arrest one John T. Dardis. What's more, Jackie identified Dardis (age thirty-eight, former mailman, former school caretaker, former security guard) as the man climbing in through the kitchen window, and he did have fifteen previous convictions, but the police maintained that "the evidence was insufficient" and released him. But what happened later caused Ben to comment that perhaps there is divine retribution after all. Dardis wound up in six meaty hunks on a railroad track. Cause of death: multiple injuries as a result of being diced by a locomotive seemed obvious—only the railroad authorities insisted that no trains had run the night he died.

The past with all the dark gravity of a dead star drew her back through time. Her parents had moved here to Taunton when she was fourteen. It wasn't a smooth transition. She seemed unable to find her feet at the new school. The other girls gave her heat on her backwoods accent, her clothes, her clunky black shoes, and most damning of all, the spectacles she wore. Maybe kids are more forgiving now. But if you wore spectacles as a teen then, my God, you might as well have had a dirty great fish head growing out your forehead.

Her schoolwork suffered; to avoid taunts she skipped lessons, got grounded, and her parents lost patience with her. Life sucked. Three years later she was out of school in the great big shining world with no qualifications.

And with a coincidence she should have relished, she found herself working in the same supermarket where Vorliss Security Systems now installed a state-of-the-art CCTV system as part of a major store refit. Then plain old Jackie Burton worked in a refrigerated room, packing raw meat, with chicken grit crunching beneath her feet, and that cloying smell of carcasses rotting in her nostrils. She might have wrapped raw animal flesh in Clingfilm until her dying day if she hadn't married TV repairman Dave Vorliss. To pay for summer vacations, he moonlighted, setting up simple CCTV systems for homeowners so they could see who the hell it was ringing their doorbell late at night simply by hitting a button on their TV remote. Then came one of those life-changing moments. Jackie happened to hear that a local market gardener was going down the tubes because so many people were helping themselves to his produce. Jackie offered to install a CCTV system out in his fields on the understanding he only paid a fee when his profits returned. Rather than the three obsolete video cameras lashed to trees, maybe the signs—WARNING—CCTV PROTECTED: WE ALWAYS PROSECUTE. 38 CONVICTIONS THIS YEAR—were the most potent deterrent (along with the fictitious claim of thirty-eight convictions). People stopped eating the man's strawberries for free, Jackie and Dave got paid, and Vorliss Security got itself born.

As if fate must balance good and bad luck in your own personal ledger, so bad fortune followed. Dave drowned in a waterskiing accident eighteen months later. Waterskiing? Hell, if the security business hadn't earned so much cash he'd never have indulged in such a bourgeois pastime in the first place. Yin balanced yang; summer followed winter, both by season and in her heart, because then came wonderful luck. Jackie found she was pregnant by Dave. Eight months after she'd buried him Caitlin was born. Jackie didn't believe she could love another human being more. Above hands that bunched into marshmallow fists was a face that became a lens that drew the whole world back into beautiful focus again. And yet fate wouldn't allow everything to be perfect. When she tried to breast-feed Caitlin there was no milk flow. She wasn't dry, far from it, but for some reason she was expressing blood. Doctors "uhmed," then concluded it was "just one of those things." Maybe it was. Anyway, Caitlin prospered on dried baby milk. She was perfectly healthy. Yet when Caitlin had her yearly eye tests, Jackie would be physically sick with anxiety. *Don't let her have to wear spectacles; please, God, make her eyes perfect.* Jackie prayed her own daughter wouldn't have to endure the ordeal of teens spent in eyeglasses. She needn't have worried. Her daughter's eyesight was perfect; as was her figure. She swept effortlessly from healthy childhood into being a beautiful blond teenager who drove boys nuts.

With new responsibility came a new determination. Jackie didn't sell the business; instead, she won more ambitious contracts. Within a few years she fell in love with one of her employees, Ben Morris, a slightly built electronics engineer who had the knack of marrying closed-circuit cameras to elaborate computer systems. His digital imaging meant that, when you got the "do you recognize this man" on most-wanted programs, you weren't presented with a figure made entirely out of smoke rings that his own mother wouldn't recognize. Felons got caught.

Of course such a relationship was tricky; the firm's dozen employees now regarded Ben with a degree of suspicion. In the world of "Us and Them," he'd definitely managed to slip away to the "Them" camp. But he was popular enough to make it all work. Better still, Caitlin took to her new "stepdad."

Jackie woke to the sound of shouting. She found she was still on the sofa. The cocktail, with its ice melted and now fizzless tonic, sat on the table beside her. The faraway shouting rose in pitch.

She'd awoken with that "monkeys in my mouth taste," as her mother put it when sleeping out of synch in daytime. Even so, it wasn't far off midnight. Rubbing her neck she went to the window to look out into the night. Lights blazed through the orange grove. Someone was taking a midnight swim. If it was those damn kids from down the street again . . . She swung open the window. Instantly, hot summer air rolled back the cool atmosphere of the room. The heat filled her lungs like hot soup, making it hard to breathe.

Two figures splashed wildly. With the window open, their shouts sounded loud and excited. Jackie angled her head to find a clear view through the orange trees. Now she could see the block of turquoise radiance that was the pool. Caitlin and Ben swam races with one another; they were laughing like crazy and spray cascaded in pearly drops.

They swam neck and neck for the deep end. Jackie watched the horse head rear up behind them. It followed them with an undulating motion that once more smoothly morphed into something cobralike. Jackie's eyes, driven by pure terror, seized on the image of the thing swelling up from the water. For a moment she saw it in impossible close-up. There was that rippling mane that wavered between purple and black. Two blazing eyes. A muscular neck engorged with veins worming their way through a mass of postmortem darkness. It sped after the two in the water, eyes locked on them, a mouth forming beneath two flaring nostrils.

Jackie didn't even know she could move with such speed. Consciousness only caught up with her as she raced barefoot down through the orange grove, her robe fluttering behind her. She heard herself screaming over and over: *"Get out of the pool. For God's sake—get out!"*

The horse's head, a fulminating thing of purpling veins that shifted, writhed, and bunched like a pailful of eels lifted high out of the water ready to strike at its prey.

At her cry the two turned, but not before the huge, dark head slipped under the water to become a torpedolike shadow.

*"Don't you touch them! Leave them alone!"*

Both Caitlin and Ben spun round in the water, shocked by the ferocity of her voice.

"Get out of the water. Now!"

"We're only having a swim, Mom."

"Get out!"

It must have been something in her mother's tone. Caitlin looked downright scared. She swam for the side in three strokes and climbed out to stand there dripping beneath the electric lights.

Ben seemed more reluctant to leave the water, choosing instead the steps at the corner. Meanwhile, Jackie neared the pool's edge with all the trepidation of someone approaching an open tomb. Looking down, she saw a shadow race along the bottom to disappear into the far end, leaving a churning wake; water bubbled there like piranha milling round a hunk of flesh. A moment later she realized it was nothing more than the outflow from the filtration system.

At last she turned to Caitlin, who stood there, that scared expression still on her face. She'd crossed her arms across her naked breasts; a sodden garment hung from one hand.

"It's my bikini top," she said in a small voice. "There's something wrong with the catch. It came off in the water."

All three set off early in Jackie's car. Even though it was only a little after seven, the sun blazed down, raising heat phantoms that rippled the blacktop.

"Whatever happens," Jackie said, "we've got to make sure the system is working properly today. Pull this one off and we get the contract for the whole supermarket chain."

Ben smiled at her. "And what will it feel like to be a millionaire?"

She didn't smile back. "It will feel safe. That's what it will feel like."

"Are you sure you need me?" Caitlin asked from the backseat. "I said I might go downtown with Sue and Bethany this afternoon."

"It's all hands on deck, Caitlin. We need you to do a full walk-through today."

She pulled a face. "Great."

Ben explained: "There are still some blind spots. For this one we need one-hundred-percent coverage." He smiled. "Even the rest rooms. It's surprising where the truly determined can hide stolen goodies."

Ben kept up the determined smile and chatted about inconsequentialities. He pointed out a woman swilling dirt from the sidewalk outside a diner. "There's Rose." He waved. "Hi, Rose."

*Yeah, Rose Spencer. We were at school together.* The words sped with dark force through Jackie's mind. *She dumped my homework assignment down the can. On my fifteenth birthday she kicked my knee so hard it still aches when a north wind blows. Yes, I know you, Rose Spencer.*

"Whoa, slow down, Jackie. We haven't got a plane to catch." Ben still wore the tooth-revealing smile. In the rearview, Jackie saw her daughter bite that full bottom lip of hers. That, now, was a guilt thing. She remembered the awkward walk back from the pool last night with Caitlin's high nervous voice saying, "I don't know how my bikini came off. . . . It's got a faulty catch. . . . It never did fit properly anyway. . . ."

The security guard met them at the staff entrance. "Morning, Mrs. Vorliss. All the workmen are out; we're just waiting on the air-conditioner engineer to finish his—"

"Everyone must be out of the store before we begin—you do realize that?"

"I do, Mrs. Vorliss. But they've got problems. The damn thing keeps—"

Jackie drove to a parking bay before he finished speaking. She climbed out of the car into searing heat, which took her breath away.

The security guard called across. "The door-locking systems are a *bitch* as well," he said, emphasizing *bitch* as he looked at her. "Once you're in the store, the doors will lock automatically. You'll be in there three hours *minimum*."

Ben said, "We might need to come out to the car for more equipment."

"Then take everything you need now. I repeat: The doors

will lock on auto. There's no way I'm monkeying around with that locking system again doing manual overrides—our guys spent all night getting that thing to run smooth."

Ben grinned. "You'll let us out if there's a fire?"

"Pray that there isn't. That thing is a *bitch*."

"Dear God." Ben rubbed his bare arms. "That guy wasn't joking when he said the air-conditioning was screwed. Watch out for polar bears, you two."

They'd piled all the gear they needed into the staff lobby. Now the doors had been locked behind them, with the security guard flipping them a salute through a tiny barred window—a gesture that he managed to make somehow offensive. Within seconds of the door closing chilled air rolled down at them like an Arctic cold front. They walked to the security pod, grunting with discomfort, their exhaled breaths turning into balls of white vapor. Jackie felt her skin run to gooseflesh.

"Hell." Ben blew into his cupped hands. "This'll freeze the ketchup in the bottles. What on earth's gone wrong with the air-conditioning?"

"It's better than yesterday, anyway." Caitlin pouted. "It was boiling down here."

"Air-conditioning's not our problem," Jackie told them. "We're going to make sure our system's fully operational. We'll start with cameras thirty-two through thirty-six in the main grocery warehouse. And we need to check those concealed microphones again. We've got some dead areas."

Caitlin sighed, bored already. "I'll go stand by those rubber door things. You call over the PA when you want me to start walking."

"Walk faster today."

"Yes, Mother." *Shall I hop on one foot, Mother? Shall I sing for my supper, too?*

"Ben, you walk the aisle route, starting from the customer entrance right through to the main exit."

"I thought I was going to run through the camera check with you in the pod?"

"I can do that myself. This way's quicker."

"Aye, aye, boss."

Jackie walked quickly along the deserted aisles. Cans of food gleamed dully in the reduced lighting, a million dead eyes watching her pass, while the cereal packets grinned their monstrous fixed grins. Her breath came in frosty white puffs and in the distance she could hear Ben faintly whistling. A moment later she sat at the console, her eyes flicking across the six screens in front of her. Two screens held diamond-sharp head and torso shots of Caitlin and Ben where infrared sensors had locked mobile cams onto their body heat. The other screens revealed empty supermarket aisles, running in perfectly straight canyons. There was something unearthly about the place now; its bone-white walls encased this block of silent, chilled air in a dead embrace. Empty of shoppers, it had become some backwater of a ghost town. Seconds ran by. A pain started in the depths of her head like the tolling of a bell. Her hand hovered above the mike as she fought to hold back the moment of revelation that had been threatening to bloom inside her mind all night.

*. . . honest, Mom, the bikini top came off by accident . . .*

Ben stood there, his skin surrounded by a ghostly aura—an effect of the low-light camera lens—his face expressionless. Caitlin, however, shifted uneasily from one foot to the other.

Jackie pressed the PA TALK button. For a moment she didn't speak, content to let the sound of her breathing spread in a pulsing rasp through the cold body of the supermarket. Caitlin rubbed her arm anxiously.

At last: "All right, Caitlin? Ben? Start walking . . ."

She watched the screens. Her daughter and her lover moved out of one screen into the next, swelling, grossly magnified, revealing every individual eyebrow hair, or tiny acne scar. She noticed Ben had a cold sore forming on his bottom lip. Caitlin had dark rings beneath her makeup from one late night too many. Their eyes were glittery . . . unreal somehow.

"Walk to the left of the aisle, Ben," she instructed. "As close as you can."

Cold currents of air ran down Jackie's back like bone fingertips.

"Caitlin. Walk to the back of the warehouse."

Caitlin scowled at the camera directly above her. At this angle there was something waiflike about the face. "Mom . . ." The voice came thinly from one of the concealed mikes in the warehouse. "Mom. There are no lights at the back of the warehouse. I can't see a thing."

"I want you to do this for me, Caitlin."

"Mom, it's pitch-black down there."

"Caitlin, I need to test the nightscope lenses."

"I'll fall over something and break my damn neck."

"You won't. Put your hand out to your left; guide yourself using those crates. I'll tell you if I see anything on the floor that might trip you."

"Be sure you do."

"I will." The *I will* rolled like the voice of Jehovah through the tomb-cold air of the supermarket.

The TV screens were unblinking eyes. They gave Jackie unnaturally clear vision. She saw a rat dart toward her daughter's sandalled feet. *Sharp rat teeth crunch through that golden skin. Caitlin screaming, clawing at the unseen thing that bites her exposed legs in the darkness. . . .*

Jackie sensed a detachment. Air-conditioning fans murmured with the voices of lost spirits.

The rat scuttled beneath Caitlin's foot, then disappeared beneath the crates. Caitlin froze; she'd felt the flick of the rat tail against her ankle.

"What *was* that?"

"Nothing, Caitlin. Keep walking."

"But I can't see a thing, Mom . . . I'm . . ." The stuttering tug of her breath sounded loud over the speaker. "I'm frightened, Mom. I want to come out."

"Trust me."

"Jackie? Anything the matter?" Ben's voice sounded over the speaker, too. He'd only caught Jackie's half of the conversation, but he looked uneasy. "Jackie, you can hear me, can't you?"

She saw his face loom to fill screen one.

"Don't worry, everyone." Jackie's amplified voice rolled through lonely aisles. "It will be over soon."

Ben started speaking. "Jackie, I think we should—"

"Caitlin. Ben. Keep walking. Only stop when I tell you to stop."

They began to move quickly. *We want this done. We want out!* Their wide eyes said it all.

Screen six suddenly revealed the parking lot. Outside, the sun blazed on cars. The security guard sat in the shade, drinking a cold soda with the air-conditioning engineer. They could have been on the far side of the moon for all they could do to influence, or prevent, coming events.

Jackie heard the sound of her own respiration go out and into that cold void and haunt it there. The dark whisper of her inhale-exhale unsettled Caitlin and Ben. They looked up, eyes darting, as if they heard nightmare creatures whirling around their heads.

"Ben. Answer me this." Now huge and somehow monstrous, her voice pounded through the store. *"How long have you been sleeping with Caitlin?"*

His head jerked round with shock. "Jackie?" His voice came through the concealed security mike. "Never. Are you crazy? You know I—"

On screen five, Caitlin had frozen, too, white vapor spurting from her lips.

Ben recovered from the shock and in that no-nonsense way of his, he said, "Look, Jackie. This is ridiculous. We'll talk about it later. In the meantime, have you seen this?" He waved his hand back along the aisle. "The air-conditioning really is screwed. The place is filling up with fog." A white mist had formed at waist height. So thick, it actually hid his legs from the knees down. Jackie rolled the camera control ball under her palm, speeding through one camera after another—aisle level, ceiling cam, wall cam. He was right. Thick mist flowed in a milky stream, engulfing aisle after aisle.

"Eldritch or what?" she heard Ben say, trying to make a joke of it. The mist rose to his chest. Caitlin wasn't immune either. Tendrils of fog, eerily luminous through the low-light lens, reached between her legs to smoothly lace about her thighs.

Jackie felt the pull of the past again, taking her mind back.

*Shivering in a northern town. Thirteen years old. Frightened. Alone. In that old warehouse with holes in the roof that let in snow. "I warned you I'd find you, Jackie." Melody Tranter's face looms toward her. "I'm going to rip your stupid face off, Jackie Burton. No one tells on me. No one."*

*Then Melody Tranter flying back through the air with a scree-eech! To hit the wall—and her blood and brains and bile splashed out to leave a pattern of gorgeous butterfly wings.*

*Dave Vorliss on water skis paints a foaming vee down the center of the lake. Then the cell phone rings as Jackie watches her husband from the car. A voice breathes into the earpiece: "Jackie Vorliss. This is Rose Spencer . . . You should know that your husband has been screwing me for months. He says you won't give head. That's his* absolute *favorite. I do it for him every single day . . . yum . . . yum . . . yum."*

*The horse's head rises from the lake behind Dave. A pulpy tumor of darkness. He looks back as it strikes, slamming him into the water. It carries him down, holds him there, until he drowns.*

*The housebreaker runs down the railroad track. Something looms out of the night. At first he thinks it's a locomotive. Only this is eerily silent. He screams when he sees blazing eyes.*

Jackie's attention snapped back to the screens. It had come.

*Yes,* she thought. *I remember you. You are my avenging angel; you are my dark destroyer.* She understood now as all those repressed memories flooded her mind. That dark shape was as much part of her as her immune system. Activated by her hurt, it flew to her defense. *Take Ben. Yes. Take him now. . . .*

She watched Ben walking along the aisle that would lead to the pod. He was perhaps a hundred paces away. While, moving like a torpedo beneath the white blanket of mist, came the dark shape. Its lines hardened as it rose to the surface. A second later it emerged, a dark horse's head veined with purple. A mane fluttered, eyes blazed from the shadow face.

"Ben. Stand still . . . Ben, I need you to stand there."

He paused. Behind him the horse's head rose higher from the mist, and as it rose above him once more, it became that vengeful cobra shape, mouth opening, eyes blazing.

His pause only lasted a moment. Sensing that torpedo shape rush at him through the mist he glanced back—then he was running. A wild headlong run with his arms wheeling as if he swam through some spectral ocean.

He cannoned against the aisles. Cans spilled to the floor; sauce cartons exploded beneath his swinging arms as he tried to run faster.

"I want you to stand still, Ben," Jackie whispered, and the whisper ran in goblin sighs through the frigid air. "Stand still, Ben. Don't prolong it. Let it come to you."

He screamed, ran harder. Vapor spurted from his lips. The steps to the pod rose out of the mist forty paces away.

On the screen, Caitlin's eyes grew larger as she stared into the darkness. In that gloom she must have been all but blind, but she looked in the direction of the noise beyond the wall that separated her from the main part of the store. Her head tilted when she heard Ben's terrified yell.

*"Mom, stop!"*

Then from a concealed warehouse mike Jackie heard her daughter begin to murmur in a voice that sounded like a prayer: *"No, not him. Not Ben. Over him. Stride over him into the pod. Go over him into the pod. No, not him. Take her!"*

Jackie roared in anger. The horse head, fulminating with purple blooms beneath the dark skin, rose higher. Now it was just five paces behind Ben. It would strike now—surely it would strike. This—*her avenger, her dark destroyer*—kept rising. It flew up out of the mist. Jackie rolled the camera control beneath her palm. Six screens were instantly full of the monstrous head. Staring eyes blazed at her through the cameras. For a split second the ceiling cam flashed on something like a serpent that soared through the air above the supermarket aisles. Then she was looking into that monstrous, demonic face. It filled the screen, grew larger, lost the eyes from the edge of the monitor, leaving the mouth that yawned as a pit of darkness—wider, wider . . .

From the warehouse mike Jackie heard Caitlin for the last time. "Mother! I know it, too. I understand it. I'm sorry. . . ."

Jackie cried out as six TV screens burst into jets of shattered glass. She tried to throw herself back from the heads as they swarmed from the monitors. Six duplicate heads that were both cobra and horse, yet somehow neither, spurted out. Bible black. Slick. Purple veins running from blazing eyes to the root of their necks. Six heads lunged.

Each pair of jaws bit deep into her body to take a sixth of her. Then six pairs of jaws bearing six bloody hunks of meat withdrew to whatever abyss that was their domain.

Five years slipped by. Fate resolutely balanced the books. And as in every household Caitlin and Ben had their good luck and back luck. Business thrived, despite the freak accident with the CCTV monitor console that had exploded with such force it had reduced Jackie Vorliss to something less substantial than ground beef. Caitlin successfully sued the manufacturer in a multimillion-dollar negligence suit. The newly married couple moved to a ranch in the hills, where along came Eddie, a blue-eyed baby boy with a giggle that could make anyone laugh. He loved the horses they kept there. He'd watch them for hours. Fate dished out bad stuff, too. Eddie fell out of the stroller one day, bloodying his nose. Of course, Ben was mortified, telling Caitlin he'd taken their son to see the horses and only left him alone for a minute when he was distracted by a call on his cell phone. Caitlin tried to reassure Ben, but of course he insisted on strapping the baby into the back of the Mercedes and taking him to the hospital. No real damage, said the doctor. Then he gave Eddie a lollipop.

That fall Ben took Eddie (a consummate little walker now) for a stroll down through the red and gold trees to the lake. With the wind suddenly blowing cold Caitlin followed, carrying Eddie's hat with the droopy Goofy ears to keep his own ears warm.

She saw the pair through the trees.

Ben sounded angry. "Listen to me, stupid. Don't do that!" He lifted his hand above the little boy's head. Caitlin clenched her fists and as the horse's head rose from the shore, she hissed, "Come now. Take Ben now."

And that was the moment Ben screamed.

# SPIRITS OF THE FLESH

## *Seth Lindberg*

The studio I rent on the corner of Eighteenth and Mission has one real piece of furniture: a futon I pulled out of a Dumpster three months ago. Even though some foreign smell still lingers, that futon's the closest I come to a home. Even the rest of the tiny apartment feels somehow foreign to me.

I sit on that futon, waiting for the end.

Sometimes I think about this broken life of mine. The wasted talent. The layers of bold lies piled on self-deceptions that led to where I am now. All those needy eyes, in pain, in fear.

"I hear you work miracles," they'd say.

"Nothing of the sort," I'd lie with a smile. "Nothing of the sort." The street has a name for me: Doctor Death. To me, it sounds like some kind of cartoon supervillain, but I know to them it's just a job title. I performed a service to those who had no one else to turn to. For the right price, of course.

Sometimes I see one of the ones I helped out on the street. They'll turn their heads and they'll favor me with a thankful smile. It sickens me to the core, each time. I just can't stand those looks. It's unnerving.

It's been months since I stopped. Since I let everyone know not to come looking for me anymore. Months visualizing the relieved looks they couldn't help but have on their faces. Months spent hating myself and lying on this futon with a bottle of something cheap and the television filled with staticy channels of saccharine bullshit.

I guess I should have known that I'd kick off and start to get scared, eventually. I'm just not really suited for a real job; I wouldn't know where to start. I don't do government assistance, and I won't work in a McDonald's. Dr. Death does not serve fries.

But they find me. They always find me, the pathetic bastards. From the thugs who try to look flashy, to the bums on the street: They all know who I am.

I wake up in the early evening, exhausted and starving. I make it all the way down the stairs before the chest pains begin to root their way through me. I start to panic. I don't want to go to a hospital. Especially not General. If you're not insured, you die there. They just forget you in the E.R. or give you the wrong blood or mess up the tests. It's an awful way to go, alone in a hospital.

I'm too young, much too young to be getting a heart attack. It's them, the ones that I channel, that did this to me. They tore my body to hell healing the poor, fucked-up creatures I thought I was doing a favor for. The Spirits of the Flesh. They took root in mine, all right. If it's not my heart, it's the blood I piss, the phlegm in my lungs, or the bile that burns my throat.

So when those two club kids find me in the hallway under the lamp that never quite worked to begin with, I think, just this once. Just this once. I know it's wrong, but . . . I need the money for the hospital. Get the money to get worked up by a real doctor and walk out with your insides all fixed.

Forget about them. They don't matter. Don't think of what the Spirits do. Think of yourself, just this once. Because no one else will.

And by talking myself into it, I've just about talked myself out of it. But they're looking at me with these faces, and I know I'll do it anyway.

That's what I hate about being who I am. You see them all come up to you over and over again, all sad and frightened and they don't understand what's just happened. It's worst when they're young, before they have a clue about things like dying.

And they say: "I hear you work miracles." Of course.

I'd laugh, but the bile rises up and burns my throat and I start coughing like a maniac. When I'm done, I tell them I don't do that kind of thing anymore. Even though I know I'm going to.

One of them says, "You have to, just this once," and I'm thinking, yeah, just this once. Just for the doctor's visit. Fuck them, fuck these stupid kids. Do it for the visit. See if there's something the Spirits did to your heart, or if this is just natural. Just get checked out. But I tell them no. I'm not even sure why.

And the girl is crying, and the boy is going to get in my face, the way boys usually do. And I try to laugh, and end up coughing again.

I take over. I tell them not to get all weird on me. I ask them how long, and it hasn't been too long. Just this morning. And she was okay just before dawn. I ask them how. They tell me it's an O.D. I'm telling myself I'm not going to do this, even as I'm thinking, good. She's young like them; that'll make it easier.

Finally I hear myself rasp, "It's gonna cost you." Like I always did before, but now I really need the cash. They balk, and I turn to walk away. Like I always used to do.

In the end, they manage to get the money together. I think I would have been relieved if they somehow didn't, but they do. Club kids. They always got some trust fund or something. They live in the same Olympic-plus-size swimming pool of shit as the rest of us, but have those nice cash-inflated water wings to keep their noses above the surface.

I get to their place, even though I'm cursing myself for doing this to that poor corpse. It's not like I didn't do it maybe fifty times before. It's not like one more matters. The damage, as they say, has already been done. But it doesn't mean anything. Back then at least I was too naïve to care. I don't have that excuse now.

And it's not fair, and I've killed myself a thousand times for not knowing and sworn a thousand oaths that I'd never do this, never in a million fucking years would I ever . . . but here I am. Because, something inside me says, I need to be here. I need the money.

For the hospital. So I don't end up like these stupid fucks.

I need it for the hospital. It's not that I . . .

I need it for the hospital.

Goddamn it.

They lead me down a side street in the Mission, about four blocks from where I live. Right in crackwhore alley itself. We take our ginger steps up rotting stairs along the side of the house that needed paint about twenty years ago. The guy's trying to make conversation. The chick and I aren't biting.

Their flat is trashed. I'm betting it's always trashed. Band posters hang on the walls, some of them falling a bit over. There's a nice, if old, stereo in the living room. They could pawn it if they had to. I step over about seven cats. The place stinks of cigarettes and cat piss. It looks like people crashed out here in the living room. I'm guessing they all took off when they found out there was a body in the place.

People get that way.

The guy goes in the kitchen to smoke, which makes no sense because there's ashtrays littered about the living room. I go in to take a leak, knowing it'll hurt. When I get out, the chick silently leads me into one of the rooms. She doesn't need to tell me that's where the body's at.

The body in question's lying on the bed, facedown and sideways. She's dressed in a miniskirt and some fairly gaudy tights. Her silvery shirt's half off, not that it shows anything but a faded sunwheel tattoo. She's not a natural blonde.

"She's dead all right," I say. It's my idea of a joke.

The guy steps into the room, taking his cigarette out of his mouth. "We didn't touch her," he offers. Trying to be helpful. Always someone who wants to be helpful.

I'm thinking about the Spirits, though, so I just kind of look at him. I realize I'm shaking. I'm excited. I'm frightened. I'm more frightened than excited. I think I feel sick, and it's not just the bourbon I inhaled last night. I try to calm myself down, though. I don't want to freak out, and I don't want to throw up. The stomach acid'll kill my throat and I'll feel it all night long, and maybe tomorrow.

I croak out, "I need the money first." That's right. Think of the money. Just keep thinking about it until this is all over. Then you'll never have to do this again.

God, I don't want to do it. The thought makes me feel like I'm sinking into the carpet. They're too busy giving each other meaningful looks to notice, however. "All right," the guy says. "I'll be right back." He pops into the other room, and the chick and I follow, leaving the body behind us. She closes the door to keep the cats out.

"I'll have to sell all of my CDs, though," he says. I shrug. He's got a pile of them down one arm. He shows me one. "I have all of their stuff, the whole collection." I look at it. The music means nothing to me. Am I supposed to be impressed by his tastes? I don't say anything. After a moment, he says he'll be right back.

I go into the kitchen to get a glass of water. Not really knowing why, I take the nastiest-looking knife I can find, and put it in the pocket of my jacket.

The chick and I settle into chairs across from each other. Just us, the seven cats, and the body in the next room. She doesn't look at me, and neither one of us really says anything. After a few moments, a couple of cats start screaming at each other over something in the kitchen. I look at her, but she doesn't do anything, so neither do I.

She's cute in a waifish kind of way. I can tell she's not wearing a bra. If I was the kind of person who could get it up, I'd be a bit more appreciative. But I'm not. The Spirits took care of that.

I kind of blank out for a few moments and try not to think of them. When I open my eyes, I see she's all curled up and crying. I don't know what to say. I never did.

After a few moments, I lie and tell her we'll have her friend back soon. It seems to comfort her, the way lies usually do.

When the guy gets back, he gives me the money right off. I don't bother to count it. I can hardly think by then. I just really want to get out of there. I want to run. The chick looks at me like she can tell what I'm thinking, but she doesn't say anything at all.

The guy looks at the chick, then at me. "So what're you gonna do?" he asks. I just try to look mysterious, but I'm too tired to worry about whether it works.

Summoning the Spirits involves rite and ritual, the way you'd think such magic would work. It helps to throw in a bit extra, the usual trappings kids like these'd expect from sorcery. Give them their money's worth, I always say. I light lots of candles, and start my Enochian invocation, mulling over the phrases and pronunciation in my head while I set things up. The candles give off the scent of burning wax, and it feels refreshing to my nostrils.

I joke to them, "No, I'm not really a doctor." They don't bother to laugh.

I take a locket from her, saying it's something close to her heart. I clip off some pairings from her fingernails, and a lock of her hair. I burn the pairings and hair in the candles I've spread out, aware of the eyes of the two watching every move I make. I begin humming, darkly, perceiving that rhythm the Spirits have. That buzzing way of "breathing" of theirs, like some alternate form of communication.

I get their help in taking the clothes off the body. It's a pretty gruesome thing, even for the freshly dead. The chick loses her cool and goes into the other room to be with the cats. The guy and I turn the girl over. Her eyes are still open, along with her mouth. She has the stupidest expression in the world, even for a corpse. I shut her eyelids. I can't take that look.

I look at the guy. He has an expression like all he wants to do is take off, but he's too macho or fucked up or whatever to do that. I can sympathize, as long as he doesn't get in the way. I take the body's hands and lay them at its sides. I take a deep breath, then invoke the Spirits.

I can feel them pull and hesitantly touch through the insides of me. I might be twitching; I was doing that a lot toward the end. I clench my jaw and try to keep control. I can feel myself tense, not relaxing like I should be, but keeping taut and shivering. I feel a grace of a touch along my stomach, the broad patina of pain and tingling starting at my extremities. I open my eyes and look down at the corpse, though I'm not sure they're looking through my eyes yet.

The tingling washes through my body, and now my hands and feet are starting to feel heavy and cold. I spread my arms, splaying fingers out, accidentally knocking over a candle. Luckily it goes out. At least I think it does. I'm feeling oddly good. Alive. On fire in every nerve ending in my body, and yet impossibly cold. But alive.

I realize I'm crying. I realize I can't stop smiling. And I hear their eerie, birdlike voices.

*You hate us,* they say. I don't know if I hate them or not; they're entities or things that are beyond my realm of understanding. Beyond what we'd call our reality. How can you hate something with the rules of emotion when no other rule of Man applies to them?

*You hate us,* they repeat, with urgency.

I'm trying to think, I don't hate you, but you lied to me. You used me. You used me so completely.

*You agreed to everything,* they say. So calm. So fucking calm.

Helpless resignation overwhelms me. I did agree to everything. I loved it. I loved being scary and weird and frightening. I loved my reputation; I loved the free money. I loved living the lie that I was helping others with magic for whom modern science and society turned their backs upon.

*We love you,* they tell me. I bury my face into someone and clench my fists.

No, I think urgently. Don't lie.

*We couldn't tell you, you wouldn't comprehend,* they say. *It was best for them.*

I hold on. I'm crying and I know I shouldn't: It's the Spirits over me, trying to puppet my body to start the rite. But I'm the one who's in control, goddamn it. Goddamn it.

The Spirits are pleading with me, a wailing chorus only I can hear. I'm singing in that birdlike voice of theirs, controlling the noises that come through my mouth the way one can try to channel a river. I give in to them.

I place my hands on the body, and let the Spirits reach through my fingers to touch into the girl. I feel my body grow even colder than it was before. I feel the way her fingernails feel while they continue to grow, feel the muscles tensed with rigor mortis. Taste what she could taste, were her nerves alive.

I'm used to this, I think. I'm a professional. The Spirits are hard at work, caressing her body from the insides, traveling along her bones. They marvel at her impurities, the flaws, the mended bones, and scarred flesh. I hear their wonder, their childlike joy. I'm choking out their song, desperately sobbing with mucus trapped at the back of my throat. Please. Stay. In. Control.

Then along the endings, and across the framework of her brain. As the random neurons fire, I'm hearing her thoughts, memories, names running past.

This is the part I hate the most. Feeling a person's life flow through you unfiltered. You get everything all jumbled together, out of step with itself. The memories are so real they blur along with your own. They feel so right, as if it all happened to you somehow.

She's hearing her parents fighting; frightened, curious, she walks down the stairs. A train going thirty miles an hour leaves New York, while a train in Pennsylvania, two hundred miles away, leaves going forty-five miles an hour. Her first kiss. Lyrics to a song she hated but couldn't get out of her mind. Bad luck. Stealing candy when she was a preteen, getting caught.

Too much for me, like always. But this time, you have to be in control or you lose it completely. And don't let them know what you have.

She remembers feeling inconsolable after her breakup with Devon. She broke all of his pictures and sold away his books. She's worried about Raven. Raven's anorexic. *Keep control, Doc. Don't let her thoughts take over.* When she was sick once, she passed out and the lamp fell and burned the futon and it's amazing she woke up at all. She really didn't mind cats.

A picture of the guy's face, the macho guy who just sold his CDs to pay me. She'd just die if Raven found out. Sensation of having sex. *Stay in control, Doc. Stay in control!* She's not into it, but when you're coming down, the last thing you want to do is just sit there, and sex is good for passing the time.

*You bastards, you never told me what you did with them.* She wishes she was in love. She never tells anyone. It'd just be so easy to just fade away, but she's too chickenshit.

*What you do with the bodies.* She tried once, she got real sick on sleeping pills and vodka. But nobody went to look for her, not that she knew. She slept for two days pretty much, felt groggy for a week. Nobody needed to know.

I hate this the worst. I don't want to know. You shouldn't have to know. I keep getting all her thoughts. There's nothing I can do but wait.

She made a girl cry once in sixth grade by telling her she didn't have any friends. That look on her face. She just smiled. "You have no friends." People can be so evil. Even she can be so evil. The girl freaked out during assembly and everyone laughed. She laughed with them.

They're in her body now, but they haven't chosen yet. They're still eating her memories. It's disgusting. I can't let them know. Even though their attentions are distracted by the flood of memories, one could still be monitoring. One of them might catch on before it's too late. Keep thinking about her:

I can't believe Chuck lost the pipe. Don't worry, I'll show you what to do with it. You take a piece of tin foil and a ball-point pen. Now pound down the crystals a bit. *They should be able to read your thoughts, Doc, but they're too busy right now.* Put the lighter underneath to melt the crystals, then inhale the smoke through the pen. *When they materialize, but before they take over, that's the time.* Watch out. It gets too hot— *All of those bodies, you gave them all those bodies, and you hon-*

*estly thought you were doing good. You believed it all, every-thing they let you believe.* You bitch! You dropped the foil; there was still some left.

*Keep the knife in your hand, Doc. Don't think about the knife.*

And she just feels so very alone, but one time she got drunk and watched the sun set from the rooftop and it was the most beautiful thing in the world. She sat next to Ralph Conners in eighth grade. She ignored him, he ignored her. *Stay in control, stay in control.* We'll be right back after these important messages. Daddy's gone for a little while, but Mommy will always love you. *Don't back out now, not halfway through.*

But I could, though. Back out, complete the ritual with no one the wiser. Let everything run its course. Let the Lazarite beast rise in her body. Her friends might see her acting a little odd, but no doubt they'd just chalk it up to the trauma she went through. I've lost track of how many bodies the Spirits have inhabited through my mockery of a resurrection. What's one more?

I'm breaking, uncertain. But before I can think things through, the memories flood through me again.

She got the tattoo when she was eighteen. It didn't hurt as much as she thought it would.

It's an American Indian design for the sun. Just a design she liked. It looked tribal. She was into that kind of thing when she was dating Devon. Feel the infusion. She's crying. She's cutting herself. She's having sex again. She's feeling him inside her and it hurts and she hopes this is the right thing and— *ahhhh . . .*

I wouldn't let go of the knife. I kept cutting it into her and crying and screaming and clutching my throat, throwing away someone or something and stabbing again. I'm desperate, now. If I'm just a little bit too early or late this will all have been for nothing.

You have just a few seconds when the thing's weak. Seconds before, and it's still on the Other Side and you can't do a thing to it. Seconds later, it's taken over the body, eaten all the memories, and you can kill the body all you want, but it'll just fade off to whatever hell spawned it. I've learned this the hard way.

I hope I've timed it right. I know the Spirits won't give me a second chance.

She doesn't bleed, but there's blood everywhere and I feel like I can't breathe. I see just a bit of it. I take the knife and dig under the jawbone up through the mouth, hissing still in Enochian. I pull out the thing, like a tiny, impossibly thin and spiny slug, but more like white sheets of mucus set to life. Its form is burning my hands blackened and smoking. I can't feel a thing, but I can hear its scream shattering in my mind, mixed with a noise I realize is the girl's voice. The corpse cries out, gasping for air, its lifeless eyes open. The gash in its neck looks odd if only for the lack of blood.

Its newfound life will fade, I know. It has to.

*Shamsha'el, shamsha'el!* the Spirits cry out, confused. A name, maybe. The name of the one I murdered.

The birdlike song of the Spirits falters into a jarring cacophony. The cries descend on me, all bewilderment and confusion. I realize, as the calls turn into terrified wails, that these things have never experienced the death of one of their own. And for the first time, I feel pity for them.

When the pain begins, it's like nothing I've felt in my life. The cold waves come rippling through me, and coughing and twitching, I fall to the floor. I am told, half aware of the muffled, unintelligible voices around me, that I've been wicked. And I can feel in excruciating detail the Spirits of the Flesh rooting about in my body, tweaking, breaking, destroying.

My muscles are stretching my face into a smile that threatens to tear my face right off. But that's okay. It's what I'd have done anyway. I knew the consequences. Like the Spirits kept explaining: She was dead already, wasn't she?

My bones are expanding under my flesh, the way metal curls under intense heat. I can feel ligaments and tendons snap as my forearms twist and my hands go clawlike. The guy keeps looking at me: He doesn't understand. I'd tell him if my jaws worked.

But the Spirits are in my body now, letting me know the pain will only get worse, and they won't let me die for an awful long time.

I know this elation will end soon, and I'll beg and whine and plead with them for forgiveness, but for now I can feel good. For a hundred bodies I unwittingly gave to them, I made them pay at least once.

I lie on the ground; the pain lacing through my body is so immediate I can't think of anything else. I scream but nothing comes out. I hear myself gagging. I wait for the end.

I don't know how much time has passed. I'm aware of so little, now. Somewhere my eyes are seeing, my skin feels sensations. Some part of me breathes.

Through the pain I focus on that dim, blurry image. It's the kid, I think. He looks concerned. I hear voices, too, but I can't really make them out.

"—happened, then?"

". . . incantations wrong . . . look at my hands . . . too old . . ." My voice. My own voice. ". . . do it any longer. If only . . ." I can't make it out. Too dim, and too much of an effort to make sense of the words.

The pain is relentless, the feeling chills to the bone. I gather up my strength and focus on the words.

". . . teach me?" It's the boy's voice, tinged with desire. Lust for forbidden knowledge, I know it well.

". . . difficult . . . hard to master. The lang . . ." No. It can't be making me say this. *No!* ". . . in time, yes. With . . . bring back the dead with the Spirits of the Flesh."

I scream a thousand empty screams, but no one can hear. The pain increases. I try to twist but nothing happens. My mind collapses, helpless. Trapped in my own body.

I wait for death. I wait for the end. It will never come.

# THE MISFIT CHILD GROWS FAT ON DESPAIR

## *Tom Piccirilli*

Fate arrives disguised as choice.

As if you could actually say, *Screw this, I'm out of here,* or just get down on your knees like everybody else.

But John's got to shrug and go, "Hmmm." He knows that even here at the end of the line, holding his pitiful check for $188.92—boss took out $40 for the broken dishes even though he was the one who slopped soapy water onto the kitchen floor—watching the teller tremble with the eleven-gauge in her face, standing behind some weight lifter with muscles coming out his asshole and piss pooling over his shoes, and despite what he knows is going to happen after this, John realizes Mr. Teddy Bear has got to be eaten.

Teddy doesn't like how slow the terrified twenty-year-old teller is moving and continues shrieking at her, "Move it. Hurry, goddamn you, hurry! I saw that! You put a dye pack in there? Did you?"

Of course, she hasn't; she can't even move or speak, hyperventilating like that. She's too much a daughter of television and can't do anything much besides keep her arms straight up over her head and pray to Christ in Spanish. The gray stretch marks on her underarms clearly mark how much weight she's gained and lost after her first couple of kids, but her pouty full lips are especially sexy now, the lower one quivering with the name of Jesus.

Teddy's rubber bear mask doesn't fit him all that well. His

beard is so thick that the mask won't rest flush against the steep angles and planes of his contorted face. It lifts an inch or more whenever he speaks, which allows the sweat that's been puddling in the curves and hollows of the rubber to drip out all at once. Spittle works its way out of the thin mouth slit. Ted tries to wipe his eyes clear, the back of his hand mopping the bulging dry forehead of the growling bear head.

Teddy's partner, Mr. Lucifer, might hold things together for another minute or two—if only his easy, muted voice can settle the situation long enough to soothe Teddy and the frantic teller. He's got to get the other cowering folks in the bank to follow his orders, lay down on their bellies, hit no silent alarms, and just face the walls.

"Ladies and gentleman, hush please." The devil repeats himself twice more, and a respectful amount of Southern flavor seeps out of his hanging cadence, friendly and mannered like he might be talking to a group at a church social. His red mask has curved horns, a wide smile, and pencil-thin mustache. The voice matches it perfectly.

"Gentleman and sweet ladies, if you'll let us get on with this, we'll be gone in no time a'tall. This here is government money we're taking, not yours. We're workingmen, too. Now just lay back and relax, and we'll all be on with our day before you know it."

"It's a dye pack. I saw it!" Teddy shrieks, hitting a high note that rings around the small enclosed room, picking up speed. "There! There it is!"

John is the only bank patron still on his feet, but the smash-and-grab thieves haven't noticed him standing there yet, as two old women and the weight lifter sob against the floorboards. John is a prime three hundred eighty-four pounds of graceful obesity and dire energy, almost as wide as he is tall (about five seven), dressed entirely in black: well-ironed jeans, a fine button-up, long-sleeve shirt and tie, standing so near the lacquered bank slip table in the center of the place that he appears to be a part of it. He is as immutable and immobile as obsidian.

His arms hang loosely at his sides, his massive hands open for when he has to hug the dead to him.

Teddy Bear isn't having any of it though, still screaming and finally realizing the teller's already out of her head, her voice rising and begging the Mother of God to save her. Those heaving, swaying breasts are doing things to Teddy, who prods one tit with the barrel of the shotgun. Without benefit of a bra, it jiggles for a while before finally settling.

Mr. Lucifer is about to say something else, but it's already too late, all the choices have been made. There's only one way out now as Teddy pokes the girl's other breast and she lets loose with a screech. The slobber pumps freely from his mouth slit, as he gives a braying laugh and pulls the trigger.

No one ever gets used to the hypnotic sight of flesh and fluid applied to an area where it shouldn't be. Everybody in the bank lifts his head and watches as her lower jaw alters into cherry gel rushing across her chest and the cash drawer in one violent splash. The corpse wheels completely around on its toes, revolving one and a half times in a pirouette, before taking a final awkward step and pitching forward.

Most of her teeth are somehow intact, though, and a handful of them do a slow slide across the floor until they stop just outside the growing circle of the weight lifter's piss. John can't help himself as her ghost floats past him, still praying as her breasts finish bouncing, adrift and being reeled towards an aurora of seething golden light that hovers and opens just over her body's left shoulder.

His enormous hand flashes out and he eats her.

The bank manager has seen this sort of thing before, and he enjoys murder. He's done in one ex-wife already and is getting ready to do in another. He hides his smile well, but not in so dark or carefully guarded a space that John can't see it.

The weight lifter is sort of thrashing around on the ground, his muscles so taut that it looks as if he might snap in seven places before this is all over. A security guard stands there with his gun in its holster and his hands straight out in front of him, wrists twirling, ass angled to one side like he's at a disco doing the bump and having a pretty good time. A few people continue to moan and murmur, so far down on the floor that they're licking it.

The dead teller is already inside John, and he can feel her settling into Gethsemane Hills, her arms still over her head and standing beside Manfred Filkes, the mailman who'd died from an aneurysm walking up John's driveway six years ago. Filkes is digging the look of the frightened teller, who sways on her feet as she touches down in the middle of Juniper Boulevard. Filkes had been a pedophile, his mail cart full of illegal photos and magazines that would have sent him away for twenty-five years if only his brain hadn't burst. His madness is palpable and unshifting, the primeval energy of hate and lust rising from him like heat from a brick oven.

Filkes goes after her, even though she's well out of his preferred age range. He manages to get one of his pale hands on her throat before John can get the thin John, the true John, down among the ghosts to slap the shit out of Filkes all the way across the cypress-lined street. Filkes can't get rid of his mindful of baby rot even now, and cowers and sobs as he goes ass backwards over a plastic flamingo planted on a well-groomed lawn.

The dead teller, whose name is Juanita Perez, is too shocked to cry anymore, staring through her fingers at the true John, muttering passages out of the Bible, but getting a lot of the words wrong. Almost everybody does. He whispers and tries to comfort her, saying, "It will be all right, Juanita. Be calm. I won't let anybody hurt you here."

This place is no different from anywhere else in the world, the John inside himself tries to explain, and he's right. When Juanita can finally move again, holding a palm to her bruised breast and glancing over at Filkes sitting on the curb, who's bleeding heavily from his broken nose, she discovers large signs looming above her in the starlight.

This is the town of Gethsemane Hills, population now 1,604, including thin John, who comes and goes, but is always on hand to keep things from spiraling too far out of control. About six square blocks of suburbia, where people occasionally still say hello to you on the street.

There are no hills, but the name is the only one this home-town could have. There is power in names. It is a perpetual twilight of coiling shadows, violet-drenched dusk, and a blood-soaked sun, always with a gleeful moon glowing. Streetlights take the form of the gaslit globes of nineteenth-century London. There is no smog, but there's a smoggy feel. The yards are flawlessly landscaped, flower beds weeded and fertilized, gardens tilled, rooftops all recently reshingled, the dogs well fed. John takes great pride in the place and does all the work himself.

Indistinct, silent people sit on their stoops and front porches, watching Juanita closely. A few insubstantial shapes rise and begin to make clumsy eager gestures, stopping and starting and abruptly stopping again. These are the ambiguous move-ments of the uncertain, who see no reason to act but are pro-pelled by memories of action. There is some laughter though, as well as angry men's giggling, and a few whispered en-treaties.

A hand flashes out, silhouetted in the always failing sun-light—the fingers are crooked, the hand little more than a claw, damaged by arthritis, tension, or heaving doubt. Juanita whirls, gazing around at the rows of dimly lit duplicate houses, each of the similar staggering shadows weaving a bit, forward and back. They are waving to her, and then they recede. Doors are closed quietly—locks are thrown, televisions squawk, and children are tapping at upstairs windows, begging to be let out.

Mr. Lucifer scans the bank one more time, finally noticing John standing there in the middle of the room. He shakes his head because he can't figure out how the hell he'd missed the fat guy in the first place. The devil points his nickel-plated .38 and says, "Excuse me, sir."

"Be quiet," John tells him, "or I will eat you."

"Pardon me?"

"Shh."

"Hey, now, we'll have none of that. You might have some trouble doing squat thrusts, but even a fella your size ought to be able to get down on the ground when he's told."

Teddy Bear doesn't look up. He's intent on getting the other

cashiers to empty the banded stacks of cash into his oversized
rucksack. Juanita's corpse propels them on so that everybody
is really moving now, shoveling money like crazy. Rolls of
change fall and break open, so Ted stomps on rolling coins and
picks them up. John sees everything that needs to occur actually happening in about eight seconds. If he had a stopwatch
he would click it . . . now. The arching, wavering lines of
chance and force of will solidifying into a pattern he can put to
use.

He takes a step sideways as thin John, the true John weaves
and thinks of ushering the lovely Juanita to bed. His heart is
hammering and the flush of ticklish heat is flooding his groin.
His breathing begins to speed up and a light sheen of cold
sweat forms on his upper lip.

Her house is already picked out at the end of the block: a
one-story cottage with a bouquet of freshly plucked forget-me-
nots already in a vase on the dining room table. Photos of her
kids are framed on the mantel, and their crayon drawings are
held in place by magnets and exhibited on the refrigerator
door. He's filled a bookshelf with some of the greatest vol-
umes of poetry and classic literature. He'll teach her metaphor
and symbolism and the definition of subtle underpinning. A
single white rose lies across the pillow of her queen-sized bed.
The vanity is laden with lace undergarments, stockings, and
garter belts. There are condoms in the nightstand drawer,
along with several different brands of spermicide and tubes of
lubrication. He likes the way her rack bobbles.

Juggling some change, Mr. Teddy Bear steps over Juanita's
lower jaw, still expecting to find dye packs everywhere. His
eyes are flitting like mad, his eyelashes swiping against the
rubber loudly. He spots Lucifer's .38 and follows where it's
pointing until he spots John calmly standing before them.
Somehow the bear mask manages to contort. "Get on your
knees!"

"I don't do that," John tells him.

A large splash of sweat falls out from the mask and threads
through Teddy Bear's beard. "You don't . . . ?"

"No. Never. Not for anyone."

"You grotesque fat piece of shit freak!"

John is lissome and quick without ever showing his speed, even while he's in motion. It's funny and impressive to see him bringing it on. He reaches into his gully-deep pocket and draws out his nail clipper, carefully stepping around the weight lifter's yellow zone of urine. Ted has been holding the shotgun crooked in his arm for so long that as he turns, he wavers and spins two or three inches too far the other way, and John is already reaching.

The devil politely says, "Hey, now . . ."

The timing is impeccable, as if John had seen this happen many times before, perhaps in a recurring dream. Ted has to correct himself and bring the shotgun back again, as if to take John in his tremendous stomach.

The bank manager is hoping for more viscera and mayhem; maybe the loan department supervisor he's been banging will get it in the head next. In his mind, he runs scenes of bloody ballets, old women being blown upwards onto their tiptoes, hoisted through the air eight or ten feet, and splattering across his desk. He's getting jittery just thinking about it.

But John has already slid inside Mr. Teddy Bear's space, too close now for Ted to do anything but growl.

The security guard lets out the squeaky yip of a toy poodle because he understands this is the moment of finality. So does everyone else, even those not looking, breathing dirt in the corners beneath the teller windows.

John grabs the barrel and pushes it aside, carefully aiming it toward Mr. Lucifer. His other hand rises, holding the nail clipper, going up and inside for Teddy's throat. If Ted hadn't been so pumped during the robbery, his arteries and major veins wouldn't now be so thick and pulsing. It would've been a lot more difficult for John to lunge in there and clip Teddy's jugular.

The pain does what it's expected to do. In his agony and panic, the arterial spray spritzing the bank counter and showering Plexiglas, Ted yanks hard on the trigger and blows off the greater percentage of Mr. Lucifer's face.

One long line of blood spurts across John's shirt before he

can move Teddy Bear's head far enough to one side so Ted's spraying throat only paints the checking account brochures and tray of free pens with the bank's name on them.

The blackness of his shirt and tie is so complete and wet with sweat that the blood doesn't stand out at all. This is also how it should be. He opens both his immense hands wide hoping to catch Mr. Lucifer's soul, but despite the fact that the devil's got considerably less face than the dead Juanita Perez, Lucifer lives on. Thick colorful fluids bubble up as his esophagus gurgles wildly to clear a path to air.

The bank manager is in such a state of arousal that he nearly passes out from the force of his orgasm. He can't wait to get home and murder his wife.

John hisses in expectation, hands clenching and unclenching, but Lucifer isn't about to let go. There's only one eye left in the sparse wedge of his face, and who knows if it can see anything. But it peers at John, gazing sullenly and all the while still blinking.

Teddy, however, is waning fast. He coughs and tries to lean back away from the counter, but John holds him there against the nice marble tile so that no more of the slackening slurp of blood gets on his clothes. Ted's heart gives three final hesitant beats before giving out.

The aurora of roiling power opens again, dragging at Mr. Teddy Bear's soul, but John's enormous arms snatch the floating Ted out of the air and haul him from the draw of the raging eddy. John can't help but give a smirk. From that golden light ushers the voice of a wounded man who suffered and offered what he could before the eyes of the world, and now rages with all the condemnation he can, claiming, *"You are not the way."*

John laughs as he always does, watching the maelstrom dissipate and diminish, because the voice is his own, but full of contrition and fear.

Mr. Teddy Bear touches down in Gethsemane Hills and doesn't take off his mask. He stares wide-eyed through the tiny slits and groans, "Oh, oh my, oh my sweet Jesus on the cross, take me home." His voice, when not incensed by frustration and cocaine, is soft and almost melodious.

Juanita Perez takes a step toward Ted because her murderer is now the only connection she has left to the lost world of the living. The sign above them is covered in a blur of black motion and soon reads POPULATION 1,605. The house across the street has an open front door.

Thin John, the true John says, "You're home," and shoves Ted toward the house. First he's got to pass some guy on the curb with a broken nose. He looks sort of familiar, like Mr. Filkes, the son-of-a-bitch mailman who sodomized Teddy when he was eight. He's still got teeth-mark scars on his shoulders and thighs.

Inside there's half a key of Coke already laid out in lines on the dining room table. His favorite video, *Scarface*, is in the VCR, and the television has Surroundsound, two motherfucking-huge speakers attached, and two others on either end of the couch. Teddy doesn't know what to do and tries even harder to hide under his mask, going a little more insane.

John eyes Juanita Perez, licking his lips. The nerve endings in his fingertips are igniting. Some of that K-Y jelly is cherry flavored, and her ass has a very nice slope to it. He smiles and takes her wrist, leading her to the new house.

When Juanita begins to struggle, he wraps his bony fingers in her hair and drags her down the block. Her mind not quite numb enough to let her pass out and fade from this awful endless twilight of corrupted colors. She starts to sob and works up to a scream, even while John's ripping her clothes off, leaving the rags draped across the perfectly trimmed hedges, the blooming azaleas.

Kids are banging on their windows, watching, excited and sick. Juanita's front door shuts and the whole neighborhood can hear laughter and squealing prayers for hours to come, with the revolting odor of cherries on the wind. They turn up their television sets and air conditioners.

John gains a full two-and-a-half pounds and goes up to the counter, slipping his check into the small deposit slot. Mr. Lucifer is still crawling and gagging on the floor, staring at John with his one eye and trying to back away.

John toes Juanita's teeth aside. The horrified cashier stares through the Plexiglas at him as he continues to click the nail clippers.

"Cash this," he tells her.

He is filled to bursting with the juice of despair and wants to buy himself a whore tonight.

# PULL

## Brian Hodge

It's like this: I guess we each grew up taking for granted that all we had to do was hang out on the corners and the stoops in our neighborhood, and day by day, year after year, the whole world would come to us a little at a time. Why shouldn't it, what with our twelve square blocks being the center of the universe and all?

You know us. Not to imply you could point at us and call us by name, or that you've even laid eyes on us before. But you've still seen us, somewhere. And if you were to ever spot us in our element, well, then you'd just *know*.

See, we're the guys who never had enough sense to know when to go inside, or anywhere else for that matter, and do something more with our lives. So we never did. We're the guys who laughed and bullshitted our way through school and came out with nothing but shit jobs to look forward to. But that's okay. Because we're the guys who grew up convinced there was no good reason why life had to be any more complicated than knowing how to get over on the next woman to bring a boner to our pants, and how to convince Davey why he should again be the one to run down to the liquor store for another six-pack while we were waiting.

And waiting for what, you might ask? Enough with hard questions already. There's one I'm still working on: *Twenty-seven years old and how did I get here?* You wouldn't think an answer would be that hard to come up with. And really, it's not. *There was never any* here *to get to because there was never any other* there *to come from. Meaning I just never budged.* You'd think there should be more to it than that. But there isn't.

Thing is, it never occurs to you to ask yourself questions like that until you're forced to. Something comes along and gives you no choice, just comes along and slams you against the wall like a cop rousting you for whatever, gets in your face and won't let the issue die. When all you'd rather be doing is sitting there with the sun on your face and the bricks under your ass, with a can in your hand and another waiting in the ringer.

For me, that something was Tommy coming back to the neighborhood.

Which came as a surprise. Nobody was expecting it, or nobody except what was left of his family, but they had their hands full with his grandmother dying, the reason he came in the first place—to pitch in, take a turn sitting with her for a few hours, help feed her when she felt like eating, or scrape out the dish after she didn't. You have to admire a family that sets a room aside for a thing like that instead of taking the old lady to a nursing home where dying is a way of everyday life. You get the idea it doesn't happen like this much anymore, that the neighborhood is one of the last holdouts where an old woman with a bad heart and bad lungs can die at home, with familiar wallpaper.

Tommy had been back half a week before anybody knew it, and then here he comes down the sidewalk and it's like seeing a ghost, just about, someone you were halfway to forgetting had ever been alive. I was about to say like someone from a different life, but just look around—it's the same old life as it always was. How else would you think Tommy knew right where to find us?

A shock to the system is what it was.

Because it was a late afternoon and business as usual, with the summer sun beating down on us as we followed the shade, and Artie, he was telling us all about something that happened that morning at work. The both of us, we work in the warehouse for this big furniture store, driving trucks and hauling people's new couches and dressers up sixteen flights of stairs for not much more than a thank-you, if that. Except Artie's telling us how this morning he delivered a bed, and the other guy he went on the run with ducked out soon as he could, to head for the coffee shop down the street, and according to Artie it really worked out to his advantage because once the bed was in place the woman gives him a look and asks him to try it out with her. And she's a fine-looking thing, too, he says, one of those squeaky clean, well-trimmed quiffs that just have to be a stockbroker, and Artie's big Dow Jones was on the rise. He actually said that.

Not a word of which we believed. But so what. Because even if we had no choice but to hoot and call Artie a liar right to his face, deep down we wanted to believe it could happen just the way he said. And who knows, maybe it really had. Stranger things, you know.

We were still debating it when here comes Tommy.

At first you don't believe your eyes—here's this guy again after all these years. Ten or so, had to be. I don't remember as any of us had seen him since he moved a year before we graduated high school. Next thing you know, here he is again, and it's like no time at all has gone by, and a part of you is wondering did he ever leave, with another part wondering did we ever know him in the first place?

We swarmed him, ganged him four on one, hugging him and slapping his back, and Davey went digging in the plastic bucket so he could pop Tommy a cold one, and we all cheered and toasted his return, because at the moment none of us knew the reason he'd come, and we wiped our mouths. Then Angelo got a scowl on his face and whacked Tommy on the shoulder, halfway in fun but maybe more than halfway really meaning it, and he said, "Hey, you moved away owing me twenty dollars, you fuck."

"Now I *know* I'm in the right place," Tommy said. "For a minute I wasn't sure." He went for his wallet, flipping through the green when Angelo told him to stop it, stop, he was only kidding. But I'm pretty sure everybody could tell that he hadn't been. Really, ten years and he remembers a thing like that right off, makes it the first thing out of his mouth, just about—it's a sore spot, all right.

Tommy reached across and stuffed a folded twenty in the little dinky pocket of Angelo's tight knit shirt, then thought for a second and followed it with another ten, saying, "Interest."

Angelo was arguing, not a bit happy about this, but then he was never what you could call happy about much of anything; it was just different degrees of calm, gloom, and annoyance: "Take the money back, you fuck. I was just joking."

"No, you were right to remind me," Tommy was saying. "Just admit it meant something to you, you go bringing it up before I can even sit down."

"You guys believe this?" Angelo was looking around for backup but finding mostly uneasiness. "A joke. Fucking guy, he can't take a joke. . . ."

"Maybe it's that you still don't know how to tell one," Tommy said.

Which went over with Angelo about as well as you would expect, and even though it was a hot day his face was redder than it should've been, and he ended up stomping off, saying he had to go, that Sophie probably had dinner ready by now, and as he left he snatched the money from his pocket and threw it on the sidewalk. We watched his back until he turned a corner and was gone, then kept watching the empty corner. . . . I guess because nobody much felt like meeting the other guys' eyes.

"Sophie, is that his wife?" Tommy asked, finally.

"No, it's his little girl," I told him.

"His wife, she's long gone," Davey said.

"Forget about it," Artie said to Tommy. "You watch—tomorrow it'll be like nothing happened."

"Tomorrow maybe. But what about ten years from now?" Tommy laughed, started imitating him: " 'What's with that day you tried to force that money on me, you fuck, was that supposed to be funny?' " And it cracked us up; he had Angelo down cold. As the laughter died, Tommy looked down at the greenbacks, starting to scoot along the sidewalk, blown by a stuffy July breeze. "I'm not picking that up."

"*I'm* not proud," Davey said, and clomped off after them, like a guy chasing his hat in a high winter wind.

And you could see on Tommy's face, how his eyes followed Davey and the way he moved now, that it was the first clue he'd had that something must have happened to Davey since we'd all been running the streets together, back when.

Davey chased the cash down into the shadows of a row house halfway up the block, then lurched back out into the sun and the glare, back to us with that one leg that was now stiffer and shorter than the other. He came back grinning and proud, shook those thirty dollars, then stuffed them into his pants pocket.

"I'll just hold it for Angelo, is what," Davey said. "In case he changes his mind. You know . . . for Sophie."

"Yeah. For Sophie," we all said, and nodded like we might've even believed him.

I had to admit, looking Tommy over and matching up the guy that came back to the neighborhood with the guy who'd left, the years had been good to him. See a guy every day— starting with the one in the mirror—and you don't think he's ever any different. Because one day's never going to make a change in you. Well, unless you're Davey, but that's not the same thing.

Let a guy show up again after ten years' worth of days, though, and you start seeing things through his eyes instead of your own. Take one look at Artie and you want to ask, "Hey, how and when *did* you get such a gut on you? You never were what you'd call a skinny guy, but didn't most of it at least used to be up around your shoulders?" And if it was a few months later instead of July maybe you'd be asking him, "So what's with the high school letterman jacket, still?" But that was Artie, could hardly ever wait for fall so he could start wearing that jacket again, a sight I was so used to it didn't even register that maybe the time was long overdue for him to leave the thing in the closet.

With Tommy, though, it was like seeing a guy jump forward from ten calendars ago and realizing that what he must've done was become the guy he'd always been meant to be. No more, no less. Same guy in the skin, but a little more carved in the bones and clearer in the eyes and confident in the walk. . . . Even if he wasn't quite the same in name, since before long he admitted that it had been years since he'd heard so many people call him Tommy, from his dying grandmother to his old friends. He went by Thomas now, but you can imagine how much trouble any of us went to to accommodate that. We'd known him as Tommy, so he'd *always* be Tommy. Anything else aroused suspicion.

"Fucking guy, he's got airs now," Angelo said when he heard that. "Airs, and short memory for where he came from."

And I said yeah, and left it at that, but really, Thomas just fit the guy better now, somehow. He'd left the neighborhood at, what, age seventeen, or maybe even sixteen, when his parents split and he went with his mom. Not just out of the neighborhood, but clear out of the country. I wouldn't have remembered this if he hadn't come back to remind, but it was Montreal that they went to. French Canada. Which, at the time, probably seemed to me and everyone else like he was going to be falling off the edge of the planet.

So maybe that was the reason Artie decided he didn't much like the guy now either—because there was something kind of foreign about him now, and the girls in the neighborhood responded to that.

Girls, well, you'd have to call them women now, I guess, but a lot of them we'd known since they really *were* girls, way before they'd had anything resembling a chest, or hips, so it's hard to get out of that mindset. Some of them had never left the neighborhood, and some of them, they had once, but were back, on familiar turf and maybe staying with their parents after their first marriages had fallen apart, and maybe with a kid or three of their own now. Some of them you got used to seeing in the bars at night, and yeah, nature takes its course sometimes, but come in a night or two with Tommy, when he's rotating an evening off from helping out with his grandmother, and it's a whole new equation: "Oh, who's *this* . . . ? No, not Tommy, Tommy, that's *you*?"

And next they'd be wanting a refresher course in what had become of him, everything he'd been doing since. How he'd gotten a business degree and now had a couple of stores selling health foods, herbs, natural remedies, like that . . . the kind of thing that totally wouldn't fly here in the old neighborhood. And for some of the women, when they got caught up with him, it was just a nice little moment, two old friends running into each other, then they go on their way and that's all there is to it. But a few of the others, when he'd go through his story, their reaction was just the saddest thing I'd ever seen. Even Tommy told it like he knew it wasn't the most thrilling story in the world, but they'd be hanging on his every word, and maybe by now they'd downed a drink or two too many, and if you looked close enough, there were moments you could see them thinking about every wrong decision they'd ever made, like getting pregnant too soon or taking up with guys they wished they'd never met, and you could see the desperate fear in their eyes over how they knew they were paying for it now and maybe always would be, with the weight of it pulling them down toward the tabletop—

—and then they'd blink back to the present moment and smile at Tommy and suddenly confess how they used to have a crush on him in high school—did he know that?—and it was like they were one more drink from saying, "Take me with you when you go back, please, please, just take me away from this life."

He could've had any of them he wanted, any night of his choosing. But his partner on those two stores he owned was his fiancée. So he didn't go home with anybody.

Artie didn't understand that at all when he heard about it.

"Must be a fag now," he said. "Sometimes they don't figure it out right away. It takes them a while."

Angelo agreed. "Fucking guy, I always knew there was something wrong with him."

And I said yeah, and just left it at that. Because, like always, it was easier than arguing with them.

\* \* \*

So we watched the sun come up one morning, right?

I'd had my share of mornings getting home by the gray light of dawn, but never had made sunrise the reason I was out in the first place. Couldn't sleep, plain as that . . . because I thought I kept hearing the apartment building settling around me, all night long, and for some reason it sounded noisy as hell. And Tommy, he'd spent the whole night up watching over his grandmother. I don't know why I called him, or even how I'd guessed he'd be awake, too—I just did.

We got coffee and trudged a few blocks east, toward the shore, to the old piers that were rarely used anymore, falling apart mostly. We looked toward the far edge of the water and waited for those first rays of golden red, and breathed in the deep saltwater scent. Back in the neighborhood, on days when the wind was right, I cold smell the ocean from there, but hardly ever came down here to see it, or listen to the waves splash against the pilings—alway seemed like too much bother, not worth the effort.

"How is she?" I asked, finally. Because he hadn't said yet.

"The nurse that comes in gives her another day or two. Her lungs—" He sagged. "She's drowning inside. A wetter cough I've never heard in my life."

Tommy talked about her a while, then put the topic aside, like he'd had enough of it for now.

"There's something I've been waiting for someone to explain to me, but since nobody seems to be volunteering it, I guess I'll have to come right out and ask," he said. "What happened to Davey?"

"He had an accident a few years back."

"Yeah, *that* much I figured on my own. What *kind* of accident?"

I'd half forgotten that Davey had ever been any other way, because how he clomped around on legs of two different lengths just seemed to suit him. He'd always been the kind of wormy little guy who tags along at the edge of whatever's going on, but there's something about him you like, even though you'll never treat him quite as an equal. The kind of guy who, ever since he was a kid, is always ready to fetch stuff for you, so he'll have a place in the scheme of things. In high school he was the manager of the football team Artie played on, which is how we ended up with him full time.

"He got hit by a car late one afternoon," I told Tommy, and explained how Davey had been on his way home after we'd all been hanging out in front of our favorite deli. He'd said later he started having trouble walking, like he was on one of those bigger planets where you'd weigh twice as much, and when he was crossing from one block to another he found himself in the middle of an intersection and that he couldn't move anymore.

"Was he drunk?"

"That must've been it," I said, even though Davey hadn't been. But really, I just didn't know what had gone wrong.

All I knew was I didn't like explaining why Davey had gone storming home in the first place . . . because if we hadn't been razzing him so hard about how he'd never had a girlfriend, maybe he never would've been in the wrong spot at the wrong time, feeling like he couldn't raise either foot enough to get even as far as the curb.

"Why's it happen like that for some guys?" Tommy wondered. "Every strike that can go against them, they get hit with it."

Like I had an answer for that. At least he didn't seem to expect one.

"They don't have much use for me now, do they?" he said then, and didn't wait for an answer. "The other guys."

I tried to stall on that one, but he wouldn't let it slide, and finally I had to tell him, "Maybe it's just they feel like they don't know you anymore. Like, whoever you were, once, you're not him anymore."

Tommy got this bitter grin. "What, they'd like me better if I was still putting bricks through windshields and stealing pints of gin?" He lost the grin, looking out across the water, and shaking his head the way you do when you're about to give up on something. "I guess we'll each just have to live with the disillusion."

So we sat on the rotting pier, and finished our coffees as all the world I'd ever known started to lighten, and the slop and slosh of seawater against pilings receded while the last of the tide ebbed out, as the moon relaxed its hold on the ocean and turned the day over to the sun.

After work, I stayed at the house with Tommy and his family during those last several hours while his grandmother let go. It just seemed like the thing to do for a friend.

But it wasn't pretty, or restful, or quiet. She couldn't breathe well, and every so often it got bad enough that the nurse who was coming by in these final days had to flip on a suction machine and snake a tube down toward her windpipe and pump out the buildup of thick fluid with a slurpy gargling sound. The first time, I watched it sputter and spatter into the jar at the other end of the hose, and then as it started to fill up, I decided not to look in that direction anymore.

His grandmother's name was Lydia. I hadn't known that until this day.

There were pictures on her wall, and some of them, you took one glance and knew how old they had to be, the people in them looking like no one from our own time. I asked about them when Tommy and I drifted out of the death room and into the kitchen, and he explained what I'd figured already, that they were relatives, long since dead, including Lydia's own parents, who'd been the first ones to come over on the boat.

I gave them a closer look when we went back, trying to keep out of the way of Tommy's dad and aunts and uncles as I stared at the haunting faces in those faded old photos, weary but with a few hopes still alive and burning. I had to have a group of faces like this in my own background, just never thought to ask who they were.

They must've been on Tommy's mind, too, when we went out for air later and stood on the porch as another day ended, a hazy summer evening closing in.

"You ever wonder what they came over here for?" he asked, then swept a hand out over the neighborhood, all of it, and his hand hung in the air as if he didn't know what to say about any of it. The parts we could see, and all the rest we couldn't, and just had to smell it, like frying peppers and diesel exhaust, or hear it, like the far-off squawk of a car alarm and the brittle smashing of a bottle and always always always someone somewhere shouting at the top of his or her lungs.

"Because it *had* to be for more than this," Tommy said.

I realized it was the second day in a row that I hadn't seen the other guys. I couldn't say I missed them, and figured they were clustered a few blocks over, maybe thinking the same about me. Three guys I'd known forever, just waiting for one day to end and another to dawn so they could get back together in their little huddle and wait for that one to end, too.

"The other morning, while she could still speak," Tommy went on, "she told me the thing she hated second most was looking out the window."

"What was tops on her list?"

"Waking up. She said for years now she's been dreaming she goes someplace called County Carlow."

"Where's County Carlow?"

"Ireland, it'd have to be. Even though she's never been there. Must be where her parents came from." He glanced off the side of the porch toward the window of her room. Nothing to see but a drawn curtain. "She says you wouldn't believe how green the grass is there."

"Grass—what's that?" I said, and laughed. "Oh yeah, that scraggly brown stuff that grows between the sidewalk and the curb."

Again he looked up and down the street, this place his ancestors had come *to*, the place he had come *from*, and said, "It had to be for more than this. . . ."

Maybe because he'd moved away before the neighborhood had sunk its deepest roots into him, it probably wouldn't occur to Tommy to wonder this, but it sure occurred to me: *And why is it so hard to leave it behind?*

Anymore it seemed like there was only one way.

So we went back inside then, to Lydia's room, and saw the rest of it through to the end. The air was filled with the rattling of her breath and the weeping of her daughters, and her eyes were like two dwindling embers as they focused on nothing anyone else could see, or maybe nothing at all. Earlier she'd tried to lift a hand to someone's cheek and you could tell how heavy she was, *so* heavy. But now in her last moments the corners of her mouth seemed to turn upwards in a grin, like she'd heard a joke told just for her, and when her last breath left her, it seemed to go on forever, and I wondered how anyone so tiny could have that much breath trapped inside her. After a few moments, when we all realized that that was it, I looked at some of the old photos again, those that I was guessing might've been taken in County Carlow, and I suppose I halfway expected to see Lydia in the background of one of them now, looking light as a rose petal and barefoot in the green green grass.

But it was just the same old faded sepia tones as before.

Once they'd had a few minutes to stay put and hold each other and absorb the moment and say their prayers for the dead, Tommy's family started moving around again. Still on the floor near the bed was the big jar, three-quarters full of what the nurse had cleared from Lydia's lungs, and one of the uncles accidentally kicked it. It bounced off the baseboard intact, but then hit the stainless-steel frame of a rolling medical tray. The whole side cracked open and all that cloudy, clotted ooze flowed out onto the floor.

One of the teary-eyed aunts scolded the guy, said someone was going to have to take a mop to it. And I spoke up and said that I'd do it, because anybody can say he's sorry and leave . . . and because I knew that Artie and Angelo and Davey would pretend they hadn't even seen the mess; right then it seemed important not to be like them.

But after a few moments, when everyone else had busied themselves with time of death and calling the funeral director, I was the only one left looking at the mess in the corner.

And it started to move again.

Not on its own—I'm not saying that . . . but like something else was pulling it toward the baseboard so it cold flow underneath, and straight down through the hairline cracks between the floorboards. It happened fast, right there in front of my eyes, faster than you'd ever expect to see something drain in an ordinary way, until nothing was left but broken glass and a wet sheen.

I caught up with Tommy in the hall, and if anybody had seen my eyes I guess they only would've thought Lydia's death had gotten to me as much as anyone.

"A mop," I said, because it felt like I had to know. "Would there be one in the basement?"

"The house doesn't have a basement," he told me.

I headed home soon after, because it had gotten to that point where you start to feel like you're intruding on a family's grief instead of helping them cope.

It had been night for hours, late, but not so late that the bars weren't still open, even though I didn't feel like stopping by any of them because I knew then I'd have to talk to someone, and really . . . what do you say after a day like this? After you feel like you've gotten to know the neighborhood a little better, what you've never noticed before because it's always been right under your feet, sucking the life out of you. I figured if I was to pry open a manhole cover and shine a light down below, I'd see what really fed this place and kept it going . . . a slow, thick river of our blood and sweat and everything else that could be squeezed from us.

So I just walked toward home, slowly, paying close attention to how it felt each time my foot left the ground. And I had to wonder how it had started that time for Davey—if he'd been so upset over the way we'd been razzing him that he'd gotten it in his head that maybe he'd just up and leave, move someplace else if he could find a place where no one would razz him over never having a girlfriend.

I'd always grown up hearing the old-timers around, the lifers, saying how the neighborhood takes care of its own.

So I walked toward home, noticing like I'd never noticed before how the buildings sounded as I passed, settling into their foundations and groaning from deep within their aged bones of iron and brick.

And I didn't dare trip and fall, because if I did, I might never stand again, and instead get pulled down and down and down, right on into the asphalt, frozen there like a bug in amber and staring up at the sun and the moon that we'd always figured were up there shining just for us.

But then, wouldn't that be perfect, too . . . because ever since I can remember, they tell you how, no matter what, you'll always be part of the neighborhood.

# MAMISHKA AND THE SORCERER

## *Jessica Amanda Salmonson*

Eastern Europe four centuries ago in a poor garden cottage. A man and woman talking.

"They say I am a sorcerer, Mamishka, but I am not, I am not."

"How can you, Anton Levi, say such a thing—to me, of all people? Of course, you are a sorcerer! I have seen you working magic many times. You do it as innocently as a child picks up a bright penny, and you mean no harm by it, but all the same, it cannot be denied you were born a mage."

"Mamishka, Mamishka, how can you bear false witness? Would you have me killed? When they come for me, you must tell them what you know, for you of all people know me best."

"Anton, do you insist? I will tell them you converse with animals—"

"No, Mamishka!"

"—and cause the wind to stop blowing under the eaves when you cannot sleep with it whistling—"

"Mamishka! How can you!"

"—and when you bless the flour by which I bake your bread, no beetle will dwell in it thereafter, but it grows finer to the taste, and its sustenance increases. Or when milk has soured, you sweeten it with your little finger and a sniff with your long nose. And if you stub your toe on some rock, you curse the rock, and it sinks into the ground where it never causes trouble to any foot again—"

"Mamishka, do I do all this?"

"—and when you made me your lover without once offering a ring, so that I became a fallen woman, despised in spite of my faithfulness like unto a wife—would I have brought this shame upon myself if not beguiled?"

"Do you bear a grudge for that? I will wed you this very night! Before any judge you select, Gentile or Jew, I care not! Only speak in my behalf, Mamishka!"

"Would they believe me if I lied for you?"

"Not a lie, Mamishka! The truth! The truth! Can you not see how desperate I have become?"

"They would burn me at your side, Anton. Or they might burn only me and let you go, for they much prefer to see a woman screaming and squirming in the flames, because it arouses them, I doubt not. You should have stayed with your people, Anton Levi—I say it without detesting you for being a Jew, but because I know my own people's feelings against yours. Had you not lived as though a convert to Christ, perhaps no one would have thought it odd, your unchristian practices. As it is, you have fed their superstition, even in your kindest moment, with your weird blessings on mothers and their babies as you pass them in the street; by your puzzling discourses with husbands who lack the least capacity to comprehend your strange ideas. Did you think they loved you in their midst because they nodded and they smiled? Behind your back they made the sign of the cross, and they prayed every night for Jesus and Mary to protect them from you."

"I did not think they loved me, Mamishka. I thought *you* loved me! You!"

"Of course, I love you. And why should I not? I have been fortunate, I confess that much. My first marriage was loveless, and I was glad when he died. Even so, mine was among the best matches in the village, although 'best' may still be nothing better than a horror. Few I know can say what I can say, that love is beautiful and lovemaking is divine—you taught me that, Anton Levi, that you are God, and I the Bride of God, when you came to me on Sabbaths singing with your pleasing voice and displaying your manhood. May I be forgiven for living in such a pretty lie and liking it! Yet for all my love, can I change your fate? You might've changed it by your sorcerous ability, but you misled yourself that you were liked. You were feared, Anton Levi, feared!"

"I have only wished to become a proponent of European culture, to show another way for my scattered people! I have tried to live as I believe good Jews must inevitably learn to live! I have explained to you, I am of the *maskilim*, who have looked into the future to discover that many of your people's ways are the ways of all peoples who wish for triumph."

"If you tell someone you look into the future, why are you surprised they admonish you as a sorcerer? *Maskil* or no *maskil*, you have emulated gentiles and you made yourself accursed to your own mother, to your rabbi, and traded them for what? A squire's cast-off shirt, and a woman you would not marry lest you displease a mother who was displeased enough, who went into her grave full of grief over her wayward only son! Anton, my Anton! I cannot lie in your behalf, for I am a good Catholic woman; but you know I would not have you burn. Run, I tell you, run, by way of the twin passes through the mountains. Then when they demand to know where you have gone, I can freely tell them, but they have only half a chance of following in your direction."

"Then come with me, Mamishka! You are all the family I have left!"

"Anton, can I leave my mother in her old age? Can I abandon my aunts and uncles and cousins and nephews and nieces and all the rest?"

"I have done all that, Mamishka."

"And look what it has brought you. Do you ask me to martyr myself for love of you? Do not think harshly of the good year we had together, as I will not regret it even if I, previously a respectable widow, find that I am shunned for having allowed a sorcerer to dwell in my house. For I will tell you this, Anton Levi, though sorcerer you are, you are a kind sorcerer, a loving sorcerer, a sorcerer who has used your magic chiefly for the good. But will that be a defense? I think not. For your magic is not of Christ, and they will answer, at your trial, that the Devil is very beautiful, even as you, my love, are beautiful; and what is not from the Father, the Son, and the Holy Ghost is inescapably from the Darkness."

"Do you believe that, Mamishka, knowing me this long?"

"I know you are a sorcerer."

"And my sorcery is evil?"

"There! With your own mouth you admit it!"

"No! No, it is a supposition, Mamishka, a supposition! The things you have seen me do, these are not sorcery, they are things of nature. I hardly noticed them myself, for I never think of such things as being magic. They are of God, Mamishka, the same God you so deeply love. Have I criticized your Jesus? We have the same God, and we both await the Messiah—you, his second coming, I, his first, and when he arrives, we will discover both are the same gentleman, one and the same, Mamishka, and his name will be Emmanuel."

"They are coming for you this moment and you argue faith with me as always. You are not only a sorcerer, but a mad one; your idealism is your undoing. *Of course*, I do not think your sorcery is evil, but I have told you, that does not matter. If you were brave, if you were strong, if you were pragmatic, you would use your magic, evil or not, to fly over their heads, laughing all the while, dropping fireballs on their stupid angry pates! But you will let them drag you away, filled with denials, and you will die rather than hurt them, though they hurt you slowly, slowly through the hours of the night. Flee this moment, Anton! Go!"

He reached toward her, as though to grasp her and hold her tight, but she turned her head, and he restrained himself. He hung his head; then he turned to flee by the back door, toward the forest and the double pass between the mountains. And when the magistrate with three strong villagers came with staves and swords drawn forth, and mindless hatred furrowing their brows, they stood before her in rank menace, demanding, "Where is the sorcerer who caused a pig to be born with three legs! Where is he that caused a child to die in the pink of health, lying in its crib? Who caused your garden, Mamishka, to flourish at the height of summer when other gardens withered? Is he beneath that bed? Is he in that closet or chest? Is he squeezed into the rafters? Don't hide him! Your life, too, is at peril!"

"I know it. I told him I would not lie for him, neither would I hide him. He is dead to me now, this Anton Levi, for I wish to live, and repent of him, and will make full breast of it in the confessional on Sunday. Until then, I beg you, cause me no grief, for I would not die before absolution."

A sword was pressed to her throat, and she leaned against a wall. The magistrate demanded, "Tell me where he is!"

"He has gone through the passes."

"Which one?"

"I only saw him flee that way. He did not tell me whether left or right when he reached the forking valley."

"Witch! You've protected him after all!" He eased back on his sword, and Mamishka sighed with relief. But then the magistrate said to his three men, "Kill the witch, summarily," and they, without flinch or query, stuck her thrice—once in the belly, once in the breast, once in the thigh. Her mouth gaped open. She looked startled. She stayed leaning against the wall, feeling wildly at the leaks in her body, dampening her hands with blood, knowing that her life was seeping out of her. She let out a keening wail of grief as the magistrate and his guardsmen left in swift pursuit of Anton Levi.

Now Anton had not as yet passed even through the first little woodland area that was second growth close above the village. From a clearing he saw ahead giant conifers of the forest proper. Suddenly he stopped, turned, and heard the keening, heard his name spoken in that keening, heard it as a prayer. And Anton put his hands together and said, "O Blessed Matrona, Bride and Presence of God, take Mamishka into your heart and keep her there for me, until I come. If she is not much, still she has loved me this long year, when not even my own mother would show affection by any means but tears, who upon her deathbed was unwilling to send for me, so that she was in her grave before I knew to come and sing for her the prayer of death. If you cannot save Mamishka's life, then save her soul; and if you will not save her soul, then give her to the Land of Fair where she can live throughout eternity in this sphere of matter, and still achieve salvation in the End."

When his prayer was done, a wind whirled out of him, and went rushing like an invisible veil of cloth through the woods. This mysterious wind knocked asunder the clutch of four men pursuing him, then came to the little shanty wherein Anton had lived with the widowed peasant. And she, braced against the bloodied wall, felt that wind as the very tangible presence that it was. For a moment she saw a glimmering woman, and the woman said, "Fear not, for I am the Ruach, Queen of Eld, called She of Good Counsel, sent by my Great Sister to snatch your soul."

"No, no," said Mamishka. "Blessed Father! Blessed Son! Blessed Holy Ghost!"

"The latter of that Three is my Great Sister," said the whirlwind that a moment before had been a glimmering, insubstantial woman. And the whirlwind said this thing with grave irony that in no way reassured Mamishka.

Then this wind broke into many parts and entered Mamishka through her three wounds, which healed instantly, and through her wailing mouth and her various orifices, so that by her ears was her mind exposed to the dark elf-light; and by her sex did she become perpetually aroused; and by her eyes could she see to the end of forever.

The fear was gone from Mamishka's eyes and laughing with a musicality that had never before been hers, she ran out of the house as though in pursuit of Anton Levi. Yet when she leapt from the ground, she vanished utterly, and was seen no more in the useless little place where she was born.

They found Anton Levi on the verge of old forest where he knelt murmuring prayers. He had after all not tried to reach the twin pass; that much was clear. They thought he must have become too frightened to continue. Or was he so foolish he failed to comprehend the full import of their threat against him?

The magistrate and his men held back a moment, worried

they were being tricked, fearful of the sound of Anton Levi's ancient prayer that was part Hebrew, part Aramaic, and wholly alien to those who overheard.

Then he left off his prayer and stood to face his pursuers, his arms open to them. He began to sing. His persecutors ran forth with swords upraised, and slashed him numerous times, but Anton Levi did not fall. His arms fell from their upward reach and hung loosely at his sides. His head hung low and he rocked slowly left, then right, backward, then forward, as blood spouted from his many wounds.

The forest became still. His slayers stood motionless, ready to give him more stabbings and slashings if they felt the least threatened. Slowly he raised his old, sad eyes and gazed directly at the magistrate. "It is not from the loss of all this blood that I am dying," he said. "It is from loss of all these tears."

At that moment, the Great Matrona opened up her womb, and took Anton Levi inside the earth, where he lies quietly to this day awaiting the blissful, waking kiss of Emmanuel. His persecutors fled in terror, certain as they were that a demon had returned to Hell, and they, righteous Christians, had escaped only by the protective grace of Mary and Jesus.

What they never knew, what they could never have understood, was how they had slain the last living relation of their own Messiah, the final Jew in the sacred line of David. For that was who this Anton Levi was, this *maskil*, whose far vision saw not far enough—and whose only son, pierced in the womb of Mamishka, was born not to save the wicked world of humanity that was beyond salvation, but was born in Eld for the sake of all who dwell immortal in the Land of the Fair.

# PETS

## *James S. Dorr*

The shelling started early that evening, the rockets and the artillery bombs. But Gregor Kubcek was used to the bombs.

He concentrated instead on the woman, blond and thin, her short hair framing an oval face with wide-set eyes, who sat across the small table from him. He concentrated on the music. The cabaret band.

He smiled when a cockroach scuttled across the table's round surface, then stopped and dashed back beneath a crushed napkin when, frowning, the woman flicked ash from her cigarette.

"That's what I'll never get used to," she said. She carefully stubbed her cigarette out in the metal ashtray, once a car hubcap, then placed the extinguished butt in her purse. She gestured grandly, first at the napkin, then taking in the whole dimly lit club, the powdered mortar that rained from the ceiling as more shells struck, scant blocks away from the cellar they drank in. "That," she said again. "Not the noise. Not even the deaths now. Not even the wounded. But the *filth*—the filth and the hopelessness. Things never getting clean. At the hospital . . ."

Kubcek shook his head, taking her hand in his. "Life goes on, though, Eva," he said. "People like us, we find ways to get through it."

The woman shrugged, then retrieved her cigarette end and relit it. She drew the smoke slowly into her lungs, letting it curl in her mouth and throat. She laughed then.

"You mean, to live for the moment. To savor each moment."

Kubcek nodded. "To savor the *smallness* of each moment. Back when I was stationed outside of Herat—"

He glanced quickly around him, but Eva knew that when he had been younger he had been drafted into the Warsaw Pact, fighting for Russia. Before events had caught up with the Soviets and set their own nation free—free to fight now among their own various groups of peoples.

To destroy their cities.

He smiled again, listening to the musicians playing American jazz on the bandstand, ignoring the crashes as more shells hit near them. And he was a teacher, he thought, not a fighter, at least until his school had been bombed out. And Eva a nurse.

"The forts were filthy. Hot in the summer. Damp in the autumn. And boring, utterly boring at times, since the main fighting was always to the east. Kabul and Quandahar. Not that we weren't glad. . . ."

Eva nodded. "And yet you *were* attacked."

"Yes," he said. "Sometimes. Between times, though, some of the men kept pets. Vermin. Things like that. Little creatures that they could take care of, just like one might a dog or a cat at home. It helped them get through it."

"Yes," Eva said. She poured more of what passed for wine in both their glasses. "And we have our cabaret, our music. And then the comedian after the noise stops, to read us the latest speeches they've made in the U.N. about us. To tell us that maybe NATO will do something for us at last. Or maybe they won't. And then we'll all go home."

She laughed again and Kubcek laughed with her. The cabaret was simply a place to be, the musicians and the comedians all volunteers. The wine he had foraged, as other patrons might have foraged sausages from bombed-out butcher shops. Bread from the counters of shattered bakeries. And no one hoarded.

Everyone seemed content with just a little, enough for the moment. Enough for the next day when Eva would return to the hospital where he had met her only that morning, getting herself ready for the new wounded. He had just brought one man in himself, helping out as a stretcher bearer. The man had been dead by the time they arrived, and she had motioned for him to go on to where the temporary morgue was. But then she had seen the lines on his tired face. . . .

And now the evening's shelling had stopped and they picked their way through rubble-strewn streets to Kubcek's apartment. They picked their way through crowds of foragers out in the cold air, leaving the shops that were intact untouched—an honor among thieves that held, too, for looters—until Kubcek stopped short.

"A moment," he said. He dashed into a burning clothier's and reemerged with a woman's coat, brushing dust from its fur-trimmed collar. He put it around her.

"It's red," she said. "A lovely color."

"It matches your lips."

They laughed again and continued on to Kubcek's building, a victim once of an earlier shelling but, to his good luck, the nightly bombings had since moved away from that part of the city. "I keep pets, too," he said, after they kissed on the rickety stairs. He took out his key and led her into a cluttered upper-floor apartment, checking the window to make sure its curtain would still block the light, then clicked on the wall switch to test the power.

Eva screamed.

Later, as they lay in each other's arms, she confessed that it wasn't so much the *idea* of roaches that had unnerved her. "It's just that there were so many," she said. "It looked like thousands, all scurrying back to their cracks and chinks—wherever it is they go when the lights come on. Swirling around us, just for that moment . . ."

He kissed her again, softly. "They're not so bad, really. And in their way, they even help keep the place clean. A bachelor like me, you know how we men are. Living alone."

Eva shuddered. "You *did* say you kept pets." She tried to smile. "And Lord knows I've seen worse—heard worse at least, hearing the doctors talk. These are the kind of pets, though, you used to keep back in the army?"

"Hush," he said. "Let's not think about armies. Some, yes, kept roaches. *Blatta orientalis*—the big ones. 'Waterbugs' as some people call them. That's where I learned they could be trained to do simple tricks. Do you know we used to lay wagers on cockroach races?"

Eva shuddered again. "It takes getting used to," she said. "Though in wartime—and here, even if it's not declared, we're in a war, too—I suppose one must. But these looked smaller."

"Yes," he said. "But more intelligent in their way too. *Blatella germanica*, the 'German cockroach,' the ones that infest European cities. They thrive on disorder—the filth, as you say, that can't be kept out even from the hospitals with things as they are now. In some ways I think they're smarter than we are, the way they adapt. The way they'll still be here when humans are long gone."

"Kiss me again, Gregor," Eva said. "Don't talk about roaches. At least not tonight." She snuggled against him, shivering once again when something moved, briefly, beneath their entwined thighs.

"Talk about *us*, Gregor."

Kubcek did more than talk. That night and nights after, even though she never, truly, got used to the roaches. But wartime was wartime: Despite his being older than her by a good fifteen years, by the second week's end she had had him help her move her things into his apartment.

These only added to the clutter. Her couch. Her bedspreads. Her bookcase and books—medical books that he would read aloud in the evenings to help her prepare for the days that followed, and each day's new wounded. These added to the room's hiding places, where roaches could gather, and more roaches came.

Gregor sensed their increase and reveled in it. More pets to care for—for him and Eva.

And yet she never herself became fully used to his small pets. "I had them, too, of course, in my apartment," she told him once. "Everyone has them. And it *is* wartime." Nevertheless she insisted they sprinkle boric powder over the bed, even though he protested. And when they sat down she would brush off the couch first. "I do love *you*, Gregor," she said more than once. "But . . ."

He nodded at those times, trying to understand.

Rather, trying to accept that she did not yet understand what companionship was like during the days when she was gone from him.

During the days he would lie on the floor, remembering what life was like before they met.

Gregor had been married once, long ago—he scarcely remembered now what his wife looked like, only that she had died. That was when they had lived in the country. Back when the first of the fighting had started.

They, like so many, had fled to the city, the roads he had used to commute every day all but impassable now from the shell holes. Practically within the city's suburbs they had been caught in an enemy ambush. Two tanks had rumbled onto the pavement. He, an ex-soldier, had crouched and run, ducking into a ditch beside the road, where he had found a dead soldier. Taking the soldier's gun, he checked the clip, then crept back, softly, to find that the tanks had already moved past.

But—what was her name?—Maria?—his wife—his wife had been crushed beneath one of the tanks' treads.

Screaming, he had fired a burst after the disappearing hulks, but the tanks, perhaps fearing they in turn were being ambushed, only increased their speed away from the city. He kept the rifle, not knowing what else to do, after he had dug out a shallow grave for his wife's destroyed body, then gone on by himself into the city where he blended in with other armed refugees.

Now, as he thought of it, he realized it had been such a waste. Now he would lie on the floor, remembering how he had sealed his wife's corpse in the good earth, having first drenched it with gasoline to keep it safe from burrowing insects, and he would feel the first roaches tickle as they began to creep into his pants legs.

He would feel them on his chest, inside his shirt, as he remembered how he had come to possess his apartment, back when his school had still been open.

He had been fastidious then, before he had understood.

He used to shoot rats with his captured rifle—bullets were easy enough to come by in those early days. And transfixed, he would watch their small corpses, until, eventually, the roaches ate them.

The roaches adapted. They only ate dead things, starches by preference, but in a pinch, even dead flesh could please them. And he had adapted, too.

Now, as he lay there, he felt tiny mandibles tickle his own flesh, cleaning away every vestige of dried sweat, every flake of sloughed-off dead skin. He felt their clever mouths suck at his fingernails, scraping the dirt out from underneath them. He felt them in his ears, chewing at ear wax, jointed legs scratching as they explored deeper. His hair. His face.

Yes, he had adapted. He had tried to poison them at first, just as Eva now tried to do. At least the ones that crept in the bed with him. But he had adapted. He had come to realize that they were just doing the same things he did. Adapting. Foraging.

Staying alive.

Even making love, as he and Eva did every night now, hungering in their own way for companionship. And who was whose pet? Or did it even matter?

In time she would understand.

Spring came early. All winter long the pattern of shellings had expanded, covering more and more of the city, even the parts that had already been hit. Exactly one month after she moved in with him, Eva's old building had gone up in flames. Then the hospital lost another wing when an enemy airplane crashed into it—and Gregor had gone back to stretcher duty, going without sleep for three entire days to help clear the dead out.

During those winter days, even the cockroaches seemed less active. Food became scarce, both for humans and roaches, but ammunition was still in supply, for those who searched for it, and Kubcek also resumed shooting rats.

Everyone shot rats now. Not for fastidious reasons this time, but for meat to put on the table. And Eva adapted with him, even to this. Even to his leaving dead scraps for his pets to eat afterward, when he could not be there to feed them himself. Even to seeing him once when she came back to their building early, and witnessing him just beginning to sit up, gently brushing the cockroaches from his arms and shoulders.

"Gregor," she had screamed. "Are you all right, Gregor? What are you doing?"

He explained it to her, how his pets helped him keep his body clean, and to her credit she only shuddered once this time.

"I love you," she said. She helped with the brushing, although, when he asked her, she flatly refused to lie down with him, to let them feed on her own bodily wastes, too.

"In time," Kubcek told her. "This, too, in time everyone will adapt to. You'll see how it is, Eva. But for now you needn't do anything you don't wish to."

He dreamed about roaches: This he did not tell her. He dreamed about them the times he was alone.

When they were together once more, they would read her books and marvel at pictures of hospital rooms where the plaster was not cracked, and doctors wore clean gowns.

But spring came early. The flowers came back first—Kubcek marveled at this as well. The earth's beauty was not destroyed. Then the trees that had not yet been shattered came out in leaves. The cabaret they used to go to reopened in a new basement, in a still-not-yet-bombed part of the city.

The cockroaches came back in increasing numbers.

And then—Kubcek and Eva were in the cabaret when the emcee had the band stop playing. "Ladies! Gentlemen!" he shouted from the bandstand. "There has been an announcement from the U.N. A cease-fire has been signed!"

Liquor appeared at all the tables—alcohol, like bullets, never had entirely disappeared, even during the worst nights of winter, but these were bottles of genuine slivovitz. Eva and Kubcek, along with the others, drank long and gratefully, letting the fiery plum sweetness burn down their throats, scarcely hearing the next announcements. A U.N. convoy approaching the city. Food and medicines would be delivered. A few dark rumors that it might be a ruse, but the enemy, surely, was as tired as their side was.

Eva and Kubcek streamed out with the others, dancing in the shell-marked streets. Swarming, like roaches, out into the spring air.

They saw the moon, bright above, full and glowing in the soft breeze, lighting the streets where the street lamps were broken.

They saw other lights go on, one, then another, as people in homes tore down blackout curtains until, exhausted, they could dance no more. "Is it true, really true, Gregor?" Eva asked, breathlessly, as, arm in arm, they climbed back up the stairs to their apartment.

"Yes, Eva," he answered. "At least for now, yes."

They unlocked the door and staggered inside, scarcely hearing the treacherous whistle of jet planes that suddenly inundated the sky.

"Eva!" Kubcek screamed.

When he woke, feeling his head ache, there had been no sound.

"Eva, are you here?" He tried to remember.

A vision came back to him, curtains shredding as shrapnel split through the tiny apartment. A section of the roof collapsing as he dove, coming up in a corner, clutching his rifle. Firing above him through the burst ceiling.

Then more of the roof coming down, searing his leg with pain.

"Eva," he called again, more softly this time. "Are you hurt, Eva?" He saw a roach creep past, its antennae quivering as if it were asking what all the noise had been, but, beyond that, there was only stillness.

He saw Eva's books spilled out of the bookcase, opened to

chapters on gangrene and blood poisoning and hepatitis—chapters he had read to her through the long winter evenings, preparing for new days.

Then he saw Eva, crumpled beneath the shattered table. Still and silent—she needed his help, but he could do nothing. He tried to stand, clutching his rifle like a crutch. Using its stock to help pull himself up.

He staggered outside, down stairs that miraculously had not yet fallen. Outside to streets littered with new rubble.

He staggered down a long, shattered hillside toward the city's center. Toward Eva's hospital, passing the corpses of burned-out buildings, the still-smoking forms of last night's revelers, until, once again, blackness took over.

He woke to a smell of carbolic acid. To crumbling, at one time whitewashed, plaster walls. Sheets stiff with sweat and only half-washed-out blood.

"Kubcek?" a voice whispered. "Gregor Kubcek?"

He looked up. A doctor. He recognized him from his stretcher duty.

"Eva," he answered. "Nurse Eva—she's been hurt. The roof fell in on her. She wasn't moving. . . ."

"Shh-h-h," the voice said. "You've been wounded badly. Don't try to move yet."

"But Eva! Doctor?"

"There's been a new cease-fire," the doctor said. "The bombing, they claim, was just a mistake—a pilot misunderstanding his orders. At least that's what the U.N. report says." The doctor shook his head. "But, Gregor, the bombing happened three days ago. You've been out that long. And we've seen your building. The rescue workers have already been through the lower floors—they couldn't get to the ones any higher. If Eva was trapped there, she's long beyond help now."

"No!" Kubcek shouted. He tried to heave himself out of the bed, to stand on his feet, to get back to Eva, but something was wrong. Then he noticed the bedsheet's strange flatness.

"Your leg was crushed badly," the doctor said. "We had no choice, Gregor." He gestured toward where the lower portion of Kubcek's right leg should have been. "We saved the knee. We could do that much. But as for below that, the damage was too great. . . ."

Kubcek stared, not speaking. He watched as the doctor suddenly turned, crushing an insect that skittered across the filth of the blood-spattered hospital floor.

"Y-you mean you had to remove it?" he finally said.

The doctor nodded. "We amputated, yes. Gregor, there was no choice. Especially given"—the doctor shrugged—"well, you see for yourself how conditions are here. So many wounded. The lack of anything like sanitation. Even saving the knee we took a chance."

Kubcek frowned, trying to take it all in. He reached down to where his right calf had been, feeling the stump beneath the sheet.

"In a few days," the doctor continued, "if the wound stays clean, we'll try to fit you with some kind of prosthetic. The U.N. claims they'll be bringing some artificial limbs in with the next food convoy. Modern plastic ones, which are almost as good as the real thing." The doctor tried to smile, tried to put Kubcek at his ease. "Before you know it, you'll be walking well enough that, if you want to, you can be helping with stretchers again."

Kubcek appreciated the try at gallows humor—he knew the doctor and knew he had done his best. But that was not the problem now.

"Doctor," he said, "I've got to get out of here, go to Eva. Even if she's dead, I have to see for myself."

The doctor nodded. "I understand, Gregor. Look, I'll tell you what. Lord knows, we can use your bed—we still have patients stacked up in the hallways. We'll get you a crutch to get around on after we've gotten you something to eat. I'll sign your discharge, but promise me this. Come back on the weekend. With luck, we'll have a limb to fit you with then. But more important . . ."

The doctor paused, and Kubcek watched as he gestured around the room. The other patients. The dirt. More insects.

"We tried to do the best we could, Gregor. But so many

wounded—so much work to do here. And sterilization procedures at best spotty. What I mean is I want you to look at your wound every day between now and then. And any sign of an inflammation, a discoloration . . . you know what I mean, Gregor?"

Kubcek nodded. He knew what the doctor meant.

"Any sign. Anything that seems to you out of the ordinary with your wound, Gregor, I want you to come back here right away."

Kubcek struggled through deserted streets that were no longer springlike. The trees, what few had been left, were in splinters. The blooms disappeared, crushed by bombs and falling rock. Nevertheless, when he got to his building, he found at least the first two floors still intact. He managed to get up the stairs that far. And then to the third, he was able to pick his way up a back stairway and, pushing broken boards and plaster out of his way, to finally get up on his hands and knees to his own fourth-floor hallway.

He tried to stand again, but found he couldn't. The floor was not level—his crutch kept slipping—so he crawled onward, leaving the crutch behind.

Roachlike, he kept on, thinking of the insect the doctor had crushed in the hospital, and wondered, as he pushed open his room's door, letting it fall from its broken hinges, if they had not all in some way become roaches. Scuttling aimlessly between the bombings. Adapting to whatever were their surroundings.

Making pets of the things real men and women recoiled from.

He did not call Eva's name as he approached his bed. Rather, he saw her, curled up at its foot underneath the table, her bones picked nearly clean in the faded sunlight that shone through what was left of the ceiling.

His leg began hurting.

He took to his bed, shaking out the sheets to rid them of the last of Eva's powder, and for the first time that he could remember since he had met her, he started crying.

He lay there through the night in his loneliness, dreaming of Eva first, then of the rats he used to shoot when he had first come here. Of how their corpses, too, would be picked clean. His pets adapting. Except even they were gone from him as well now.

He lay in silence, and when morning came, he inspected his wound, discovering a slight inflammation. And who was whose pet now? He had cared for the roaches, but now, in turn, they had cared for Eva, making her substance a part of themselves, then left when they had done all they could do.

He lay there wondering, and the next morning, he wasn't surprised to find that his right leg, above the knee, had taken on a dusky-blue color. He tried to get up, remembering the doctor, but then he saw the first roach.

*His pets had come back!*

He saw it approach what was left of Eva, scuttling over an open textbook, then chewing at the few fibers left of her right hip. The hip he remembered so warm against his own.

When it was finished, he eased himself painfully from the bed and lifted her bones onto the mattress. He looked at his leg, saw the first signs of pustules, and realized the page the roach had crawled over had been that which described the symptoms of gangrene.

He laughed as he climbed into the bed beside her. He did not need a textbook to tell him that his stump had become infected.

He lay and he kissed her, the skull of his Eva, and thought about what his pets had done for her. Made her a part of their own immortality through their succeeding generations, even when humankind left the planet. When all else was poisoned.

Then later, when darkness had come again, he felt the first tickling at his diseased stump. Cockroaches never attacked the living.

But flesh was dying . . .

The next day the blisters had crept up past his thigh, leaving it swollen, a vast, black balloon-shape attached to his torso. He knew the symptoms: He had read them out loud to Eva often enough in the evenings. The way the anaerobic bacteria,

*Clostridium perfringens*, fermented the very muscle they bored into, drinking its sugars like people drank liquor, leaving just gas and spent tissue behind them. The odor of rot that crept up past his stomach.

And even by day now the cockroaches followed, branching when blueness infected his left leg, tickling, scratching, as the gangrene spread. How many amputees died in the First World War, just from his symptoms? He ought to know that—he had once taught history.

How many others had died in the Second? Fewer in that war, with antiseptic field medical stations, but nevertheless some. And in this new combat, despite its cease-fires and its U.N. convoys . . . ?

He thought about Eva, about immortality, as the disease spread up both his sides, toward his lungs and his heart. As cockroaches followed, eating the tissue as soon as it died, but never the living. Patiently, waiting, until it was ready, making his flesh a part of their own bodies. And Eva, too, waiting.

*Would he recognize her?*

And who were whose pets now?

# THE LAMB

## *Paul Finch*

It was quite an array of filth.

Everywhere Damien looked, gasping women—with bright red lips and thick, spider-leg lashes—were clutching rock-hard penises. Milk spurted in frozen jets; there were spread thighs and gaping vaginas, black leather masks, PVC trusses. . . .

Damien was astounded by it, though he didn't know why he should be, for it was now his sixth week in Rome and he'd seen this sort of thing—in shops, on open-air market stalls—almost every day. Of course, it was still incredible that here, in the Piazza Venezia, only half an hour's stroll from the Vatican itself, in an otherwise pleasing spot, where the religious—priests, nuns and lay folk alike—could enjoy espresso in the gentle shade of limes, this horrendous display was openly to be viewed, unremarked on by anyone. Even children passed it by without noticing; worryingly, the message of this seemed to be they'd seen it all before, and to such an extent that it no longer made an impression.

Damien glanced up. The man behind the stall, a short, thin Roman, with a leathery face under his dour flat-cap, wore a vaguely amused expression . . . as if he knew exactly what the young seminarian was thinking, as if even though Damien was in a short-sleeve shirt and jeans, it was evidently clear what he was doing in the city, and why he was lingering by this sordid storefront. Damien would have been tempted to say something indignant, to demand to know what the man was smiling about . . . were his hot hand not already embedded in his pocket, toying with a pile of *lire*, his nervous eyes not already scanning the price tags on the magazines. Fifty to sixty thousand—ridiculously cheap. Equivalent sums back home in England, where hard-core pornography was not even legally available, would come to three or four pounds each. It was bewildering . . . here he was, at the beating heart of Christianity, yet temptation had never been so easy.

It was a struggle to walk away without buying something, though in the end it owed more to Damien's fear that someone from the college might spot him, rather than the triumph of his spirit. Even though he'd only glanced at the glossy covers, his penis remained a steel rod in the front of his jeans.

A lecturer at junior seminary had once told the young priests-in-training that sins of the flesh would be the toughest to resist in a world where sexual imagery was so blatantly prominent. It was something they'd simply have to live with. Wise words perhaps, though interestingly, that wisdom had then dried up; when asked by a student how it was that young men, filled with hormones, driven virtually by Nature to seek sexual outlet, might find the strength to ignore such enticement, the scholarly gent had told them that each one would have to find his own way—a good method to resist temptation, apparently, was to concentrate on something mundane, such as polishing one's shoes. Damien still remembered glancing down at that moment and noticing the lecturer's own shoes . . . perhaps the most fastidiously polished he'd ever seen.

Of course it was easy to snigger at such things, but the truth was that six weeks into his course, Damien was struggling. He'd never doubted his vocation, yet on his first week in Rome he'd succumbed badly to sinfulness. Within two days of arriving, a simple walk along the riverfront had become an ordeal. Quite by accident, he'd glanced down a side alley, and had spotted a prostitute at business with a client. First of all, the sight had startled; then it had entranced. . . .

The girl, stunning to look at in a short clingy dress, high white shoes, and flowing platinum locks, had been on her haunches, her shapely knees wide apart, her miniskirt pulled taut, showing firm thighs and a tight sheath of lacy gusset. Standing beside her had been an ordinary-looking man— somewhere between thirty and thirty-five, probably a father and husband—clad in tan slacks and a white shirt, holding a briefcase. His eyes had been closed, his mouth agape . . . gasping and grunting. The blonde had been working his exposed erection in and out of her mouth, pumping it like a piston with a delicate, pink-fingernailed hand. So absorbed was he, that Damien hadn't even realized he'd approached them. Only then had the girl's eyes flickered toward him from under their heavy brocade of blue-gray shadow, immediately registering shock and anger. Her trick had then turned as well, his own surprise quickly giving way to rage. He'd begun shouting and gesticulating, apparently unconcerned that such a disturbance might bring other spectators.

Damien had stumbled away, white and breathless, gagging with revulsion at the flagrant scene he'd just witnessed. A couple of minutes later though, he'd gone straight to a public lavatory, locked himself into a cubicle and masturbated. And after that, he'd wept. Not just there in the privy, but all the way back to his hall of residence. It was because he was alone, he'd tried to tell himself . . . alone and strange, far from the Lancashire home he'd shared for so long with his loving mother. But none of that had cut much ice with his conscience. There were some vices the Roman Catholic Church would tolerate among its clergy—so long as kept to moderation—but not . . . *that*. Never, ever . . . *that*.

An hour after his torment by the market stall, Damien took a bus out of the city to the catacombs at the Ardeatina. As always, he hoped, the sense of peace which pervaded these hidden places of reverence and refuge would aid him in his struggle.

It was late afternoon when he arrived, the October sun luxuriously warm in the narrow lanes and verdant gardens, beating up from the white stones of the old Appian Way. But once he descended below ground, that familiar cool—just faintly damp, scented with ancient dust—enveloped him. The ceilings down here were low and arched, the walls smoothly cut, but in many parts rippled and rutted, the red turgid clay in some places moist and held together only by complex steel braces.

"The Catacomb of Saint Callixtus is one of the largest and most important Christian shrines in Rome," said the English-speaking tour guide, as she led Damien and several other pilgrims down the steep entrance stair. Already, carved epigrams and preserved fragments from the lids of *loculi*, or burial niches, were visible embedded in the walls. "These labyrinthine galleries run for twelve miles under the city, and contain perhaps half a million tombs," the guide added. "And these are only the ones we know about. Many more await discovery and excavation."

Like so many Italian ladies, the tour guide exuded sex appeal, yet seemed unaware of it. Damien watched her carefully. It was the first time he'd visited here and been guided by a woman, let alone a woman who looked like this. She was forty perhaps, with flowing, shiny brown tresses, dark eyes, and a face that was handsome rather than beautiful, but flawlessly tanned. Her respectable jacket and skirt of cream linen served only to accentuate her buxom figure. Even the small crucifix at her throat added its own sultry message—its sleek gold contrasting sharply with the soft bronze of her skin.

"These catacombs were basically cemeteries," she added. "The word 'catacomb' is actually Greek, meaning 'near the hollow.' They were dug in the soft clay outside the city walls in the middle years of the first century by Christian journeymen called *fossores*. The pagan practice of cremation was frowned upon by the early Church, as it was widely believed Christ would shortly return and that all bodies must be ready to resurrect. Hence . . . this vast underground network, where as many bodies of the faithful as was humanly possible could be preserved."

In the next chamber, they saw an *arcosolium*—an infinitely larger niche with an arched ceiling. To either side of it, frescoes depicted biblical scenes. Carved onto the tomb's marble lintel was a monogram, a symbol bearing two figures from the

Greek alphabet, *X* and *P*—the first two letters of the Greek word *Christos*, carefully woven together.

"Of course, the catacombs are probably better known as a place of sanctuary during the persecutions," the tour guide said. "This was not their original purpose, but as the violence grew, many Christians had no option but to hide down here."

Damien knew this part of the story well . . . not just as seminarian and student but as a member of a faith whose dynamism owed much to the sacrifice of its first practitioners.

"Dedicated to lives of charity and social justice, the first Roman Christians were in many ways impeccable citizens of the great metropolis," the tour guide explained. "The year A.D. 60 was of signal importance to them, however. Lucius Secundus, Prefect of the City, was murdered by one of his own slaves, and in response, in accordance with ancient laws, the entire household of slaves was sentenced to die by crucifixion. This barbarous law hadn't been enacted for generations, and many Romans were repulsed, but the Christians were openly outraged, holding candle-lit vigils and drawing themselves, for the first time, to the attention of the emperor Nero, who, having grown to manhood in the Machiavellian world of the patricians, was suspicious of all sects and secret groups."

They walked through into the Crypt of the Popes, where the now-empty sepulchres had once contained as many as nine pontiffs at the same time. Beyond that lay the Crypt of Saint Cecilia, then ever more burial galleries. The party pressed on resolutely.

"The Christians weren't alone in their dismissal of imperial divinity," the tour guide added, "but they alone had dared to challenge Nero's authority on the streets of his own capital. All at once, phrases like *strana et illicita*—strange and unlawful, or *tenebrosa et lucifuga*—mysterious and opposed to light, became common parlance. As with the Jews in Nazi Germany, first it was the Christians' property that was damaged rather than their flesh, their names dragged through the gutter rather than their corpses. But after the great fire in A.D. 64, things became much worse. Unfounded accusations were made that the emperor himself had started the blaze, to clear space for his new Golden House, so in a panic, Nero blamed all on the Christians. Almost overnight, the bullying became genocide. Images of Christians being hurled into lion pits or burned as human torches are all too familiar."

Damien had now visited the catacombs several times since his arrival in Rome. The lesson of the place was inspirational without the lecture—in many of the niches ranged along the endless passages, bones were visible which bore signs of calcination through heat, which had been severed by blade or smashed by bludgeon. He couldn't suppress a shudder as he thought about it. At every junction now, narrow tunnels wound away into dimness, the bulbs placed at progressively less regular intervals on the ceilings, shedding only minimal light into the shadows cloaking the *forma* and *loculi*. It grew colder, danker; footsteps echoed eerily.

"Equally brutal emperors would come after Nero . . . Domitian, Decius, Valerian," said the tour guide, "though the detail of their atrocities is unnecessary. Look around you, and wonder what terror might have driven ordinary people to leave their homes and shops and eke out a molelike existence hidden down here. Of course, even then, they weren't safe. . . . There were massacres in these very catacombs, the Praetorian Guard— pagan Rome's own version of the SS—hunting through them." She stopped and looked keenly at the party. "Who knows . . . the blood of martyrs may have soaked into these very stones beneath our feet."

Then she turned and strode on, her round hips swaying beneath her tight linen skirt. Hot-faced, Damien glanced down. He wasn't thinking about that down here . . . *for God's sake, not down here!* The Cubicles of Sacraments would come next— that was something to anticipate, then the Region of Saint Miltiades. To take his mind off it completely, however, he meditated on the ghastly conflagration of those primitive times, and the despot who'd sparked it.

Of all pagan tyrants, none had been darker or more feared than Nero Claudius Caesar. The name alone was seared into the fabric of faith. A common misconception held that the "Beast of the Apocalypse," or "Antichrist," as described in

Revelations, referred to Satan himself, whereas scholars held it to mean Nero. That infamous number, 666, meaningless in any common study of demonology, was actually a coded Greek reference to Nero, and had been widely understood as such among anti-Caesarian groups at the time. The insane emperor had attacked the Christian faith with such fury that fear of him would linger long after his suicide. For centuries to come, even during other reigns of terror, Christians would dread that somehow Nero might return. Subsequently, their writers demonized him in text after text, until no crime or depravity was beyond him.

Damien almost smiled at one story he'd been told. In his private life, the emperor had reputedly been a rapist of voracious appetite. When the mood was on him, it was said, no servant or slave in his palace, regardless of sex or age, was safe. Allegedly, Nero had been so excited by the spectacle of lions feasting on Christians, that he'd had himself a lion-skin outfit made, which he would don and prowl his palace in, leaping upon any person who took his fancy. A removable codpiece had been stitched into the costume, enabling the emperor to then fully penetrate his victim. Damien wasn't sure where he had heard this tale, or who from, but it always made him smile . . . until now.

Now it had a different effect upon him.

He could scarcely believe the stealthy movement in the front of his jeans. Even here, it seemed, in this holiest place, he wasn't immune. Once again, the sight of the tour guide—with her handsome face and lush brown locks, with her big motherly breasts pushing against her smart blouse and jacket—set his loins astir. He tried to listen to her, but it was hopeless. She spoke beautiful, modulated English, yet even her voice was alluring—breathy, husky. When he stared down, to avoid eye contact, he found himself gazing at the bare feet in her heeled sandals—they were clean and brown, the toenails glossed. Above them . . . sturdy calves, shapely knees, then that tight linen skirt, which clung to the curve of her thighs. Doubtless, some man or other had enjoyed the womanly cleft concealed up there. Probably more than one . . . she was Italian after all—a sensual, sexually aware race—and just touching maturity . . . which meant widely experienced, probably with men both young and old, maybe even with women. Damien's erection was now painful. He wondered if she might spot it as she spoke, and then grow wet lipped and hoarse at the sight. He glanced up to look directly at her, knowing that he was dark haired and dark eyed, that he was young and virile, and that when he wanted to, he could call upon a wolfish, even devilish smile.

Disappointingly however, she wasn't looking at him . . . neither his face nor his crotch, but was smiling beatifically. "Here we have a fine example of early faith in Our Lord's promise of afterlife." She indicated a carving on the lid of a propped-up sarcophagus. Crudely drawn, but clearly visible, it depicted a human figure with a lamb held over its shoulders. "The Good Shepherd," the woman added, "whose gentle love was a source of inspiration even in times of the most acute fear."

Damien felt his lust deflate like a balloon. All of a sudden he remembered who he was and where he was. His cheeks flushed with guilt. He thrust his sweaty hands into his pockets . . . where they found only the clammy heap of lire he'd earlier planned to purchase pornography with. Helpless, he hung his head.

"Dark and dingy they may appear, but these halls must truly be imbued with Jesus's love," the woman continued. "Many times agnostics visit us here, and without fail I think they are moved by the aura of peace and purity. . . ."

Damien slipped quietly away. He had no option. A moment later, he was around a corner and walking fast; he didn't know where to, and for the moment at least, it didn't concern him. He wouldn't even look up or from side to side, for on every surface it seemed, litanies had been inscribed . . . Greek and Latin for the most part, but all exalting God or those put to death in His name. Unending lists of martyrs were scrawled there—*Eusebi, Phoenella, Severa.*

Damien wouldn't read any of them . . . he couldn't. His eyes weren't fit to gaze upon them . . . or indeed upon anything else down here. He'd first visited after the incident with the prostitute on the riverfront. He'd thought it would bring him forgiveness . . . in fact, he'd actually *expected* that. For the first time in this strange, foreign, bustling city, he'd believed that he'd find himself among brothers and sisters. How presumptuous, he now realized. He knuckled a tear from his eye . . . he'd always thought his calling genuine. As a child he'd been inspired by Father Tilton's aggressive sermons on Sundays; he'd gone to the cinema and sat awestricken through New Testament extravaganzas—*Ben Hur, Barabbas, Quo Vadis . . .*

Hollywood, of course: stirring music, epic crowd scenes, lashings of fake blood. It had its role and purpose, Damien supposed. But down here in the dust and stillness, it was a distant charade that, like so much else in his life, was little more really than a pretense of devotion.

He strode on . . . and came suddenly to a barred gate.

Damien stopped. His tears were partially dried. In none of his previous visits had he noticed this before. Beyond it, another gallery led away, curving quickly into shadow. From what he could see, no electric lighting was fitted down there—at the gallery's farthest end, a single torch flickered in a bracket.

Damien was not thin—at junior seminary he'd excelled at rugby and soccer, the regular training for which had gifted him a sturdy physique. In consequence, the barred gate appeared to present an impassable barrier. But as well as being strong, Damien was also supple. Sideways, and with some twisting and turning, he was able to slide himself through it. Once on the other side, oddly, he felt better . . . safer to wander with his thoughts maybe, without the lovely Italian lady to distract him.

Cautiously, he began to walk. As he'd seen through the bars, the gallery bent sharply right. Beyond this, it then passed under an arch into a small crypt or chapel. This too was lit by torches, and immediately Damien was able to see why it was currently closed to the public . . . spades, brushes, chisels, and other archaeological paraphernalia were strewn about the flagged floor. He strode on, passing through farther vaults . . . seeing more *loculi* filled with bones, more scarred and broken sarcophagi, and now—in addition—hearing a distant "crashing" sound, like hammering or the tramp of heavy feet. He stopped for a moment, to listen. It was difficult to work out exactly what it was . . . he imagined someone marching. Whatever, it only lasted a moment or so, before gradually dwindling into the distance.

Shrugging, he set off again, crossing another junction of corridors, entering a farther crypt where, to one side, fragments of mosaic were marked out with pins and tape. Damien only glanced at them as he passed . . . their images were indistinct, their once bright colors all but faded. As far as he could tell, they depicted a martyrdom . . . a female, possibly Saint Perpetua or Saint Rhais, bound and helpless in the hands of men wearing helms and breastplates.

Either a martyrdom . . . or a rape.

Damien stopped to consider this. Perpetua had been thrown to a bull, which had gored and tossed her, and then been finished off in the arena, hacked to pieces by gladiators; Rhais had been nailed to a cross, then set alight . . . but only after being smeared with pitch first, so she'd burn slowly like a candle. Had the brutish Praetorians made it even worse by raping those holy women as well? Damien backtracked and looked at the crumbling mosaics again. This woman here, though no facial features remained, was very feminine, described with flowing locks and a richly curved form beneath her simple shift. Was it unreasonable to expect that before they'd put her to death, they'd yanked her legs apart and invaded her saintly body?

Damien suddenly realized that he was breathing heavily.

Then he wondered what in God's name he was thinking.

*Even here . . . in this sanctified place.*

Cursing himself, he blundered away, staggering through to the next chamber. It wasn't his fault, he tried to tell himself. It had been her body . . . that firm, rounded body. . . .

*Bitch, harlot . . . big-titted whore!*

"No!" Damien shouted as he ran. "I didn't say that! I didn't think it!"

*Slut, strumpet,* the crackling old voice continued, *this is what your hot little quim deserves!*

He didn't stop running until he reached a stairway plunging downwards, where he came to a sliding halt, his skin moist with sweat. From what he could see, the level below was less well illuminated; fewer torches threw dark and writhing shadows across the foot of the steps. Distraught as he was, Damien might not have gone down there, had that distant tramping sound not suddenly assailed his ears again. . . . He glanced back uneasily. Narrow ways seemed to lead off in all directions, each one indistinguishable from the next. The noise could be coming from any one of them . . . but it was definitely drawing closer. Suddenly Damien was certain that it was leather soles he could hear, slamming on the ancient stonework . . . leather soles and the repeating clink of mail harness.

Without another thought, he tottered down the steps, to find himself in damper, narrower galleries. He set off into them all the same. Could he really be blamed if he found women desirable? Wasn't it natural? How had the Lord managed? Damien wondered. He'd been a man, hadn't He! How had He felt when He'd stood in front of the adulteress the mob had wanted to stone? That was another movie moment to reckon with . . . Claudia Cardinale, that most beautiful actress, hurled at the feet of ranting, rock-wielding men, clad only in some filmy chemise, her naked body entirely visible beneath—huge breasted, dusky skinned, her lustrous brown tresses spread out around her as she wept in the dust.

But what had the adulteress looked like in real life? Probably similar. And then . . . those fucking hypocrites! They'd genuinely wanted to kill her. But they'd probably wanted to fuck her first. Many there present probably had fucked her, and royally. . . .

An image on the wall brought Damien up sharp. He stopped in his tracks, the breath caught in his constricted throat. Seconds passed, then he glanced around. He'd entered a low anti-chamber, he realized, carved all over—ceiling, walls, and pillars—with arcane graffiti. Much of it ran higgledy-piggledy, messages cut sideways and backward, repeatedly crisscrossing, so that to make sense of it was a near-impossible task. It was even harder to tell which language the writing was in . . . probably Greek, though some of it must have been unintelligible even then. One thing easily recognizable, however, was the mural which had first caught Damien's eye. It was large and occupied a prominent position on the wall facing the entrance. From what he could tell, it was the Good Shepherd again, the sketchy outline of Jesus coming in from the fields, crook in hand, though on this occasion, no lamb lay across His shoulders. Curiously, it seemed to be following Him. And it didn't look much like a lamb either. For one thing, it was much, much bigger. . . .

Even as Damien stood there gazing, there was a low groan from somewhere close by. He looked sharply left, and through a narrow arch, spied an adjoining chamber. From this position he could see virtually nothing of it, but even the little he *could* see froze him rigid. For there was movement in there . . . some figure in rough, tawny garb was stirring as it lay prone upon a stone slab. Fiery shadows flickered over it.

Damien rubbed his eyes to ensure that he wasn't dreaming, but when he looked again, the slab was bare. Still half-dazed, he walked through. He had definitely seen movement . . . what was more it had been silken, orgiastic movement. The groan he'd heard . . . it had been male, but it had also been a groan of pleasure. He remembered the married man as the street girl engulfed him with her ample mouth. Damien half-expected the room to smell of sex when he entered it, perhaps to be bathed in soft, sweaty heat. But it wasn't. Instead, he found another small crypt or chapel, its roof and arching walls smooth and unblemished, its air dank and cool. In the center, the thing he thought a slab was in fact an old altar table . . . where terrorized people had probably once celebrated the Holy Eucharist.

The seminarian felt revulsion at his own thoughts. Was he really so lost as this?

For several moments he stood there helpless, wondering if he could utter a prayer or two, but so muddled that he couldn't think even of one.

Then he heard the growl.

It was low and rumbling . . . as if it came from some deep throat, some heavy, fur-flushed belly.

Damien started. He turned wildly, his heart thumping. . . .

On all sides, however, there were blank, empty archways, filled with shadow. The growl came again, this time more a snarl . . . as before, it was bass and powerful, rolling slowly. Damien felt his hair prickle. He backed to the table. Was it a dog perhaps, which had strayed in? That was a nice idea, but Damien knew this was no dog. It was more reminiscent of trips to the zoo he'd made. Damien began to wonder if there were other reasons why certain sections of these vaults might be caged off.

Even as he thought this, the growl rose in volume, until it became a roar. Without even thinking, he dashed madly for the nearest doorway, scrambling up a steep stone stair. It was very dark and slippery, but within a minute he'd made it to the top . . . only to find himself in a cul-de-sac—a small, circular chamber, dripping with water and lit by a single torch. Upright *loculi* had been dug into the walls, each one containing a sarcophagus. There were ten of them in total, and all but one stood open . . . their stone lids broken or fallen over. Ash and fragments of bone were all that remained inside them.

Damien felt his spine crawling. From somewhere below he could now hear footsteps. And they were growing louder. They were ascending behind him . . . *right behind him.*

In a panic, he retreated across the crypt, until he collided with the lid of the one enclosed sarcophagus. He turned and looked at it, his mind working furiously. That lid would be heavy, but it was also old, which meant that it was probably loose. Hurriedly, he fit his fingers around its edges and tried to haul it free. With effort, it would come away, and then he could hide in there . . . he'd be safe. It took *considerable* effort however, and only then, with a sharp grating sound, did it finally dislodge. Grunting, Damien shifted it aside, and at once, a waft of stale air enveloped him. He coughed, almost choked . . . and then he stared, aghast.

He'd expected rubble, disintegrating bones, at worst a complete human skeleton . . . but nothing like this.

Inside the coffin, almost completely preserved, there was a corpse . . . but such a corpse. It was tall and lean, but instead of a shroud and hood, it was encased in skins, one skin in particular in fact . . . a skin of sleek, tawny fur, which clothed it entirely, having been cut and stitched along the arms and legs to form trousers and sleeves, and drawn into gloves at the hands. More horrifying still, though, was the corpse's head . . . now hidden beneath the huge skull and clamped jaws of the original magnificent beast. Even after all this time, the thick golden mane was as full and lustrous as in life.

Damien was so stunned that he no longer heard the feet padding up towards the room.

In a near-stupor, he reached out and placed his fingers on the thing's chest, lightly pressing. It was stiff and cold, the rib bones beneath at first resisting, and then yielding with a faint crack; dust puffed out. Damien stepped back, still bewildered. This was all wrong, this abomination couldn't be here, not in a Christian necropolis. . . .

"Hallo?" said a small voice behind him.

He turned slowly . . . and beheld the tour guide, the Italian lady. She was holding a flashlight and gazing at him with puzzlement. By the looks of it, she was alone, but that didn't stop her from coming warily forward.

"Why are you here, sir? This part of the catacomb is closed to visitors. . . ."

Damien could only blather. "I . . . see why. What is this . . . some bizarre find which doesn't fit the bill?"

Her puzzlement seemed to grow. "I'm sorry . . . The catacombs are dangerous; you must come back now."

. "I'm talking about this," he said, turning. "This thing here. I—"

To his confusion, the sarcophagus now stood empty . . . save for a few crumbs of dirt. "Where . . . where is it?" he stammered.

"Sir?"

"Where's it gone?"

"You must come now, please."

"Where the devil is it?" he exploded, rounding on her. "What have you done with it?"

Startled, she backed away a step.

"You're playing some kind of joke—is that it?" Damien snapped. Then he lunged at her, catching her by the wrist. "*You bitch!* Get over here . . . See how you like *my* jokes. . . ."

She shrieked in terror and flailed at him with the flashlight, but he knocked it from her grasp, then flung her bodily into the empty cubicle, grabbing up the heavy lid and slamming it over her. Her screams became hysterical, but were audible only as muffled wails. Damien leaned against the lid with all his weight. He could hear her frantically on the other side.

"Bang all you want, you sow! This is what you deserve. . . ."

Slowly, his words tailed off. An icy second passed. Then abruptly, he stepped away, pinpricks of sweat all over his ashen face. He could scarcely believe what he'd just done! Hurriedly, with much grunting, he wrestled the lid aside again. This time it crashed onto the flagstones and shattered. The woman came out like a cork from a bottle. Eyes bulging, hair streaked across her scarlet face, she rebounded from Damien's chest, screeching wildly.

Desperately, he tried to grapple with her. "Wait . . . no. I'm sorry . . . It's not what you think."

But she was already past him, fleeing down the steps.

"Damn you!" Damien bellowed, as he chased her. "Don't you women understand anything!"

The moment she sensed that he was following, she began shrieking again, at the top of her voice.

"Jesus Christ!" Damien roared. She'd make it worse . . . She'd give everyone the wrong impression!

He bounded in pursuit, but already she'd vanished from sight. He couldn't afford that . . . He had to catch her, or at least get to the surface first, so that he could explain.

His descent became headlong flight. He slipped and fell twice, so when he reached the bottom he was breathless and in agony. He kept going, all the same, and stumbled back into the chapel with the altar table . . . only to be greeted by a streak of glittering metal and a crashing blow to his forehead.

For a split second his vision blacked out, his mind went reeling. A second blow followed . . . same ferocity, same implement, but this one detonated like a bomb. There was a blinding flash, then Damien—in flickering, ticker-tape imagery—saw the woman backing away from him, a hefty spade dropping from her hands.

In slow motion, the tool descended, turning over and over in midair, finally landing with a furious clatter. The next thing Damien knew, a cold flagstone lay against his cheek. His entire body was heavy, numb . . . like clay. Nothing made sense, yet as his vision faded, he still saw the woman, turning and staggering away.

And a half second later he saw something else . . . something shapeless and tawny, but moving at terrible speed. It emerged from somewhere behind him, and in one bound, had cleared the altar table. With a reverberating growl, it went hurtling after her. . . .

"*. . . you've made a genuine pig's ear of this one, haven't you, boy!*" *said Father Tilton, but not in the fond and friendly tone he normally used when he came for tea on Sunday evenings; in the aggressive, scornful voice he used during RE lessons at school, usually just before his hard hand swept to deal a stinging slap.* "*A genuine pig's ear!*"

*This was strange, Damien thought, because he wasn't in school. He was at home . . . in the living room of the small terraced house he shared with his mother. He knew he was there, because so many things were familiar . . . the worn rug with the brown patterns, the shilling-operated gas fire, the framed photo of his late father on the mantel above it. And Mum. Of course, Mum . . . in that prettiest summer dress of hers.*

"*I think you should go to bed now, Damien,*" *she said from the couch. She often sent him to bed shortly after Father Tilton arrived, but now it was without the usual hug and peck. Now she looked disappointed, despairing even . . . and he realized why. It was because of the* woman . . . the one he'd attacked and imprisoned. And why not? He'd be thrown out of seminary for certain after something like that . . . though surely he wasn't at seminary yet? Still, there was no excuse . . . no argument.

Without a word, he trooped to the door, glancing back only once. The four-square Father Tilton, with his gray sweater and head of chalk-white hair, could only scowl from the armchair, his face dark and pinched but somehow unsurprised by the terrible turn of events; Damien's mother, on the other hand, seemed too upset for words. She laid her cup of tea aside, uncrossed her shiny legs. Tears now trickled mascara down her dusky cheeks, dripping into her cleavage. Sniffling, she took a handkerchief from the table. He longed for her to look at him, but she wouldn't. Her mass of glossy brown hair fell over her face, as she dabbed at it.

As Damien ascended the cold, narrow stairway to bed, he heard the couch springs creak.

"There there, my dear," said Father Tilton in his crackling old voice. "The boy may come to something yet. Who knows what plans God has for us. . . ."

. . . Damien was slumped against the wall in the crypt, his joints cramped, his head splitting.

Weakly, he tried to sit up . . . and instantly felt sick to the pit of his stomach; his neck ached, at least one of his eyes was solidly buried under mounds of bruised and swollen flesh. Gingerly, he felt at it . . . his entire face was crusty with blood, his fringe hung down in matted, gluey strands. When he probed further, he found a wad of damp cloth, and below that several deep gashes.

Very slowly, his sense of balance tilting, he struggled to his feet. More whoozy moments passed. Things shifted into focus only gradually . . . but when they did, it was no great surprise to see that the woman had been brought back. Not only that, she'd been brought back, despoiled of her clothes and now lay spread-eagled on the altar table, fastened by her wrists and ankles with ragged strips of linen.

Damien approached her, still too disoriented to fully appreciate her flaunted charms. He *did* notice, however, that she was conscious and watching him . . . once again, wide-eyed with terror. Only the additional strips of linen, thrust into her mouth as a gag, prevented her from crying out. Her body was beaded in perspiration, and wriggled violently in its bonds. Damien saw bright finger marks on her ribs and thighs—rows of red welts, indicating rough handling.

"Well, at least you can't blame me for that," he mumbled. "What's the matter? Why're you frightened?"

At that moment, the makeshift poultice slipped down from his injured scalp . . . and he partly understood. He held the item up for inspection . . . It was a pair of female panties, cute—rather lacy in fact, for a woman of God—but now drenched scarlet. Damien pulled a face, then glanced at the various dark doorways. "I hope that's *my* blood . . . you sick bastard!"

From some distant place, there was a renewed *clump* of feet—heavily shod, crashing with military precision.

Damien snorted. "You can't frighten me with your jack-booted soldiers! What I do now . . . I do for myself." There was no point denying it—the woman's sumptuous body, so crudely displayed, filled him with desire. Man could only resist his natural impulse for so long.

So thinking, he placed a bloodstained hand on her left breast, and tweaked its brown nipple. Then more softly, hoping to both tickle and titillate, he ran his fingertips down her ribs, across her belly, and finally to the moist hairy grotto between her thighs. He would have enjoyed prodding that private place, inspecting it in minute detail, but time, Damien knew, was not on his side. Instead, he turned and searched the chapel floor. Almost immediately he found what he was looking for: the workman's spade she'd struck him with, its dusty blade still spotted with blood. He picked it up and hefted it.

The woman regarded him with even greater consternation. The eyes bulged from her waxen face, muffled exclamations came through her gag.

Damien nodded, understanding her horror, but assuring

himself there was no other way. "I'll make it quick," he told her.

From some deep recess in the nearby passages, there was a low, contented growl.

"Those who are about to die, we salute you!" Damien shouted with a raucous laugh, and then he raised the spade above his head.

The woman writhed; the growl became a purr, rumbling from tunnel to tunnel.

Damien swung the spade like an ax, driving it down with all his might. And his aim was true.

With that first blow, he slashed clean through the linen strap at the captive's right wrist. There was a deafening clang, sparks flashed. Before even the woman had realized what was happening, he'd raised the tool a second time and swept it down again, this time severing the bond at her ankle. Instantly, the growl rose up into a furious roar, blasting through the galleries like cannon fire.

"Hurry!" Damien shouted. "Get out of here!"

Still regarding him with dread, the woman yanked the gag from her mouth, sat up hurriedly, and began to work at the remaining knots. Her supple body ran with sweat, the claw trails flushed a livid crimson. But all of a sudden, those tramping feet sounded closer . . . much, much closer. Once again, arms and armor clanked.

*"Hurry!"* Damien screamed, and now the woman screamed as well, hoarsely, cowering away from him . . . as if for everything else, *he* was still the greatest threat to her.

In fact, she was so terrified, it was miraculous she could concentrate sufficiently to loosen her remaining straps, but she somehow managed it, finally leaping from the table and haring naked through the nearest arch. Damien gazed after her, elated that she might survive.

And then mortification struck.

The passage she'd taken . . . she'd taken it blindly, with no concern for direction. And suddenly, without any doubt, this passage was the one from which the approaching footfalls echoed . . . *She was dashing right toward them.* Fleeting images beset him: tortured bodies transfixed to crosses; women and children wrapped in bloody fleeces; Saints Perpetua and Rhais, raped and scourged as they went to their deaths. . . .

*"No!"* he cried, giving frantic chase. *"Come back!"*

Seconds later, he caught sight of her—now hobbling with fatigue, but still rounding corner after corner, keeping well ahead. Damien called again for her to stop, but her only response was to throw him a fearful back glance.

Gasping, but determined, he raced in pursuit. Even when he saw the group of burly men intercept the woman from an adjacent tunnel, he continued. In fact, it gave him new purpose. Raising the spade over his head, he charged madly, bellowing. He saw her fall into their arms. Then she was lowered gently to the flagstones, but he wasn't fooled. Torchlight gleamed on their leather boots and gauntlets, on their thick belts, on their drawn steel. . . .

Three muzzle flashes followed in quick succession, each one accompanied by a thundering crash.

What seemed like several minutes, but was probably less than a second, passed before Damien realized what he was actually facing. It brought him to an immediate if stumbling halt. For a further second he was too perplexed to speak. He felt embarrassed, even foolish . . . Then he felt rather frightened. It wasn't going to be easy explaining this. In fact, at this moment—as one of the officers came slowly forward, his Beretta leveled—it probably wasn't a good idea even to try.

Without a word, Damien turned and ran, throwing the spade aside. A shout rang out, but he ignored it. Surely he could elude them down here? If he could just do that . . . at least long enough to get his thoughts together, to concoct a story?

But his strength was ebbing badly by the time he'd returned to the chapel.

He walked weakly to the altar table, at which point his knees collapsed. He slumped heavily down over the smooth surface, his elbows taking the brunt of the impact, but pain lancing through every portion of his being. His head drooped, his eyes began to close. And he sensed rather than saw the great tawny beast come needling into the chamber behind him, snarling under its rancid, blood-soaked breath.

Almost silently, it sprang up onto the table. Within a moment, its hot snout was next to his face. The hideous belly growl grew slowly more menacing, but Damien could only shake his head. "I'd . . . never have made a real priest," he sniggered. "I'm a lost . . . little lamb . . ."

Again, the snarl . . . deep fury reverberated like a throbbing engine.

Damien thought about Father Tilton . . . black-and-blue, kicked unconscious in his own sacristy.

Velvet jowls drew back to expose incisors curved like cavalry swords.

Then there was the married man near the river, the one who'd shouted and gesticulated. He too had bruised easily; he'd fallen among the trash cans like a rag doll.

Damien shook his head again . . . took a strangled breath. The animal was set to pounce; he could sense it. At any moment.

So *he* pounced first.

As his broken body fell limp across the table, he rose up in wrath and sprang upon the thing, bringing it down with savage force.

"But the Lord is not *my* shepherd!" he spat into its dense, golden curls. Then he clamped his jaws, and he sank his ivory teeth through its yielding skull.

Its growls became whimpers, then shrieks . . . and they echoed and echoed through the endless catacombs of the night.

*"Vengeance is mine," saith the Lord. "I will repay."*
                                        Romans 12:19

# THE MANNERLY MAN

## *Mehitobel Wilson*

At noon on Tuesday, Gregory took a break for lunch and discovered that his bathtub drain had not swallowed the water from his morning shower. He removed his sunglasses and looked at the standing water, which was milky with shed cells and fragrance-free soap. He did not sigh or frown. He tried to plunge the drain clear, without success. There were, he calculated, three options: He could ignore the problem, he could risk calling the landlord, or he could brave the grocery store in search of chemical relief.

The landlord was a calm man, a mannered man, who had always seemed safe to Gregory. But one never knows, does one? thought Gregory, and deleted the landlord from the list. If he ignored the tub, it might eventually overflow and leak through the floor, staining the ceiling of the apartment below. Gregory had never met the tenants, though he'd seen them, nodded through his dark lenses at their own implacable, sunglassed faces. One never knows.

He should have considered this eventuality and ordered some drain cleaner from an Internet site, but he had not. The only remaining option was to brave the store.

At times, being in public seemed more safely anonymous than did staying alone. Gregory tried not to test this theory often. No one tested anything anymore.

So he went to the door, smoothed his jumpsuit, adjusted his sunglasses, and opened it. He passed no one on the stairs. His drab sedan was dirty enough to be dull, but not so dirty as to offend anyone, he hoped. He got into it.

En route to the store, Gregory kept pace with the traffic. He slowed once to let a car merge into his lane, and peered over the tops of his sunglasses, checking the rearview mirror for any signs of aggression from the motorist directly behind him. There were none. He kept his face placid and did not sigh in relief.

His holster chafed his calf every time he pressed the clutch.

Gregory reached the store and found a parking space without incident.

While crossing the parking lot, however, he tensed his shoulders as he caught sight of a group of young teenage boys loitering outside the automatic doors. They were wearing primary-bright sweaters, jeans, and boots. Their postures were open and easy. One smoked. One sang. The third picked his nose. None of them wore sunglasses. All three of them turned their heads this way and that, their uncovered gazes casting sightlines that mannerly folk could nearly visualize, like rifle-mounted lasers streaming through smoke.

There was no other way into the store.

Gregory's own head balanced on his neck in the same position it always did, his face tilted down just low enough to be polite. Others he passed had their own faces tipped down into the meek zone. Gregory found that as dangerous as he found aggression.

He approached the doors. The boys stared at him. He felt a measure of fear, but not too much. There was never too much of anything anymore.

If any of them had a Legal left, and chose to exercise their Right against Gregory, he would feel no pain. So he hoped, anyway.

And he knew that the boys had nothing against him personally, that they were just looking for attention. It was rude, but not so rude as to attract the kind of attention they were looking for. Perhaps that was their point, Gregory realized. Perhaps they weren't obnoxious kids, but activists, trying to prove by example that survival did not depend on manners, after all.

Perhaps they each hoped to sacrifice themselves in order to waste the Legals of strangers, thereby potentially saving other, better lives. There were, Gregory had heard, people like that.

Gregory stepped onto the concrete walkway leading to the shaded doors of the store, and the boys pivoted their heads and let words through their sneery grins, words all running under each other, low and easy-mean. "Do you hate me? Do you? Want me dead? Want to kill me? Motherfucker, want to take me down? Am I bothering you? Are you scared? Think you bother me? Talk to me, talk to me, sir, give it up, hand it over, sir, where's your eyes, where's your gun, whatcha packin', am I rude?"

He walked through the words, ignored the adrenaline seething in his cheeks, and the doors sucked apart and let him in.

Very few customers shopped in the store. Most had the same agenda as Gregory: get in, get out, offend no one. Some were nearly furtive in their movements, which drew Gregory's attention and made him wish them well. One man held his smooth chin high and shoulders back, but his brave stance made him look all the more afraid. Gregory walked down an extra aisle to avoid that one.

In the six years since the Right to One had become final, the country's population had been cut in half. Everything was going according to plan. The equal-rights people were made happy by the fact that everyone had the Right to One, the choice-loving people were happy that they could choose whether or not to exercise their Right, the pro-life people had been thrilled that they could act as the fist of God and remain on the good side of the law. Citizens who preferred government aid appreciated the money liberated now that prisons were nearly obsolete; those who preferred to handle things themselves liked the freedom to do so.

And everyone was very, very polite.

You never know.

Fear of the ultimate retribution had made the remaining members of the population very considerate. Please, thank you, yes, sir. May I come in? Do you have a moment? Is this a good time?

It was hard. Gregory still wasn't sure, after all this time, whether he had the game down right. One mustn't bother anyone else or offend them. No interruptions of their private trains of thought, but no ignoring them, either.

The sunglasses were a big help. That way, everyone could gauge one another's moods without being noticed. The jumpsuits kept the fearful anonymous.

When the Right to One was put into effect, twenty percent of the population died within two weeks. Twenty percent of the population had inflicted wrongs, imagined or real, so deep that their murderers came for them immediately. More than one news story featured a man or woman who had crossed the country to exercise their Right and discovered that the person against whom they bore a deadly grudge had already been Legally killed. Most of those stories ended with addenda stating that, in fits of rage, the frustrated killers had wasted their Right on the next person that passed.

Thousands of people were then executed by the Authorities for surpassing their limit of One.

Over the years, the people who had prudently decided to save their Right for when they might really need it started to snap. Twelve items in the ten-items-or-less line could get you killed. Road rage exploded. Saying hello to a stranger could earn you a shot to the face; not doing so could result in the same end.

You never know.

Now that the country was paranoid, and now that the pensioners had killed the drug dealers, and the meek had killed the bullies, and abused and abusers killed one another, things had settled down a bit. Everyone tried to remain invisible, as Gregory did. Those who had exercised their Right hid the fact that they had, for they would be easy prey. Even a killing in self-defense was call for execution if it was not the One.

Some citizens refused their Legal Right because they feared that the whole law was a trick, that the Authorities executed all who exercised it and claimed that they were punishing people for their second kills, when each kill was the first.

The Authorities frightened everyone. They were executioners who could not themselves be killed.

Gregory had wanted very badly to be a police officer. The killing would bother him, but the relative immortality would have been worth it. But he had been afraid to apply, because it would bring him to their attention. What if they had not let him join the Force? What if one of the police he met hated him? The fear of being noticed was too much to bear, so Gregory stayed at home and telecommuted, delivering spreadsheets and calculations on the hour to the warehouse whose stock he tracked.

He had never exorcised his Right. He was a prudent man.

He carried his drain cleaner to the cash register. There was no clerk. Clerks drew ire too easily: made incorrect change, perhaps raised an eyebrow a millimeter if someone bought hemorrhoid cream. Editorials in the newspaper often commented upon the unforeseen way the Right to One had affected technology. Now Gregory waited as the placid, jumpsuited young woman in front of him fed her four purchases through the laser screen. Toothpaste, mouthwash, dental floss, and menthol lozenges. Gregory looked at the clean brown hair on the back of her head and wondered what was wrong with her mouth. Her total appeared on the LED readout; she agreed to pay it, and slotted her card in the reader. The gates opened and she crossed through. No alarm sounded. She turned her mirror-lensed face to Gregory, and her mouth looked fine to him.

He nodded at her, just barely, the slightest hint of congratulation in his movement, and pushed his bottle of cleaner through the red-light screen.

Her face was still turned towards him. Her mouth looked less fine now. It looked curly at the corners.

Then it cracked open and showed him teeth so white they looked tinged with blue, and he dropped his gaze to her hands. No gun. She was gathering her purchases into a mesh bag. He looked at her face again and realized that she was smiling.

Gregory was so stunned to see a living person smile directly

at him that he faltered for a moment. The customer in line behind him shifted and Gregory heard the squeak of shoe leather
against the linoleum. He turned quickly and said to the generic
man behind him, "I'm sorry, I was a bit distracted for a moment. My apologies."

The man's head ticked forward, as if he'd seen something in
Gregory's face that bothered him. "It's quite all right," he said.
His voice was pleasant.

Gregory was quick to pay, and anxious as he waited for the
gates to part. No alarm sounded.

The girl with the menthol lozenges stood waiting for him.
Her breath smelled of medicine. Her smile was huge and, now
that Gregory had assimilated it, genuine.

He was terrified.

She took off her sunglasses, revealing bloodshot eyes, and
said, "I've missed you very much. I fucked up, I know that. I
can't sleep without you next to me. The nightmares are worse
now that you're gone. Please have coffee with me? Please let
me talk to you? I know you must be hurting, but I need to explain some things."

Gregory had never seen the girl before in his life.

You just never fucking know.

He clenched his bottle of cleaner and wished for the first
time that he kept his gun in a shoulder holster.

Possibilities: She could be nuts, and he could die. She could
have mistaken him for someone else, and the confusion and
embarrassment she might suffer if he told her so might get him
killed. She might have used her One already, but that was not
a chance he was willing to take. He could play along, and she
might kill him for it. She might be trying to trick him and kill
him anyway.

"Coffee," he said. "That would be nice. Let me drive you."
He wanted one of her lozenges. His throat was so tight with
fear that the words hurt as they left him.

The smile vanished, her lips tightened with emotion, and
then the smile came back, smaller now, grateful. Nervous. Her
eyes filled with tears and she cut off his access to them with
her sunglasses.

They left the store. Behind them, the three boys stood in the shade and tried to draw attention. One of them said, "That's that fucking guy, man!" Gregory told himself that they could not mean him, that he had done nothing, and he did not look back.

Together, they walked toward his car.

She was very small.

His bottle of drain cleaner was heavy. Eighty fluid ounces.

"Thank you, Marcel," she whispered, and touched his wrist. He flinched. When was the last time he had been touched? Smiles, eyes, speech, and touch all in the space of four minutes, maybe five. His heart beat incorrectly. His breath was wrong. "You're welcome," he said, wishing he knew her name, wishing he knew whether or not a blow to the skull would knock her unconscious.

They reached his car. No one was parked in the space in front of his.

"Let me open the trunk," he said, "so you can put your groceries in the back." He unlocked his car, got in, and started the engine. He left his door open. He pressed the trunk release and the pneumatic struts raised the hatch. He leaned out of his door and saw her walk to the back of the car, saw his brake lights turn the legs of her khaki jumpsuit a sour mauve.

Gregory dropped the brake and hit the gas. The car jumped forward, the engine stammered a moment, and then he shot across the parking lot. His door banged into his left elbow and he gritted his teeth, caught it, closed it properly. The tires hit the canary speed bump guarding the exit and the trunk lid sprung wide, then slammed shut. He braked at the street and checked the rearview mirror. The girl stood, stunned, where he'd left her. Her mesh bag dangled from her hand. She made no attempt to pull out a weapon.

He signaled, turned onto the street, and drove home.

A dusty green car was parking parallel on his street. He idled behind them, giving them plenty of room to maneuver. Once they had parked, he steered past at a distance so they could open their car door without having to wait for him to pass.

He parked and got out of the car. The bottle in his hand seemed heavier now. He carried it to the steps of his building, where another tenant stood, an older man, graying, fumbling with his keys. Gregory hung back for an instant, having had enough interaction for one day. But that might make the man feel tense, watched, and it's never wise to cause tension in strangers.

So Gregory stepped up and the man turned his head a bit, his beard rasping against the collar of his starched jumpsuit, and said, "I'm sorry about the wait. I'm having a little trouble with my keys."

"That's quite all right," said Gregory. "I'm in no hurry." An offer to help would be friendly, but might also be considered insulting. He was torn.

The man did not turn back to the door. Instead, he stared at Gregory through smoke-gray lenses. "Pardon me, er. I must say I'm surprised to see you here. Please accept my condolences. She was a lovely woman."

Gregory, at a loss, raised his bottle of drain cleaner. "I live in this building, sir. You may have mistaken me for someone else."

The man looked grave. "I understand. Please forgive my intrusion. I will, of course, be discreet. No one will know that you are here." He turned back to the door, fitted his key into the lock, and entered the building, letting the door fall shut behind him. Gregory felt a flare of annoyance at the fact that the man had not held the door, and was surprised at himself for it.

He gave the man plenty of time to get inside his apartment and out of his way before he entered the building himself.

His hands shook a little as he unlocked his apartment door. Once inside, he allowed himself a moment of release: He shook openly, breathed deeply, lost control of his expression, and let his face tighten upon itself with relief.

No way would he leave the house again. Never. Not for weeks, at least, he told himself. People were too unpredictable. They spoke. They demanded engagement. They threw blue-white smiles at strangers and said things that made no sense. They killed. They put him in very uncomfortable situations and he hated them for it as much as he feared them. You never know.

Then he seized control of himself, smoothed his jumpsuit, and took off his sunglasses. He inspected the instructions on the bottle of drain cleaner. He followed them. Chemical fumes filled the bathroom. He considered opening the window an inch for ventilation, but feared that the fumes might bother a neighbor, so he turned on the exhaust fan instead. The bottle suggested he allow fifteen minutes for the treatment to work.

He logged onto the Internet and went grocery shopping. Along with the canned and frozen goods he chose drain cleaner, throat lozenges (cherry), and aspirin.

He also ordered three jumpsuits and a new pair of sunglasses, a pair styled differently than his own.

Thirty minutes had passed. Gregory was a prudent man. The drain cleaner had not worked.

Gregory frowned down at the still, clouded water and then flinched as he heard a sound he hadn't heard in years: the sound of a fist rapping on his door.

It was not even one-thirty yet. He couldn't pretend to be asleep. He crept to the door and craned his neck toward the peephole, trying to stay as far away from the door as possible, but still see into the hallway. This never worked and didn't work today. He had to put his eye right to the door.

A woman stood in the hallway, a brunette, his age. Her sunglasses were tortoiseshell. In these times, those were as much of a statement as musical fuschia cat's-eye sunglasses would have been seven years before. She wore lipstick. It was a neutral beige, but it still caught his eye. She liked attention. This meant that she either had a death wish, or that she had little to fear.

Gregory wondered if a woman like this, a jumpsuited, sunglassed woman who still had an edge of individuality, might touch him. Her mouth was pretty.

Her hands were pretty, too. She raised one and knocked again.

Gregory relished the fact that he was, physically, inches away from her, staring directly at her face, and that she didn't know. Even in sunglasses, on the street (never!) he never allowed himself to fully turn his face toward a stranger. Toward anyone. Everyone was a stranger now.

He thought of the confused girl from the store and remembered how his blood had felt when she'd smiled at him.

The woman in the hall made her glossy beige lips twist around, hesitated, then knocked once more.

Gregory raised his own fist and knocked back at her.

She laughed. She laughed aloud and her teeth weren't scary at all. Her throat was long when she threw her head back. He wondered how he could make her do that again.

He opened the door.

"Oh!" she said, and took a step back.

"Hello," said Gregory. "May I help you?"

"Hello, yes. No. I actually came to help you, I believe." Despite the coverage of her sunglasses, he could tell that she was staring at him. He stared back. He saw his reflection in her lenses and blinked at himself. Blinked: He'd forgotten to put on his own shades.

"I see. Well, thank you very much. How so?"

"I live in 221B. Your package was delivered to my door by accident. It is addressed to 221A. But it says Gregory Binford." Her forehead pinched and flushed.

"I'm Gregory Binford," he said. "This is thoughtful of you, thank you."

"Gregory Binford," she repeated.

Something oily rose inside him. His joints felt slow. He wished that the sick oil would reach them and make him fast so he could shut the door.

The woman pulled her canvas satchel around her pelvis and pulled back the flap. Gregory felt tight all over and knew that she could see his eyes, would read the fear there. Shut the door. Kick her and shut the door! Hit her in the face! Blind her with broken tortoiseshell!

Her hand slid into the satchel and he heard the rush of enormous wings in his ears and she pulled out a flat brown package.

"Gregory Binford, 221A." She held the package to her face.

Her fingernails were painted with clear gloss and Gregory stared at them. They looked crystalline and he wanted to tap his teeth against them and hold her fingertips on his tongue.

She raised her hand and pushed her sunglasses up to crown her head, and then Gregory was eye to eye with another human, and she said, "Please forgive me for being forward, but I would like to come in for a moment, if you don't mind." Her words were appropriate, but there was no formality in her voice at all. Instead, she sounded exhilarated, nervous.

She stepped forward and stood on his threshold. If he slammed the door right now, right now hard, he could knock her out, maybe she would even fall down the steps and break her neck. That would be an accident, not his Right. Even if it were his One, it would stop her from looking at him, from doing this to him. He gripped the edge of the door down low and his shoulder tensed to swing it shut.

But she came into his home and reached out as if to touch him and then he couldn't move at all. Her hand stopped and hung in the air, her fingers twitched.

"You used to be famous," she breathed. "Does that mean you still are? Once known, always known, I guess." Her teeth, scarier now, dented her lower lip for an instant. The tip of her tongue flashed out and licked beige lips wet. Gregory backed against the wall opposite the door and she toed the door shut. God, alone, alone with bare eyes and a woman. He wanted to tell her that he had never been famous at all. He wanted her to touch him.

"Famous," she said, in a fugue. Then her eyes grew bright and she snapped her gaze to his, cocked her head sideways. "I don't blame you for changing your name, for going anonymous. But I've seen all of your movies. I was a fan even before you did *Cold Scars*, in fact—I watched you on the soaps. And the fact that you've survived . . . oh, you don't know how glad I am. I watch your movies and I mourn for you. They're all dead now, you know. Lovers and fans and—oh, Mickey, don't ever think that I'm one of those fans, never ever think that."

She forgot herself and put her hand on his arm. She drew a

fast, hard breath and shook as she exhaled. Her voice grew heavy. She had to expend effort to lift it into words. "You have always been so strong, so beautiful. The fact that you've survived proves how strong you are."

Gregory disagreed with this, but agreed very much with the flutter of her fingertips on his forearm.

The woman was bats, he knew, but this would be so easy, and she was so convinced of her delusion that she would never notice.

Gregory put his hand on hers and said, "What is your name?"

"Ann," she said, and it didn't sound like a name, it sounded like a noise that had fallen out of her.

Her hand moved under his, cool and trembling. He wanted to keep it. But he was a prudent man, and he said, "Would you like to have dinner tonight, Ann?"

Ann's eyes grew wide and wet, as did her smile. She nodded and gave an affirmative hum.

"Would six o'clock be a comfortable time for you?" Oh, it would, it would. "I'll see you then, Ann. Thank you for bringing my package. I'm very glad to have met you." He dared to put his hands on her shoulders and as he gentled her toward the door again, he marveled at the flex of bird bones beneath his thumbs. She was cooing.

"Good-bye, Mickey," she said, and he smiled at her, nodded, and closed the door. Locked it. Pressed his forehead to the wood and focused on the stretch of his lips. A smile. The air dried his teeth and he put his lips over them, where they belonged.

Gregory returned to the bathroom and stared into the mirror. Work could wait. What was making these people look at him funny, mistaking him for other men? He examined himself. Brown hair, brown eyes, and a face. Clean guy. Bland guy. Utterly normal and unremarkable guy. He could be any one of a thousand men.

Sunglasses, jumpsuit, please do pardon me, I'm so sorry to have bothered you. No smile, no eyes, no expression, no self-expression. He was just a man, purely manners and anonymity.

He was nobody.

He could be anybody.

Gregory unholstered his gun and weighed it, tipping it from one hand to the other. Who would the Authorities see, if they saw him?

He frowned. Ann and the girl at the store, could he have known them once? No, of course not. He would have remembered the terrible magnesium teeth of the shopper and the gaudy colorful frames of Ann's sunglasses.

It was two o'clock. Water stood in the bathtub, still. He had no mind for work.

He passed the time on the Internet. He ordered a shoulder holster. He researched the film *Cold Scars* and its star, Mickey Samson. Samson was four years older than Gregory, and six inches shorter. Ann would not know about the height difference. Samson's whereabouts were unknown. This was typical of personalities famous before the Law was passed. There were few stars now; television displayed reality footage, and entertainment shows were most often animated. News shows contained footage and voice-overs instead of anchors and live reporters. Movies were reminiscent of 1950s films, wherein much of the story was dialogue based and set in homes. The cooperation among the sheer numbers of crew members needed for long shoots on location had made effects-heavy action films obsolete. The primary tool of entertainment was the State Internet, a closed system for citizens only. Text was king.

Despite the physical suggestion of anonymity cultivated by the jumpsuited population, the laws demanded that individuals take responsibility for their words and actions. Online, for instance, all users operated under their own names. Their home addresses and private phone numbers were available to the public. Manners reigned on the State Internet, too.

At five o'clock, Gregory shaved, dressed, combed his hair. He polished his sunglasses. His jumpsuit was crisp. His boots were clean and glossy, but not too glossy.

At five-forty, he sat down to wait.

Fourteen minutes later, he heard movement in the building hallway, and saw the shadows of feet at his door. He waited for Ann's knock. It did not come.

Once again, Gregory crept to the door and peered through the lens. Ann stood outside. Her upper teeth pressed into her lower lip. She pinched her earlobe. She drew back the cuff of her fawn jumpsuit with her fingertips and examined her watch. She looked at the door, then back at her watch. The watch was scarlet. Gregory's own watch was matte black. He wondered how Ann had survived for so long with all her attention-getting accessories.

Her chest swelled, deflated, then swelled again, and she held it that way and knocked on the door.

Knocked again.

Gregory stared through the peephole until she could hold her breath no more, and just as she let her posture slip, he thumbed the lock and opened the door. Her shoulders were still caved in, but her eyebrows rose above the tops of her sunglasses, and she squeaked.

"Good evening, Ann. I'm honored that you returned."

She wobbled her head a little and then regained her composure somewhat, and said, "Good evening, Mickey. Gregory. Which do you prefer?"

"Gregory please. Mickey must be our secret."

"Of course." Penny-sized jowls rose at the corners of her mouth, indicating her disappointment. They faded as she controlled her face.

"I would be happy to ask you in, under normal circumstances. Tonight I thought you might like to come with me to see Shakespeare performed in the park. *Othello*, I think. The Web schedule says there will be dim sum vending kiosks there."

"That sounds just wonderful," she said.

Gregory nodded. "It begins at six-thirty. We can walk to the park. There may be a crowd," he warned. He could barely speak the word "crowd," so unnerved was he by the possibility.

Ann could contain herself no longer. "Who cares?" she asked, reaching for and catching his hand. "Six-thirty? Not much time. Let's go!" Her smile was broad and eager.

Mistake, thought Gregory. Being in public with this woman

was like taking an alligator for a stroll. She was all teeth and quickness, but even when quiet, she wanted attention. The skin that gloved her dangerous flesh felt nice against his, but not nice enough to stop him from fearing her.

They left for the park.

The walk took five minutes. Ann chattered the whole time. Her plumbing was bad, too (perhaps Gregory would bother the landlord, after all), and she detailed the stagnant contents of her kitchen sink to him. Her toilet was clogged, too. She told him that, until it was fixed, she tried not to eat or drink much at home, to keep her body from forcing her to use the restroom. He would rather not have heard this and thought it appallingly uncouth of her to have told him. Her tongue was death. He wanted it far away from him.

They entered the gates of the park and passed through the arbor. Ahead lay the parade grass. The air was indigo with dusk. The grass was populated by quiet people wearing sand-colored coveralls. The dim sum kiosks were tastefully lit, and each stood as the heart of the wheel spoked by queues of polite citizens. Here and there white-suited Authorities monitored the quiet throng.

"Oh, Mickey honey, the play's going to start soon. Let's eat during intermission, or afterward, we can eat afterward if you want." Ann's hand gathered the fabric of his right sleeve at the elbow and bunched it up as she hauled him toward the small stage. The button that held the cuff closed popped off as she dragged the fabric up his forearm. He was glad he'd ordered new jumpsuits.

Gregory offered apologies and excuses to each person she brushed against. He doubted his words could be heard over her own, which were growing shrill.

People.

He had brought this upon himself. It had been an experiment. It had failed. His eyes watered behind his glasses.

It would be rude of him to yank his arm away from her. It might anger her. Anger is danger.

But Gregory was angry himself. That, too, was danger. Danger to her. And, he thought, if she was too stupid to realize what she was doing to him, it might be polite to enlighten her.

So he did.

"Ann. Ann." He stopped short and she stumbled back into him, her momentum interrupted. Her hair bounced against his chin. "Pardon me, but you seem to be growing a bit overexcited. I am concerned that your talking is bothering other patrons."

She whirled around and struck him in the sternum with the heel of her open hand. "Fuck you," she snapped. "I have the upper hand here. I know who you are, Mickey fucking Samson. I know you used your Legal two years ago, right before you disappeared. You killed that movie critic." She fingered the collar of his jumpsuit and smirked at him. "Sorry, you're embarrassed. You'll have to get used to it, lover. Now let's sit here. It's a nice place. We're as close to the stage as we're gonna get. I know you don't want to be right up front because the actors might recognize you, right? Here's good."

She sat down on the grass, her legs crossed. Her hip bone pressed the toe of his boot.

He thought about kicking her in the back of the head.

He thought about her mouth. He'd wanted so badly to feel her lips, earlier.

So he knelt down behind her and drew his knife from his boot, folded his left hand over her slick beige talkative lips and brought his right one around to shove the knife through her larynx.

Her hair smelled like lemons.

Her lips moved against his palm and her blood moved down his wrist. Her shoulders bucked hard against his own throat. It felt nice. He stirred the insides of her throat with the blade, crushing and severing her windpipe. The sounds were bad.

Then his One was dead.

Gregory pulled the knife from her neck and wiped the blade on the grass. He slid it back into the sheath in his boot. He wiped his wrist on the grass and pulled the sleeve down over it. The cuff hung loose but hid the blood.

He checked behind him and saw that the crowd was standing. The play was about to start. They stood to honor the players. Gregory stood, too. Two men in white suits strode toward him from the stage, their eyes hollowed by dusk.

Gregory took four steps backward, then four to the right. Five back. Three left. He stopped when a man touched his shoulder and said to him, "Pardon me, but aren't you Professor Brooks? You taught my class last semester. It was an excellent class."

"Thank you," said Gregory. "I remember you. You were a talented student.

The man looked very much like Mickey Samson.

"Excuse me," said Gregory. "I must be going." He walked another dozen yards, then turned to face the stage.

The Authorities fixed hard stares on a man twenty paces closer to the stage than Gregory. The man's posture was calm and confident. The Authorities approached him and stood before him, spoke to him. His posture did not change. He drew forth identification and one of the men in white scanned the chip with their ID databank device. The second Authority listened to the verdict of the first, then spoke at length, face fixed and mechanical, to the man. The man's shoulders twisted and his head turned from side to side. The first Authority extended his hand to the man's neck and administered the lethal dose via syringe.

Gregory watched all of this, but he was calm. He did not stare. It's not polite to stare.

Subdued applause came from the crowd, then, as the curtain rose.

The man next to Gregory smiled at him and said, "I'm so glad we came here. This was a lovely idea, just what I needed. Thank you."

Gregory smiled back. "I'm glad you're happy."

He continued to smile.

# JUST SOMEONE HER MOTHER MIGHT KNOW

## *Michelle Scalise*

I found an index finger on the front porch this morning. It was just lying there next to the Sunday paper like a grizzly insert. The end looked ragged enough to have been bitten or maybe even torn off. For a moment I considered calling Errol and asking him, casual-like so he wouldn't think I was some kind of freak, if he might have lost something at my house. But I knew better. His hands were long and thin. This digit was more like a small fat sausage tipped with pale pink nail polish.

Mama wore that shade for as long as I could remember. Even when the sickness was eating out her stomach like screw worms in a cow, she would demand in a raw, pain-twisted voice that I paint them for her. Mama said the Lord wouldn't fault her such a tiny vanity. I think she may have been wrong.

While I used the sports section to scoop the finger up, I recalled a funny dream I had last night after Errol left. I was sleeping on the couch and I thought I woke up to a slow, steady scratching noise on the window right above my head. Actually, it sounded more like something was trying to dig through the glass.

I carried the digit like a wedding ring on a velvet pillow into the kitchen. One more quick look just to make sure I wasn't imagining things, then tossed it in the trash. I almost made it out to my truck before I threw up the scrambled eggs with ketchup I had for breakfast.

\*     \*     \*

About noon Errol Flynn Pederson walked into the hardware store with his girlfriend hanging on his arm. Traci Lynn looked as misplaced as a hooker at a high school prom. I continued stocking boxes of nails and screws until her phony, baby-doll voice forced me to grip the shelves to keep from tackling her skinny ass right into the new power mower display.

"Errol Flynn," she said. "You promised you'd take me shoppin' today. I want a new dress not a damn set of drill bits." She was wearing the same black miniskirt and tiny white T-shirt I'd seen her in last night before she went storming out of the bar, yelling something about finding a real man who'd treat her with respect. I should have known she didn't mean a word of it.

I wanted to crawl under the shelves or launch a hammer at her head.

Reaching into the pocket of his grease-stained jeans, Errol handed her a twenty. "I need to take care of somthin'. Go shop . . . and try to find an outfit that'll cover your back end for a change."

Traci Lynn primped her short, dirty brown hair and sashayed out the door. Mr. McGee, my boss, looked like he might jump the counter just to get a taste of her.

In high school, Errol Flynn Pederson was so pretty it almost made me cry just to stand behind him in the lunch line. But time has a way of evening out the haves from the have-nots. A badly healed broken nose from a fight, a chipped front tooth from an illegal tackle he swears he should never have been called for, and years of drinking had given him a hard edge that only dim bar lights could disguise. Or perhaps I just didn't want to see the flaws so I smudged them out like fingerprints on a windowpane.

His mama—he'd told me last night when he couldn't think of anything else to talk about—loved Errol Flynn movies so she thought she was being real sophisticated when she named him. I didn't bother telling him that his namesake was a Communist who enjoyed doing unwholesome things to young girls.

Errol walked down the aisle as if he were still the center of every ugly girl's universe. "Well, if it ain't Eleanor Rose. You look like you got lucky last night."

Mr. McGee glared.

Grabbing Errol's thin muscular arm, I pulled him down the fans and portable heaters' aisle. "Are you tryin' to get me fired?"

"I was just playin' with you." He looked me up and down like I was a damaged car without any hope of repair and shook his head. "I wanted to make sure you wasn't goin' to say anything to Traci Lynn about what happened. See, I had too much to drink and after she went stormin' out like that . . . I mean, I'd never . . ."

I ran my fingers through the mess of short dark tangles on my head, giving my best impression of an inviting smile. "I thought you might come over again tonight. You know . . . if you're not busy. I could make you dinner."

"Well, I got plans with Traci . . . maybe afterwards if I ain't too worn out." He smirked. "What the hell kind of woman works in a hardware store?"

The kind not pretty enough to work in the clothes stores over at the mall, I wanted to shout. Instead I mumbled something about Mr. McGee's benefit package as he left me standing there alone, pushing dust with my black boot.

"You are one strange girl," Errol was saying as I led him down the hall into Mama's old bedroom. "We ain't doing it in your room just cause you got a picture of Jesus over your bed? I mean, hell, it's just a cheap paint-by-numbers. He ain't actually crucified up there, you know." I could smell Traci Lynn's perfume on him. "I think you just get off fuckin' in your dead mama's bed. Yeah, one of them fetishes like that Farber kid in school, who used to pay my sister to take off her shoes and socks so he could suck her toes. You know if you'd have acted a little bit normal in high school you might have gotten laid once in a while."

"This is my house now," I said, turning on the dim overhead light and closing the door behind us. "So we can make love anywhere we choose."

"Trust me, Eleanor, what we're doin' ain't called 'makin' love.'" He fell across the bed, raising his arms behind his head. Black hair, soft as feathers, fell across his cheek.

It almost made me cry, the harsh glare he put on us. But God, he looked like a prince waiting for me.

"What'd your mama die of?" he asked while I was untangling the knot in my boot laces.

I pushed the question aside. "How come you picked me over Traci Lynn tonight?"

"Who says I didn't choose you both?" he laughed.

Pulling my shirt up over my head, I said, "Mama used to think I was sneakin' boys into my room at night. Once, when I was readin' comics, I crept up and opened the door quiet as a spy and found her on her knees with a water glass up to her ear. She didn't even have the sense to act ashamed. 'I know you're a dirty whore, Eleanor Rose,' she used to say. 'The Lord speaks to me and He tells me all the nasty things you do with boys.'"

My bra, held together on one side by a safety pin came next. Errol emptied his pockets and unzipped his jeans, but left them on. Dark red love bites like welts covered his neck. It didn't really matter much. The night distorts everything; sometimes it even shapes and shades a lover.

Errol laughed. "I remember your mama from church. She was always talkin' in tongues. My daddy said she was just fakin' it to get attention."

I knelt above him, straddling his thighs with my scraped knees. But when I tried leaning down for a kiss, he turned his head as if he too was searching for a softer hue of reality. I got myself wet with a little spit, knowing after last night that Errol wasn't much for foreplay, then pushed hard until I felt him inside me.

Wrapping his arms around my waist, he pulled me down. Traci's perfume was everywhere, like a foul presence hovering over the bed. I licked her stain from his throat as if it would fade.

Errol grabbed my shoulders so rough it forced me to stop. "Did you hear that?"

I did. It sounded like something scraping at the bedroom door. But I needed to finish first before I gave a damn.

I think I heard someone cry my name when Errol came.

Afterward, I feigned sleep, watching him sleek as a snake in the shadows as he quietly riffled through my wallet on the nightstand.

Everything has its price, Mama would say. It was the only quote she had that didn't come directly from God's own majestic mouth. Though I suppose the Lord might have told her that, too.

I curled up in the damp comforter that smelled of sex, Traci Lynn's drugstore scent and, like a ghost, my mother's dying breath.

In the morning, I found a water glass outside the bedroom door.

And an ear.

I should have known better than to think she'd take it lying down.

I pressed the ear down the garbage disposal with one of her silver-plated spoons she never allowed anyone to eat with besides the preacher when he'd come visit on Saturdays.

The next night, in Mama's bedroom, I was showing Errol what I could do to him on my knees when something shook the door. He grabbed my head before I could stop, pushing into my mouth again, saying, "It's probably just the heater kickin' on."

"Eleanor Rose, you dirty whore!" Mama said as clearly as if she were standing next to me. "You think I don't see your wickedness?"

I jerked my head up and looked around. From the joyous look plastered on Errol's dark face I could tell he hadn't heard a thing.

With a low grunt, Errol forced me back on the cold wood floor. I felt myself tearing apart as he entered me dry. Each thrust coming faster as if I were a punishment he wanted to get done with.

Gazing up into the window, I looked for moonlight to bleed a little romance into the moment. Suddenly my body shook as if a current had been shot through my brain. Mama's haggard face, flesh hanging off like someone had taken a potato peeler to her skin, watched me through the dirty pane. Her right eye hung from its socket, dangling like a Christmas ball. Most of her matted grey hair was gone, torn out in bloody patches like a hideous quilt. Pieces of her black lips flapped at her chin as she called out. "You know where harlots and murderers end up, Eleanor Rose? I can show you plenty of them in that fancy graveyard you threw me in."

And then she was gone.

I was coming and screaming even as I tried to push Errol out of me.

He refused to spend the night, though I begged him, even offered him money to stay.

Once he left, I pulled the blanket up over my face. Like a frightened child, I listened to the house moan along with the wind outside. Angry shadows from the swaying weeping willow danced across the water-stained ceiling. Mama's old windup clock kept beat next to my ear.

"Mama, leave me be," I cried. "You was dyin' anyway. I didn't do nothin' the Lord wasn't tryin' to do Hisself."

Something was tapping on the window.

"This is my house now," I hissed. "And if I want to bring a man in here I can."

She was pounding with a strength she'd never had in life, as if she were going to break in the glass. I laughed hysterically, then quickly covered my mouth.

After an hour, Mama got tired and left me weeping on the pillow I'd used to smother her complaints two months ago.

I waited thirty years for her to stop breathing. Then another eight months listening to her fool doctor tell me, "I just want to prepare you, Eleanor Rose. Disease is gonna take her any-day now." So how much of a crime is it to kill a dying woman? Christ, she was in pain . . . at least I suspect she was. And I was tired.

\*   \*   \*

I found Mama's foot, still wearing the orthopedic, black lace-up shoe she'd always favored, the next day. I threw it through the living room window, watching as it tumbled off the porch like a dog's rubber toy. "Go fetch," I hollered.

At dusk I drove out to the Resthaven Memorial Cemetery. A hard, cold rain slapped my cheeks as I dragged a brand-new shovel across the graves of dearly departed and those no one much cared about at all. Mama's gravestone was small and simple, "BELOVED WIFE AND MOTHER," the usual stuff. Not quite honest but I couldn't exactly ask them to carve "CRAZY BITTER OLD WOMAN" on her stone. Some of the dirt and sod was pushed aside, but I knew she was still down there. Before I left the house, I searched inside and out for her just to be sure she wasn't hiding out in the damn bushes again or lurking in a closet.

"Mama, I'm sendin' you to Jesus's open arms whether you like it or not," I said tossing shovelfuls of wet soil over my shoulder. "And then I'm goin' home to fuck Errol Flynn on your pink bedspread. I may not even wash it this time when we're done." The sky turned black and starless before I finally struck something solid.

"Eleanor?"

I jumped at the sound of my name.

Errol stood behind me, rain drenched and beautiful, like one of those lovers in a movie who rushes through a violent storm to save his woman. "What the hell are you doin'?"

Brushing the water from my eyes, I glanced around. "How'd you find me here, honey?"

"I drove by and saw your truck parked with the lights on."

"I'm always forgettin' to shut them off. You think my battery's dead?"

"Christ, Eleanor! You're as fuckin' crazy as your mama." He tried to grab the shovel from my hands as I crawled up out of the hole but I pulled back.

"No!" I cried. "You don't know what she's been doin'. She watches us at night. I may be a whore but she's a damn pervert, starin' through the window. Mama don't want me to be with you but I ain't gonna let her tell me what to do no more. I'll cut her up like a piece of meat and feed her to the dogs before I'll let her kill our love."

Errol's hand fell to his side. A drop of rain clung to his bottom lip. I wanted to kiss it off so bad, wanted to hold it on my tongue like a jewel. But I could see he didn't believe a word I was saying. "I'll prove it to you." I jumped back into Mama's grave, pushing the wet dirt from her coffin. "You see here on the sides? She's broken the hinges to get out." I glanced up and smiled.

He was gone.

"Errol?" I called.

He was still up there. I could hear him moving around.

I stood on tiptoes, peering over the edge of the grave.

Mama threw Errol's head at me so hard I slammed back onto the coffin and screamed.

"You can kiss him all you want now," Mama said, glaring down on me. "I left his mouth for you, not that you deserve it considerin' how you killed me but the Lord says turn the other cheek." She smiled, using the stump of Errol's blood-drenched arm to wipe her lips, then bit into one of his fingers. I could hear her teeth crunching through bone like a dull wood saw.

I gazed down into my lover's startled, frozen face. Still so pretty in the distortions of moonlight.

I couldn't help myself.

Closing my eyes, I kissed his parted lips.

# THE OCEAN

## *Poppy Z. Brite*

*For Neil Gaiman, with gratitude*

It was right after the fight with Niccolo that Eli went for his last drive.

The fight wouldn't have been such a big deal under normal circumstances, if there was such a thing as "normal circumstances" for the members of Fly anymore. There had been fights before, and plenty of them. But this particular one touched on a lot of things that had preyed on Eli's mind lately. Such as the champagne and the feather pillows.

Eli had come back to his hotel room late one night after a concert, dead tired and lathered with dry sweat, sure he'd be asleep before he hit the mattress. He'd found Niccolo in his room with a very young Asian girl. Each had a bottle of champagne and was trying to pour it into the other's mouth. Most of it was going all over them and the bed. Eli's bed. Niccolo's trousers were drenched with it. The girl's breasts were slick with foam. The room reeked of champagne, sharp and sour. The floor was covered with a creamy pale fluff. Eli couldn't figure that out until he saw the flaccid pillowcases in a heap at the foot of the bed.

"We had a pillow fight," said Niccolo.

"Looks like a blizzard hit, hey?" said the Asian girl, and giggled.

Eli went to sleep in Niccolo's room. He woke at seven the next morning with a silvery-delicate headache and a sense of heaviness and warmth and rancid champagne on the bed beside him. The Asian girl had gone into a leaden doze on Eli's bed, and Niccolo couldn't stand to sleep on the wet mattress next to her. His tangled brown hair was spread out on the pillow next to Eli's face, and his legs were sprawled out under the covers, flung across Eli's. Eli kicked them away.

Then there was the blurb in the fan magazine. It was one of those magazines that had words like "PIX" and "INFO" and "SIZZLING COLOR" plastered all over its cover, and foldout posters of himself or Niccolo, or sometimes Bailey or Jock, or any combination of the four. The magazine was in Niccolo's suitcase; people gave those magazines to the guitarist, and he saved them to pore over obsessively when he was alone. There was a tall stack of them in his bedroom at home that he kept saying he was going to throw out, but Niccolo hadn't been home for months: The other four had taken a week off in the middle of their world tour and gone home, but Niccolo had gone to Paris to shop for rare occult books. The fans, who had nicknames for all of them, called Niccolo the "Spook."

Eli picked up the magazine and flipped through it. He knew it would put him in a bad mood for the rest of the day, and was about to toss it back onto Niccolo's bed when he saw a picture of himself and Marie. The caption said:

*Elijah Stiles of Fly, resplendent in black velvet trousers and leopard-skin jacket (fake—eccentric Eli labels himself a hardcore animal lover and is even considering becoming a vegetarian!!!). But that gorgeous mane of blond hair is always real! He attended this Broadway opening with an unidentified beauty.*

"Unidentified beauty." That was his girlfriend of two-and-a-half years, and the magazine writers knew it, and Eli knew they knew it. But the fans didn't know it, and didn't want to. It might disturb them. The fans, all the little girls, had to be sheltered from gossip column scandals and innuendo. They might get upset, tear the pinups off their bedroom walls, stop buying the records. No, you couldn't break the little girls' hearts.

Marie had to stay reduced to a nonentity, an unidentified beauty.

And there were the natty clothes, velvet frock coats, flowered silk shirts, trousers made of fabric that looked like striped Christmas candy. He got so sick of beautiful clothes that he went around naked at home. There was the way his hair felt stiff and dry at the ends because he hadn't cut it in two years; the fans liked it long. There was Niccolo's lovely young-old face. Early in the tour, Niccolo had fallen into a drunken sleep at an all-night party. When people began pouring half-empty glasses of beer over his head, Eli decided it was time to get him out of the way. Niccolo was so slight and thin that Eli was able to pick him up like a child and carry him back to his room. As he was draping a blanket over Niccolo, he looked at the small familiar face, the smooth cheeks, the impossibly straight nose. And he realized with something like dread that there were tiny lines around Niccolo's eyes. Niccolo often wore dark eyeliner for performances. That night's layer was still smeared around his eyes. It had crept capillary-like into the creases of his eyelids, forming a spiderweb pattern around his eyes. The breath from between his parted lips was sweet and spicy with wine. One hand was flung up on the pillow next to his face, loosely curled, with a delicate golden chain looped twice around its wrist. In the sleep of alcohol Niccolo was childlike, but the lines around his eyes made Eli see him ten years from now, wrung dry, his life the equivalent of a few faded rose petals on the floor of a ballroom. Then Eli became afraid that he would lose his own looks, and hated himself for caring. But Niccolo was twenty-five, and that was too young to have lines around your eyes.

Yes, it would have been a rough life if they weren't all hugely successful at their chosen career and filthy rich to boot. That was one of the things Niccolo told Eli during the fight. "Right," Niccolo said with that annoying quirk of his Cupid lips that Eli had become so used to. "Right. I bet there are lots of workers in South Africa who would just *love* to hear you pull the covers over your head and moan about how tough it is to be Elijah Stiles. They'd really feel for you, my friend."

"That isn't the point. No, I'm not going to give it up. I'm not going to go live on a kibbutz and raise fucking soybeans. But that doesn't mean I want the leopard either."

They were arguing about a public appearance Fly was scheduled to make at a record store in Virginia. Their publicist had hired an animal trainer to bring a full-grown leopard to the gig, a play on the fact that the big single from their album was called "Danger Spots." Usually Eli endured the hype, comforting himself with the notion that anything went as long as they didn't prostitute their actual music. Usually he wore the costume of golden rock god without complaint, cut whatever ribbons needed cutting, obligingly turned the bottle toward the photographers and let the champagne foam into Niccolo's glass.

The leopard caused him to rebel. In the first place, he told the publicist, the song's lyrics were about symbolic spots, not the real things on a leopard's hide. In the second place, the animal would obviously have to be drugged to the eyeballs and didn't need to spend an afternoon in a hot mall full of screaming teenage girls who would inevitably want to pat its head. It was the sickest form of conspicuous consumption, he told everyone, the degradation of a living thing. Finally Eli said he would only attend the appearance if the leopard did not, and the contract of trainer and beast was canceled. In the world of rock music, a band without its singer was a handicapped band. The trainer had to make up for the lost gig, and someone later told Eli that the big cat had ended up appearing that afternoon at the grand opening of a supermarket.

Eli spent most of the day in bed, at peace in the shady room until Niccolo stormed in, flicked on the overhead light, and accused him of trying to take over the band. They railed at each other for what seemed like several hours, until the others were lured in by the sound of their raised voices. Jock lounged on the bed next to Eli, interested. Bailey faded uncomfortably into the bathroom. Soon tiny plops and hisses were audible; Bailey liked to toss aspirin tablets into the toilet and watch them explode. Eli and Niccolo paused for breath and went on arguing.

Jock jumped up and slipped out the door, heading down the hall toward Niccolo's room. In a moment he returned with one of Niccolo's guitars. He perched his considerable bulk on the floor and began to strum. Jock was widely acknowledged as the hardest-hitting drummer on the scene, but he played guitar very badly and sang worse. "All we are saaaay-ing," he wailed, "is give peace a chaaaaaance."

He was so ridiculous that they had to laugh, which dissipated most of the tension in the room. Eli threw the bedclothes back and crossed the room to put his arm around Niccolo. Niccolo's shoulders were stiff, and when he wasn't smiling, his lips still had that hateful quirk. Eli knew there would be plenty of juicy arguments before the matter of the leopard and all the overtones Niccolo supposed it had were settled.

Eli wasn't up for it today. He cleared everyone out of his room under the pretense of taking a nap. Then he rose and dressed (a plain white T-shirt and old faded jeans with a red bandanna patch at one knee, and God, didn't they feel better than velvet jackets and pants so tight his balls couldn't breathe?) and left the room.

There was a crowd of teenagers outside, completely surrounding the hotel. They were holding a vigil, boosted every few hours by a glimpse of Eli, Niccolo, Bailey, or Jock. At the concierge desk, Eli arranged to rent a car for the afternoon. Driving had always relaxed him, especially if he could drive fast. They were in California, and the concierge informed him there was a Jaguar XKE coupe with a 4.2-liter engine available. He could take it out to the desert and let it rip.

As Eli turned to leave, the concierge looked worried. "Are you sure you don't want me to find someone to accompany you to the car, Mr. Stiles? Kids get excited and don't always know what they're doing. . . ."

"They're my fans. I can handle them." He refrained from pointing out how many times and in how many ways he *had* handled them, and simply asked the man to have the car brought around for him.

The girls were upon Eli as soon as he stepped outside. He was overwhelmed with the scents of perfume and watermelon bubble gum. Rose petals wafted around him and settled in his hair. A bunch of grapes was shoved into his hands, a reference to a Roman bacchanal in his lyrics. Brave little fingers touched him as lightly as wings. He smiled tolerantly. All of them had been through this too many times to count. He pressed gently through the crowd, afraid they'd hurt themselves if he moved too quickly. He was almost to the car when the pain stabbed through his wrist.

*"Jesus!"* For a few seconds he felt as if a white-hot needle had been pushed into his vein. He whirled on the crowd and studied their faces. Brushing him with their fingertips was one thing, but he was damned if he was going to let them hurt him. Their faces were all alike, innocuously pretty, heavily made up, very young. An occasional hand poked out of the crowd, grabbing at him. He dropped the bunch of grapes. They pounced on it immediately. He heard the fruit squelching as they fought over it.

Only when the car's door handle poked him in the small of his back did Eli realize he had been backing away from the crowd. He gave a feeble little wave, which elevated the girls to new heights of gasping and pointing, and fumbled with the key. A sense of relief seeped through him when he was inside the locked car.

Eli examined his wounded wrist. No wonder the girls had pointed at it when he waved—a fat worm of blood was running down his inner forearm. Tiny threads of scarlet crept through the fine blond hairs there, reminding him of the fine lines around Niccolo's eyes . . . which had most likely been from simple exhaustion. And the scratch on his wrist, which was already clotting up, hadn't been maliciously inflicted upon him by a groupie with blood lust. Probably one of the girls had been wearing a pin that had come undone, or had had something sharp sticking out of her handbag. Marie once had to have three stitches after gashing her finger on a razor blade buried deep in her purse. She used razors to cut her canvases and scrape paint off her wooden palette, but this one had hidden and turned on her. Eli had made her dump her purse out and throw away all the superfluous junk. Even now he smiled at the memory of some of the crap she'd had in there. Ads torn from magazines because she liked the colors, felt-tip pens and minuscule sketch pads, a red rubber dagger. She swore she'd never seen the last item before. Like Niccolo, women were natural packrats. Eli himself always ended up throwing things out and needing them later.

Girls fell across the hood of the Jag as he pulled out of the parking lot. He beeped the horn gently and inched away, one sneaker-clad foot poised over the brake pedal in case any of them should jump out in front of him. They flung grapes and roses after the car. He raised a hand—the uninjured one—in thanks.

Eli drove and drove, passing glossy storefronts, box-format office buildings, hotels like their own, but not as comfortable or well located. He drove past a bus station and thought about how well he liked flying. Niccolo hated it. His slender, skilled fingers would dig into the leather of his armrest as the plane took off, and though he liked watching the heavenlike formations of clouds and sunlight outside the window, he refused to look down if the crisscross pattern of roads and buildings on the ground were visible. Flying over bodies of water was out of the question unless Niccolo had had at least three drinks in the airport lounge.

The car drifted toward the center of the road. Eli righted it. He had left the middle of the city and was driving on the outskirts, past dingy convenience marts, Bowl-a-ramas, nightclubs shut darkly against the daylight. Soon the only buildings were gas stations and fruit stands scattered along the highway. The air was clear, but there was a faint reddish haze in the distance where the mountains met the sky. Niccolo and the leopard and Jock's funny-desperate attempt at peacemaking began to fade. He rolled his window down and drove out into the desert. The powerful engine purred beneath him, responsive as a groupie's body. The sun seemed to sear away all his earthly concerns. The landscape was cleansing: so empty, his eyes might have been filled with sand.

It was dark when he got back to the hotel. The others weren't around; no doubt their manager had dragged them off to some club and they would all be wondering loudly where he was. Eli took a long shower, fell into bed, and dreamed of empty, shifting sands. His sleep wasn't long enough. It never was.

"Time to be Elijah Stiles," said Niccolo.

They were backstage at a massive arena, could have been anywhere in the States. Eli had just shared a massive line of coke with Jock, and the walls of the dressing room seemed to swarm with motes of sand. Niccolo examined himself in the mirror. His hair was a wild dark cloud, his eyes sunken shadows in his face. Eli closed his eyes and shivered. He was wearing a white silk suit embroidered with astrological symbols; it was indeed time to be Elijah Stiles, to play the role. But most of all it was time to sing. No amount of hype and false glory could dull that feeling.

And it was glorious. He was in full voice and the music poured from Niccolo's fingers with the smoothness of sex. The band was utterly together. Bailey and Jock laid down a solid base of rhythm. Niccolo peeked from under his eyelashes and filled the stage with strange chords, pyramids of a thousand notes. Midway through the show, Eli leaned his body against Niccolo's as their respective instruments howled together, and things were all right between them again.

And the boys banged their heads, and the little girls cried and reached and screamed.

Eli woke the next morning with a fresh sense of purpose. He felt good. He had partied after the show, but only for a few hours; he'd had little to drink, less to snort, and hadn't touched the smack at all. Best of all, he had woken up alone. Marie's beautiful face would not hover accusingly before him today.

He showered and washed his hair. The scratch on his wrist pulsed. He felt drawn to the desert again.

Today's concierge—a woman this time—smiled up at him. "Same car as yesterday, Mr. Stiles?"

"Yes, please, ma'am," he said, making her his for life. "Can you have it brought round?"

The car wasn't there yet when he stepped out of the lobby. The girls still circled the hotel. Love was in their eyes as they surged forward to greet him. Their hands reached; some of them were almost touching him now. Their fingers were tipped with sharp slivers of red, and their mouths were wet, and their sound was one communal babble that rose in pitch and volume as they approached him.

A soft little hand closed on Eli's wrist. The wounded one. There was a flash of pain. He felt the lips of the cut part, the blood begin to flow again. The girl's head bowed over his hand. Her hair was an impossibly pale shade of blond, but natural right down to the roots; it would darken before she turned sixteen. Other pneumatic young bodies pressed against him. Their softness surrounded him. He cursed himself for not having his manager beside him, or the concierge, or *someone*.

The girls. The red slivers at their fingertips. Their wet mouths.

Eli looked at his wrist, at the girl's mouth on it. The flesh had separated from the bone in a curious way, in two neat flaps. There was only a thin lather of blood, but the pain was deeper, more personal, more surely *his* than he had ever imagined pain could be. It went beyond pain, beyond emotion. He was only looking on. He closed his eyes and felt delicate tendrils of agony, as fine as the lines around Niccolo's eyes, wrap around him and lift him away.

The little girls snapped at anyone who tried to come near. The police were summoned, but even when it became obvious what the girls were doing, no policeman would club them or shoot at them. There were so many, and they were so pretty, and none of them was over sixteen.

At last they had to be allowed to feed until they were sated.

# THE ORIGIN

### David B. Silva

It happened.

Not by accident.

Not by plan.

But simply because it had been inevitable.

It happened like this:

Like he often did on his way home at night, sixteen-year-old Dylan Wakefield went the long way, which took him three lanes over, past April Parker's trailer. He was in luck tonight. It was rare when her mother and little sister weren't hanging around. But tonight, as Dylan watched from across the gravel road, he realized she was alone.

He took a swig from the can of warm beer he had been carrying around with him for the last hour or two, gained a little courage, then left the can at the base of the oak tree and crossed the road.

She answered the door, wearing a sweater and a pair of old jeans. He had never seen her up close like this before, and she was beautiful. "Yes?"

"Hi." He glanced uneasily back toward the road, not knowing quite what to say. "My name's Dylan Wakefield. I live a couple of rows over."

"Yeah," she said. "I've seen you."

"I've seen you, too. That's why I came by, because I guess I thought maybe we could . . . you know . . . like maybe go out sometime? You and me? Maybe over to the Burger King or something? If that was okay with you?"

"I'm sorry," she said sympathetically. "But we're moving back home tomorrow."

"Tomorrow?"

"In the morning."

"Oh." This was it then. The last time he would ever see her. "You think like maybe I could come in anyway? Just for a little while?"

"I'm busy packing. Besides, my mom's not here."

"I could help you pack."

"I'm sorry. I really shouldn't."

He nodded, looking off at nothing in particular and thinking that he didn't want it to end like this. Before it even got started. It wasn't right. He had been polite. He had said all the right things. What more did she want?

Dylan stuck his hand in his pocket, brought out the knife and thumbed the blade open. "I think maybe I'll come in anyway."

She didn't scream like he had thought she would, but she did take in a sudden, startled breath. She backed away from him, deeper into the trailer.

Dylan followed her, closing the door behind him.

The inside of the tiny trailer was a confusion of boxes and clothes, kitchen utensils and silverware, books, knickknacks, packing tape, and more. The smell of her and her family was strong and pleasant. He motioned with the knife toward the back bedroom.

She moved ahead of him down the tiny hall. "What are you going to do?"

"Don't worry. I'm not going to hurt you."

The bedroom was a mess as well. He told her to clear the boxes off the bed, which she did, though she was purposefully slow and deliberate, which angered him. They didn't have forever. There was no telling when her mother would be back.

"Hurry up!" He tossed the remaining two boxes on the floor. "Take off the sweater."

"No, please."

"Take it off!"

She took it off and let it fall to the floor, then self-consciously crossed her chest with her arms. There was a spattering of freckles across her shoulders, and more freckles across her belly. Her arms were trembling. She stared downward at the floor.

"Now the jeans."

No argument this time, just a slow methodical process of unbuttoning the jeans, unzipping, then gradually pulling them down over her smooth thighs.

"Hurry up!"

She stepped out of the pants and he pushed her back across the bed. Her arms crossed protectively over her breasts again. She began to whimper.

Dylan straddled her, mesmerized by the closeness of her nearly naked body. The adrenaline was pushing hot through his veins now. His hands were trembling, and he was already hard. He asked her to place her arms at her side, which she did, then he used the knife to cut away her bra. There was nothing else handy, so he used the bra to tie her hands together. He left her ankles free.

He started to slide her panties off.

For the first time, she let out a scream. Then she rammed a knee into his groin.

He groaned, stunned and in momentary pain. Before she could strike again, he pinned her legs under the weight of his body. In a flash, his adrenaline turned to anger. He reached back and slapped her. She screamed again, louder this time, then flailed at him with her arms. He slapped her a second time, which only made things worse. She caught him across the face with the back of her hand.

Then it happened.

Reflexively, absent all but a single thought—*I'm losing control*—he plunged the knife into her belly.

Her face froze, caught in a startled, openmouthed expression. Then her eyes rolled back, and her body went limp.

"You stupid bitch. Why'd you have to do that?"

He pulled the knife out of her belly. There was blood on his hands, on the sleeve of his jacket, and covering the knife. He crawled off her, wiped the blade on the bed sheets, and stared down at the body. For a moment, nothing existed outside of this room. He found himself caught between wishing things could have been different and being completely captivated by the sight of this death he had brought.

When reality stepped back to the fore, he went down the hall, out through the door, and into the night, where an eerie stillness belied what he had done. He crossed the road to pick up the beer can he had left by the tree, then took a long walk to Lexington Park, where he tossed his jacket and the can in a Dumpster. He washed the blood off his hands in the public restroom.

*Never again*, he told himself.

*Never.*

He would struggle against this promise, against the images and the thoughts and the reality that were now a part of his psyche for another six years before he would kill again. Then he would kill nine more times before he would be caught.


## BEFORE

He had been having trouble sleeping lately. Whenever he closed his eyes, his head would fill with these . . . these images and thoughts. Sometimes it felt as if they were boring deeper and deeper into his soul, nasty little parasites feeding off the last remaining hold to his sanity. Could a person spend his entire life hiding what's inside him? He had managed to keep it buried for eight long years, but he was beginning to lose control now. He could feel himself giving way to the hunger. God, he was such a fucking loser!


## BEFORE

Dylan found the photograph album at the back of the cabinet over the stove while looking for a couple of bucks for beer. His mother had passed out in the bedroom. Her purse was empty, but Dylan was sure she kept change hidden somewhere in the trailer in case she ever ran out of booze. Instead of change, he found the album.

H sat on the couch and thumbed through the old photos. Most had been taken of his mother—on a swing with this man, on the hood of a car with that man, faces that had come before his time and of which he had little recollection—but a few were his childhood pictures. One photo in particular caught his attention. It had been taken on the front stoop of their apartment, long before they had moved into the trailer. His mother sat on the steps, shading her eyes from the sun. Dylan sat next to her. He was maybe five years old. He remembered the day clearly, though. It was the day she wore her new red scarf. After the photo, he had reached up to touch it and she had slapped his hand away.

"That's not a toy," she had said.

He started crying, and she slapped him again to shut him up. "Quit being such a little baby."

## BEFORE

The absolutely perfect fantasy went something like this:

He would meet her somewhere nearby, usually at the My-T-Fine or the Burger King, and they would hit it off immediately. He would be all smiles and politeness with a little shyness thrown in, and she would be completely taken by him. She would be dressed in pure white, with a tight blouse that showed a modest hint of her breasts, and a short white skirt that wasn't too short. She was a girl with some class. Not stuck up, but friendly and nice and . . . *interested*.

Most often, it was April who he imagined as the girl.

They would make some small talk for a while, laughing politely at each other's jokes. He would ask her if she'd like something to eat, and he'd treat her to a hamburger and fries, or if they were at the My-T-Fine, they would walk down the street to Dell's Burgers and maybe he'd throw in a milkshake for them to share.

After the meal, they would take a long walk around town, maybe spend some time sitting at one of the picnic tables at

Lexington Park. They would not hold hands. He didn't like the idea of holding hands. Just the thought made him uneasy. But they would talk and he would get to know her, and eventually he would ask her if she would like to go back to his place.

She would say, "Yes."

He would live alone in the trailer. There would be no photographs, no empty rum bottles, nothing to remind him of his mother. Even the scent of her would be washed away.

He would offer the girl a beer. It would be her first. She would like it, and she would like him for introducing her to it.

They would talk at the kitchen table for a while, flirting a bit, though never crudely or suggestively like you saw so often at the movies. This would be sweet and innocent, just two strangers who felt attracted to each other. Her smile would be angelic, her lips inviting. She would laugh easily. They would be completely comfortable together.

Eventually he would lean across the table and kiss her.

She would kiss him back.

They would make their way to the back of the trailer, to the bedroom. She would lie across the bed. He would bring a red scarf out from a drawer and ask her to wear it around her neck. She would tie it herself.

They would kiss some more.

His hands would roam her body.

Her blouse would come off, followed by her skirt. Her skin would be milky white. Soft and warm and pure. Touching it would send a tingling wave of electricity through his body. He would kiss her belly, her thighs, then bring out two lengths of rope. One to tie her hands. One to tie her ankles.

"Do it," she would say eagerly.

And he would tie her.

And she would like it.

He would be in total control now, in complete command, and from a pocket he would bring out the knife, sliding the blade out with his thumb until it locked into place. Her eyes would grow wide with a mix of fear and excitement.

"What's that for?"

"You'll see."

He would use the knife to cut away her bra, and suddenly her breasts would be exposed. Perfect, full breasts with nipples that were already hard. He would cut away her panties, and she would protest, but she wouldn't mean it.

Then he would unzip himself and climb on top of her.

And he would be in complete control.

For the first time in his life, he would be in complete control.

## BEFORE

There were ugly things going on inside him.

He tried not to acknowledge them, but they were there. They had been there for a long time, though lately they seemed to show themselves more and more often.

None of this was apparent when he stood in front of the bathroom mirror. On the outside, he was your typical male teenager. Medium-length hair, clean and well-kept. No pierced ears. No pierced nose. The idea of poking holes in himself to impress others seemed slightly insane. No tattoos. He had spent an afternoon at the Body Shop once and had come close to getting a skull and crossbones needled into his left arm. Across the top it said: DEATH BECOMES YOU. Definitely cool. But he had decided against it. He didn't want people to be able to look at the tattoo and know what was going on inside him.

Were the same things going on inside others? Did the same thoughts pass through their minds? The same images? Did they think about death the way he sometimes did? As if it would bring a final sweet reprieve from all the ugliness?

There were such ugly things going on inside him.

Such ugly things.

## BEFORE

Sometimes at night, an edginess would overtake him and he would find himself out on the streets, wandering aimlessly. April had been on his mind a lot lately. So had his mother. And other things he would just as soon not think about.

This night, he went out shortly after eleven, carrying a book of matches from Jack's Bar and Grill in one pocket, and a plastic bottle of Royal Oak Charcoal Lighter in the other. Nervous energy kept him walking for nearly an hour, until eventually he found himself standing outside a boarded-up duplex on Hazelnut. Abandoned. Neglected. A place you tried not to notice as you walked by. The past had been short and brutal here. There was no future. It seemed like the perfect metaphor for his life.

He started the fire in the back of the second unit, after squeezing through a missing window where the plywood had pulled away from the siding. It was a small bedroom, with a closet off to one side. Carpet scraps, chunks of sheetrock, and old newspapers littered the floor. Water spots stained the ceiling. A damp, musty odor lingered thick in the air, making it difficult to breathe. Still, the duplex was in better shape then the trailer had ever been.

The thick black smoke began to pour out of the windows within minutes, and the first sight of flames followed closely behind, bringing a false morning to the sky. Dylan watched from across the street, gradually mingling with the crowd as people began to emerge from their homes.

This was nothing like the Dumpster.

Nothing at all.

This was power.

## BEFORE

April.

She seemed at odds with the misery of the trailer park. She dressed nicely. Went to school every day. Seemed almost . . . *happy*.

Dylan's mother told him that Mrs. Cooperman had told her that April's mother was in the process of getting a divorce and their stay at the park was only temporary. Just until some of the settlement was in place. Her father had hired an army of lawyers and he was making life miserable for them.

"No-good bastard," Dylan's mother said. "Oughta string

him up by the balls. You can't trust a man. Not a word he says. He'll try to screw you every time."

Dylan thought she had her genders confused. It was women you couldn't trust.

Except April.

He thought about her all the time. Sometimes late at night, he would sit across the road from her trailer and watch her silhouette against the curtains as she moved around inside. And sometimes when he became hard, he would jerk off right there, out in the open, the late hour and cold temperatures the only things keeping him from being discovered. Most of the time, though, he just watched, imagining what it would be like if a girl like April took an interest in him.

On Valentine's Day, he lifted a box of chocolates from the Wal-Mart on Gleeson Street. It was a one-pound box in the shape of a heart. He wrote her name across the top and signed it "Secret Friend," then left it on her doorstep. Her little sister discovered the box. Dylan watched her pick it up and carry it back into the trailer. He thought it would make him happy, but when he realized he was still on the outside looking in, all he felt was anger.

April.

She didn't even know he existed.


## BEFORE

The magazine was called *Detective Stories*. Dylan found it while rummaging through one of the Dumpsters behind the Down Home Cooking restaurant at the truck stop. On the cover, a woman appeared to be hanging by her arms, her wrists bound by a pair of panty hose. She was gagged with what looked like a white sock. The headline read: KIDNAPPED AND TORTURED IN KANSAS. There were other, smaller photos on the cover. Two of men, one of another woman who appeared to be in peril. The headline next to her photo read: FIRST VICTIM OF A SERIAL KILLER?

Dylan had never seen a magazine like this.

Inside, there was one true detective story after another,

everything from fraud to murder to rape to bank robbery. It was all fascinating, especially the black-and-white photographs. But the stories that interested him the most were the stories about murder.

It was the first time in his life he realized he might not be alone.

Maybe other people in the world had *thoughts*, too.

### BEFORE

There were empty bottles of rum and cans of Coke lining the small counter next to the stove. Dirty dishes were stacked above the rim of the kitchen sink. Shopping bags, filled with the boxes and trays of consumed TV dinners, sat next to the front door. Linoleum curled up around the edges of the floor. Stacks of the *National Enquirer* and the *Star* and the *Weekly World News* made places for themselves wherever there was space.

It was his mother's private little corner of the world.

It was also where he learned that the smaller you made your world, the greater your chance of controlling it.

### BEFORE

April Parker moved into the park on October 3, a day that was bitterly cold, made all the colder by winds up to thirty-five miles an hour. Dylan watched her arrive with her mother and her little sister, taking over the Howard space. James Howard, a man well into his eighties, had died of a heart attack while showering almost a month earlier.

She was one year older than him. Blond, medium-length curls. Blue eyes that shimmered like sunlight across water. Always the hint of a smile on her face.

He followed the old Toyota Corolla down the graveled, single-lane road that circled the park, staying far enough back so he would go unnoticed. From behind an old oak, for nearly an hour, he watched the family of three unpack boxes from the back of the car and carry them into the trailer. She was the most beautiful thing he had ever seen.

It was as if he had been living in a black-and-white world and suddenly there was color.

## BEFORE

When he tried to imagine his life ten years down the road, it was nearly impossible to see past the trailer park, his mother, the day-to-day drudgery. Maybe if he got lucky and hit the Lotto or won the Publisher's Clearinghouse Sweepstakes . . .

But the truth was, ten years from now, he imagined nothing much will have changed. He supposed his mother would be dead. Either the alcohol would have killed her or he would have. He would probably still be living in this hellhole of a trailer. Where else was he going to live? Or maybe if things went his way, he might end up on the road like his father, traveling the country's highways in an eighteen-wheeler, free to do as he pleased. No women to keep him down. No lies. No tears. Nothing but the road.

Sometimes he could close his eyes and see the prairies, the snowcapped mountains far in the distance, the city lights, the little towns with their two-lane main streets.

That was freedom.

Any place but here.

Any time but now.

## BEFORE

He had started collecting red scarves when he was fourteen, lifting one from the Penny's in the mall, another from Gottshcalks, yet another from Sally's Boutique. He kept them under the couch cushion, wrapped around the two knives.

He assumed they would always be safe there. It wasn't as if his mother was likely to discover them while cleaning. She never cleaned. But apparently she did eventually find them. She never said anything—by this time they had both learned that most of their conversations ended with her crying and him storming out—but she put them back with the scarves out of order, so he knew she had found them.

The odd thing was . . . he wished she *had* said something. Maybe if she had yelled at him a little, grounded him, and taken the scarves and knives away from him, maybe that would have put a stop to it. But she did none of those things.

He had the knives now.

And the scarves.

Gradually, the *thought* was inching its way across the boundary between imagination and reality.

He prayed that someone would stop it, because he didn't think he could stop it himself.

### BEFORE

A week after his mother had told him about his father, Dylan set his first fire. It was a small fire, confined to one of the Dumpsters behind the My-T-Fine. He didn't understand why he did it, only that feeling the heat against his face, watching the flames stretch toward the night sky, hearing the crackles and pops . . . these things took some of the edge off his rage.

He should have killed her.

He should have killed his mother when he'd had the chance.

He should have set the trailer on fire.

### BEFORE

He never spent a single day in high school. His mother brought it up a few times: Then they would argue, but he refused to go and she never cared enough to force the issue.

That made for long days with nothing to do.

### BEFORE

The *thought* wormed its way back to the fore of his mind one day after he had watched a Lance Burton special on television. It occurred to him that he didn't really know anything about tying knots. If he wanted to restrain someone and do it right, he needed to learn how to tie the right knot. That made sense, didn't it?

He asked around at the My-T-Fine and over at Gus's Heating and Air-Conditioning, even over at the city's Youth Center, where all the idiot skateboarders hung out. No one had a clue about tying knots, but one of the counselors at the center suggested he try the library.

"The library?"

"On Court Street. The other side of the tracks."

He knew where it was. He'd just never been there. Reading had never been one of his favorite activities. But there must have been a dozen books on knot tying on those library shelves. He settled on *Knotcraft: The Practical and Entertaining Art of Tying Knots*. The cover looked arts and craftsy, but there were plenty of knots, with plenty of pictures showing how to tie them.

At the checkout, they wouldn't give him a library card without his mother's signature. It was because he was only fourteen, they said. Not yet an adult. He was more adult than his mother, of course, but he didn't argue. There was no winning in arguing. Not when the person you were arguing with held all the cards. Instead, he disappeared back into the stacks and waited until the checkout got busy again. Then he started out, stopping to pass the book between the alarm pedestal and the wall, and picking it up on the other side.

It was a good book. Almost made him want to read.

He spent weeks practicing the knots.

Got fairly good at it, too.

## BEFORE

The first time Dylan killed, he killed a cat.

He was thirteen.

The cat was a stray that had been hanging around the trailer park for a couple of months, getting into garbage bags and terrorizing Mrs. Garcia's two tabbies. Twice it had crossed in front

of Dylan on his way home, a superstitious omen he considered
both unlucky for him and dangerous for the cat.

He trapped the black cat in a cardboard box, using a can of
tuna fish as bait and some chicken wire to make sure it couldn't
escape. For a week, he kept it under the trailer, not sure what
to do with it. Then one afternoon, he found a knife he liked at
the Big 5 on Oak Street. It was called a Disc-Kicker. The blade
was only three-and-a-half inches, but it opened as smooth and
easy as a drawer on rollers. Just by the pressure of his thumb.
Stainless-steel handle. Only $28.95. He used some money he
had saved up from mowing lawns and collecting aluminum
cans, plus a few bucks from his mother's purse.

The cat was the first test of the knife.

Over the next six months or so, eleven other cats were discovered hanging from trees in the neighborhood with their
throats slit.


## BEFORE

The only time he ever used the Bowie knife, besides whit-
tling away at some of the fallen branches down by the pond,
was on his mother. They had both been doing some drinking
that day, though Dylan had done his secretly behind the My-T-
Fine and his mother had done hers out in the open, like she always did.

It was after eight when he got home, which was usually late
enough that she would be passed out, either on the couch or in
bed. But this time, he found her awake. She was in a particularly nasty mood, mixing her drinks with bouts of crying and
screaming. He closed the door and leaned against it, debating
if he should turn around and go back out again.

"There he is. There's my baby." She was already blubber-
ing. The booze did that sometimes, when it didn't make her
angry. "Where have you been, Dylan Lee Wakefield? I've
been waiting all day for you. Your mommy needs her baby."

"I'm not your baby."

"Yes, you are. You'll always be my baby. Come here, give
Mommy a kiss."

"I don't want to give you a kiss."

She fell back against the couch, pouting like a spoiled brat for a moment, then working the pout into more tears. Finally the tears worked into anger. "You don't know. You just don't know what I have to go through. Have you ever said thank you? Once in your life? Ever? Who do you think puts food on the table? A roof over your head? Not your fucking father, that's for sure. He doesn't even know you exist. But I'm here for you. I've always been here for you. You'd think you could at least show a little appreciation."

"What do you mean he doesn't know I exist?"

She laughed derisively, her eyes half-lidded from the booze. "Never told him. How do you like that, you ungrateful little shit? I never even told him about you."

Dylan didn't want to hear it. Not a word of it. He escaped back into the night with his mother screaming behind him, "He would have hated you anyway. He would have hated the idea of you, and he would have hated you, too."

For the next four hours, after he'd lifted a couple of beers from the grocery store, he walked the neighborhood in a rage. By the time he returned to the trailer, it was a little past midnight and he thought the booze had given him the courage to do what he needed to do. He fished the knife out from under the couch cushion, and carried it with him to the bedroom, where his mother was sleeping off the rum. He sat on the edge of the bed, staring at her through his hate, until he finally placed the knife across her throat.

She swallowed and rolled away.

He pulled the knife back.

Why he didn't slit her throat that night, he never fully understood.

But there would be many times when he would live to regret his decision.

## BEFORE

Out by the highway, there was a truck stop. All the drivers of eighteen-wheelers stopped there to gas up, get a bite to eat, maybe catch a little shut-eye before they took back to the road again. It was a good seven or eight miles from the trailer park, but sometimes when the weather was good and he needed to get away for a while, Dylan would make the trip on foot. He had tried to hitch a ride a few times, though after a couple of weirdoes (one old geezer in his sixties had flashed him, and another guy had placed his hand on Dylan's thigh), he had learned to prefer to walk.

The truck stop was a huge old thing. Arco pumps. A parking lot the size of a couple of football fields. A restaurant called Down Home Cooking, which served runny eggs no matter how you asked for them. And the Easy Sleep Motel, which looked like it had gone out of business in the fifties by the height of the grass growing up through the asphalt covering the parking area along the front of the place.

Dylan spent most of his time in the restaurant, nursing a Pepsi or sometimes a chocolate shake. He liked to listen to the truckers' stories, and he liked to listen for the truckers' names. The name he was waiting to hear—hoping, even praying to hear—was Duncan Wakefield.

It was a name that never did come up.

### BEFORE

He had started doing some drinking of his own around thirteen. He tried a little rum once, out of a bottle that was almost empty so he didn't have to worry that his mother might miss it. Basically the stuff tasted like the worst. It burned like hell going down, and he never tried it again. Instead, he settled on beer. It was cheap when he had to pay for it, easy when he had to lift it, and it didn't take much to give him a buzz.

The more he drank, the less crappy life seemed.

And the less often he had to deal with the *thought*.

### BEFORE

Junior high was hell.

Dylan was small for his age, an easy target, so he went

through the motions of getting up to go to school, then spent most of his days out roaming around instead. There was no telephone; they were living on the bare necessities by this time: rent for the trailer space, food, and of course, booze. Even if the school could have called, Dylan didn't think his mother would have cared. She would have yelled a bit, most likely, and mixed the yelling with some rum and Coke. That pretty much would have been the extent of it.

## BEFORE

The first time he ever saw a woman's snatch was out of a *Penthouse* he had lifted from the newsstand at the Liquor Fair off Jefferson Street. It was a straight-on shot of the woman, her legs spread, her knees bent, her hands opening the lips of her secret place like it was an invitation to rush in. It was pink and moist and glistening, and it looked to Dylan like some sort of alien mouth.

He thought it was the creepiest thing he'd ever seen.

## BEFORE

He experienced his first wet dream when he was twelve, on a night when he was still sharing his mother's bed. As bad as it sounded, there was nothing nasty about sleeping with her; the trailer was small and only had the single bed. Every once in a while, when she brought some guy home with her, Dylan would sleep on the cushions around the kitchen table. They were covered in a worn orange-and-brown material that smelled like grime and booze. And even though they were lumpy, after the wet dream, he started sleeping on the cushions regularly.

Fully awake now, he thought at first he had peed himself. He crawled out from under the covers, embarrassed and praying his mother was still asleep. In the bathroom, he stared down at the cold, wet spot on his underpants, then pulled them off and realized it wasn't pee after all. This was something else.

He wasn't sure what it was. No one had ever talked to him

about sex and he had cut most of his classes at school, but he knew this much: he was still hard. The emission had brought him out of a dream in which he had coaxed a girl out of her clothes, tied her feet and hands together, and wrapped a red scarf around her neck. She appeared to be enjoying herself, until he brought out the knife. Then her smile had disappeared and she had started to scream. He woke up, not just suddenly aware of the semen, but also wondering what would have happened next.

He washed his underpants in the bathroom sink, tossed them onto the pile of dirty clothes in the basket sitting in the bathtub, then cleaned himself off and put on a clean pair of shorts. He slept the rest of the night alone on the couch, the Bowie knife under the cushion.

## BEFORE

He didn't do it often, but every once in a while, toward the end of the month when the money had run out and there was no food left in the house, Dylan rummaged through the Dumpster behind the My-T-Fine Foods store, two blocks down from the park. Most of the time he found old fruit, sometimes some lettuce or carrots, occasionally some bread or pastries or a half-empty bottle of soda pop. And sometimes he would find something he wasn't even looking for, like the time he found the knife.

It was an old Bowie knife, around eight inches long, a round-barrel India stag handle with obvious signs of wear. Someone had owned the knife for a good many years. Probably used it for hunting and fishing. Maybe had even killed a wild animal with it. A wild boar or a cougar or maybe even a black bear.

There were rust stains on the blade.

He turned it over in his hands a couple of times, feeling an exhilarating sense of power, then stuck it between his belt and pants at the small of his back and made sure his T-shirt kept it hidden. He had found two unbroken eggs and a couple of ears of corn before he found the knife, and that seemed plenty for the time being.

When he got home, he dumped the food in the kitchen sink, then went to the bathroom (the only place of privacy in the small trailer), and took out the knife to give it a closer look. The stains on the blade weren't rust. They were blood. A little scrubbing and they washed right off. He never knew for certain whether the blood belonged to an animal or a human being, though several months later he heard that two guys had gotten into a fight at the apartment complex on the other side of the My-T-Fine and one of the guys had been cut up pretty bad. They never did find the weapon.

## BEFORE

This is what he wrote on the cover of his fifth-grade binder before Mrs. Finney, his teacher, took the binder away from him and locked it in the bottom drawer of her desk:

*I hate this place.*
*I hate every fucking thing about it.*
*Especially the idiots like that Randy Gardner fag who's always in my face.*
*Sometimes I can close my eyes and see him with a huge, fucking hole in his head. Blood covering his face. Brain tissue all over the place.*
*It makes me smile.*

Inside the binder, Mrs. Finney discovered page afer page of crude drawings, depicting women's breasts, most often the size of watermelons. She took Dylan's binder to the principal, who suggested she show it to the school counselor, who looked it over and said that while it appeared disturbing at first glance, the expressed sentiments (both written and drawn) were typical of a boy Dylan's age.

"You might want to keep an extra eye on him," the counselor said, "but I wouldn't worry too much. He's an adolescent boy. These are the thoughts that pass through their heads at that age."

## BEFORE

By the age of eleven, Dylan had come to realize that he wasn't like other kids. He had no close friends. His mother was an alcoholic. They lived in a run-down trailer, in a run-down trailer park. He hated school, especially the teachers, and did just enough work to get him from one grade to the next for fear if he was held back a year, he would be an even greater freak than he already was.

He had already become a loner, eating his lunch (on those days when he was able to find enough food in the house to pack a sack lunch) by himself, out on the far reaches of the baseball field, where he was seldom bothered. His nickname around school had become Skeletor, not because he resembled the Masters of the Universe character, but because he was as thin as a skeleton. Secretly, he liked the nickname.

He once shoplifted one of the action figures from the Shopko toy department. He kept it under his bed, where he brought it out at night and fantasized about being the real Skeletor, ruler of the world. The action figure was everything he was not: big, strong, courageous. Someday that was going to be him. Someday, people were going to fear him; they were going to do whatever he told them to do.

Someday.

## BEFORE

No one ever knew this.

Dylan was only ten when he started peeping. It happened one winter night when his mother had sent him to the store to pick up some cigarettes. On the way back, he passed by the Coopermans' and heard a strange noise coming from their bedroom window, which was open just enough to let the sound out. It was going on ten o'clock and cold enough to freeze the snot in your nose, so there weren't any people out besides Dylan.

Curious, he went to investigate.

Through a crack in the curtains, he could see old man Cooperman on top of his wife. There were sheets and covers strewn everywhere, so he really couldn't tell if they were naked or not. But the old man was grunting like the pig he was and the little woman (that's what he always called her: his little woman) was letting out these little gasps every once in a while as if she needed to get some air in her lungs.

He didn't see much—there wasn't much to see—but it was exciting just the same. After that night, whenever the opportunity presented itself, he dropped by the Coopermans' bedroom window for another look. A couple of times he caught Mrs. Cooperman changing clothes. That was generally cool enough to bring him back for another visit, and eventually he started visiting other trailers in the park.

He was never discovered.

## BEFORE

They lived in Willow Creek Park, a small trailer park at the edge of town. During the summers, Dylan spent the length of his days at Swinging Tree Pond, a small alcove off the creek, about a mile upstream from the park. Most days, he would bump into one or two other kids he knew. They got along well enough, though he never had any close friends.

One summer they built a dam at the feeder end of the pond, with mud and broken branches from the surrounding area. It raised the level of the water about a foot, which was cool because some of the kids couldn't stand on the bottom after that and suddenly there was an element of danger to the pond. No one ever got hurt. Still, just the *idea* of danger seemed to make the swimming more fun.

Another summer, in late August, just two weeks before school, he met Curtis Gallagher, a boy his same age, who liked to swim naked. Dylan tried it and liked it, too. But when a girl from the trailer park ran home and told her mother, the mother made a big fuss about it and the boys both got in trouble.

Curtis worse than Dylan.

Dylan rarely got into big trouble.

His mother had made friends with rum and Coke that summer, after she had been fired from her job as a checker at the 99 Cent Store on Athens Road. That had happened just before summer started, and she had spent the rest of her summer watching television and drinking until she passed out. It could have been worse. She could have been a mean drunk. Instead, she was just dead to the world most of the time. Dylan didn't like to hang around the trailer when she was like that. He usually left before she got up and didn't come back until well after dark, when she was likely to be passed out on the couch, with the television on in the background.

That same summer, only a couple of weeks after the girl had told on them for swimming naked, she showed up at the pond again. Dylan was swimming alone this time, as he often did.

"You swimming naked?" she asked.

"No." He stood up in the water and showed her the pair of jeans he was wearing. At the beginning of summer, he had cut the legs off, around midthigh. As good as swimming trunks. "See?"

"Okay." She was a year older than him, and though he didn't know her name, he knew where she lived: Space D-13, two rows over from him in the same trailer park. She found a level area, covered in dirt, but clear of any weeds or debris from surrounding trees, and unrolled her towel. Then she unbuttoned her shirt and slid out of her pants, which covered a bathing suit underneath, and waded into the water.

"It's cold," she said.

"No, it isn't. You're just a baby."

"I am not."

"Then how come you told on Curtis and me?" Curtis had not been allowed back to the pond after his mother found out he was swimming naked. He also hadn't been allowed to play with Dylan anymore.

She shrugged. "I don't know."

"You got us in trouble."

"I didn't mean to."

"Well, you did." They stood face-to-face in water just above Dylan's knees. She wore a one-piece bathing suit with a pattern of white, green, and yellow flowers. Impulsively, Dylan reached out and pushed the strap off her left shoulder. "Maybe you shouldn't be allowed to swim here now. Not until *you* swim naked."

"Don't." She returned the strap to its place.

Dylan pulled the strap off the other shoulder. "It only seems fair."

"I said *don't*." Again, she replaced the strap.

This time, he reached out and pulled both of them off her shoulders, and this time instead of putting them back, the girl let them dangle freely. She folded her arms across her chest. Dylan became instantly aware of the change. "Just once. You gotta go naked just once. Then you can swim here."

"I don't know." She glanced at the surroundings.

*My God, she's thinking about it.*

He reached out and grabbed the straps again, tugging on them until they were free from her arms this time, then unrolling her swimsuit down to just below her navel, where she stopped him. "Come on. Just once."

"You, too, then."

"You've already seen me naked."

"You, too."

"After you."

"Okay." She did the rest herself, slipping the suit off one leg first, then the other leg, until she was standing there in front of him, completely naked.

Dylan stared at the tiny mound between her legs, and wanted to get a better look. He had never seen a naked girl before.

"Your turn."

"What?"

"Now it's your turn. Take off your pants."

He started to unsnap his jeans when he realized he had become hard. It was the first time in his life he had ever become hard, at least that he was aware of, and instantly he felt a mix

of excitement and embarrassment. He closed the snap again.
"Fooled you."

"You said you'd do it." She reached for his jeans and he
slapped her hand away.

"Did not."

"Yes, you did." She started to reach out again, but pulled
back when he raised his hand. "You're a liar, Dylan Wakefield.
A liar and a cheat and I'm telling."

"Go ahead. See if I care."

She slipped back into her bathing suit, grabbed her clothes
and towel off the dirt, and went trudging down the path like
the spoiled brat she was. He didn't think she was really going
to tell on him. After all, she had taken all her clothes off, which
meant she was just as likely to get into trouble as he was. But
she did tell, and according to her story, he had *forced* her to
take her clothes off.

There was a big stink about it after that. The police came to
the trailer the next morning and gave both Dylan and his
mother a long lecture about letting it go this time, but next
time . . . next time they were going to throw him into juvenile
detention and he was going to rot there for years.

"There won't be no next time. I promise you that," his
mother said. She was lucky—they were *both* lucky—the cops
hadn't come around in the evening. Odds were she would have
been passed out on the couch and he would have been hauled
off to live with some foster family from hell. As it was, as
soon as the cops left, she gave Dylan the beating of his life
and ended up keeping him inside for a week until the swelling
and bruises disappeared.

In bed that night, he listened to the sound of the ice cubes
against the glass as his mother poured herself one drink after
another, sobbing half the time, grumbling the other half. He
thought about the girl at the pond, standing in front of him,
naked, and he began to get hard again.

He closed his eyes.

And from his thoughts of her, came another thought: *I wonder what she would look like dead?*

## BEFORE

His name was Dylan Wakefield. He lived with his mother. He never knew his father, who (according to what little he had learned in his nine years) was a truck driver back east somewhere. Dylan thought about him at times. He fantasized about riding in a big rig with him, the road ticking by like endless hours, nothing else mattering, just a father and his son out traveling the country.

Just the guys.

No women.

The way it should be.

## BEFORE

It began as a whisper.

He was playing in the dirt outside the apartment, waging a military battle with a set of plastic army soldiers his mother had bought him for Christmas. Tommy Dunn, who lived in an apartment on the other side of the building, had been playing with him, until his mother called for him to come to dinner. So now he was playing alone as the car pulled up to the curb on the other side of the street.

He looked up and watched a woman climb out. She was dressed in jeans, a fashionable hole in one knee, and an oversized sweatshirt that hung loosely off one shoulder, exposing a white bra strap. She crossed the street, wearing a pair of platform shoes with stars and a moon painted on the sides, and approached him, shading her eyes against the late afternoon sun.

"Hi, sweetie," she said.

"Who are you?"

"I'm looking for Millie Farmer. Do you know where she lives?"

He shook his head. The name Millie Farmer didn't sound familiar at all.

"She has a little boy by the name of Jeremy."

"I know Jeremy."

"Oh, good. Where does he live?"

He pointed out the second-floor apartment on the end. "Right there."

"Thanks."

He watched her climb the stairs, her heels methodically counting off each concrete step as if they were meant to keep time. She knocked on the door, looked around uncomfortably, then smiled with relief as the door finally opened. A moment later, she was inside the apartment and the door was closed again.

He watched all this, with a plastic soldier held in one hand, and hardly noticed the thought that crossed his mind next: *I wonder what she would look like dead?* It was as casual as wondering about what was for lunch or reminding himself that *Mork & Mindy* was on tonight. But it was planted now—a seed that would come back to him, stubbornly, repeatedly, for years to come.

He was only eight years old.

Too young to realize the change had started.

But it was part of him now.

Part of his soul.

# AFTER THE FLOOD

## *Joel Lane*

Ironically for a town that had built its reputation on water, Leamington Spa had no provision for the flooding that took place on Good Friday 1997. Torrential rain caused the picturesque river that crossed the lower end of the town to overflow its banks, drowning several square miles of roads and surrounding fields. Commuters driving home for the bank holiday abandoned their cars in three feet of water. Houses, shops, and restaurants were flooded out; cellars brimmed like teacups; and bookcases exploded with the swollen volume of soaked paper. The battles over liability for the damage raged on for years.

Matthew had spent that weekend at his parents' house in Cardiff. By the time he came back, the flood had drained away. Most of the shops around the train station were closed, shutters and blinds hiding the damage. His bedsit was nearer the north end of town, higher up. The house clearly hadn't been affected. The newsagent at the end of the road told him: "Lucky you were nowhere near the station. Trains didn't run all night. There's people drowned, cars ruined, no end of pets gone missing." In the local paper, a Jehovah's Witness was quoted as saying: *It's a foretaste of things to come. This town must purge itself of the decadence that infects our streets.*

The house was quiet; most of the other tenants would be away for the whole Easter break. Matthew wanted to spend some time with Karen before the exam term got under way.

She was his first proper girlfriend, and the passion they'd shared in the last couple of months had made it hard for him to focus on work. Karen wasn't a student: She worked in a little bookshop off the Parade. They'd met at Warwick University cinema, after a screening of *Bladerunner*. She'd changed everything for him: Leamington, his studies, being alive. Everything glittered with fragile sunlight.

Karen lived with two friends in a flat in Russell Street, not far from the station. He'd better call and check she was okay. The telephone rang four times; then he heard Karen's voice asking him to leave a message. He was about to speak when Sally broke in: "Hello? Who's that?"

"Matthew. Hi. How are you?"

"Okay. Is Karen with you?"

"No." He could still hear her voice in his head, wanted to answer it. "I've been away since Friday."

"So's Karen. We don't know where. Thought she might be with you. Her mum rang from Telford, so she's not there." Sally breathed in anxiously. "Shit . . . I hope nothing's happened to her. You know, the flood."

"Jesus." Matthew felt like he was drowning. "Surely . . . surely by now . . . I mean . . ." She'd have been found, he wanted to say.

"You're right. Don't worry. When she comes in, I'll ask her to phone you straight away. If she's not here tomorrow, I'll go to the police. She'll be here, though. I just know it."

But she wasn't. There were no leads to follow. No body was found. Sally talked to the police, who sent a DC to talk to Matthew. The young officer's questions were polite, but very detailed; Matthew knew he was under suspicion. It was hard to talk about Karen. They'd gotten very close quite quickly. He'd never expected to have to make factual statements to a stranger about sleeping with Karen; it felt cold and alien, a code for loss.

At the end of the interview, the DC said: "We'll keep you informed. Let us know if you remember anything that might be helpful." April slipped into May, and the police didn't get back to him.

As the weather grew warmer, the damage to the south side of town was gradually repaired. Shops and restaurants closed for refurbishment; cellar contents were piled in skips; and the smell of rotting wood and plaster hung in the air like the ghost of last night's take-away. Matthew was supposed to be preparing for his exams. But when the library closed, he'd drop off his books at home and then wander downtown towards the river. Maybe he'd pick up some clue about what had happened to Karen. But more, it was a way of keeping her alive.

One Friday evening, instead of having dinner, he drank four pints of Guinness at one of the pretentious new bars on the Parade. It was full of shouting Yuppies from local offices, grins like pale sharks. The bar was full of polished pseudo-rural artifacts: carvings, horseshoes, framed photos of show-jumping. The toilets were scented with pine. Staggering a little, Matthew walked down the Parade towards the river Leam where it came through Jephson Gardens. He'd expected the fresh air to clear his head, but it wasn't fresh. It seemed heavy, polluted by the traffic that clogged the town like cholesterol in blood vessels.

On the bridge, he gazed down at the waterfall. The setting sun and the tainted air made it look slightly yellow. He remembered standing there with Karen, around the same time in the evening. Her arm linked through his. How she'd said: "I love rivers. They make me feel connected to the sea. It's a part of us, the sea. It's inside us." They'd kissed then, and walked down past the station into the industrial part of town.

The canal ran parallel to the river, a shadow of it, like a sepia photograph. In between was a fault line of ruined or condemned buildings. That evening, they hadn't waited to get home. They'd found a bricked-up alley by the viaduct, out of sight of the road. The wall was tattooed with images and words. He remembered how she'd giggled when he'd stood on tiptoe to enter her: "You're the wrong height." And the way she'd bit his shoulder through the cloth in the last feverish moments, drawing blood.

Remembering, he was painfully aroused. Which only made him feel more wretched. He walked stiff-legged down to the end of the Parade, and along the viaduct. There were huts in the arches, pigeons nesting on corrugated-iron roofs. Blue plastic sacks were fixed across the gaps. Here was the alley, paved with broken glass and used condoms. Griffiti covered the wall: PIGS SUCK, KERRY SMELLS OF EVERYTHING, COLIN IS FIT BUT HE TREATS GIRLS LIKE SHIT, GOTHS LIVE FOREVER. To one side, a wire fence was overgrown with some white flower he couldn't name. It smelt bad here.

Further south of the river, away from the grand architecture and the gift shops, most of the buildings were post-war: tenement houses and blocks of flats, workshops and little factories. A lot of students lived here. Karen had told him that this was supposedly the bad part of town, where it wasn't safe to be. It reminded him of the inner-city district where he'd grown up and gone to school. The "spa town" part of Leamington—or, to give it its full Empire-building name, Royal Leamington Spa—left him cold. It made so much of its literary heritage; but the local branch of W. H. Smith's didn't stock a single literary journal. The town's sense of civic identity was embodied by the dark statue of Queen Victoria opposite the Municipal Baths, and the omnipresent signs banning drinking out of doors. The local paper had recently announced, with some pride, that a gay club had been denied a license. The town's center had a faintly decaying air of fifties pomposity that made him feel violent.

Out here, without a guidebook or tea shop in sight, he was overwhelmed by thoughts of Karen. Her short reddish hair, pale blue eyes, freckles, conspiratorial smile. Her face on the pillow, asleep. Her frankness in bed. "You can do anything you like, but don't make me pregnant. It's not up to me to take precautions, it's up to you." The fact that most of what he remembered about her was sexual depressed him. He began to walk back towards the station, thinking about the first night they'd spent together. They'd been to see a film, and she'd come back to his room for coffee. Suddenly they'd started kissing. Then she'd drawn back and asked him something about the film. Without thinking, he'd said: "Let's discuss it later."

She'd raised her eyebrows. "You mean in the morning?"

He'd wondered if he'd gone too far, and said awkwardly: "You're reading my mind."

Then she'd smiled, put her mouth to his ear and whispered: "No, just looking at the pictures."

The weekend before his exams in June, Matthew decided to allow himself a Saturday night out. One of the tackier North Leamington bars was having a student night, with reduced prices and lots of gloomy 1980s music. He didn't intend to find someone, just to get drunk with his friends. But he was so hyper from studying and loneliness that he drank a lot without feeling the effects, and ended up drifting back and forth through the long venue on his own. The music made his grief sustainable, made it part of a world where everyone wore black. It mattered less that he and Karen wouldn't live together, have children, share a sunlit life.

There was a little bunch of Goths at the end of the bar, probably discussing whether it was worth the effort of forming a band. One of them glanced at him and smiled. She was short, stocky, with black hair and eyeliner—nothing like Karen. But in her brief smile, there was something that made Karen leap out of her face. He couldn't look away. She joined him at the bar. "Are you having a bad night?"

"It's a long story. I'm okay." He had to see that smile again. "Are you in a band?"

"What, them?" Her teeth were smaller than Karen's; yet, somehow, the same smile. "Yes, but we haven't put anything out yet. We're still absorbing influences."

"What do you play?"

"The bass. Sometimes I sing. We swap roles quite a bit. We all live in the same house, so it's easy to work together."

"Are you at the Uni?"

"I work in the library." He supposed she was a little older than him, but not much. "You probably won't have seen me there. I'm an archivist. I've got my own office." A graduate, then.

The barmaid was moving towards Matthew. "Do you want a drink?" he said.

"Bacardi. Thanks." They moved away from the bar. They talked about the university, his course, the bands that had played there recently. Her name was Terri. He couldn't place her accent; there was a trace of West Country in it—a diet lilt, so to speak—underneath the flattened Midland vowels. She seemed in no hurry to rejoin her housemates. They sat down together in the twilight of the lower bar, where it was quieter. Suddenly he was telling her about Karen. Her hand on his arm. Her face blurred by the tears in his eyes, changing.

"It must be dreadful," she said. "To lose someone and not even know where they are. But if you remember her, she hasn't completely gone." Very gently, her fingers stroked a tear from his cheek. They looked at each other for a few seconds. Then they began to kiss.

Her mouth tasted of Bacardi. Like her smile, her kiss held faint echoes of Karen. He supposed that was how it always worked with new girlfriends. The same, but different. It didn't matter that Terri was a stranger, or that doing this made him think of someone else. She probably felt the same way. Why else was she giving herself like this? He felt her tremble in his arms. "Are you all right?" he said. Her eyes were shut.

When the lights came up, she asked him: "Do you want to come back with us?" They walked together through the back-streets of shuttered shops and glowing restaurants; across the park, where the pale bandstand stood like an empty cage; and down Brunswick Street, over the dark ribbon of the canal. Terri's housemates, two boys and a girl, walked with them—quiet, protective, almost like a family. Maybe he should get into this Goth thing. Terri gripped his hand. It was unusually quiet for this part of town: no dogs barking, hardly any traffic.

The house was one he'd walked past without really noticing. It had an overgrown front garden with poppies and hollyhocks. There was a small wooden gargoyle above the black front door. The windows were leaded. Inside, it seemed oddly formal: a hallway with a tiled floor, a bare staircase, blank walls. There was a peculiar smell of rotting wood and stagnant water, over-laid with chlorine like swimming baths. "Sorry about the smell," Terri said. "The cellar was flooded. We're leaving it open to help it dry." She put an arm around Matthew's shoulders. "Let's go upstairs."

Her room was almost as sparse as the hallway, though it had a double mattress under a duvet and a few Cure posters on the off-white walls. As he sat down, Matthew realized how drunk he was. The cracks in the ceiling were blurred. Terri bent down to kiss him. "Would you like some vodka?" she asked. "Russian."

"I don't want to get too drunk," Matthew said.

Terri looked steadily at him. "Don't worry. We can make love in the morning."

Matthew felt himself blushing. "You can read my mind."

Terri smiled. "No, I'm just looking at the pictures." Matthew felt a momentary chill. She took a bottle with a Cyrillic label from a small cupboard and filled two fluted glasses. It must be a line from some film they'd both seen. He kicked his shoes off.

The vodka tasted peppery and was exceptionally strong. It stung his lips. Gradually, he forgot the smell of the basement. They undressed each other in between sips of vodka. The tiny bedside lamp gave Terri a giant shadow, a face like paper over darkness. The room was cold; they slipped under the duvet, and Matthew fell asleep at once.

Towards dawn, he drifted in and out of sleep. There was a dripping tap somewhere, floorboards creaking, muffled voices. His limbs felt too heavy to move. He could hear Terri's steady breathing, but couldn't feel the warmth of her body. In his dream, he was walking down the house's uncarpeted staircase. It was twisted into a spiral, and it seemed to go on forever. People were climbing past him, but he couldn't make out their faces. They seemed no more than shadows.

When he awoke, it was twilight. His muscles were tense, a reaction to the vodka. He was breathing fast. Terri slipped an arm across his chest and murmured: "Relax, darling. It's all right. You're with me." He lifted her onto him, and they kissed slowly. Her hand moved down his chest to his crotch.

"Wait," he whispered, reaching for the packet of condoms he'd left beside the bed.

"Leave them," Terri said. She caught his hand, guided it back under the duvet, pressed it to her taut belly. "I want everything. Every trace of you. I can't have children." He held her tightly; she was trembling again.

As the morning brightened outside they made love furiously. Matthew was crying when they finished. A thousand sounds, movements, and sensations reminded him of Karen. Was it his imagination, or was it always like this? The second time, it was easier to lose himself in the experience and forget what it meant. As he washed in the austere bathroom, he felt a sense of uneasy contentment. As if his loneliness hadn't gone away, but had been subdued by some kind of local anesthetic. Sunlight melted through the net curtains, making indefinable shapes.

Over breakfast, they talked about work. "I've got half a dozen books about narrative theory to look through for tomorrow's paper," Matthew said. "You never get time to actually read primary sources. Might as well be studying organic chemistry."

Terri shrugged. "What are you carrying books around for? This isn't the nineteenth century. You can get all that stuff off the Web."

"I can't stand reading off a screen," Matthew said. "You lose any sense of context. A printed book is more meaningful. The way it looks tells you things. Besides, the Internet's making the use of sources totally confusing. At least before, to rip off somebody's ideas, you had to write them out. Now you just cut and paste, nobody's got any idea who's written what."

"But what does it matter? It makes no difference whose words they are, if they're the right ones."

They argued halfheartedly for a few minutes. In the kitchen, the alkaline smell from the cellar was hard to ignore. Matthew wished he'd got more sleep. "I'd better get back," he said. Their hands linked across the table. The shadows under Terri's eyes reminded him of her makeup the night before. They agreed to meet on Friday, after Matthew's last paper. In the dim hallway, they kissed good-bye with a passion he found almost frightening. She waved as he shut the garden gate and walked off in the burning, unreal sunlight.

All through the week, the staircase dream kept coming back. He never reached the foot of the stairs: They twisted down forever, past an unlit landing just a few steps away. Thoughts of Terri distracted him from work, especially in the library. His exams didn't go very well. And behind it all he still felt the loss of Karen, like a silence that nothing could fill.

An hour after completing his last exam paper, Matthew was standing on the bridge at the bottom of Jephson Gardens. He felt exhausted, relieved, and nervous at the same time. Nervous because he'd not seen Terri since the morning in her room. Would she want to cool it? After all, she'd had a week to find someone better looking, more experienced, taller. But here she was, still dressed in black, waving as she came towards him through the Gardens' quilt of fertile colors. She embraced him. Their faces leaned together, hesitated, then kissed hard. The waterfall sang in his ears.

They walked along the riverbank, holding hands. Terri seemed less nervous than before; the sunlight had brought out a quiet energy in her face, a sense of self. Leaves cast faint, tattered shadows on the water. Up close, the yellow tinge of pollution was clear. He shivered. "Are you all right?" she said.

"Yes. It's just . . . I can't seem to get away from water. Rivers, floods, canals."

Terri gripped his arm. "We're still in the sea," she said. "Wherever we are. Like crabs in pools. Just waiting for the tide." He turned and looked into her eyes. They were dark, murky, but with a skin of light where he could see trees reflected.

They went for a drink at the Station Inn, which was just beginning to fill up with office and shop workers making a start to the weekend. The buzz of conversation mingled with the bleeping of mobile phones and cyberpets. Terri said her band, Forbidden Janet, were playing at the Haunch of Venison on Thursday night. Matthew said he'd be there. They both knew he only had nine days left before he went back to Cardiff for the summer. Under the table, their feet carried out their own slow, nervous conversation.

As they left the pub, Matthew suddenly knew what was going to happen. He didn't seem able to make decisions anymore. They walked slowly to the crossroads at the foot of the Parade, and on to the canal and the traffic-blackened viaduct. The familiar smell of stagnant water. The broken glass in the alley. A scrap of torn plastic raised its head and flapped away. Terri backed against the wall, held him against her. As he lifted her in his arms, she giggled. "You're the wrong height." They made love quickly, without foreplay. Matthew was shaking so much that he hardly needed to move. Terri bit his shoulder when she came. Her teeth were sharper than Karen's.

They went back to Terri's house, where they shared a bath and made love again, splashing in the antique, claw-footed tub while steam drew ghostly figures in the mirror. Then Terri cooked them some pasta with mushrooms and shredded chicken. She seemed to sample food, eating a little bit of everything without getting through much; but she drank a lot of wine. They both did. At the back of his mind, Matthew thought he should ask Terri what she really knew about Karen. But he couldn't find the right words. Instead, they talked about records. Terri's favorite Cure album was *Disintegration*; Matthew's was *Faith*. They both thought Nirvana's *In Utero* was a better album than *Nevermind*.

Around midnight, they climbed the naked stairs to Terri's room, where they drank some more Russian vodka and listened to a tape of Forbidden Janet. It was strong on rhythm, but weak on dynamics. Like most Goth bands. Terri said the rest of the band were off to see the bright lights of Kenilworth. They'd be back later. Matthew knew only the alcohol was keeping him awake. Fibers of smoke from Terri's cigarettes made the air seem tangible. He could still make out the faint odor of bleach and decay from the basement. When the music faded, they lay together on the mattress, naked, not moving.

The air was damp and cool. He could hear something from below, within the house: a whispering like the sea, a gradual sifting of layers. The smell of rot was stronger now. It must be rising through the walls. He could feel sunlight on his back and the side of his face. His mouth was so dry that his breath seemed to stick to it. He sat up and rubbed his eyes.

Terri was sleeping beside him, stretched out on the duvet. Her face was shifting, changing its expression. She didn't look like Terri. The mouth twisted, and something moved under the skin of her cheek. One eyelid swelled like a blister, then fell inward. He didn't know what he was seeing. It was the vodka, he realized, tasting his own sweat in his mouth. He reached out to touch her arm. It was cool: no sign of fever. Then the arm lifted towards him, coiling. It seemed to have no bones. It was hardly an arm at all.

He backed off, pressing his hand to his mouth. A thread of darkness flickered behind his eyes. With shaking hands, he pulled on his jeans and walked as quietly as possible out of Terri's room and down the stairs. Light hung in the dusty air by each window, like patches of cloth. The smell of decay was stronger in the hall, mixed with something else: flesh and brine, like a crowded swimming pool. He could hear water swirling round and round, very slowly. The sound was coming from the basement.

He pushed at the door under the stairs. Paint flaked away on his fingers; the wood felt soft, yielding. It wasn't locked. A wave of decay hit him. Somehow, it didn't seem like a smell of death. He walked down five cold steps. There was a faint light in the basement, but he couldn't see any window. No light bulb either. Just four walls, and the bluish tint of whatever was covering the floor.

It was like a swamp of some kind: mold and peat and stagnant water, with crusts and ripples on its uneven surface. It smelt brackish, like seawater left out in the sun. Like rock pools. And it was moving. He could make out shapes just under the surface: hands, shoulders, the curve of a spine. And then he could see the faces. A dozen of them, more, their eyes filled with a faint violet glow. And among them, Karen. She saw him and smiled.

Suddenly he understood what the staircase dream meant.

And what Terri had meant about working in the library. The library was here. His hands began to unfasten his jeans. There was no choice to be made. It had already happened. Naked, he stepped forward into the murky pool. It lapped around his feet, gripping them. The steps went on under the surface. He could feel the pool absorbing him, reading his flesh like a phrasebook. It was deep enough to drown in. Its texture was dense, blood warm, intimate. It was memory.

In the last moment, her face slipped over his.

# THE NIGHT CITY

## Wilum Pugmire and Chad Hensley

The night encircled the city's citadel tops, tiny fires flickering from the windows high above. A lukewarm wind whirled earthward from skyscraper darkness, carrying muffled moans to the street. A lanky shadow shuffled down a cracked concrete incline. Sickly green light flashed neon vulgarities upon the stark, angular face of a man. His hair was a mass of unkempt nigrescence curling around thin, oily ears. A hand of bone and callused flesh brought a sheet of tattered foolscap to wide nostrils. Michael Ashton inhaled deeply, savoring the scent of death and lavender, which was imbued in the paper. The words, penned in crabbed hand by his old friend, danced in the faint glow of the street lamp.

The gleam of passing headlights illumed a hunched form. A sea of rusted safety pins held together a jacket of shredded black fabric. A jaundiced face emerged from the dark folds of the garment. Angular patches of hair dotted a bald, wrinkled head. Incandescent pinpricks of color swam in clouded eyes. A frail froglike hand reached out to Michael and he knew Manly Davis had found him.

"Hello," said a soft, croaking voice.

Thoroughly pleased, Michael wiped a scab-encrusted palm on black denim pants and gripped Manly's slightly webbed fingers with a gentle squeeze. "Nice to finally meet you," gurgled Michael in a phlegm-filled voice. He gazed around furtively as if expecting other forms to stumble out of the darkness.

"Yes," replied Manly solemnly, purple-veined pupils dilating in streetlight glare. He turned and gestured with a thin, branchlike arm toward the darkness. "Where shall we go?" Manly asked, a bit of excitement betraying his sternness. "I have not been outside in a long time." His voice took on a sad, somber tone. "I am afraid I have forgotten the city."

Anthracite eyes gleamed with anticipation. "Surely, you have some sights of interest to show me?" A fat, pointed tongue darted across dry lips, exposing a mouth of unnaturally white teeth. "Lead the way. We can talk as we walk."

"Well . . ." Manly said, pondering for a moment. "We can go to my place and look at my newest acquisition, and there are numerous points of interest along the way."

Michael pressed his hands together, knuckles cracking loudly. His tall, lean frame fell behind Manly's slithering shadow as the pair wandered off into the night. "It is so nice to finally meet you," Michael repeated nervously, "after our years of correspondence."

"Yes, isn't it?" Manly replied, rounding an unmarked street corner, red brick walls covered with cryptic spray-painted symbols. An alley materialized out of the darkness. Overturned trash cans filled the small quarters with rancid garbage. A pile of rotting cardboard quivered and a pale, trembling form crawled into a wedge of moonlight. "Look!" Manly snapped gleefully, pointing a long, shriveled finger. "It's a night child."

Michael stared into the alley, curious at this new discovery. A small, androgynous, childlike shape scurried toward them, its dirty knees soiled and bloody. The naked adolescent stood and smiled, sapphire eyes sparkling with strange recognition. Michael noticed the absence of sex organs between the child's legs as Manly kneeled.

Tiny, unblemished hands clutched leathery cheeks and pulled Manly's face to moist, black lips. The child stepped away from Manly, the skin of its smooth, hairless chest beginning to bubble. A shower of sparks shot out of the child's chest cavity as the flesh fell away and a pile of fragile bones clattered noisily to the ground. The musky scent of semen filled

the air and a sudden wind scattered glittering ashes. Where the
child had kissed Manly's forehead, drops of blood seeped
from an open, raw wound. Manly's face became a wide, wrinkled grin and he stood. He motioned for Michael to follow and
they resumed their slouching stroll.

The night child was forgotten, as Michael had other concerns. "How is the collection coming?" Michael asked.

Manly took a long, wheezing breath and increased his pace.
"There is, of course, the new acquisition with which I've been
preoccupied. You'll see it in due course." Manly pointed to a
building ahead of them. "Hmmmmm. What is that?"

A neon billboard blinked with a thousand yellow bulbs. A
marquee in the center proclaimed a live peep show waited
within the theaterlike entrance. Michael stopped and gazed
hungrily at a wall covered with Polaroids of topless women,
their faces completely scratched out. His muscles tightened
between his legs and his heart began to pound uncontrollably.
"Can we go in?" said Michael, attempting to restrain himself.

"Certainly," Manly replied with a whimsical smile. "I've
never experienced this sort of establishment."

The doors were open and a change dispenser sat on a black
masonite counter. Michael pulled a dollar bill from his pocket,
slid the paper into a tray, and gently inserted the tray into the
machine. Four coins clanked into a leather catch. Sweaty fingers took two and placed a pair in Manly's upturned hand.
"My pleasure," said Michael proudly.

Manly shuffled into the hall, his boots dragging new stains
onto the soiled carpet. Michael followed, his face softly blushing. On either side of the hall, swinging doors led to narrow
booths. Twitching feet stood below some of the stall doors.
Faded red letters explained that some booths allowed their occupants to watch the show through one-way glass, while in
others, the viewer could also be seen.

Michael looked about nervously until he found an unoccu-
pied booth. The cramped room allowed little more than elbow
space. At shoulder height a black panel covered a small window. A coin slot occupied the wall below the window. Without
hesitation, he put a coin into the slot. A hum of electricity

filled the room and the panel began to rise. Michael squinted as a dimly lit circular chamber filled his vision. A single, bare bulb dangled from the center of the ceiling. Michael held his breath as shadows congealed on the fringes of the room's darkness

Two round pink eyes peered pensively at Michael. The eyes were attached to two large fleshy orbs and he giggled childishly, realizing they were a woman's breasts. He tried to discern the features of the woman's face, but there was only blackness. The breasts pressed against the glass and Michael watched expectantly as the woman began her dance.

The woman pulled away for a moment and then pressed her crotch against the glass. Michael found himself unable to feel even a stirring of emotion, the sight of the sex organs so close to his face was neither stimulating, nor repulsive. He felt nothing. Suddenly he wondered if Manly was similarly bored with this tawdry display. Why had he brought Manly here? Embarrassed, he turned quickly and left the peep show to find Manly outside, gazing into the night.

Manly smiled as Michael approached. "I can find no inspiration in such a place, I fear. It sings neither to soul nor loins. Still, I'm glad we came, as it has brought to mind another place that might amuse us. Are you game?"

The two wandered to an alleyway near the waterfront. Manly led the way into the dark alley, to a door made of ancient wood. He lightly touched the wood with trembling fingers. Then he turned and touched those fingers to his companion's lips.

"Can you taste it, the old, old oak, an elder taste that hints of death? This door is made of wood from a hanging tree that stood in a town where witches and wizards were put to death because of arcane wisdom that dreamed within their skull-space." He oddly smiled. "There are traces of the past in this mad, modern world; one merely needs to know how to find them. Come."

Michael entered the drear place, and slowly his eyes adjusted to the darkness. He found himself in what looked like some forgotten wax museum. Manly reached toward a wall, and the room suddenly filled with dim blue light.

"This is my little gallery of dreams and nightmares. You see, in this corner, this weird work of iron and steel, and from that bar there hangs a studded leather belt. Gaze deeply at that belt, my friend."

Michael did so. The steel studs of the belt eerily caught the dim reflection of strange blue light. The belt began to sway, as if blown by wind. Michael looked, and thought he could detect a bulk of shadow forming by the swaying belt. A human shape, dark and still. A dead boy, hanging from a length of leather belt wrapped around his broken neck. He felt a gripping pain wrap around his own throat, and suddenly Michael could not breathe.

Manly placed a hand over his friend's eyes. "It isn't wise to gaze too long upon these memories of exquisite death," he whispered.

Michael found himself pulled away from the exhibit. Staggering, he followed his companion to a dusky corner of the room. He beheld the waxen figure of a young man, and thought that this was a more mature version of the pale, trembling youth whose form had hung from the leather belt. He could not be absolutely certain because the figure's eyes were concealed behind opaque glasses. Something wet gleamed upon the figure's mouth. He stepped closer, and saw that the thing's mouth was stained with blood. As he stared at the image, a taste of blood tainted his lips.

"The taste of blood, that elixir of life and death. A rather captivating sensation, don't you think?" Manly sadly smiled, then walked away. He wandered to a doorway that was labeled CARNIVAL OF FREAKS. "This is my current nightmare, a curious phantasmal glimpse of the creature who now haunts my life. It broke my heart to create this one. It is an image of pain and rejection. Do you care to see it?"

"Of course," Michael eagerly gasped.

Manly secretly smiled. "Yes, the angst-ridden images of decadent passion are intoxicating, are they not? Well, this is one of which we can deeply drink. But first let me prepare myself. My love for this creature has turned me into a foolish clown, and to look upon it I must dress the part."

He knelt before a cardboard box from which he took a tin of white greasepaint. He smeared the substance over his weary face. He reached into the box and brought forth a tube of crimson lipstick, with which he formed a clownish mouth. Reaching one final time into the box, he brought out a pair of huge rubber ears, which he fastened to his own. Slowly he rose and faced his companion. The sight of this tragic, mirthless figure broke Michael's heart, and he had to fight so not to weep.

Together they entered the doorway. The room was very large. The walls and ceiling had been painted to resemble evening sky. As Michael looked at it, he thought a nighttime chill embraced his skin. He thought the tiny silver dots painted here and there on the dark ceiling twinkled like starlight. He thought he could hear the faint sighing of evening wind whisper in his ears.

They approached an animal cage, the kind wherein lions and other such beasts were once kept at circuses. They could smell the straw that littered the cage. They could see the small, dim shape of the thing that slept upon the straw, the thing that stirred awake and slowly rose.

Manly trembled at the sight of the beautiful boy inside the cage, at the dark eyes that gleamed with a reflection of starlight.

Windsong played at his floppy ears. The creature in the cage began to sing a low, whispered song. Manly sank to his knees, and his body shook with longing. Weakly, he crawled toward the cage. His shaky hands clasped the cold metal bars. He watched the beautiful lips that moved in quiet singing. He watched the twilight eyes set deep within an impious face, those eyes that beckoned yet refused him.

His face, pressed against the bars, was inches from the creature's naked loins. He could smell the sweat that stained the penis set deep within its thick pubic mound.

The creature in the cage raised a dainty hand. Manly watched in wonder the crimson stain that began to spread upon the palm. He watched as the beautiful creature bent to him, offering him the bloodstained hand.

Manly kissed the stigmatic palm. His lips tasted richly of blood. The caged thing's beautiful face bent to him and kissed his dripping mouth, then pressed crimson lips against Manly's forehead. The wound obtained from the night child closed, leaving only a tracery of scarlet droplets trickling down Manly's face. He blinked the blood from his eyes and beheld the hand before his face. The dainty hand was raised over his head, and from it dripped a black rain of blood.

"I am his, my soul blends with his, and yet he will not love me. He cannot love me, nor ever will I taste his love. I am doomed to feel this unwanted ecstasy for the remainder of my wretched life." Manly shook and wept. Unable to withstand the sorrowful sight any longer, Michael grabbed his friend and took him from that room, that building, into the nighted city where reality awaited them.

Side by side, Michael and Manly left the dirty tarmac and walked toward the whispering shore. A horned moon split the sky into patches of slatelike darkness. Moonlight flickered like sparkling diamonds on the dark surface of the lapping waters. The towering city fell away behind them as the ocean approached.

Michael was the first to break the silence. "You will always be an inspiration to me," he said sincerely. "If I can master the craft half as well as you, it will have been from my eyes upon your efforts." Michael balled his right hand into a fist and shook it in the air. "Meeting you has been such a pleasure."

Manly's sad, swollen eyes glimmered softly for a brief moment. "Thank you, my friend. Maybe you will be an inspiration for me." He slowly slid to his knees, the damp sand clinging to his tired flesh. The tide licked at the shore, tickling his legs. He suddenly plunged his hands into foamy waves of chilly water. He splashed water in his face, clown makeup melting away.

"But no matter what, you will never be satisfied. The work will never be enough. Achievements will turn empty and you will long for the final ecstasy of death's embrace." Tears streamed down Manly's face and into the tide.

A loud flapping of wings echoed from the shore and misty shapes rose from the undulating waters. Shimmering apparitions composed of droplets resembling beaded mercury soared into the night air. A humid wind blew shoreward and faint echoes of people drowning rolled off the distant depths. Manly stood, smiled at Michael, and waved farewell as he walked into the beckoning waters.

Michael smiled fondly. Thin, papery dragonfly wings unfolded from the flesh of his back. The wings vibrated rapidly and Michael rose into the air. He watched until Manly was swallowed by the ocean and then he departed. He caught the scent of dried sex wafting from a forgotten hotel room on the early morning horizon. He allowed the currents of lukewarm air to carry him toward the city. Beneath him, a red tide washed upon the shore and stained the beach around him.

# THE PLAGUE SPECIES

## *Charlee Jacob*

Intermission.

Territory.

Counterpoise.

After the last brass trumpet sounds, the walls have fallen and the ground is saturated with blood—what becomes of the descendants of angels?

Going to bed on the island of Timnah, not thinking about justice, lending not the slightest consideration to the troubles of a poisoned nation, I gazed out through the glass walls and ceiling of the greenhouse. This conservatory was attached to a traditional home, which itself had standard bedrooms. But I had moved my bed in here, shunning all other pieces of furniture, save for a nightstand and telephone. I could see the yards and front doors of several of my neighbors, porch lights glowing. I could see the street with its dark curbs, like extra midnight-water horizons pulled close to the heart of our block. I could see the sky replete with moon and stars—something I hadn't been able to do at all in our old country where the cities were so dirty.

Back then, we would picnic on the beach, staring out across the waters of the Aegean at the island of Timnah. Some atmospheric condition caused the isle to be ever wrapped in a rosy mist, not brown and noxious as the clouds which hung over our land. The sunrise and sunset turned the sea a bright red, and at night there was a flashing, bright peculiarity around Timnah—not unlike the aurora borealis I saw when visiting Sweden for a symposium on the relationship between environment and precipitation. Streaks, hazy fire, scarlet mirage.

I remember taking my son, Micah, out on a boat, getting as close as we could without actually landing. So we could stare with wonder at the paradise rich with olive and pistachio groves, a silver-blue waterfall visible through our binoculars, and black sand! I once took a trip to the Hawaiian Islands in America—studying heretofore unrecognized nuances of fire and water. They have a black beach there as well.

"Why can't we go all the way there, Daddy?" Micah would always ask me.

"The Timnians turn people away. They discourage visitors," I explained, gently brushing the soft hair out of his eyes where it always seemed to fall. I would worry because he seemed to be losing weight again.

"But it looks so pretty. Our land is dirty and smells. Why is that?" he wanted to know.

How did a father explain pollution to a five-year-old? How did I get him to understand that our own country was once beautiful? It was development, progress from a medieval system to an industrial one, business. . . . Not so long ago countries in the Balkans were considered backward, feudal. Old World "charm" made few of us rich. We began to see factory smokestacks as more elegant than minarets and pillars. We upped production to rival giants of commerce such as Detroit, Munich, Tokyo.

I just told him what the rumor was—what we'd all laughed about for years. "The islanders claim they are the descendants of angels. So maybe that is a little bit of heaven over there."

Now, in my bed, I recalled the movement of a ship beneath me, the side-to-side rolling of the leviathan's own gestalt, stuffed with us. I remembered a harbor made from the bones of the dead. I recollected my cock erect with rage in the moonlight, even as my balls shriveled with revulsion, and wondering how those two opposites were even possible. My hands were then straining, fingers testing a strange metal. My face was contorted until my own soul wouldn't have recognized it.

It was amazing how little time it actually took for the stench of burning to leave one's nostrils. Clean air and roses could work wonders.

The mind might not forget horror, but could at least set it aside, relegating it to recesses within the transport boats and cleansing camps, the burial pits and the weeping of children. The earth starts over, a piece of space turns to reveal an unsullied side, and we begin anew.

I crept between clean sheets, crisp and unwrinkled pajamas smooth in flannel against flannel. I placed the back of my head upon the pillow so I could face the clear ceiling and heaven beyond. I murmured a prayer, wondering how many of the neighbors did the same. I hissed it out between my teeth and felt it turn humid a few inches of air beyond my lips. I stretched my legs and wriggled my toes, feeling old, yet healed, scars crackle like morning frost.

When I felt the first pain in my ankles, I also heard the first screams. It seemed as if the bones were grinding together, turning within their tendon shrouds. I shouted and tried to throw back the covers to see what was wrong, but the intensity of the agony paralyzed me. I barely managed to look down. Had some animal gotten beneath the blanket and attacked me? I could see movement, a sinuously violent twisting at the other end of the bed.

A loud jangling began to fill the air, looping between the spaces which scorched with shrieks coming from neighboring houses. I was adding my own startled and tormented voice to this great noise as I finally convinced my body to act, to at least struggle to rise. I grasped the headboard and tried to pull my legs up from the end of the mattress. I wrenched my shoulders, thinking I would fling myself onto the floor and thus escape whatever rodent or serpent had invaded my bed.

But my legs were pinned, flesh tearing as bones audibly snapped. The pain was so terrible I almost fainted. I watched helplessly as the movement at the end of the bed shifted, the savage undulation now gliding toward the edge, rippling the covers, then emerging from beneath them to slip free.

There was no animal. It was only my feet, no longer attached to my legs. They hovered in the air for a moment and then began to float toward a glass wall, leaving a trail of bloody smoke behind them.

The screams outside and the jangling increased, so loud that the glass panes of the greenhouse shuddered as if from thunder. But my feet simply passed through the wall, not unlike a passage in water, treading the air and leaving red smoke in their wake.

Staring through glass, I could see many other pairs of feet, bloody, with shattered bone ends sticking up like thin pale ankles emerging from boot tops. They were all sizes, from smooth and little bigger than thimbles to great hoary bunioned ones with rippled yellow nails. They came from the other houses, moving toward the street. Here and there a front door opened and someone crawled outside in agonized pursuit, with face sculpted into a crescent rictus, mangled ankles leaving thick, crooked trails of gore.

Screams and jangling.

My phone rang. That was when I realized what the jangling was. It was thousands of telephones going off, as frantic people tried to call for help.

I picked up, gasping into the receiver

I heard a phlegm-thick voice ask, "My God! Zethám, what is it? What's happening? I've lost my feet. . . ."

"Kataren?" I fumbled, trying to identify the caller out of her hysteria. I knew the voice. It belonged to another researcher I worked with at the lab. "I don't know. . . ."

"Where are the police? No one answers there. And I've heard no emergency vehicles, no sirens. . . ."

"Have you looked outside, Kataren? There'll be no one coming to rescue. All help is walking away!" I replied in an almost shrieking giggle. I choked on the laughter, trying to make myself believe this was a dream. I simply didn't realize that I'd fallen asleep. Yes, that was it.

But I wasn't asleep. I never suffered so much pain, even in the worst nightmare.

I felt that agony, saw the feet outside, and made myself

throw aside the covers at last. I saw the mutilated shape of my crippling.

Of course, she probably couldn't look outside. She was likely lying in her bed in two pools of blood or collapsed on her floor. I knew of no one other than myself who slept inside four glass walls.

I heard her sob as she hung up. Reluctantly, I let my gaze drift back beyond the greenhouse windows. The street was filled with feet! The red smoke had evaporated. Curious—it was usually feet that went away and footprints which remained. But now the prints—if this crimson smoke could be called that—were disappearing and the feet were still there.

They floated up in pediform march, across the lawns, over the sidewalks, lining up along the horizon curbs. They were queuing before the openings to the sewers which gaped beneath, slipping inside and down into the cloacal hollows, vanishing from sight into the gutters.

Weak from loss of blood, I passed out.

Inquisitions.
Celebrations.
Incumbency.

The sound of wings fluttering against glass is of a pure white noise. Unless it's night and there's no light to see that the wings might not be black.

I ought to have bled to death. Those I could see who had managed to crawl from their houses also should've bled to death. We hadn't. The wounds had clotted, blood dried into hard brittle.

I missed dawn's arrival and the sun's departure into dusk. I awoke to twilight's fading, disconcerted to see there were no stars and the moon never rose. But the sky was streaked with the aurora which always hovered above the island. Incandescent. Like rainbows on coals.

I'd been having a dream about being at the old lab where I used to work. We were very excited because our team had invented a process which would eliminate the acid rain that had become such a problem. Clouds would be seeded with it before a storm and the corrosive properties would be neutralized. Then I went home from work as usual . . . only to find that our house had melted. It was like a tiny sea in our yard, with only the fireplace with my wife's collection of porcelain angels on the shelf bobbing in the center of it like an island.

My son came running into my arms, his face half gone.

"Can we go to the beach? I've a boat we could journey to the island on," he asked, holding up a toy ship with a bright red sail, a sail like a flame.

And then it began to rain and everything—even the sea in our yard, which had been our house—caught fire. Only the fireplace didn't burn.

I had no doubt this was a dream because things didn't happen that fast. No buildings actually dissolved. That's ridiculous—no matter what the foreign media said. And I didn't know anyone who was burned that badly.

After that, I'd been having a dream about boats and the bomb-melted edges of battle trenches, which sometimes filled with seawater. In it, I listened to the sounds of someone crying softly and the noises of clothes being torn. My skin buzzed, as if it had been flash-fried. It sparked with electricity as I hurtled through the passive currents of night.

Then—in my bed in the greenhouse, awakened by a sudden new terror—the crotch of my pajama bottoms ripped, rupturing at the seam. There were razors between my legs, doing a backward scroll along the downy underside of my groin. I heard a skitter as of the manic teeth of shrews. This ought to have been drowned out by my screaming but, incomprehensibly, wasn't. My balls vibrated, spewing clots into the open air (I was no longer lying between covers, having kicked them off in my struggle of the previous evening), blood flashing before me until I had the sickened impression of hundreds of scarlet fireflies. My penis erected in agony, shot out a wad of sanguine sperm, and then bobbled limp again.

Outside the shrieking had begun along the street, and there was the raucous jangling as telephones rang. Floating in the air through walls, doors, and windows were genitals: cocks with testicle sacs sagging below . . . triangular gouges of uteruses, framed with ragged clitoral folds, and trailing scrappy ovaries like the optic-nerve stalks of eyes. Some of these wombs were visibly occupied with fetuses, floating like half-formed dolls inside water balloons. In a few they hung out, as if half-born or half-aborted, or crucified upside down like St. Peter. Many of the genitals—both male and female—were clearly diseased. And again, as with the feet, they were of all sizes, the most graphic proof that none were spared.

A singularly long protracted moment and my own organs were removed, leaving me flopping on the bed, convulsing as I howled.

Still, I turned my head, looked through the greenhouse glass, seeing people spasming on front lawns, sidewalks, the street. The genitalia inched wormlike through the air, or swirled through it like so much detached dandelion seed. But there was something else in the air now, too. I watched it rush up in a long black streak, heard the rustling even above the screams and telephones. Ravens I took them to be at first, or crows. Yet as some dashed themselves against the greenhouse windows in feeding frenzy, I saw the blackbirdlike bodies had the heads of locusts. The greasy ebon feathers ended at the shoulders and then chitin exoskeletons rose from there. Pressed against the glass, they stared in at me with compound eyes, antennae twitching, labra and mandibles working in graceless appetite. The night turned red with fleshy tidbits torn apart, tissue-thin membranes peppered with dark pubic hair shaken into atoms before being swallowed down, the unborn gobbled like pickled suckling pigs.

(Locusts? I remembered them from my younger days. Sometimes they used to savage the crops which grew in summer fields. They would come across in a giant black shadow, leaving the land gray and empty afterward. Our fathers created strains of grain which made their bellies swell until they burst. But I couldn't remember if locusts ever swarmed on islands.)

The birdthings didn't attack people lying in the street, who gazed up with pain-shocked eyes, trying to crawl back inside their homes—but too weak to do anything past floundering like the drowned. Blood and skin filtered down, falling into their eyes, into open mouths, choking them. The locust-headed birds landed on them, pecking up these trophies, then flew back into the sky to seek more meat. Everywhere, from all across the city—the island, too, perhaps—generative organs floated like flotillas of grotesque valentines. The birds fed until all had been devoured, then gathered back into their streak and were gone.

I'd somehow managed to prop myself into a semi-sitting position, shoulders and head balanced precariously—dizzily—against the headboard. I stared at the wound between my legs, nested between the torn remnant of my pajamas, rendering me a sexless thing.

Why? What demonic force attacked us? Surely I wouldn't fail to die from this night's sundering. Between the loss of my feet and the unexplainable castration, my body evacuated more blood than I thought it possible my veins had ever contained.

I took one of the pillows and stuffed it against this new scoop of outrage, watching as the dark red stain spread through the case to sodden each feather within. The stench was foul—of rotten eggs and ruined cheese, of slaughtered lambs and children decaying before the shovel turns the earth.

My phone rang. It made no sense to answer, but I did.

"Zethám . . ." It was Kataren. "What's going on? Something's torn me apart, cut me open like men with knives. Only there was no one there. . . ."

I could hear panic shaking apart her words. She was normally such a reserved woman, a scientist. We were a rational group, usually, seldom given over to chaos. But had I tried to sort things out? Had I developed theories about what might be going on here, analyzing the possibilities calmly?

How could anyone be calm when their feet twisted off and walked away, and when their genitals detached and floated out to feed monsters?

"Kataren, are you a mother?" I asked.

"Y-yes," she stammered. "They live on the other side of the island with their father. I can't have more now. . . . Why?"

"Weep for your children," I replied.

"What does it mean?"

"The descendants of angels. What tears do they shed?"

I don't know which of us hung up first.

I didn't pass out as I had before.

I hung in a blood-misted fog, waiting to die as dawn came, trying to close my eyes so I couldn't see the carnage in the street. I heard locusts, the songs the plague species makes using their stridulatory mechanisms, hunger-chant of Orthoptera. Swarming to claim what they must have to live. There were none to be seen, neither in bird form nor grasshopper shape. The sun rose on streaks of blood which had dribbled down and dried on the greenhouse glass, on a sifting confetti of sexual aspic turning to damp dust along the horizon curbs.

Those who had been in the street the night before were still there. They hadn't drowned in the peccant fall of gore. They lay where they were, rubbing weak hands across their faces to clear the mess away from lips and noses, rubbing strings of it from their eyes so they could look out at the destruction. Then they wept because there was nowhere to wipe their stained hands clean.

The phone rang once. I picked it up, said nothing, heard only gurgling, as of black bile pregnant and come to term in the throat. It made me ask myself, *Where and when does rot begin?*

I hallucinated: from blood loss, physical trauma, emotional shock. I thought of:

Corruption.

The Tolls of Grief.

Jericho.

I thought of several years ago when Micah was sick, skin gone too white, hair falling out, baby teeth going without permanent ones replacing them. The doctors couldn't make up their minds whether or not his body failed to produce enough red blood cells due to radiation from the nearby nuclear power plant, or from toxins which had been dumped in the river. They were certain it had nothing to do with the rain project, which at least gave me some relief from my guilt.

At least my work hadn't done this to him. Not directly anyway.

My wife and I kept him in the living rom in his last days, his bedroom not being large enough to accommodate all the machinery he was hooked up to. Near where we'd moved his bed was the fireplace. Up along the hearth was where Nari kept her collection of porcelain angel statues.

When I was just a boy myself, I remembered hearing about a poll which had been taken among the citizens of the United States, finding that over seventy percent of their people admitted to a belief in the existence of angels. Our own media followed up with a similar survey, reporting that most of our country did, too.

Micah liked looking at Nari's statues.

Then one day, Micah asked me through bleeding gums, "Daddy? You said the people on Timnah Island claim to be descended from angels. What does that mean?"

I sat beside his bed. "It means they think they're better than everybody else. It's why they don't do business with the rest of the world. They don't even trade with us and we're right across the water, their closest neighbors on the sea. They grow olives and nuts, like we do, but they don't use them for commerce. No one has ever even seen a fishing boat from there. That is very strange since all the other islands on the Aegean have fishermen."

"Then why don't we ever have fish?" he asked.

I threw a knowing look at my wife. "Well, let's just say that no one who knows what's in them now will eat fish."

The boy blinked slowly, not really understanding the concept of international business or of toxins dumped in the water. But he went on. "I heard Dr. Hiel say that the Timnians live in the past. There's nothing modern there, like a third world country—only on purpose. Like a third world country—only nobody ever gets sick because they haven't messed things up. He said people have taken pictures that prove the garbage in the sea never reaches their shore. It always stops a certain distance out, all the way around the island."

I decided to have a talk with Dr. Hiel, about making such

comments where my boy could hear them. Because it was treasonous even if it was true. Because it was cruel to make a child think he lay dying due to wrongness committed by his people, his family.

"Can't we go live on Timnah, Daddy?" he asked me.

It was a question a lot of folks had been asking of late.

A week after the child asked me, "If we aren't able to live on Timnah, mightn't we visit? I know you said they don't like visitors. But if they're the children of angels, can't they make me well?"

Nari and I were desperate. Wasn't it worth a try? So we bundled him up and drove to the beach hoping a charter boat would take us all the way to the island. Many others from our country were there, camped out, pressuring the boat captains.

A few finally took us over, convinced by the money we promised. Sailors were a superstitious lot. They said it would have to be strictly during the day. The flashing red lights at night around the island frightened them.

It was a strange feeling entering the pink mist. A sense of euphoria swept over us as if there were a drug in the air. The waters at the shoreline glittered and glowed as flames.

They were almost too bright to look at directly.

"Like in drawings of holy fire," Nari commented, genuflecting from right to left as the Orthodox Church instructed.

"Several perfectly rational things might explain such a phenomenon," I said. "Some unusual species of plankton, for example. Large amounts of a particularly vivid coral on the bottom. Some quality of the island's soil seeping into the water."

She sighed. "Oh, Zethám, you take the magic out of everything."

Four large boatloads of us were ferried over. We landed and spread out on the black sand. A delegation came to meet us, wearing cumbersome flowing robes. A strange-looking race, tall and beautiful in an angular sort of way, but they were always looking at the ground, very pious, extremely humble. It was odd to think a simple people would wear such elaborate hairstyles, even on the men, puffed and curled upon the tops of their heads.

"We can't help you," they told us, heads bent. "You must turn away from here. This island is restricted."

"We need miracles," someone spoke up in protest.

"You claim to be of angelic heritage. . . ." another argued.

"Yes, we are," they admitted. "But we cannot heal your sick. What comes as the force of either a heavenly justice or damnation through your own foolishness is not for us to interfere with."

We were, of course, greatly insulted. What self-righteous arrogance! And they would not meet our eyes, gazing ever at the ground as if none of us was anything to look at.

"I don't care if their ancestors were angels or not," Nari complained hotly. "It's very rude not to even look at us."

"But, Mama," Micah said, "maybe their eyes would burn us down."

He was feverish, his own pupils reflecting red.

As they left the beach to move back into the interior of the island, we noticed that they still didn't look up, even after their backs were long to us.

Grumbling, we boarded our boats and were taken back across the sea. From time to time the captains had to stop their boats, to move trash out of the way. The smell of rotting fish was horrible.

Nari and I took Micah home again. He died a day later. As Nari cried inconsolably, I strode to the fireplace, snatching up each porcelain angel and throwing it hard to smash against the wall.

I rented a small speedboat and piloted to the island. I turned off the motor and climbed out into the shallows, dragging the boat in with me. I shot the first Timnian I saw. Many of our people—who'd sought help for their loved ones in vain—were there also. There were at least fifty assorted craft at the beach: sailboats, sloops, small fishing vessels, even rowboats. The people were armed and angry. This was how the war started. Or perhaps I should simply refer to it as an invasion—for the Timnians didn't fight back.

It didn't matter. We didn't believe in angels anymore.

\*    \*    \*

Night dogged the heels of day, arrived with fear of what would happen next. It took little time, lying on the mattress stiff with blood, unable to move except to pant, desperate for water. From time to time, I flailed my hands, as if reaching out to the air for spirits, arabesques in gray swirls. I would gain enough strength to invoke with them, inarticulate signs that my pain-shocked mind was convinced would create the magic of deliverance. Then I let my hands fall to the bed, thinking I'd see the blood on them—not my own, but spectral stains from those I'd murdered.

Out, damned spot! Was I imitating a high-pitched Lady Macbeth? I laughed hoarsely, then clutched the bed as new centers of pain began in my shoulders. Whirling internal galaxies of excruciation, memories untangled from coils of nebula like combing snarls from the nuclei of rainbows. Recalling a line from the Book of Joshua in the Bible—able to command it because I had once been a devout boy. I'd believed in angels before I learned so much at university. The quote was from 6:26.

*And Joshua charged them at that time saying, "Cursed be the man before the Lord, who riseth up and buildeth this city, Jericho. . . ."*

It meant that those were cursed who would *rebuild* Jericho, after the Lord had seen to its destruction. We'd assured ourselves that God was with us, even as He'd been with the army of Joshua, marching in to take whatever land they needed for themselves. God had decreed that none in Jericho be spared. The army had marched in as a shadow across the land and left a gray emptiness behind.

Pain shot down the arms, flesh and bones beneath buckling like concrete. To wrists which warped and snapped like downed powerlines. Skin popped, shook in crepe gloves, veins and tendon wet in sunburst. The hands writhed at the ends, fingers twitching like gigged salamanders.

The hands twisted off, flapped like inexact and fledgling

wings, rustled through the weight of blood, then floated away from me.

I heard my own screams and shrieks beyond the greenhouse.

No jangling this time. No phones. Who had hands for them?

I saw them outside, gathering with all the others, ripped uncleanly from the wrists. So many sizes: only little doll's hands . . . and then those large enough to pull triggers, to jab with bayonets. No distinctions were made. Across the board.

"My Lord," I shouted, "they look like starfish!"

There had been nothing in the sky for the last nights: no moon, no stars. Only the rippling aurora.

Now there were stars, in hands going up and up, five-pointed pentacles ascending to spot the flashing darkness. All digits were splayed, yet pointed accusingly down at us. I don't know who else was able to look at this—except for myself through the glass ceiling and the wounded who were lying in their yards or in the street, whom I could see through the glass walls. But those of us who could look heavenward.

Not like the ones we'd invaded, gazes always down whether they were old or children. Even if they were thrown on their backs, clothes torn from their bodies, quiet or weeping, they still managed to have those eyes averted downward.

Even as we lined them up to be shot, bodies tumbled into ditches. As white men had done to American natives two centuries ago. As Nazis had done to Jews and gypsies, and Serbs had done to Muslims in the last century. And in this century and new millenium, how many times done one to another? Who was to say, I wondered, who were truly the descendants of angels?

On one occasion we'd marched into a village on the far side of the island, with a distant view of the coast where ancient Troy had stood. We hustled everyone out of bed. During the usual confusion, some women were raped, men were beaten, a stray memento severed.

We set up the duck row. They stood there, shivering in the cold morning, miserable, eyes cast to the earth. And as we raised our rifles, one of them with tears streaming down her cheeks—all salt in the salt-sea air—this single woman actually looked up. She didn't gaze at us but let her sight move beyond our soldiers. She kept tilting her head until it was fully back, eyes pleading toward the sky and whatever heaven lay beyond.

We paused, slightly lowering the barrels of our weapons. We heard the other Timnians gasp, as if they knew what she'd done without actually witnessing it.

There was a clap like thunder, but no bolt of lightning. She reached up her hands, imploring the thin ceiling of pink mist, a smile spreading across her bruised face.

Then she burst into flame, a writhing column of it, beginning somewhere in her chest and spreading out to the four limbs as if to four winds. She fluttered like a party flag on a cruise ship, burning quickly.

The other Timnian prisoners shuddered, peeked from the corners of their eyes, and sighed. Then they brought up their faces and threw back their heads, staring skyward, crying, grinning, catching fire—it was a mess. We moved back from the scorching wall of spontaneous heat. It became our turn to shudder, hair prickling at the backs of our necks as any hair on our faces singed. Nari and I both unshouldered our rifles and glanced at each other. A fool decided to fire into one of the living torches. His bullet ricocheted or exploded, flattening a tire on one of our jeeps.

In my bloody bed, I relegated the memory to its proper place, tucked between concepts of fable and reality, an image caught between the lies we tell ourselves and the whispers we ignore.

Cognition.
Epos.
Infinity.
Day and night. The sun came up, and the hands were stuck in the sky . . . like dead butterflies pinned on pink mist board. They seemed to wave hello to us. The sun set and they replaced the stars, only a few hundred feet up or so. I probably

couldn't have seen them at all if there weren't so many. They seemed to wave good-bye.

I was too terrified to think of what could be taken from me—from *us*—next. And yet a strange calm had overcome me. I found myself waiting, nervous, curious about and anticipating what fourth shape this retribution would take. For I knew we were being punished. Still, as I was lying in my bed, I asked no forgiveness, felt no remorse. We'd needed this new place to start over in. And the Timnians had refused to help my dying son, haughty with their eyes averted from us.

(Unless they were really only powerless, without miracles.)

I consoled my conscience with the fact that it was a bitter world. That God Himself had commanded the slaughter of innocent women and children, ordering genocide in the Old Testament.

I had another memory. We'd just moved into this home, freshly built from razed earth. I was working for the new lab, and our team had come up with an odd reason for the color of the sand around the island.

"It isn't what we would have expected. It isn't a product of a volcanic eruption on the island," Kataren told our superior.

"No," I added. "Apparently the beach itself was once on fire. As was the area now underwater a short ways out."

"Well, there must have been underwater eruptions, fissures opening, back in antiquity we believe," Kataren went on to say. "The seabed immediately surrounding the island isn't black like the sand on the beach. It is turned quite to glass and is an interesting red color. This is why the sea seems to flash."

"And the mist? The aurora?" asked our superior.

Kataren and I both shrugged. I replied, "We're still working on that."

Nari wanted a greenhouse because she had a desperate need to grow life. She was depressed after the war—the *invasion*. I didn't seem to be able to make her understand that the feelings of guilt would pass, that survival had dictated our actions. She'd wanted to have more children, but the doctors found a cancer inside her uterine wall. They could cure it, but she wouldn't be able to get pregnant again.

We'd had the greenhouse built, adjoining our new home.

I'd been taking a nap on the sofa when I heard Nari come inside. It was raining out, and she was soaked to the skin. There was an acrid stench in the air. Perhaps the storm was blowing the smells of pollution from our old country, in dusky tendrils across the sea, shaped like anemones and jellyfish— and just as poisonous.

When I realized the odor was gasoline and that it wasn't raining, I tried to get up quickly to stop her. I called out, "Nari!" but it was too late. She lifted her face, frowned as she realized she couldn't see the sky through the living room ceiling, and flicked the lighter. She then smiled, as if understanding that the ceiling made no difference. It was the gesture that mattered. She didn't spontaneously combust at the sight of heaven, but she died in a blaze of glorious light.

I glanced outside now, night down around us. Those who had crawled out and were lying in yards or in the street were on their backs. No matter how they'd collapsed, everyone had managed to roll to where they could see the sky. And I slept in a greenhouse so I could always see it. I had little trouble imagining that those still trapped within buildings with regular roofs were also on their backs, faces to heaven.

No remorse? No belief? No nagging suspicions?

I recalled the first Timnian prisoners being stripped naked. We were so startled to see the cloven hooves, the tails which had hitherto been concealed under those flowing robes, and the horns which had been hidden in the masses of stylized hair.

No one had guessed they might be the descendants of *fallen* angels.

This was why they'd not dared raise their eyes to the sky but remained meek, as if in the pose of eternal atonement. Sins of the fathers.

And now the latest agony began. My face seemed to erupt with fire, yet there was no flame. The edges at the cheekbones and jawline peeled, cellophane layers crisping. My mouth filled with blood . . . until I couldn't even scream for trying to spit it out, or swallow it down to keep from choking. My eyes filled with it until I couldn't see anything but red. My skull-bones ground in protest, and part of my throat collapsed. My face was leaving my body, pulling away in a taffy stretch from the slick muscles beneath, securing tendons snapping like rubber bands, my teeth biting out to attempt a last grasp on the lips. The eyes unscrewed from their sockets, sending white-hot bolts of torment backward through my brain. My spine arched, contorting until the back of my head touched the crimson crusts of my footless legs. It was the worst pain yet, more than the last three nights combined. For the face is the pinnacle to both body and mind, the seat of our consciousnesses. To defile that was the most terrible of the insults.

The most peculiar thing was that I still seemed to see it float up away from me, even with my eyeballs removed from my head, no longer sending messages to the brain. I saw it the way a spirit sometimes watches its own departure from the corpse, yet I wasn't dying nor was I rising. I was still in that devastated body, which certainly looked as if it ought to be dead. (Yet wasn't. Would I never die? Could none of us die?)

There were so many faces outside, like the surreal masks of souls. They fluttered strands of gore-flecked hair in masquerade ball ribbons. They might have been filmy papier-mâché, with cracked glass marbles inserted as popping-with-surprise eyeballs.

And then there were other faces, *other* faces. Beautiful and horrible, smiling and cruel. They took their form from the night itself, erupting out of the aurora and the memory of their own burning sea which it represented. The ancestors had come at last to avenge their own, I was sure.

I was now seeing from two places at once, from my body lying on the bed . . . and from my face rippling boneless and anchorless in the cold air. I saw the black mouth of an angel who has fallen, sired children, and lost them (not necessarily in that order), lean down close to that helpless face of mine, and then felt it kiss me hotly on the lips, breath hissing a pink steam. After this, the mouth opened chasm-wide, abyss-large, and swallowed me down.

Suddenly I couldn't see from either my face or my body.

How remarkably silent the night was. Were none of us able to scream?

By the morning, that facility would likely be returned to us. One didn't need lips to scream, only to fully articulate the pain. A poetic and erudite rendering of our agony wasn't necessary.

But perhaps we wouldn't cry out, wouldn't bellow blood clots from our lungs, nor gnash our teeth and rend the wind with our outrage.

Do not be deceived: Every man and every woman knows what justice is.

Yet rage or not, the night would come again. What would we lose the next time? I guessed nothing.

Our invading feet, raping organs, stealing hands had met vengeance . . . with a vengeance.

And we couldn't see the sky, couldn't see heaven. No, that wasn't for the fallen nor for their children.

# TEN BUCKS SAYS YOU WON'T

## *Richard Laymon*

"Ten bucks says you won't," Ron said.

"Let's see it."

Ron leaned toward the door of his car, squirmed, then sat up straight behind the steering wheel and lowered his head.

Jeremy, in the backseat, heard quiet, papery sounds.

"Got it." Ron raised a handful of bills, looked back, and waved them.

In the darkness of the car, Jeremy couldn't make out their denominations. "What've you got?" he asked.

"A five and five ones. What do you say?"

"Are you sure you want to lose it?" Jeremy asked.

"Not gonna lose it. Let's see *your* ten."

Jeremy leaned sideways and pulled his wallet out of his jeans. Holding it in the moonlight, he found a ten-dollar bill. He showed it to Ron. "Here's mine."

"Wait, wait, wait," said Karen from the front passenger seat. "I want in on this. I've got ten bucks says you won't do it."

Tess, in the backseat with Jeremy, said, "Me, too."

"*Et tu?*" Jeremy asked her. "*Against* me?"

"I'm hardly *against* you," Tess said. "I just happen to know you won't do it. You obviously *think* you will, but you won't."

"Oh, ye of little faith," pronounced Jeremy. Though trying to make light of it, he couldn't help feeling a little hurt.

"What do you think I am, some sort of wuss?"

"I'm not saying that," said Tess.

"I am," said Ron, and laughed.

"Just saying you won't do it," added Tess.

"I'll do it. And I'll be delighted to win your money."

"Can you cover all the bets?" Ron asked him.

Jeremy found a twenty-dollar bill in his wallet, pulled it out and put it with his ten. "You want to hold the stakes, Tess?"

"Sure."

Ron and Karen reached through the space between their seatbacks and passed their cash to Tess. Jeremy handed over his. Tess removed some money from her purse, folded all the contributions together, then reached inside the neck of her white blouse and stuffed the cash under a cup of her bra.

Ron whistled. Karen punched him in the shoulder.

"Ow!"

"What about you, Ron?" Tess asked him, suddenly smiling.

"What *about* me?"

"Do you want to do it?"

"Me? Are you kidding? This is Jeremy's gig, not mine."

"I don't see why the betting has to be limited to Jeremy," she said. "He'll never do it, anyway."

"Hey!"

"Well, you *won't*."

"Will, too."

She shrugged, then said, "I think it oughta be open to anyone. First person to do it gets all sixty bucks." Turning her head toward Ron in the front seat, she added, "And gets to personally remove the prize money from my person."

"Hey, hey, hey!" said Ron.

Karen punched his arm again.

"Ow! Stop that!"

"You stop being an asshole." To Tess, she said, "And you can lay off teasing him, okay? He's with me."

"Sure, sure. I know."

"If he wins, you can hand him the money."

Ron said, "I'll still know where it's been."

"You!" Karen punched him again.

"Ow!"

Jeremy laughed.

Moaning quietly, Ron rubbed his arm.

"You know," Karen told him, "you're not the only guy in town. If you don't appreciate what you're getting, I bet I can find somebody who would."

"I appreciate it, I appreciate it! Them."

Jeremy and Tess laughed.

"I mean," said Karen, "every guy in school wants me."

"Plenty of girls, too," Tess added.

"You wouldn't believe all the offers I've turned down. And why? Because I'm your girl, Ronny. I am your girl, aren't I?"

"Yes! Of course!"

"All right, then. Nobody touches me but you. Nobody touches you but me. And I'm the only one you touch."

"That's right!" Ron blurted.

"So much," said Tess, "for everyone bolting out of the car in a mad rush to win the money and feel me up."

"No feeling up," Karen said. "Unless Jeremy."

Tonight was Jeremy's third time out with Tess. So far, the most he'd done was hold her hand and kiss her good night. He'd been trying to work up the nerve to sneak a feel, but he'd been afraid Tess might be offended.

*She'll let me tonight,* he thought.

*But only if I win the bet.*

"I'm still gonna go," he insisted.

"Oh, sure," said Tess.

"I am."

"Then why are you still sitting here?"

"What about the rest of you?" he asked.

"Not me, dude," said Ron.

"Not me," said Karen. "Wouldn't catch me dead doing that. This is about as close as I ever want to be to the creepy old bitch."

"I'm thinking about it," said Tess. She patted her breast. "Feels like a lot of cash. I might want to keep it for myself."

"Wanta do it together?" Jeremy asked.

"No fair!" Ron blurted out. "I've got no problem with opening it up to everyone, but no collaborating. It has to be the first one to do it, or the bet's off."

"Jeremy's the one who said he'd do it," Karen reminded them. "I think the only fair thing is to let him give it a try. By himself. Then if he chickens out, he can come back to the car and Tess can try. How does that sound to everyone?"

"Sure," Tess said. "I don't have a problem with going second . . . since I *know* Jeremy won't do it."

"That's what you think," he told her.

"That's what I know."

"Oh yeah?"

Without waiting any longer, Jeremy threw open the passenger door. He climbed out and eased it shut. Standing beside the car, he took a deep breath. The air smelled fresh. It carried a sweet flowery scent.

When he walked toward the front of the car, his legs felt shaky. He tried not to make any sounds on the pavement. Past the edge of the roadway, gravel crunching under his shoes. Then he left the gravel behind, and the grass was nearly silent.

I must be out of my mind, he thought. Why did I say I'd do this? What the hell was I thinking?

Never thought they'd take me up on it.

*But man, they sure did.*

No big deal, he told himself. A few minutes from now, it'll be over and done with. I can climb back into the car and help myself to the sixty bucks in Tess's bra. And help myself to a little feel.

And they'll know I'm not a wuss.

*They really think I won't do it. Man, they've got another thing coming.*

He wished he had a flashlight, though. There were just too many shadows from trees, bushes, monuments and burial vaults. Too many patches of total darkness. Where someone might be lurking, watching.

Maybe not a person. Maybe a graveyard dog.

*Or a ghoul?*

Sure thing.

*How about some of those* Night of the Living Dead *creeps?*

Stop that!

*They'd love a fucked-up old cemetery like this.*

Knock it off!

Suddenly, he saw his destination.

Old lady Flint's burial place. It was easy to spot; the senior class had donated a special monument to mark her grave.

*And here it is!*

Jeremy stepped up to the monument—a brass apple the size of a giant pumpkin—on top of a marble pillar about five feet high.

At the dedication ceremony a couple of weeks ago, everybody'd ragged on the apple. Though obviously intended to symbolize Flint's dedication as a teacher, it reminded all the kids of the poisoned apple in Snow White . . . with old lady Flint as the wicked witch. Ron had said, "Forget an apple, they should've made it brass balls." And Jeremy himself had suggested, "A brass anus."

Tess, overhearing his anus remark, had laughed and started talking to him . . . the first time she'd ever shown any interest in him. Within about five minutes, she'd made it clear that she might like to go out with him.

Thus, their first date.

And now, their third time out together, they were back here where it had all started.

Looking over his shoulder, Jeremy saw Ron's car directly behind him and somewhat closer than he'd expected.

*They're all in there watching me.*

Well, he thought, I knew that when I said I'd do it.

*But I'm really out in the open.*

Though half the graveyard seemed to be shrouded with black shadows, there was nothing near the grave of old lady Flint.

Nothing but moonlight.

*Fine. They're supposed to be able to see me.*

He smiled, waved, then turned his head away. Reaching out, he patted the apple. Its brass surface felt cool and slick.

Leaning closer, he found that he could read the plaque in the moonlight:

*AGNES EILEEN FLINT*
 *1941–2001*
*DEDICATED TEACHER*
 *LOVED BY ALL*

Real good one, Jeremy thought. Loved by all. Loved by all who weren't her victims, maybe.

His face burned as he remembered the time only last semester when he'd raised his hand and asked her for a hall pass. She'd smirked up at him. "Oh, I don't think so, Mr. Harris."

"But I really need one. Please?"

"I'm afraid you'll have to wait till after the bell, Mr. Harris."

"Please. I . . . I can't wait that long."

"Perhaps you should've come to class in diapers, Mr. Harris."

The other thirty kids in the biology class had gotten a big laugh out of that one. And so had old lady Flint.

"Should we perhaps take up a collection, class, and buy Mr. Harris a box of Huggies?"

Clenching his teeth so hard that his jaw muscles ached, Jeremy turned around to face the car, then unbuckled his belt. He opened the waistband of his jeans, lowered the zipper, then squatted, pulling down his jeans and underwear.

Elbows on thighs, he folded his hands between his knees.

He lowered his head.

Saw his hands and his drooping shirt-front. No sign of his penis or testicles. However, his jeans and underwear, gathered around his ankles, were definitely in harm's way.

*I'll look like a real asshole if I crap on my own pants.*

*And what'll I do about toilet paper?*

Maybe this isn't such a great idea, he thought.

I've gotta go through with it or they'll say I'm a wuss . . . and I won't get to put my hand in Tess's bra.

He took a couple of small, waddling steps forward, then sank down on the grass. It felt dry and ticklish against his buttocks and scrotum. Leaning forward, he tugged off his shoes.

*I've got my pants down and they're all watching.*

*Tess is watching, trying to see what she can see. Karen, too.*

As he struggled to pull his jeans and underwear off his feet, an erection began to rise and push against his belly.

*Uh-oh.*

Free of his pants, he continued to lean forward while he pulled up his socks.

*Everyone's watching.*

He seemed to be growing stiffer.

*What'm I gonna do?*

It'll be all right, he told himself. My shirt hangs down far enough . . .

He kept an eye on the front of his shirt while he rose to his feet. About to straighten up—and recognizing the probable result—he remained bent over at the waist.

He took a few steps backward. His bare rump touched cool marble.

The pillar.

Wait, wait, wait, he thought. I don't want to do this on her *monument*, I want to do it on *her*. On old lady Flint's face.

He moved forward slightly and squatted.

Nothing but grass between his widespread feet.

Like most of her students, Jeremy had come to her funeral. He'd watched the casket being lowered into the ground.

*Right here.*

*And this'll be her face . . . ground zero.*

*Too bad there're six feet of dirt in the way. And a coffin lid.*

Best of all possible worlds, he thought, I do this plop! On her bare face. And she's nice and alive while I'm doing it so she gets to enjoy every moment.

Even as he thought about it, however, he knew that he never could've done such a thing.

*I must be nuts even trying this.*

*Everybody watching.*

*Hell, they hate her as much as I do. They'd be doing it themselves if they had the guts.*

Tess still might, he reminded himself.

*Not if I make it.*

As he strained, however, he imagined Tess crouching out

here naked from the waist down. The thoughts made him harder.

*Stop thinking about Tess!*

Why?

*Gotta concentrate, take care of business.*

WHY?

*It'll be Tess's turn next!*

But they'll say I'm a wuss and I'll lose my thirty bucks and their thirty bucks. A total loss of sixty. Plus, there goes my chance to take the money out of Tess's bra.

*Maybe she'll take off all her clothes before she squats over old lady Flint.*

Oh, sure . . . as if.

The car horn blasted.

Jeremy gasped and flinched.

Two more blasts raged through the night.

In the silence after the honks, he heard laughter from Ron's car.

"Very funny!" he called.

"Just trying to help," Ron called back. "Did it scare the shit outa you?"

"No! And don't do it again, okay? Jeez! Somebody might've heard that."

"You worry too much."

"I'm the one who's out here . . ."

"With your pants off!" Ron yelled in a very loud voice.

"Shut up!"

In the car, Karen said, "Quit it, Ron, okay? Jeremy's right. We shouldn't even be here, much less honking the horn. Somebody might call the cops."

"Nobody's gonna call any cops."

"How do you know?"

"Stiffs don't call 911."

Sounding very calm and reasonable, Tess said, "We probably should keep it down. We might not be the only people out here. You know?"

Ron was silent for a few seconds. Then he said, "Yeah, well.

Guess I can knock off the honking." Turning toward his open window, he called, "How long is this gonna take, Mimi?"

"How should I know? And don't call me Mimi."

"I mean, you got something on the way?"

"Shut up!"

Ron giggled.

Tess leaned closer to the back window and yelled, "Anything we can do to help?"

"I just need a little more time, that's all. Rome wasn't built in a day."

Jeremy heard laughter from inside the car.

After they quieted down, he said, "I'll be as quick as I can, but it'll help if I have some peace and quiet."

"Want some reading material?" Ron called.

"It's a little dark for that." Then he realized that paper would come in handy. "What've you got?" he asked.

Waiting, he noticed his legs were starting to ache. Also, his erection had subsided.

"I've got some maps," Ron called.

"Are they expendable?"

Karen said, "Oh, gross."

"Nothing gross about it," he heard Tess say. "He just wants to see where he's going."

They all laughed, even Jeremy. "Good one!" he called.

"Thanks."

"So," Ron said, "you wanta come over and grab a map?"

"I haven't got my pants on."

"What are you, modest?"

"How about bringing me a map?"

"Dude, no. Not me. You haven't got any pants on."

"Ha-ha-ha."

"Here," Tess said. "Give me that." Louder, she said, "I'll bring it to you."

Jeremy heard a rattle of paper. Then a back door of the car swung open and Tess climbed out. She shut the door. A dark rectangle in one hand, she walked toward him.

Her white blouse and skirt looked bright in the moonlight,

and she wore no shoes. Her deeply tanned skin was so dark that the clothes seemed to be gliding along without her.

As she stepped over Jeremy's pants, he stood up straight. With one hand, he held the bottom of his shirt in front of his groin. With the other, he reached out for the map.

Tess stopped in front of him. Her teeth showed. She held out the map. "Here you go, sport."

He took it. "Thanks."

But Tess didn't turn away. "I must say. I didn't think you would do it."

"I haven't done it."

"I didn't think you'd go this far," she said. "I mean, you've done it all but the grand finale."

He blushed. "Does that mean I win the bet?"

"Hah! No! The bet's the bet. But win or lose . . . I'm proud of you."

"Well, thanks."

She stepped forward. As she moved in against him, he took his hand away from his shirt and put both his arms around her. He kissed her and hugged her, feeling her lips and breasts. Her belly was flat against his. The fabric of her skirt was soft against the bare skin of his thighs and penis.

He tried to back away, but she held him.

"It's all right," she whispered.

Rising, his erection lifted the skirt between her thighs.

"I tell you what," she whispered. "I'll sweeten the pot."

"Huh?"

"Throw in a little something extra."

"Really? Like what?"

She answered by easing back and forth, rubbing herself against him.

"Mmm."

"Give her a big one for me," she said, and stepped back.

"I'll try."

"The bitch deserves the very best."

" 'Dedicated teacher,' " Jeremy said. " 'Loved by all.' "

"I don't know how many times I dreamed of killing her."

"Really?"

Tess nodded.

"Dream-dreams or daydreams?"

"Daydreams."

"Me, too," Jeremy said. "I thought a lot about how I'd like to kill her. And it wasn't just because of what she did to me. It was . . . a lot of things. Especially how she treated you."

"Really?"

He nodded. "Especially that time she pinched you. Right there in front of everybody. I wanted to rip her apart."

"That's so sweet," she said softly.

"I don't know why they never fired her," he muttered. "Teachers aren't allowed to do that sort of stuff."

"Teachers aren't allowed to molest students in the supply closets, either."

Something sank inside Jeremy. "Flint did that?"

"Yeah."

"To who?"

"Me."

"My God," he muttered. "Did you tell on her?"

She lowered her head, shook it. "No. I haven't told anyone. And you can't either."

"I won't."

"Nobody else knows about it."

"Not even Ron and Karen?"

She shook her head. "You can't tell them. Or anybody. Promise me."

"What'd she do to you?"

"Do you promise not to tell?"

"I promise."

Tess glanced over her shoulder.

Jeremy looked, too. The way the moonlight glared on the windshield, he couldn't see into the car. He supposed that Ron and Karen were probably still in the front seats, watching them, waiting for more action.

Maybe they're having some action of their own, he thought.

In a low voice, Tess said, "What happened, Flint called me up to her desk one day after class. She said I should come in at the end of the sixth period so she could talk to me about my grades. And she was in her supply closet when I got there. You know, putting away beakers and stuff? Next thing I knew, she was all over me, kissing me and . . ." Tess went silent. For a few moments, Jeremy heard only her quick breathing. When she spoke again, her voice was a quick, trembling whisper. "She stuck her hands under my clothes and pinched me and twisted me. She hurt me so much she had me crying. And she put her fingers in me and then she used her mouth. Her tongue and teeth. She bit me. Down there. All over. And she made me do things to her."

Shocked, Jeremy stared at Tess.

"She had me in the closet for . . . more than an hour. And then . . . then when I thought she was done . . . you've gotta promise you'll never tell anybody, Jer."

"I won't. Won't tell. I promise."

"Cross your heart."

"I do." He quickly crossed his heart.

"She took an empty test tube . . . one of the big kind . . . and she put it in me."

"Huh?"

"Slid it up inside me. You know. And said if I ever told on her, she'd do it again only she'd break it in me. And maybe she'd have something extra in the tube like maggots or even acid."

Jeremy groaned.

"You asked."

"That . . . that *bitch*."

"Yeah."

In a low voice, he said, "But you should've told someone. The cops . . ."

"And have her do that to me? Thanks anyway. Besides . . . she just would've denied everything. And I'd be the one getting in trouble. You know. You've seen how that stuff goes. They'd make me look like the bad person. Trying to ruin Flint's good name. So even if she didn't carry out her threat, I'd still be fucked. And then *this* happened." She nodded toward the monument.

"What do you mean?"

"You know. She got killed. In her supply closet, no less. Thank God I hadn't told anyone what she did to me. The cops would think I'm the one who killed her. Who could have a better motive?"

Jeremy felt a coldness stirring through his bowels.

"I don't know," he murmured. "A lot of people, probably. She was so awful. And maybe you weren't the only one she . . ." He tried to think of a way to say it.

"Raped?"

"Yeah."

"God, no. I think she had the hots for lots of her students. Probably didn't take the chance of actually attacking many of them, but . . ." Tess shook her head. "I know she tried to get Karen."

"Jeez."

"She told Karen to come in after school. This was after what she did to me, so I went along and she didn't dare try anything with two of us there."

"So there must've been others."

"More than likely."

"Maybe one of them killed her."

"Could be," Tess said. "Anyway, I'll be okay as long as it never gets around that she did that stuff to me."

"But . . ."

"What?"

"Why'd you tell me about it?"

Tess shrugged. "I guess because . . . I think you hate her almost as much as I do. I mean, it was your idea to come here. 'Let's go out to the bone orchard and shit on Flint's grave.' And you really meant it."

"Guess I did."

"And you really mean to do it."

"Guess so."

"My hero," she said and smiled.

Jeremy laughed softly.

"You didn't kill her, did you?" she asked.

"No," he said. "Did you?"

"No. But I'm glad somebody did."

"Same here."

"Do you mind if I join you?" Tess asked.

"Join me?"

"We can do it side by side."

He contemplated it, then said, "I don't know."

"What's not to know?"

"You mean . . . ?"

"Yeah."

"Jeez."

"I want to. Don't you?"

It would be so weird, he thought. And embarrassing. And gross. And exciting?

"But what about the bet?" he asked. "I'm supposed to do it alone."

Tess reached down and took hold of his hand. She guided it into the open neck of her blouse. "Take the money," she said.

He slipped his hand underneath the cup of her bra, feeling the stiff folded bills, feeling the heat and soft firmness of her breast. He slid the money out, let it fall, then put his hand again inside her bra.

The tight fabric cup loosened against the back of his hand.

"What the hell are they doing?" Karen muttered.

"What does it look like?" said Ron.

He reached forward and put on the headlights. The pale beams reached into the graveyard, illuminating Jeremy and Tess as they finished removing their clothes.

"That's enough," Karen said.

"Yeah," Ron said.

"Shut the lights off."

"Okay." But he didn't.

"Ron."

"Just a second."

Naked, Jeremy and Tess embraced and kissed.

"You want to look at someone, look at me."

He glanced at Karen. She started to unbutton her blouse.

"All right!"

She opened her blouse. Glimpsing the white of her bra, Ron turned his eyes toward the graveyard.

Jeremy and Tess broke away from each other and waved toward the car.

"Eyes on me," Karen said.

He watched Karen reach up behind her back and unhook her bra.

"Lights off," she said.

"Okay, okay."

He looked out the windshield again.

Now Jeremy and Tess stood side by side in front of old lady Flint's apple monument. Holding hands, they squatted.

"Here they go," Ron said.

"Shut off the headlights, damn it!"

"Okay!"

As he reached for the knob, he noticed something just beyond the place where his two friends were crouching. Just behind them. And higher.

A scrawny, naked woman with dead white skin and drooping breasts seemed to be perched atop the brass apple, hands on her widespread knees, leaning forward, leering down at them.

"Fuck!" he gasped and shut the headlights off. "Did you see that?"

"More than I cared to."

"I mean her. Flint!"

"Gimme a break."

She seemed to be gone now. The profiles of Jeremy and Tess, however, were still fairly easy to see in the moonlight—pale shapes squatting in front of the monument.

Ron started to reach for the headlights' knob.

"Don't you dare," said Karen.

And suddenly in the dark the pale hag was again perched atop the apple . . . then springing from it with her arms out wide, her white hair flowing behind her.

"Look out!" Ron yelled.

\*       \*       \*

Jeremy flinched and stood up straight, hardly aware of Tess still holding his hand.

"What?" he shouted.

The driver's door flew open. Ron jumped out, put his back to the graveyard, and ran.

"What's going on?" Jeremy yelled.

Karen called from inside the car, "He went nuts! I don't know!"

Tess pulled at Jeremy's hand. "Come on!"

Leaving their clothes on the ground, they took off running after Ron. As they neared the car, Karen shouted, "He just all of a sudden freaked out!"

"We'll get him," Jeremy said.

"Me, too," said Karen. "In a sec. Don't wait for me."

Running past the open door, Jeremy glanced in. She was trying to fasten the buttons of her blouse.

"I'll be right out," she said.

Jeremy kept running. Tess had pulled ahead of him slightly, and he watched her sprinting along in the moonlight and thought how magnificent she looked and wished something like this could be happening without fear.

And Ron was missing it. Far ahead of them on the graveyard road, he didn't look back at all.

"Ron!" Tess shouted. "Stop running! What's the matter with you?"

He cried out in a high, shrill voice, "*Flint!*"

"What?" Tess called.

"*She's after me!*"

"Slow down!"

"*No!*"

"Why's she after you?"

"How the fuck should I know?"

"Did you kill her?" Tess called.

"No!"

"Are you sure?"

"Didn't kill anybody. Never touched her! Maybe that's why she's pissed!"

"Don't count on it," Tess yelled to him. "You're not her type."

Jeremy shouted, "Anyway, she's dead!"

*"Her ghost, dude! Her GHOST!"*

And Tess called out, "Where?"

And Ron looked over his shoulder.

Whether because he saw no sign of Flint's ghost or because he realized he was being pursued by Tess wearing nothing at all, he quit running.

Tess stopped. Jeremy stopped. They stood side by side, huffing for breath as Ron walked slowly back to them. Sweat was pouring down Jeremy's skin. The soft night breeze felt good.

"You okay?" Tess asked Ron.

"I guess so. Except . . . I think I'll take my pants off."

"Hey," Jeremy said.

"Don't get excited. I had a mishap."

Jeremy chuckled.

"Yeah, real funny." Ron started to unbuckle his belt. "You try getting chased by a fucking maniac spook, see how you like it."

Frowning, Tess shook her head. "Why the hell was she chasing you? I don't get it. If you're not the one who killed her . . ."

"I tell you, she's hot for my bod." He pulled his pants down. "They all are."

"Not Flint. She strictly likes . . ." A scream interrupted Tess.

And she was in the lead running faster than Jeremy had ever seen her run. And he was behind her, sprinting but not nearly fast enough, and Ron was somewhere to the rear and Jeremy could see the car in the moonlight but he couldn't see Karen.

He could hear her, though.

Hear her screams. Hear her cries of, *"No! Oww! Don't! Please! No! Don't do that! No! Ahhh!"*

*WHAT'S HAPPENING TO HER?*

Jeremy tried to pick up more speed, but Tess ran faster.

"Slow down! He shouted. "Wait for me!"

But she didn't.

Karen screamed and pleaded while Tess raced closer to the car.

She's gonna get there first, Jeremy thought.

*Oh, dear God! Don't let her get there ahead of me . . . !*

I've gotta stop her!

I've gotta!

Ten bucks says you won't.

# ARMIES OF
# THE NIGHT

## *John Pelan*

"It never ceases to amaze me what some people collect—" I looked at Ian as I went on—"matchbooks, hatpins, refrigerator magnets, all sorts of worthless junk." We were sitting at the bar of The Smoking Leg, enjoying iced tea and air-conditioning and I was doing my best to recover my spirits after having wasted most of the day assisting a lawyer friend with an estate appraisal. I'm not really an expert on antiques in general, but I do know enough to be able to walk through a place, poke around, and tell the heirs whether they ought to call Sotheby's or The Jolly Junkman.

The Smoking Leg is the perfect sort of place to escape the heat of a summer's day, quiet enough during the afternoon that one can enjoy conversation without having to shout over the jukebox. After a disappointing morning clambering around in an attic for the privilege of looking at worthless books, an iced tea and some conversation was definitely called for. As usual, my friend Ian was working and with few customers on hand, we could have a chat and enjoy the cool of the air-conditioning.

I wondered momentarily if this might be the day that I would be successful in prying the real story behind the tavern's name from him. Thus far I'd heard three different stories from employees, ranging from a commemoration of a grotesque accident to a tribute to a little-known British author. The third version, which dealt with an overcooked entrée, seemed even less likely. . . . Ian didn't seem inclined to want to talk about the bar; instead he seemed quite interested in my unsuccessful morning.

Ian sipped at his iced tea and queried, "I take it that there wasn't anything of particular note there?"

"Not really. I was just asked in to look at the books, but there didn't seem too much else that was noteworthy. Their 'library' consisted mainly of the entire oeuvre of *Time-Life* Libraries and an assortment of Book-Of-The-Month Club titles and similar stuff. If there was anything of value, it certainly wasn't in any of the areas of expertise. The furniture was just a tad shy of being able to be described as 'vintage,' and as far as anything else, they seemed to have a good bit of vinyl, but it was all the most common stuff imaginable. I expect that these folks sat up late nights dialing into the shopping channel for whatever junk caught their fancy."

"Not really collectors then? More of the sort that accumulates stuff without rhyme or reason? Perhaps just as well—sometimes collections can get out of hand and monopolize one's existence. Take yourself for example, you've got literally tons of books. It would be a major undertaking if you ever had to move. Me, I've more CDs and odd recordings than I know what to do with; that and all the film scripts where I've either helped with the score or consulted in some way. Hell, I've given over one of my two rooms to the stuff and I never consciously set out to *collect* anything. . . . Imagine the sort of things that can occur when a person really puts some passion into acquiring things. . . ."

"Well, books have an intrinsic value, as does your music collection, but some of the stuff people collect makes little or no sense. Old kitchen utensils, cigar bands, animation cels . . . I mean, do the people that buy animation cels have any *idea* how many of the damn things there are for one ten-minute cartoon?"

Ian smiled and refilled our glasses. "People opt to spend their money on strange things. Perhaps you recall the older couple that used to come in here, the Mohans? Always sat over by the dart room and drank Pimm's Cups?"

"The guy that was always reading up on military history?"

Ian nodded in affirmation. "Sure, I talked with him a time or two when I was writing a piece set during World War I."

"I suppose that you didn't know that his interest wasn't in history per se so much as it was getting detailed pictures of the uniforms. You see, Bill Mohan was a miniaturist."

"A what?"

"A miniaturist, specializing in military dioramas and the like, had a huge collection."

"I note that you're using the past tense, is he . . ." I let the sentence trail off, pretty much sensing what the answer would be.

"They're both dead. He died from an overdose of his medication some weeks back. At the time it seemed like an accident, but based on what happened later, I'm not so certain. Near as I can figure out his hobby drove her mad, perhaps mad enough to poison him. A week or so after the funeral she was in here asking around to see if there was anyone willing to haul off the whole collection. There's a good bit of money to be had in military miniatures, so I stopped round to have a look at the lot and it was really amazing what he'd done. It was the way she went on about the stuff that led me to think that perhaps Bill's death hadn't been an accident.

"I'll tell what I know of it, as soon as I take care of these folks." He nodded toward a couple that had just wandered in and taken seats by the pool table.

I waited while Ian drew a couple of pints and thought about the Mohans. Bill had seemed a friendly enough sort, always eager to talk about the one subject which he seemed passionately interested in, that of military history. His wife, on the other hand, seemed to be one of those people that decided early on that they'd been handed a bad hand of cards by life and was convinced that the only way to improve her lot was by being highly critical of everyone else. I remembered in detail a fairly nasty row that they'd had in the bar; she snapped at him like a wolverine while he did his best to calm her. . . .

\* \* \*

"Now you've got your damned toys in the living room as well as the study and the extra bedroom, what's next? Your toy airplanes hanging over our bed?" Neve Mohan was obviously infuriated with her husband, and the soothing balm of a Pimm's Cup was not alleviating her mood.

"Dear, I've explained that it's quite impossible to have the Kandahar diorama in either of the other rooms. It would clash terribly with the other displays—different time periods, you know." Bill Mohan seemed as though he was reciting this explanation by rote, that this was a conversation that they'd had many times in many variations and always to an equally unsatisfying result.

Ian's return jolted me out of my reverie.

"As I'd been saying, Bill was a fanatical hobbyist. I guess that military miniatures had been an interest of his for years, but until he took early retirement he'd never had much of a chance to pursue his hobby in earnest.

"Most collectors start out fairly reasonably. Bill was no different; he had a table in his study that they'd set up to work on jigsaw puzzles and never quite got around to using for that purpose. It occurred to him that he could set up a little display on half the table and use the other as a work area without too much difficulty. It all began with a static display of a dozen Confederate soldiers manning a Gatling gun. The kit was inexpensive enough and purchased from a mail-order firm for around fifty dollars. Bill bought the metal epoxy and paints that were called for and set about working on his soldiers. Neve was even encouraging in the early days of his modeling work.

"After a time he had the soldiers painted and the artillery piece assembled, but the effect wasn't quite what he'd hoped for. Rather than an accurate depiction of a slice of life from the War Between the States, it was merely a handful of lead soldiers with their artillery piece looking woefully out of place on the corner of a table.

"Bill was disappointed. He'd followed the directions meticulously, even blending the colors to give an appearance of wear to the uniforms. It just wasn't right, at least not without some additional embellishments. Calling up the hobby shop he explained his dilemma and followed the helpful clerk's recommendation and soon had another kit of some Union soldiers on the way, along with some materials to construct an actual diorama. This cost a bit more, but Bill figured the effect would be well worth the expense, and after all, he could always use his desk as a work area and leave the whole table free for the display.

"The Civil War project actually took several months and several calls to the hobby shop. It wasn't any good having the Confederates with their Gatling gun firing on more-or-less defenseless Federals. To set the equation right, he thought that superior numbers on the Union side might balance things out a bit, but when he'd finished the second lot of eight Union soldiers, it still didn't seem right. He added some cavalry and another two dozen infantrymen and some more accessories to give it the appearance of an actual battlefield. The diorama was starting to shape up nicely and his wife wasn't objecting overmuch to the credit card bills. By the time Bill was done with his 'small display' piece, his table was no longer recognizable as a piece of furniture; he'd run out of room so he chopped several inches off the legs and constructed ramps from plywood (covered with paint, sand, rocks to emulate a real hillside). Now he had a stunning battlefield scene with over two hundred soldiers including artillery, cavalry, and even a remarkably lifelike figure of General Lee astride Traveller, brandishing his saber.

"Neve didn't object much at the time. After all, the den was Bill's sanctum sanctorum and she really had no idea that the diorama now had well over one thousand dollars' worth of figures and accessories tied up in it. If he'd stopped there, it might be that there would have been no problem, but being a collector by nature, Bill could have no more stopped there than an alcoholic would stop at one beer.

"Apparently what really started things going to hell was the kindness of a stranger or at least of a passing acquaintance. One of the hobby shop owners that had spent a good deal of time with Bill on the telephone and had been very appreciative of his patronage had some figures that were fairly slow sellers, which he sent on to Bill as a gift. Bill was in equal measures pleased and peeved with the gift. The man had sent him a hodgepodge: a piper of the Black Watch, a sapper from Napoleon's Old Guard, a hussar from Crimea, and an officer of the 3rd Sikhs of the British Indian Army; nothing that you could really make a display of, more of a representative sampling. However, the colorful uniforms would be far more challenging and interesting to paint than the prosaic blues and grays of his Civil War tableau. . . .

"That's where it really got started, Bill had to have proper displays of the Charge of the Light Brigade, of Kandahar, of Tournay, and of course, Waterloo. . . . He started off as he had with his Civil War display—rather smallish, just a representation of the trenches of Tournay and the Highlanders with their muskets facing the French line. Of course, being a stickler for accuracy he realized that the Scotsmen were only a small representation of King George's army at the time and that he'd need to add several of the more traditional British regiments to go along with the kilted infantry. . . . And so it went, each small grouping invariably led to a profound dissatisfaction and the need to add to, expand, and have *more*. That's the way of the collector, when one's succumbed to the passion, be it for cars, model railroads, Pokemon, or what-have-you, there's always a compelling need to have *more*. . . . In Bill's case, he was financially able to keep adding to his collection and wasn't the least deterred by his wife's remonstrances or the expense. The main problem as Bill saw it was that it was a matter of *space*. The den just simply wasn't large enough to encompass the four displays that he was working on.

"To bring the matter to a head was the aesthetic problem as Bill saw it. Having Kandahar, Tournay, and Shiloh in the same room looked more than a bit odd. The anachronism was absolutely jarring. Something simply had to be done. . . .

"Bill resolved the situation by invading the dining room— or rather the British Indian Army invaded the dining room. As with most couples of their age, Bill and Neve took their meals in the kitchen or dined out. The dining room table was a barren expanse ripe for occupation. It took Bill most of two days to move the Indian diorama piece by piece to its new home. Neve objected that they'd be without anywhere to entertain guests, and Bill countered with the reasonable answer that anytime they had guests, everyone eventually wound up downstairs in the TV room rather than sitting in the dining room.

"What he'd failed to mention to her was that he had already conducted a good bit of reconnaissance regarding the TV room as a future target for occupation. After all, Waterloo was the pivotal battle of its time, and to scrimp on the display was simply niggardly. Quietly, without calling undue attention to his project, Bill went about modifying the TV room to suit his purposes.

"He continued in this fashion for several months; they'd come in from time to time and, while Bill seemed pretty chipper, Neve would clutch her drink like she was seizing a life preserver and just sit and glare at him as he thumbed through modeling magazines and catalogs of miniatures. There's all sorts of crises that can occur in a marriage when one or both partners retire. In some cases the husband starts chasing younger women. I think that Neve might've coped with that a bit better than she did with being cast aside in favor of thousands of lead soldiers.

"Bill really loved his hobby to the point that he pretty much let his interests in anything else fade away. After a time Neve would come in occasionally by herself. After all, there wasn't much point in bringing Bill if all he were going to do was sit and read magazines; he could (and did) do that well enough at home. She broke down and cried at the bar on more than one occasion; claimed he'd started talking to the soldiers, that late at night he'd be in the den, the dining room, or the basement and she could hear him muttering as he moved the displays around as though he were leading troops into battle. The sort of activity that's charming when you see a ten-year-old doing it, but rather disturbing when the ersatz general is a man of late middle years. . . .

"Eventually he ran out of room for his displays, and had to try another tack. Since there was no longer any space for elaborate battle scenes on the surface, he turned to lining the walls with shelves, where he could display an even greater range and variety of soldiers. The ceiling offered an entirely new vista for representations of war in the air. The Fokker DR-1 of Werner Voss faced Eddie Rickenbacker's Spad XIII, with Oswald Bolecke in his Albatros DIII engaging a Sopwith Camel in another dogfight. Within a few short months, every room in the house boasted an aerial display to rival the best museums. By this point Bill was so obsessed with his hobby and writing articles for the modeling magazines and posting to collectors' groups on the Internet that he no longer even had time to make the models himself, but instead purchased them ready-made from other hobbyists. I've no doubt that Neve really started to hate her husband then. . . .

"I can't really say if what happened to Bill was an accident or not. Bill had a number of health problems that he took a variety of prescriptions for. Blood pressure medication, insulin, and who knows what else. A lot of stuff that can be deadly if taken in the wrong amounts or wrong combinations, which is just what happened. Neve found him dead one morning, sprawled across the diorama in the basement, facedown on Blucher's cavalry. . . . The M.E. wrote it up as an accidental death and that was that. I suppose if the police had wanted to push it, they might have come to the conclusion that maybe Neve helped him along by adding a bit of this or that to his food or coffee, but there was certainly no history of threats or a pending divorce or anything of that nature. If called upon to testify, I'd have had to say that I saw them argue in here, but I can't think of any couple that comes here regularly that I *haven't* seen argue at least once or twice."

I had to concede the wisdom of this statement. While Neve Mohan had the look of a woman who was desperately unhappy, I couldn't really say that their argument that I'd overheard was any worse than any of a dozen others I'd seen over the years. Certainly nothing that would suggest murder as Ian seemed to be hinting at.

"I'd have really thought no more of it if it weren't for what Neve said in here one night. It's the only time that I could say that I had any concern about serving her. Sure, she'd had her moments when she'd cried at the bar on a couple of occasions, but this was the only time that I actually considered her to be more than a bit tipsy.

"She wandered in late one afternoon and asked for brandy, not her usual drink, and she gulped it down as though she were desperate to get the drink into her system. Now I'd never known either of the Mohans to be heavy drinkers, two Pimm's was about their limit. It was a little unsettling seeing her drink this way, but after all the woman had just lost her husband under tragic circumstances. (Though it could be said that she'd lost him a long time before for all practical purposes.) She tossed off the brandy as though it were ginger ale and asked for another. I poured her another one and it was then that she asked me if I'd go to her house and dispose of Bill's collection. What she told me was as odd as anything I've heard. In light of what happened, I feel badly that I dismissed it as the drink talking.

"She asked me if I believed in ghosts, if I'd ever seen or heard one. . . . I asked her to explain what it was that she thought she'd seen and here's what she told me near as I can remember. . . .

" 'They move around at night, you know, thousands of the damn things, shifting positions, maneuvering for battle like Bill was still there playing with the damn things. They're worth a fortune, but I just want them out of the house. I'll even pay to have them removed.'

"She'd had more than a bit to drink as I'd said, and she was talking about throwing away thousands of dollars' worth of stuff. I suggested that she just write to some of Bill's hobbyist friends and there'd certainly be someone willing to take the whole lot for a good price.

" 'You don't know what it's like to sit in that house and feel thousands of sets of eyes on you, watching and hating. I lock the door to the bedroom, but even in there I'm not safe. I can *feel* them watching and hating just outside the door.'

"I assured her that I'd call a couple of antique dealers that might be able to help out and send them round on the weekend to pick the whole lot up. She seemed buoyed a bit by this and left with the air of someone who's glimpsed a bit of light at the end of a very dark tunnel.

"The next day I called the appraisal firm of Eatman & Suggs, reasoning that I'd be quite out of my depth advising her on the disposal of such a large collection. They sent an appraiser round to visit the Mohan house with me, an older chap name of Hainey who specialized in this sort of material.

"I don't know what I'd been expecting. The Mohan place was one of those huge wood-frame places built in the twenties and when they'd been in the bar, Neve had always claimed that Bill had filled the house with his collection. Anyway, Neve greeted us at the door; she was limping, a huge bandage around one foot. Hainey was as stunned as I was by what we saw in the house. . . .

"There were thousands of pieces. I think that if there was ever a time that more than two people got into a fight, Bill had made a model of it, right down to the weapons used and the clothes they wore. There was a fortune there, and all Neve wanted was to get them out of the house. She took us on a brief tour and offered to brew up some coffee while Hainey took notes and tried to make some calculations. I guess that I'd thought in terms of his making her an offer and loading up a few boxes. . . . However, it was apparent that the cataloging and removal of the collection would be a major undertaking that would require a good deal more effort than that of two men working on a Saturday afternoon.

"Neve poured me a cup of coffee as Hainey scurried about, writing things down in a big three-ring binder, occasionally stopping to pick up a figure and examine it closely. Curiosity got the better of my manners and I inquired about her foot.

"'One of the damn monsters stabbed me, one of his soldiers. The bayonet went right through my foot when I stepped on it.' Neve's voice shook a bit as she related the story, whether due to anger or something else, I wasn't quite certain.

"'Well, that's an unfortunate accident, but I imagine with so many of the things around, it's easy for one of the things to get underfoot, so to speak.'

"I'll never forget the look she gave me. It was as though she was explaining something to a very stupid child. 'Ian, you don't understand . . . I stepped on one of the damn soldiers in my *bedroom*. It's the one room in the house that I never allowed Bill to put the damn things in. I've told you, I hear them *moving around at night*!'

"I wasn't sure how to respond to that, and muttered something about seeing if Hainey needed a hand with anything. Hainey was ooh-ing and ahh-ing over the Waterloo display when I caught up with him and confirmed what I'd suspected—this would be a project that would require several laborers just to pack everything up and the better part of a week for him to catalog everything.

"Walking through the house I couldn't help but be amazed at the sheer volume of the pieces. The amount of artistry and scrupulous detail that had gone into each figure was remarkable. Despite being just lumps of lead, paint, and epoxy, the miniatures were so lifelike that I could empathize with Neve's feelings of being watched. I wouldn't enjoy staying in the house by myself with all those rows and rows of unblinking, painted eyes staring at you. One could almost fancy the soldiers all taking careful aim and . . . Well, it didn't bear thinking about. . . . I dismissed these absurd ideas and went to find Hainey again.

"Neve was none too pleased to hear that we wouldn't actually be taking the soldiers away that day. Hainey talked in terms of several thousand dollars, which didn't seem to cheer her much. I think she'd have been happy to have us just take the soldiers out in wheelbarrows and dump them in the trash. Hainey assured her that he'd be back on Monday to begin cataloging the collection and we took our leave.

"Sunday night she showed up here at the bar, bandaged foot and all. She looked like she hadn't slept much and there was a wicked-looking scratch on the side of her face. One of the miniatures, that of a Zulu warchief with an assegai, had fallen from the shelf and the tiny weapon had given her a deep scratch. Or as Neve put it, 'One of the things sprang at me, and if I hadn't just turned, it would have put out my eye.'

"She was desperate to have the things taken away as soon as possible. She said that she felt that Bill would've wanted his armies to stay undisturbed, but that they knew she hated them and in turn they hated her. I put this down to being the talk of a woman under a great deal of stress and possibly with a guilty conscience. She stayed until nearly closing time, not really drinking to excess, but just sipping at her drink and eyeing the clock on the wall. When last call rolled around, she had me call her a taxi and promise that I'd make sure that Hainey would be on hand first thing in the morning.

"I never saw her alive again. Hainey came to the bar around noon complaining that she wasn't home. It so happened that the owner was in and I was able to get him to cover for a bit while I went over to the Mohans' with Hainey. We ended up having to get in with a spare key from a neighbor.

"She was there, just inside the doorway. It must have happened as soon as she entered the house. A freakish accident—one of the planes had fallen from its wire and the razor-sharp metal wing had hit her neck in just such a way as to sever the jugular. . . . She must have bled to death in a matter of minutes.

"I have to wonder, she'd asked me about ghosts and I have to dismiss that notion. Bill didn't have an ounce of malice in him. I can't see him returning from the grave as a vengeful specter. . . . I do wonder about other possibilities, though. Is it possible that if one develops such a bond and love for inanimate objects that part of his essence imbues them? That perhaps even bits of wood or plastic or metal can take on a strange sort of sentience? Bill really loved his little armies, and I suppose that it's just possible that the feeling was reciprocal. . . ."

I finished my tea and left the bar, resolving to not make any further disparaging remarks about my wife's doll collection.

# UNSPEAKABLE

## *Lucy Taylor*

*Never underestimate the power of words, Christine,* my stepfather, Dr. Peyton Eads, used to say. *We think they're only symbols, only sounds, but the right word is like a rare perfume—it has the power to evoke the feelings and sensations from the past and make them real again.*

I was just a kid then. I didn't know what he meant, only that Dr. Eads was a renowned psychiatrist and unquestionably the best of the various "uncles" and boyfriends who had preceded him through the revolving door to Mother's bedroom. But that was because he hadn't yet started to "train" me. Later on, I learned only too well what he meant about the power of words.

Ricky Calloway, as I was to find out years later, understood the power of words as well or better than Dr. Eads and demonstrated that knowledge more dramatically. Unlike in the case of my stepfather, though, I knew Ricky was dangerous and crazy from the start.

It had been over a year since I'd last seen Ricky Calloway when I came home one night to find the lock on my apartment door jimmied and Ricky sitting in my living room, naked, in the dark.

I knew it was Ricky by the bulk of his outline, backlit against the aquarium-green glow from the computer screen that threw the only light in the room—his sheer heft was unmistakable; his nudity—when viewed in silhouette—was shockingly ap-

parent. His only concession to clothing was the biker bandanna holding back the mass of black hair that slid over his
shoulders like an Apache warrior's.

The first question that popped into my mind—*did you do
it?*—was the one I was afraid to ask. So instead I said, "Jesus,
what are you doing here? Why'd you break into my place?"

"I didn't know what time you got off work, and I didn't
want to wait out in the hall. Don't worry, I'll fix the door before I go."

"Damn right you will. And you'll get dressed."

"When I leave. But maybe you won't want me to leave.
Maybe you'll want me to stay the night. I've got something to
show you that might change things for us."

*Us. What us?* I thought.

"What could you show me that could change anything?" I
said. "I can't be with you. I can't be with anybody. We tried
that once, remember?"

"Well, let's try again," said Ricky. He held a big hand out to
me. "Come over here and touch my cock."

"Do *what*?"

I knew Ricky Calloway was a little nuts and I knew I should
be afraid of him, but I wasn't. If he'd come back to kill me or
extort money, I figured so fucking be it. Considering what I'd
set in motion, maybe I deserved it. On the other hand, I knew
Ricky was once in love with me, so maybe he still was. Or
maybe he just wanted to get laid and figured that I owed him.
Big time.

"Christine," he said, "did you hear me?"

"Yeah, I heard you." I sidled into the room and sat across
from him on the couch, looking him up and down, trying to
assess the extent of his dangerousness. "Give me a minute. I
need to think about this."

I first laid eyes on Ricky Calloway at my brother Andrew's
funeral. Andrew committed suicide two years ago by hurling
himself off the roof of the ten-story apartment building where
he owned a condo. He didn't jump feet first, which I was told
by the police—who tend to know about such things—is the

norm, but dived headfirst, like a Mexican cliff diver—an aberration even for an act that is itself an aberration.

The funeral was modestly attended, the priest drafted for the occasion a tufted-haired old Benedictine from St. Paul's, the church that Mother used to attend before her gait grew too tipsily unsteady to make it up the broad, pink-marble steps. My sister, Anne, and her husband, Robert, were there and Andrew's colleagues from the legal firm where he'd worked as a criminal defense attorney. Our younger brother, Barnett, the baby of the family and a little slow in the head, came to eulogize his elder sibling and did so with such fervor and at such length that the priest's head drooped upon his chest and snores emanated from his ribby torso.

"Whatever the magnitude of his sin, *God* loves Andrew," Barnett yelled, fist raised as though challenging anyone to argue the point. "*God* has saved Andrew, and he is sitting at the feet of our most merciful *God* and His son, our Lord and Savior *Jesus Christ*."

I'd never heard Barnett rant like this, churning himself into such a spiritual lather that his listeners were either appalled or simply agog at the display. Barnett shook sweat from his hair like a wet spaniel and rolled his eyes and trembled each time he invoked the name of the Lord. At a certain point, his ferocity began to make me uneasy and I searched for distraction by looking at the reactions to my surviving brother's diatribe in the faces of the predominantly well-groomed and tastefully attired mourners who had made up Andrew's social set.

A couple of people, who didn't fit in any better than Barnett did, caught my eye.

"Who's that?" I said to Anne, indicating the hulking biker type whose glaring black eyes would have been scary if not for his copious weeping.

"That's Ricky Calloway," she said. "When he was sixteen years old he caught his father molesting his sister and stabbed him to death."

I absorbed this, then said, "How'd he know Andrew?"

"Andrew defended him on an assault charge a few years back and they got to be buds. Stop staring at him, Christine.

He's a career criminal. Not your type. Even if you haven't been with a man in ten years," she added, squeezing my hand to show she wasn't trying to be nasty, just acknowledging what she viewed as my bizarre and stubborn celibacy.

"Make that fifteen," I said.

Chastised, though, I stopped sneaking peeks at Ricky Calloway and turned my attention to the other person who looked out of place here—the one I figured this Calloway guy would probably end up going home with—a short, zaftig woman whose brassy blond curls stood out like yellow neon and whose dangly minichandelier earrings twisted in the breeze like tiny hanged men. She must have felt my eyes on her, because she turned suddenly, looking directly at me. Her hand came up in a tiny wave, fingers only, as one waves to a child.

After the service, as everyone drifted back to their cars, the blonde came stumblingly up the hill behind me. She wore a long black skirt, slit to the thigh, and a grey sweater unbuttoned to allow a glimpse of her pink lace bra. She was easily twice the age I'd guessed—blond hair framing a coarse, fatigue-lined face, her limbs stocky and muscular—factory worker limbs, well larded but at the same time powerful.

Then, closer still, I reassessed that thought—not a factory worker at all, but in a manner of speaking, still assembly line. She reeked of brandy and her steel-gray eyes looked slightly out of focus from a lifetime of seeing selectively.

"I'm Katrina," she gushed, forcing a sloppy hug on me. "Andrew and I were close friends, *very* close." She dabbed at her dry eyes to show sincerity. "You're his sister, right?"

"I'm Christine. He mentioned me?"

"Yes, well, not exactly. Not really, no. He wasn't a big talker, Andrew. He more liked me to talk."

She gave me a crafty sideways glance. "He left a few things at my apartment, some clothes and a few books, and you know, some other items, items of a sex'shul nature."

"Whatever things you have of Andrew's, I don't want them," I said. "The only thing I'd appreciate, if you have it, is information. Why would he do something like this?"

Her eyeballs rattled around in their sockets as though she'd taken a blow to the chin. "He had a lot of secrets," she managed finally, "but, like I said, he wasn't much of a talker."

I turned and strode away from the stench of her hundred-proof breath. I have nothing against hookers, but I'm intolerant of drunks, my mother having been one.

"Hey, wait!" she called.

Incredibly, she was grinning as she staggered after me. "Look, Christine, I liked Andrew a bunch and I got only respect for the dead, whatever way they go, but I have to ask. I gotta know . . ." She ran a pointed pink tongue along vermillion lips and whispered slyly, "I mean, I thought maybe you could tell me, what does— what did— there were some words he made me say over and over every time we were, you know, intimate—it was the only way he could get it up—but they weren't sex words. They weren't dirty. I wondered, maybe you could, you know, like satisfy my curiosity, what did they—"

"Stop it. I don't want to know."

But she was drunk and one thing I learned from my mother was that drunks neither see nor listen nor care, so she told me anyway. Three words—my brother Andrew's dirty little secrets. They weren't the same Words given me, but I damn well knew where they'd come from and how they'd gotten hardwired into his brain. Just realizing this brought up such rage in me that for an instant I stood looking around for Ricky Calloway, patricidal son, no longer feeling shy or grief stricken, but ballsy and sexy and hot on the make.

I wanted something from Ricky Calloway.

Thank God, when I spotted him, he was roaring away on a Harley, and I watched him go, imagining what kind of knife he might have used to stab his father with, how it must have felt when he shoved in the blade.

At night, I dream Words. Not Andrew's words. Mine. The consonants whisper against my clit like the stroke of a feather, the vowels ooze wetly like a seeking tongue. I chant them in my mind, these Words that I never say aloud, that no one else has ever heard me utter except the one who first inflicted them on me.

"Say them, Christine, pronounce them slowly, lovingly," says Dr. Eads as his fingers rove and wander. He has long, beautiful pale hands capable of elegant, almost balletic movements. In my dream his hands flow over me like cool wine. They weave a lurid tapestry across a befouled loom, uniting sounds and synapses, hot-wiring lust and potent shame to sounds that, in standard English, are almost pathetically innocuous. A child could say these words and not be scolded. To the world at large, they are just words.

But to me they are Words that suck and stroke, Words that evoke my darkest memories, that set me on fire and immolate me with shame. Magic Words. The Words that accompanied my introduction to sex and to shame and to secrecy.

A few weeks after Andrew's funeral, I went over to my sister Anne's to keep her company while her husband, Robert, was out of town. We were hanging out, eating popcorn, and watching TV. I knew she was worried about something, working up to telling me. Finally, she said, "Barnett is giving me the creeps. When he gave that eulogy at Andrew's funeral, it seemed to have an effect on him."

"What do you mean?"

"I heard he's been going to the cathedral, preaching sermons, ranting and raving, God-this and Jesus-that. The priests are being good-natured about it—they like Barnett—but it's got to stop. He's interfering with the masses."

"You want me to talk to him?"

"Would you?"

"No."

We both laughed. "That's what I thought you'd say."

We talked some more, Anne trying to persuade me to pay a visit to Barnett, me coming up with reasons not to. Barnett and I are ten years apart in age and miles apart in temperament and lifestyle. "He's eccentric," I said to my sister. "It's why he can't hold down a job. This preaching thing—it's just a phase."

The sitcom we were watching ended and a trailer for a new movie came on, something about the flood of the decade in a small northwestern town. *"Hundreds in danger of drowning,"* a grim-faced actor was saying to a panicky crowd.

Anne started to giggle, stifled it, and stuffed some popcorn into her mouth, almost choking in the process, and then spitting it back out into her hand.

The giggles pealed out of her like a wildly rung bell.

"Anne, you okay?"

Anne clamped her thighs together and doubled over as the TV voice went on, *"Water rising! A town inundated . . ."* The giggling wasn't giggling anymore. It had transformed into something else, a jagged, helpless laughter with as much gaiety as a death rattle. She wrapped both arms around her belly, fighting for breath as the compulsive laughter racked her, and hissed, "Where's the goddamn remote?"

I tossed it to her

She must have been trying to hit *mute* or change the channel, but in her flustered state, she increased the volume by mistake. *"Floodwaters drown an entire valley . . . "*

She lurched to her feet and staggered into the bathroom. When she came out, her hands were trembling, and she couldn't look at me.

"Anne, what's wrong? What just happened?"

"Jesus, it's so embarrassing . . . why do they let them *talk* like that on TV? How the fuck can they allow it?"

"Allow what?"

"The obscenities! The dirty talk just then. Didn't you—" She covered her face. "Jesus, you have no fucking idea what I'm talking about."

Something cold passed under my heart. "What obscenities?"

"Oh, *you* know." She leaned toward me conspiratorially, body language and tone of voice that of a woman confessing to something torrid: banging her brother-in-law, embezzling funds from the school soccer team. "You know, the nasty words that everyone pretends aren't. Hearing them like that, when I don't expect it—fuck, I had to go jerk off. My goddamn cunt was throbbing. Why does everyone pretend those words aren't nasty when they *are*?"

"Anne," I said, "when Mom was married to Dr Eads, she was drinking more than ever, and he'd spend a lot of time with us, each individually. Making up for her absence, he'd say. Did he do something to you? Those words that made you laugh—did he link them in your mind to— other things?"

For a second, she looked at me as though I'd just landed from the moon. Then her face drooped like a crone's. "You, too?" she said, her voice barely a whisper. "Oh fuck—he did that weird shit to you, too?"

"And Andrew," I said. "I'm pretty sure."

"I always thought it was just me he played those sick games with, and I was too ashamed to tell anyone. But why the words? If he was into molesting kids, that's one thing, but why did he hook the sex up to words that aren't even sex words, that he probably picked out at random?"

"Maybe that was the point. He wanted to see if he could take ordinary words and make them erotically charged—for-ever—for his victims. He was always talking about the way the brain processes language. I think we were his own private experiment."

Anne folded her thin arms around herself. "The son of a bitch. I always felt so ashamed, so crazy. I mean, just hearing those stupid words sometimes will make me come."

"Did you ever ask Robert to—you know—say them when you're making love?"

"You kidding? I know those really aren't dirty words to anyone but me. I'd feel like an idiot. What about you? Have you ever asked a lover to repeat whatever it was Eads said to you?"

I tried to smile, but the corners of my mouth turned down. "It's been fifteen years, Anne. Does that answer your question?"

Her small, freckled hands curled into fists. "It isn't fair. He molested both of us, maybe Andrew, too. We should track him down to wherever he's living now and make him pay."

"I've thought about it," I said, "but I'm afraid to try that. I'm afraid it would come back to haunt me."

           *      *      *

But God has a sick sense of humor and He proved it by letting me run into Ricky Calloway, in the least likeliest of places for either of us to be—a church. Ricky grew up in the same Irish-Catholic neighborhood that I did and, even though far from devout, he still managed to get to confession and mass a few times a year. I'd gotten a strange call from the priest who gave the eulogy at Andrew's funeral—apparently Barnett was at the cathedral delivering a sermon. He'd commandeered the church steps and was giving some sort of extemporaneous rant. *Could I please come get him?* the old priest wanted to know.

By the time I got there, Barnett was gone, and I was nearly knocked down the pink-marble stairs by a huge man with angry black eyes who came barreling through the door. Later, Ricky would tell me that he'd forgotten to put the safety lock on his Harley and had bolted out in the middle of mass, afraid hoodlums would be taking off with his prized bike. He knew how easily and profitably such a theft could be accomplished because it was one of the ways he supplemented his own income.

"Watch where you're going," I snapped.

"I *was* watching," he said, stopping to look me up and down the way he might appraise a communion goblet he was getting ready to filch. "I saw you at Andrew's funeral. You're his sister."

"Christine," I said. "I remember you, too. You're Ricky Calloway." Astonished at my own boldness, I added, "You headed anywhere in particular?"

He grinned. "Straight to Hell, according to the priest."

"Me, too."

He looked me over again. "That's kinda hard to believe."

"You'd be surprised."

"Surprise me."

I did—but not, undoubtedly, in the way that he'd been hoping.

Considering that we were both, in our own way, desperate, we observed an unlikely regimen of self-control, postponing sex while we became friends. I hadn't had a lover, male or female, in years, and Ricky had just broken up with a girlfriend and hadn't been with a woman in nearly a week—which somehow, for the two of us, approximated the same amount of deprivation. And we had Pasts. His, he liked to boast about. Mine, I preferred to hide. We'd meet for dinner or drinks, catch a movie. I learned his story, not little by little in dribs and drabs, but in large, nearly indigestible chunks of such mayhem, intrigue, and substance abuse that it resembled an action/adventure series. After the stint in juvie for murdering his dad, he'd worked construction and sold drugs on the side, got busted and gone to prison for drug dealing and assault, weathered two divorces, countless breakups, and the death of his mother, survived a gunshot wound to his thigh that almost severed his femoral artery.

We didn't have sex for four months, partly because I was in denial about what I really wanted from Ricky Calloway, partly because I cherished the fantasy that this time, because he was so different, so outside the conventional norms, I would be different, too, and the act of sex itself would be different. Not shameful and sordid and embarrassing, but full of raw lust and vigor and sheer animal exuberance.

When I judged that Ricky could be put off no longer and I had to take the risk, we finally lay together in his bed, kissing and caressing. His body was a tapestry of scars from various mishaps and altercations, fistfights and motorcycle accidents and bullet wounds, in addition to a number of lurid tattoos and painful-looking piercings. While in prison, as part of a gang initiation, he'd notched his right shin with a knife—three equally spaced vertical lines—and carved some sort of Celtic–looking symbol into his forearm, and he seemed proud of this self-mutilation, as though it marked some sort of rite of passage.

My fingers kept returning to the scars, especially the self-inflicted ones, tracing them over and over.

"What was it like when you killed your father?"

"A rush," he said. "Better than sex. Then later on, I just

went numb, spaced it all out. But I was never sorry for what I did. He deserved it."

I knew for sure then that I wanted Ricky Calloway. From the neck up, anyway. Now if I could just convince the rest of me to want the rest of him.

But the moment he started to penetrate me, I froze and my mind seemed to exit my body like a parachutist abandoning a doomed plane. I invoked my Words, saying them in my mind, but in another human being's presence that only caused a paralyzing shame that numbed my limbs and pelvis. It was as if I was afraid that he could hear me thinking, that he would *know*.

He propped himself on his elbows. "What is it, Christine? I do something wrong?"

"No, you're fine. It's just that . . . I'm so sorry. I can't—"

"Tell me what's wrong."

"It's not your fault."

His face contorted. "It's me, isn't it? Because you're scared of me. I shouldn't have told you all the shit I've done. That stuff turns women off."

"Not necessarily."

"What is it then? I can force my way inside you, but it'll hurt you and probably me, too, and I don't want to do that."

My mouth was as dry as my pussy; the only part of me that was lubricated was my eyes.

"Ricky, I'm sorry. I haven't had a lot of practice at this. I think I'd like sex if I could just be good at it."

"Something happened to you to make you afraid of sex. Tell me."

So I did—most of it anyway.

Ricky listened with a mournful expression on his face, then asked, "What happened to the bastard?"

"The marriage to my mother fell apart because of her drinking, and Eads divorced her. The last I heard, he'd gotten a job at a psychiatric hospital back east and moved away. We never heard from him except at Mother's funeral. He sent me a condolence card. On the back he'd written a sonnet that contained the Words. His little joke. I had to leave the viewing to go masturbate."

"Christ, what a bastard," Ricky said. "Where the hell does the son of a bitch live?"

I almost told him that he'd have to track Eads down, that I wasn't really sure where he lived, but something stopped me. Maybe the fact that I really liked Ricky Calloway and didn't want him to risk another prison term in some possibly misguided quest for vengeance on my behalf. Maybe because I'd planned to at least make love with him first.

Or maybe I just wasn't angry enough.

It took a call from Anne the following week to accomplish that. She told me that Barnett had quit his job as a custodian at a local middle school to "preach" full time—on the steps of the library, outside a day-care center, in the rose garden behind city hall. His spiritual intoxication seemed to be reaching apocalyptic and dangerous new heights.

"I'm afraid for him," said Anne. "When I tried to talk to him myself—well, put it this way: When the priest talks about having a passion for God, I don't think this is what he means."

When I went to Barnett's apartment, I found him sitting in the middle of his living room with three TV sets turned on—each one to the same religious channel. On each screen, a florid-faced, pompadoured huckster-for-Jesus exhorted his audience to let God provide for food and rent and send cash *now*. The TV screens were blurry with handprints, which puzzled me till I remembered that TV preachers often exhort viewers to "pray" with them by touching the screen.

"Cut that nonsense off," I said, perhaps too harshly, for Barnett looked like a mother who's just been told her blessed newborn resembles a toy troll.

"That's God's message, Christine," he said. "Have some respect."

"Bullshit," I said. "What's going on, Barnett? I know you've always been religious, the only one of us who went to mass, but I never knew you wanted to be a preacher."

"Till Andrew's funeral, I never realized what it feels like to get up in front of a crowd of people and talk about *Jesus* and *God* and the *Holy Spirit*." He put an emphasis upon the words, drew them out across his tongue, and licked the final consonants. "I always said those words alone in prayer, never out loud. I never dreamed the thrill that comes from calling out the name of God and God's son Jesus Christ and Lord and Saviour."

As he went on, a cold finger of dread wended its way up my spine. "You like to say God's name, don't you, Barnett?"

His mouth stretched wide in a parody of ecstasy.

"The Lord God is my savior. I sure as hell do. It lifts up my spirit."

*Not to mention your cock,* I thought, to judge from the hard-on that had tented up his pants the first time he said the word *God.*

"Tell me something, Barnett. When we were little and Mother was married to Dr. Eads, did he touch you and do things to you? And did he maybe talk about God while he was doing it?"

Barnett scrunched his forehead as though deeply perturbed. "Why do you always call him Dr. Eads? I call him Dad."

"I know you do, Barnett. So tell me, did he?"

"Did he what?"

"Touch you."

"He calls me sometimes, you know."

"He does?"

"At night, real late. He likes to call me up and talk."

"Where does he call from?"

"A pay phone."

"A pay phone where?"

"Near Noah."

"Noah? Like Noah's ark?"

"Yeah, but new."

"New? Newark? Is that where that scumbag lives now, Barnett? Newark, New Jersey?"

"Why do you hate him, Christine? He's a good man. When he calls, we talk about God. He says God must love me a whole lot, because I haven't forgotten anything."

*Oh, Barnett,* I thought, *you were just a baby. Oh, fuck.*

I went home and called up Ricky Calloway and told him Newark was where he could start looking for Dr. Eads.

* * *

"Christine," says Ricky, sitting in my darkened living room almost a year later, "come here and touch my cock."

I see his hand move toward the darker shadow of his lap and look away. I want to want him, but the cold is coming over me, climbing my spine like some inner ice age, numbing my heart.

He holds out a hand. "Come here."

I shake my head. "It won't be any different than before. Nothing's changed."

"Give it a try. Please, Christine, just once."

So I do. In the bedroom, I cut off all the lights and peel out of my clothes with my eyes shut, as though this means he won't be able to see me. Then I crawl under the covers, where Ricky, having nothing to do in the way of undressing, is already waiting for me.

"I found your Dr. Eads," he says, "and I made sure where I put the body, nobody's gonna find it for another twenty years. But before I used the knife on him, we had a talk." In the dark I feel him smiling. "And then I used the knife on me."

"You what?"

"I had to stay away until I was sure the scars were going to heal up good and raised. I think you'll like the way they feel. I think you'll want to touch me now. I think you'll want me inside you."

"I don't see—"

"I know your Words, Christine," he said. "I made him tell me."

I move to clamp a hand across his mouth, but he pushes me away.

"Don't worry. I don't need to say them," he says. "They're as much a part of me now as they are of you. Run your hands over me. Feel the scars." He takes my hand and guides it down. "You can start with my dick."

# STANDING WATER

## *Caitlín R. Kiernan*

Monday afternoon and Elvin Sloss is having a cigarette behind the bookstore when he notices the mud puddle for the first time. The narrow alley that runs between Twenty-second and Twenty-third streets, alley of broken, rustbarred windows and dented trash cans, high walls of brick laid and mortar set when Birmingham was a steel town and the mills belched fire and sootblack fumes. Elvin takes a thoughtful, long drag off his Winston, holds the smoke in his lungs like a drowning man's last breath, and watches the mirrorsmooth surface of the puddle. Then he glances up at the sky, exhales and a gray nicotine ghost hangs in the stale and scalding summer air trapped between the rear of Second Chance Books and the empty warehouse on the other side of the alley.

There isn't a cloud anywhere in the high, whiteblue sky, the narrow slice of it he can see draped between the buildings. There haven't been any clouds for almost two weeks now. No clouds and not a single drop of rain, just ozone alerts and the mercury climbing above one hundred day after day, hardly dropping below ninety at night, but here's this mud puddle anyway.

Elvin takes another drag and flicks the butt of his cigarette at the oily-looking water. There's a brief, faint hiss and the Winston's filter bobs and floats on the surface, sends out concentric rings of tiny ripples to lap against the edges of the puddle, the crumbled asphalt and limestone gravel margins of the pothole; here and there the sticky, yellowbrown clay beneath the blacktop is visible, like an old secret the city's trying to hide from itself.

Elvin chews at his lip and stares up at the sky again, the dog-day sun only an hour past noon, and there's no end at all to that dry shade of blue.

The back door of the shop slams open, then, releasing an unexpected draft of staler air that smells like dust and silverfish, old paperbacks, and coffee grounds, bookscented air that's only slightly cooler than the summer day. Shanna sticks her head out and squints at him, her hair the color of a dead mouse and chopped off almost down to the scalp.

"Didn't we have a copy of *Bleak House*?" she asks and blinks. "Didn't someone bring one in just last week?"

"English lit," Elvin says and when he looks back at the puddle there's no sign of the cigarette butt and the water is as smooth as melted plastic.

"Yeah, I already looked there. The only Dickens I can find is five copies of *David Copperfield* and one of *Great Expectations.*"

"Did you look in the B's? It might be there," he says.

Shanna clicks her tongue loud against the roof of her mouth, a curt, annoyed sort of a sound and "Why the hell would Dickens be stuck in the B's?" she asks.

But instead of an answer he points at the mud puddle and asks another question.

"Was that there yesterday?"

"What? What are you pointing at, Elvin?"

And he almost tells her, but it is only a mud puddle. Only a mud puddle in the alley behind the bookstore and Shanna sighs and clicks her tongue again. There are already little beads of sweat standing out on her forehead. •

"Never mind. It's nothing," he says and "You're gonna bake your brains if you don't come back inside," she grumbles in a voice that almost sounds like his mother's, almost sounds like she might actually give a shit.

"You must'a read my mind, Ladybug," he says, smiles, and Elvin follows the girl out of the blinding August glare and back into the mustywarm shadows waiting on the other side of the door.

She got him the job in May, about three weeks before they split up, and this grudge match has been going on ever since, Elvin refusing to quit because he needs the job and Shanna refusing to quit because she was there first. And it's usually not that bad, except for the days when Mr. Culliver's arthritis is bothering him, or his bowels are acting up, and he doesn't come in to the store and so they both have to work. Days when they have to pass the awkward hours trying to stay out of each other's way, ten o'clock to four-thirty and maybe it wouldn't be so difficult if there were a few more customers. But hardly anyone ever comes into Second Chance and so they take turns sitting behind the antique cash register and pretending to sweep the floor or tidy up the rows and rows of books that are hardly ever out of order.

Sometimes Elvin gets a bunch of them out of order on purpose, ignores Mr. Culliver's obsessive categories and alphabetizing, and sticks *Bleak House* under the B's or *Gravity's Rainbow* under "New Age" just so they'll have something to do. Once he hid all the Ayn Rand and Germaine Greer together under "Ichthyology," but it was almost two months before anyone even noticed.

Mostly, he does the work, or lack thereof, that Mr. Culliver pays him to do; better than flipping burgers so he ought to be grateful, even when it's 102 degrees in the shade and the old electric fans suspended from the ceiling of the shop do little more than rearrange the heat.

On Tuesday Mr. Culliver is feeling better again and Shanna has the day off. Elvin spends half the morning slowly unpacking boxes of encyclopedias from a flea market, three whole sets of *The World Book* from 1970 and not a single J–K volume in the bunch. And so maybe Mr. Culliver plays a few games of his own, maybe he doesn't actually *want* to sell any of these moldering, dog-eared books, or he's just really fucking curious to see how many people don't care whether or not their ten-dollar set of Nixon–era *World Book*s has listings for "Jet Engines" or "Kuwait."

At noon, Elvin retrieves the brown-paper Piggly-Wiggly bag with his lunch from the little refrigerator in the stockroom and opens the back door, steps out into the sundrenched alleyway, and the mud puddle is still there. If anything, it seems a little wider than the day before, never mind the heat or the drought or the trucks and cars that use the alley every now and then. He thought about the trucks and cars last night, lying in bed, thinking because it was too hot to sleep, and he thought how water would get splashed out of the puddle whenever anyone drove across it.

The water in the puddle is the color of chocolate milk and there's a definite iridescent sheen to it.

Elvin sits down on the wooden steps and opens his brown paper sack, takes out a Ziploc baggy with a white bread and egg-salad sandwich cut diagonally into two neat triangles, takes a big bite, and watches the puddle while he chews. The sandwich isn't very good, because he forgot the black pepper and didn't have any pickle relish, so it's just boiled eggs and mayonnaise mushed together. He thinks that there's a small tin of black pepper on top of the refrigerator, but doesn't want to go back inside to look for it, doesn't want to take his eyes off the chocolate-colored puddle that long.

Elvin takes another bite of his sandwich, another gooey, bland, yellow-white mouthful, and the puddle shimmers and glints wet beneath the Alabama sun. *Yes*, he thinks, *it is wider than yesterday*. At least two feet across now and the water's risen over the edges of the pothole. So maybe it's a leaky pipe under the alley, not busted but just a slow leak or there'd be a lot more water. He smiles, feeling stupid because he didn't think of that before.

Elvin finishes his sandwich and there's still a Hershey bar at the bottom of the bag, but it's already started to melt in the heat, going soft inside its wrapper, and he decides to put it back in the fridge for a while, save it for later. He lights a cigarette instead, stares at the spray-paint graffiti on the other side of the alley and then at a stunted patch of dandelions and clover that's managed to push its way up through a crack in the asphalt. Keeping his eyes on anything except the mud puddle, that mystery solved and tonight he'll only lie awake because of the heat. Tonight he can toss and turn and only think about the things he could have said to Shanna, the things that might have kept her from walking out on him.

He glances at his watch and stubs his cigarette out against the bookstore wall, leaves an ashy, black smudge on the bricks, and then Elvin starts to flick the butt at the puddle. But there's a sudden ripple across it, like a gust of wind, when there isn't any wind, when there's nothing but the stagnant, broiling air. For a moment the iridescent water seems to twitch, prism bands of oily color stretching out and winding quickly back upon themselves. And then the puddle's calm again, as if it had never been anything else. Elvin drops the butt of his Winston on the ground, grinds it back and forth with the toe of his right sneaker, and he reminds himself about the leaky pipe somewhere under the alley, and goes back inside the shop.

Wednesday and that's almost always Shanna's day, so Elvin sleeps until nearly eleven o'clock. Up half the night until he took an icy-cold bath at three a.m. and drank two bottles of Sterling with some allergy pills and when he finally wakes up, he only feels like shit. He lies naked in bed, wondering if there's enough sugar left for coffee and if he's ever going to get off his ass and find another air conditioner. There used to be a window unit in the bedroom, a huge, noisy contraption that rumbled and whirred and thumped like some ridiculous cartoon gizmo, but Shanna took that with her when she left. She'd paid for it so Elvin didn't argue with her, but sometimes he wishes that he had.

After breakfast (four frosted blueberry Pop-Tarts and bitter coffee, because there wasn't any sugar after all), he goes back to bed and sits staring out the open window that used to hold the air conditioner. The sun is burning the city alive out there, roasting it up for some feast the sky has planned, the sky or the stars, and from here he can see all the way across the

tracks, past the first row of buildings, and right there's the roof
of Second Chance Books. Shanna under that roof, so at least
she's safe from the sun, safe inside the bunker with all the dust
bunnies and Mr. Culliver's applestinking pipe smoke; safe
until the sun stops fooling around, gets its act together, and
there's nowhere left to hide. Elvin imagines the city wrapped
in flames, the brick-and-glass skyline turning soft as a melted
candy bar.

"Jesus," he whispers, laughs a very dry, dishonest laugh,
and wipes at his face. Sweat that stings his eyes and dissolves
in salty drops on his tongue. He wonders if the heat has ever
driven anyone insane, is wondering if there's a word for that
sort of insanity, and if it's true that more people commit murder and suicide in the summer, when the phone begins to ring
in the next room.

*It'll stop soon*, he thinks, no more than six or seven rings
even if the caller is very determined, even if it's his mother or
the landlord because he's two months behind on the rent. So
Elvin sits staring at the sun and the city, counting the shrill
telephone rings. Five, six, seven, and there, *that* ought to convince them he's not at home or at least that he has no intention
of picking up. But then it rings again, eight, and again, nine,
and he frowns and spits out the window; Elvin gets up and by
the time he makes it all the way out to the coffee table with the
old, black rotary phone, it's rung exactly thirteen times. He isn't
superstitious, but he waits until it rings once more, just in case.

"Are you drunk or something?" Shanna asks, her voice
small and tinny and seeming farther away than it should.

"No, I'm not drunk," he says, too relieved it isn't his mother
or the landlord to be annoyed that it's Shanna. "I'm only
medium rare. I won't be drunk for at least another hour and a
half."

"Ha-ha," she says and clicks her tongue against the roof of
her mouth.

"What do you want, Shanna? I'm not coming in today, so
don't even ask."

"I wasn't going to, asshole," and there's a pause then, familiar pause that he knows means she's working up to something,

and maybe she's only going to ask if she can borrow twenty
bucks or if he still knows someplace cheap to score a bag of
weed. Maybe she wants to borrow twenty bucks to *buy* a bag
of weed, he thinks, and reads the cover of an old issue of
*Wired* while he waits for her to get it over with.

"I'm not getting any younger, Ladybug," he says and she
clicks her tongue at him again.

"Day before yesterday," Shanna says, "Monday afternoon,
you were pointing at something out back of the store. Do you
remember doing that?"

"Yeah," Elvin mumbles, "I remember," and that's the first
time he's thought about the damned thing since leaving the
store on Tuesday; he wishes Shanna were standing in the room
with him so he could kick her in the ankle just for reminding
him.

"It was just a mudhole, wasn't it?"

And there's a cold, empty feeling deep in his belly then, his
guts full of ice water even if the weathermen will be frying
eggs sunny-side up on the hoods of cars on the six o'clock
news.

"Elvin? It was, wasn't it?"

"So what?" he says, trying too hard to sound like he really
doesn't care. "I was pointing at a mud puddle behind the
store."

"Do you even know the last time it rained?"

"I think Noah was building an ark," and oh, Christ, that was
clever, he thinks, that was smoother than oyster shit on
greased Teflon, and starts reading the magazine cover over
again.

"Well, *I* know how long it's been. I checked," Shanna says
and she's whispering now, like Mr. Culliver's walked up or
there's a customer at the register, someone she doesn't want to
hear what she's saying.

"I left something on the stove," Elvin says, glancing towards the kitchenette, the dirty dishes heaped in the sink, the
garbage can overflowing with fast-food bags and beer cans
and Chinese take-out boxes.

Another long pause from the other side of the line and

Shanna clicks her tongue twice. "Sure," she says, sounding nervous, almost sounding scared, but that might just be his sweltering imagination, might be nothing more than wishful thinking.

"Look, Shanna, I've *got* to go. Right now. A pot's about to boil over."

"August third," she whispers. "That's the last time it rained, Elvin. Seventeen days ago," and then Shanna hangs up before he can say anything else. And Elvin stands there holding the telephone receiver and feeling like an asshole, listening to the insistent dial tone and staring out the living room window at the endless, fireball day.

Almost four o'clock on Thursday afternoon, and they're sitting together on the back steps of the bookstore, smoking and watching the puddle. Shanna's holding a black umbrella over both their heads, stifling scalloped-edge shadow and the two of them huddled underneath. She came by after her Greek and Roman history class let out, rode the bus downtown instead of walking because the air's so bad and it's better to give up a dollar and a quarter than risk a heatstroke.

The puddle's nearly half as wide as the alley now, five feet across at least, and the muddy water's gone the mottled black-green of overripe avocado skin.

"Sewage would smell," she says, reluctantly dismissing his latest explanation. "I don't smell anything at all."

"Then maybe it's only water," Elvin says and cigarette smoke leaks slow from his nostrils and chapped lips. "Maybe the rust or something from the broken pipes is making it turn that color. Doesn't copper make green rust?"

"I don't think they use copper for water pipes. I think it's poisonous."

And then neither of them says anything else for a minute or two, just sit watching the puddle and the sun glistening off the rotten avocado-colored water. The surface of the puddle is perfectly smooth, even though there's a hot wind blowing down the alley today, coughdry wind to send the pages of a discarded newspaper flapping noisily past and stir up clouds of grit and dust.

Shanna sighs, a long, exhausted sigh, and Elvin takes his eyes off the puddle and looks at her; she's staring down at the scuffed leather toes of her boots, and there's a fat bead of sweat dangling from the end of her nose.

"When I was a little girl I had a Dr. Seuss book," she says and "Yeah, *Green Eggs and Ham*," Elvin says for no particular reason, the first Dr. Seuss book that comes to mind, and she shakes her head. The drop of sweat falls off the tip of her nose and leaves a dark splotch on the knee of her blue jeans.

"No, Elvin, it wasn't *Green Eggs and Ham*. I never had a copy of *Green Eggs and Ham*. It was called *McElligot's Pool*."

"I don't think I remember that one," he says.

"It was about this pool, and this kid that was trying to catch fish out of it, even though everyone kept telling him there was nothing in McElligot's Pool but old bottles and cans and shit."

"So, did he ever catch anything?"

"No, but that's not the point of the story. He kept saying how maybe the pool might be connected to an underground river that ran all the way to the sea, and there was no telling what was at the other end, what might come swimming up into McElligot's Pool if he sat there with his fishing pole and waited long enough."

Elvin turns back to the puddle then and it hasn't changed at all.

"That damned book used to scare the bejeesus out of me," Shanna says very quietly.

Elvin rubs at his chin, the stubble there like sandpaper to remind him how many days it's been since he's bothered to shave. A lot easier to forget without Shanna around to bitch about his beard scratching her face, and "This is fucking bullshit," he says and puts out his cigarette on the side of the steps. There's a broken broom handle leaning against the wall of the bookstore and Elvin reaches for it, ducks out of the sanctuary shade of the umbrella, and walks quickly to the edge of the puddle.

"What are you doing?" she asks, but he doesn't answer her,

his heart beating too fast now, adrenaline and the faintest silver taste at the back of his tongue like a new filling. Fucking ridiculous, scaring themselves like children telling spooky stories when it's just a goddamn mudhole, a busted pipe or something, and Elvin holds the broom handle right out over the puddle, as close to the middle as he can reach.

"Elvin, just come back and leave it alone, okay?" But he ignores her and lets go of the broom handle instead, and it sinks straight down into the dark puddle and disappears. Not even so much as a splash or a ripple, only those restless, iridescent greens and blues and reds writhing across the water. *Dragonfly colors*, he thinks, *June bug colors*, and he stands there, waiting for the broom handle to pop back up again, because it doesn't matter how *deep* the thing is, wood still fucking floats.

"Come on, Elvin. Let's go back inside now," Shanna says. "Mr. Culliver will be wanting to close up soon," and she's standing beside him, shielding him from the laughing sun with her big, black umbrella. "It isn't ever coming back," she says and takes his hand, her sweatslicked palm against his, and when he's sure that she's right, Elvin steps away from the edge of the puddle and lets her lead him back inside.

And "It's gone," she says again. "It's just *gone*." Elvin is standing with Shanna on the sidewalk outside Second Chance and the wind blowing down the street smells like rain and lightning. Friday afternoon and the sky hangs low and furious above the sunblind city, the violetredyellowchartreuse sky like a bruise, something beaten and battered and finally, *finally*,This is enough, it might have said, and the civil defense sirens have been wailing their tornado-warning cries for almost an hour.

"Just come and see for yourself," and she herds him roughly through the front door of the shop; the brass cowbell nailed above the door jangles loud and now there's the musty, wordy smell of books instead of the smell of rain. Past a bargain bin of coverless paperback mysteries and romance novels, between the towering, overcrowded shelves of science and history, philosophy, and more occult conceits, and she's squeezing his hand so hard it almost hurts. Shanna tugs and hurries him through the inkscarred, paperpressed belly of the shop and right back out its ass and then they're standing on the steps and the air smells like rain again.

"See? It was still here this morning, Elvin, but now, now it's just fucking gone," and she sounds frightened and confused and disappointed all at the same time.

He stares up at the stormy sky and then back down at the alley, the very dry place where the mud puddle was a day before, and the day before that. But now there's only an empty pothole no bigger around than a hubcap, no deeper than any pothole has a right to be, and "Let go of my hand," he says and she does.

"I heard something back here, and when I came to see, it was gone. Have you ever heard a rabbit screaming?"

"No," he tells her, because he hasn't and never wants to, and in a few more minutes the rain begins to fall and they stand together behind the bookstore and watch as the hole fills up again with nothing but rainwater and the soggy bits of trash washing down the alley.

# GRAVE SONG

## Brian A. Hopkins and Richard Wright

*The mass of men lead lives of quiet desperation and go to the grave with the song still in them.*

—Henry David Thoreau

Sixty miles southeast of Macon, the cemetery lay draped in Spanish moss, cypress, and pine, bordered on three sides by a dogleg in the Ocmulgee, in ground so swampy-soft that it was a wonder the coffins hadn't long ago risen to the surface.

Murphy found the cemetery on a whim. Twice a month he made the drive up to Atlanta, never veering from the monotonous ribbon that was I-75, but today he'd been struck by a quiet desperation. His life was an endless loop of seldom-rented VHS tape. He was going nowhere. With no one. And in absolutely no hurry. It was as if at some point in time he'd been told he would never amount to anything and he'd set out to personally ensure that this prophesy came true. He woke every day to the same breakfast, went to the same office, saw the same people, returned home to watch the same television programs . . . and twice a month he drove to Atlanta. He might have continued his tedious pattern today were it not for three completely unrelated statements.

His mother, on the phone that morning: "William, on your way up to see me, could you pick up some pecan divinity from the Stuckey's in Valdosta?"

Brett, a coworker at the office in Jacksonville: "Big weekend planned, Bill? Oh, wait, this is the second Friday of the month. You'll be going to spend the weekend with your mama."

And, finally, the guy at the gas station where he'd filled up:

"Holy shit. Is that a Pinto? I didn't know there was a single Pinto still on the road . . . thought they'd all been melted down and made into beer cans. Shit, that's even a Pinto wagon!"

Each was a statement on William Murphy's life: his mother's question, the same question she asked every time he called to let her know he was leaving and would be there in about five hours; her concern for the candy, which he always brought her (even now, as he stood contemplating the cemetery, the box was tucked out of the heat beneath the passenger seat); Brett's jibe and the snide look on his face as he'd said it; and the gas station attendant, who'd obviously thought only the lowest form of life would be caught driving an old Ford Pinto.

So he'd taken an exit just north of Tifton, completely at random, and worked his way northward via Georgia's scenic side roads. Somehow he'd wound up here, at the end of a dirt road, staring at a cemetery that looked to have been forgotten about a hundred years ago. Most of the headstones dated back to the Civil War. Moldy and canted in the soft earth, they spoke of Southern gentlemen who'd been hastily buried and mostly forgotten in a nation's attempt to hide its guilt. Many of the stones were completely unreadable, the names and dates long obscured in wind and rain and fungus, but a few—those that faced away from the prevalent wind or lay sheltered in the lee of a larger stone or tomb—still spoke to Murphy. Names and dates. "Beloved father." "Cherished son." "Loving husband."

He was nearly to the banks of the river when he stumbled across the one that bore his name.

Without that significant lapse in concentration, his diversion might have ended with a cemetery, a different set of road signs, and pleasantly different views. Instead, he found himself grappling with a root that refused to lie beneath the sodden soil, that reneged with climbing willfulness as though knowing full well it had a meeting with Murphy that day.

Snagged, he fell, expecting to be cushioned by dark, sodden humus, wondering how he was going to explain his stained suit to his mother. Once, long ago, he had arrived at her porch wearing jeans and a T-shirt. After two days of frowning disapproval, he had sworn never again to thwart her expectations so, and had bought a beige suit specifically for these monotonous visits. It was useless trying to explain to his mother that his job writing music scores for computer games at DeltaSoft Entertainment didn't require a "professional" wardrobe. His mother, product of a South that refused to die in spite of the Civil War and all the reform that had followed, equated blue jeans and T-shirts to the "servant class."

Solid stone was his painful savior, knocking the wind from him, bruising his chest. He lay there for a moment, trying to gather his senses. What lay beneath him was an ancient headstone, one which had toppled during its long stay in the shifting ground. His nose brushed the faint indentations of words. When he pulled back his head and saw the name "Murphy," he almost smiled at the coincidence.

"Thanks," he told his ancient ancestor, pushing himself up on his elbows. Then his breath, so recently reclaimed, caught in his throat. The first name on the headstone was William.

Still, perfectly still, he stared, his mind cavorting through myriad possibilities. A bird cawed roughly somewhere to his left, a reaper noise, harsh and damning. Or so his imagination painted it. And there was a thought to shock him from shock. Who would have said that William August Murphy had an imagination? How many times, as he grew from boyhood into the great beyond of adult life, had his mother told friends and relatives alike that he was "a bright boy, but not particularly creative"?

Shaking his head, he climbed to his knees. It was a coincidence was all, an even stranger one now that he shared not one but two names with the cadaver beneath him. Not even a cadaver now, most like. Rather it would be nothing but mineral deposits for the creeping, reaching roots of trees—those that weren't intent on doing him an injury anyway.

He reached out with a shaking hand and brushed dirt from the old stone. There was a middle name there, too, fainter than the others, impossible to read, but not impossible to touch. His fingers traced what his eyes could not make out, the art of Braille given whimsical purpose.

The first letter was an "A," and he brushed the possibility

away with another hesitant grin. What a story this would make when he went to the office on Monday! The second was a "U." His smile faded. "G." Then another "U." Now his hand was trembling furiously. The next letter was impossible to deciper, though he knew it would be an "S." The last letter was a "T."

The instant he finished deciphering the name, his own unlikely, foolish middle name, he was on his feet, suddenly breathing in a ragged pant. Coincidence now seemed too convenient a word, too unlikely a dismissal. Scanning the headstone for information, for explanation, his eyes settled on the date. Whereas the name had been worn soft and subtle by time, the date was deeply engraved, was solid and real.

And completely impossible. Murphy had been a poor student of history in school, but there were some facts he had retained, so fundamental had they been. One of those was that Christopher Columbus had only made his great discovery in 1492.

The date on the headstone was March 12, 1067.

He wanted to laugh at the utter absurdity of it all—not to mention the final coincidence of his own birth date being March 12—but he couldn't. He decided it was the suffocating heat, that he'd lost his faculties. A blow to the head perhaps. He'd taken a nasty fall, hit his head, and had unknowingly lain sweltering in the sun for hours. Sunstroke. That had to be it. The trick now was to cool off. The air conditioning in the Pinto had died years ago, but the sparkling, sun-teased surface of the river looked cool and inviting.

Murphy shuffled toward the bank of the Ocmulgee, his loafers sinking in the mud. Vines and creepers caught at his legs. Querulous insects assaulted his ears. He knelt beside the river and splashed water on his face, heedless of the mud soaking into the knees of his slacks. The water was tepid, but still much cooler than the stagnant air beneath the trees. He felt it evaporating from his face, taking with it some of his anxiety. He'd misread the date, he decided then. It had said 1967, instead of 1067. The name had been a coincidence. Bizarre, yes, but certainly not terrifying. Life was full of such one in a million coincidences. Sooner or later everyone ran into one.

Closing his eyes, Murphy splashed his face again. Water ran down his neck, soaking his collar and shirt. It dripped from his chin and splashed back into the river with a soft music, scattering a team of water bugs racing across the surface.

His eyes shot open.

It was actual music he was hearing. It was coming from the graveyard behind him.

Not knowing what to expect—a danse macabre scene from Poe perhaps—he turned and looked back into the cemetery. Everything was as he'd left it. The scattered tombstones. The sun-draped moss. The wavering clouds of gnats and the croaking of frogs. Even the pinto sat exactly as he'd left it, the driver's side door ajar. Nothing had been disturbed. Except . . . he was definitely hearing music. A soft piano concerto. Strings. A clarinet. The mournful tune was completely unfamiliar.

Wiping his hands on his ruined trousers, Murphy rose to his feet. That's when he saw it. William August Murphy's tombstone was standing, the engraving on its surface crisp and clean, the stone as smooth and polished as the day it had been made.

I should panic, he thought, as his legs shuffled him away from the bank of the Ocmulgee. The stone was beautiful, now that the markings of time had been erased, sharp and defined, proud and gleaming. If it were his own headstone, he would have been pleased. The year on the stone, he noticed as he drew near, was indeed 1067. He accepted that fact with a certain surrender, resigning himself to whatever bizarre fate the day had in store for him. He was done with doubt.

The music was enticing. He wondered briefly if there could be some hobo concealed behind the markers of the dead, a graveyard musician with Spanish moss for a seat and ghosts for company. The strings burrowed deep into his soul and gut, summoning innate emotions as they dragged wistfully on, pulling rapture through his muscles, leaving them trembling and weak and delicious. Tears glossed his eyes at the beauty within him, the desperation that wanted to respond to the music, to be one with it.

The clarinet, flippant and whimsical, curled into his heart, altering its beat with subtle precision, until it danced a glorious, irregular frenzy. His breathing was suddenly a race to find the air he needed to tame the wild joy surging within him. Muscles across his back and chest tensed and fluttered, tripped by intrusive passion. Pushing his head back, closing his eyes, he hungered to laugh and cry, unwilling to do either lest he release this glorious, caressing tension. Nothing had touched him so in his dull, soulless life. Nothing had moved him with such awful exultance.

While the strings threaded his emotions, while the clarinet took his heart from him and recalibrated its rhythm, the piano was the world, was time and place in one penetrating concerto.

Opening his eyes, not knowing whether to sob joy or pain, Murphy saw that he was standing beside the tombstone that bore his name. Noticing that the earth before it was freshly turned, he wondered if there was a body below. Whose body?

In answer to the thought, the music found a new, exhilarating tempo. This time Murphy did sob his desperate joy, bending over in an agony of thrilling sensation. The music wanted him to find out, would reward him if he did. But if he didn't . . .

Would this passion leave him? Would he ever recapture the feeling he had been bequeathed today?

Dropping to his knees, he scooped a handful of warm, moist dirt from the top of the grave. His fingers sank through the loose soil, burrowing ever deeper, the earth growing cooler with every inch of penetration. His heart and breath were held in check as he waited expectantly for that first contact. What would his probing fingers encounter? The hard impermeability of a coffin or the cold give of dead flesh? Elbow deep, he fumbled for a clue. He could smell the richness of the damp earth. He found himself suddenly and inexplicably intoxicated with the full aroma of verdant decay and burgeoning life, a glyph of paradoxes that overpowered his senses. He fell forward, his arm plunging to the shoulder in the loose earth, his face burrowing into the grave.

Still, at the tip of his questing fingers, wriggling nearly thirty inches below the surface like pale worms, there was nothing. The grave was empty.

Murphy extracted his arm and rolled onto his back. Skeletal branches and dead-gray moss swayed against the sky above him. The turned earth was cool at his back. The frogs resumed their cacophony. A bird shrieked. It was only then that he realized the mysterious music had died. His back began to itch and he squirmed against the earth to scratch it. The ground parted, moist folds of humus opening to receive him. He squirmed some more and the dirt lapped at his sides. Unafraid, he wriggled like a turtle caught on its back. The earth shifted up over his legs . . . up over his abdomen and chest. It encircled his neck. Clogged his ears.

When he stopped moving, only his face remained exposed to the air above. Buried within the earth, he'd relocated the mysterious music. It echoed through the banks of the river, reverberating among the tombstones and the cypress roots, filling Murphy's mind with that same relaxing peace. He lay there and he listened, entrenched in the cool confines of the earth.

And he knew what the "1067" on the tombstone meant.

Her name was Anna Davinsky, pale, fragile daughter of an immigrant carpenter. Her family had relocated to Atlanta during Murphy's senior year in high school. Her mother had taken a job cleaning Murphy's house, and Anna had often gone home with Murphy after school. Tall and bony, with a gazelle's cautious grace, Anna never spoke above a whisper. Her movements were always small and precise. The few times that she'd touched Murphy, her contact had been no more substantial than a lighting butterfly. But her eyes had been a blue that he'd seen nowhere else. And in those eyes, he'd seen something warm and comforting, a quiet place where a man's thoughts took on infinite clarity. Talking to Anna, he'd found someone who actually listened to him, someone who seemed to understand the things he wanted from life. Or maybe it was that, while around Anna, he was first able to understand himself what it was he wanted. To Anna, he revealed his desire to compose music—not the tinny inanities he created for video games at DeltaSoft now, but *real* music.

He'd composed his first piece of music for Anna. "Ten Sixty-seven," he'd named it. Only she knew why.

"A bright boy, but not particularly creative," his mother had echoed, time after time. "Reliable—not like some of those airy-fairy types." She had been so very determined, so very sure. Slowly, her enormous will had wreaked havoc on his own wants, leaving nothing but crushed hope behind as her prophesy self-fulfilled. Could he have been a musician? A real musician? Perhaps, given another, different life. You could not choose your family. Anna had known this, known him, better than anybody.

She had approached him tentatively one day, in the school library as he crammed for the exams that would take him on to the university of his mother's choice. Soberly, quietly, she sat down beside him as he worked. Like a wistful caress, her scent drifted over him, his first sign of her presence. Though he knew she was there, he pretended not to notice at first, pretended that the work was engrossing, enthralling. All the better to prolong her nearness, to feel the relief she brought from a thousand school-day stresses. Eventually, he turned to her with a shy smile.

"Anna. How are you?" She smiled, illuminating the library gloom, and the smile broke his heart, for it held a depth of sadness he had never seen there before, a great sorrow that was for him. Fear lit like fire between his ribs, and he reached out a hand to snatch Anna's hand to him, not thinking of the teenage stigmas that witnesses may bring to bear later.

"What? Anna, what is it?"

She hesitated, seeing in him many possibilities, seeing only one probability. Suddenly she was eager, her eyes darting, her words halting.

"Billy, I have a favor to ask, if I may?" Perhaps that was it, the reason for the sudden anxiety, an awkward question she needed to pose. Yet the thought brought no comfort, no relief.

"Of course, you can. How can I help?"

The hand grasping his tightened with the strain layering her words.

"I want a piece of music, Billy. I want you to write for me."

Stunned by the enormity of that simple request, he stared blankly at her, his face expressionless. She had long known of his music, his desire to perform, to further his skills. His mother had never been keen on it though, had always frowned on what she considered a worthless hobby. William relaxed and sighed. "Anna, I don't know. I don't really compose stuff, you know? I just play in my room, and—"

As she cut him off, her eyes were frantic. "Billy, I need this! I trust it to be a special song. It must be from you and about you. It must be your passions, your dreams, and your soul—in one soaring piece. Can you do that for me, Billy? Will you?"

He sighed frustration, and started to release her hand. "Anna, my mother's putting a lot of pressure on me to get through these exams, you know? I haven't really got time to—"

She yanked his hand back to her, clutching it to her sleek breasts. "Your mother must not know!" She realized she had raised her voice, that heads were turning their way, and lowered his hand again. "Please, Billy, do not tell her of this. I want the song because I am frightened. Frightened that if you do not record this, ensnare it, she will set it forever free, and you will never see it again." Staring into Anna's pleading eyes, William had been truly afraid then. Though part of him tried to dismiss the implication of that suggestion as girlish foolishness, another had known, had been resigned to the future laid out before him.

In the grave, in the now, William shuddered as damp soil slid through his clothes, covering him like cool, black skin. A beetle skittered across his exposed cheek like a bleeding tear. When had he forgotten this? After composing the tune, sweating and raging away a fortnight to get it right, he had astonished himself with the result.

"10:67," he had called it. The time when his aspirations would be finally realized. An impossible time, when the implausibility of his hopes might yet manifest themselves beneath the oppressive spirit of his mother.

When he had presented the finished piece to Anna, she had wept, and he had joined her. Then she had thanked him, holding him for blissful minutes, and promised to keep the best of him safe until she could return it. William August Murphy, not having the slightest idea what she had meant, smiled pleasure and held her back. When the exams were finished, Anna had moved away, and despite the usual promises to keep in touch, he had never heard from her again.

Billy's hopes and joys flocked into William from the dead mush of the swamp and the cemetery. Anna had taken the best of him, long ago, while it was still fragrant with possibilities, and then buried it deep, just as his mother had buried it deep within his infinite mundanities.

Beneath the earth, the alarm on William's wristwatch sounded. He did not need to unearth his buried arm to know what time it was.

# TWENTY MILE

## *Ann K. Schwader*

The developer's sign by the front gate took Cassie like a punch in the stomach. Phil had told her about it, but seeing it was something else. Something that clenched her fingers white on the steering wheel. Made her swear all the way down that long dirt road, because cussing was better than crying and that asshole Phil was *not* going to see her cry.

TWENTY MILE RURAL PROPERTIES—YOUR PIECE OF THE WEST.

*Your overpriced shed, anyhow. And none of it mine.* Maybe Twenty Mile had never really been hers, but it had still been in her family. She'd worked up here every teenage summer, helping her aunt with cooking when she had to and riding fence as much as she could.

Now there were no cattle left to fence in. No branding crews to cook for. Just miles and miles of dry grass and brush, stuck full of orange plastic flags flapping in a Wyoming wind. The kind that meant thunderstorms coming—maybe a bad one, since it was barely past mid-June.

Good thing she didn't have much farther to go. After driving almost nonstop from Denver, even staying under the same roof with Phil sounded better than another three miles up to Bear Lodge, Montana. So long as Phil hadn't shut off the electricity and sewer yet, staying at the ranch was bound to beat accommodations there.

Of course, there was still the problem of talking to her cousin.

She and Phil hadn't spoken since the memorial service back in January.

The one that had left him the last heir to Twenty Mile.

Strictly speaking, of course, the service hadn't done that. A drunk in a 4X4 had, on a twisting road in a snowstorm. Her aunt and uncle and Phil's two brothers—plus their wives, one with a baby on the way—had been returning from a neighbor's holiday dinner. All in one van. One target.

When the Barrett family lawyer called Phil in L.A., only her aunt had still been alive. He'd flown in just in time to say good-bye in the ICU.

By the time the will cleared probate, Twenty Mile was already history.

Raindrops spattering her windshield told Cassie she'd better stifle her grievances for now. Not easy, when the very emptiness of the landscape kept reminding her of why she was here. She'd just come to collect a few things her aunt had set aside for her—things Phil had "forgotten" to send down for months—and close the door on too many memories.

By the time she pulled into the graveled front drive, it was raining steadily. The clouds were darker than early dusk could justify, and thin lightning stabbed at the distant hills. Grabbing her windbreaker from the backseat, she pulled it over her head as she ran for the porch.

There was a scrap of paper taped to the front door.

Cassie read it, reread it, then tore it off and threw it into a nearby lilac bush. She tried the door anyhow, but found it locked. *"Shit."*

She was just turning around when bootheels sounded on the porch steps. "Cassie? Cassie Barrett?"

Glancing back quickly, she saw an older man in jeans and a work shirt. The band of his battered straw hat held a single feather.

"Noboby else, Frank," she said, smiling recognition. "What are you still doing around here?"

"Closing up. Selling out." The Crow looked tired and disgusted. "Your cousin wanted somebody to stay through the summer, at least until that developer brought her people out from California."

His expression hardened. "I'm not staying much longer, though. You'd better not, either."

"Doesn't look like I'm staying at all—at least not tonight. Phil went to Sheridan for another business meeting. He was supposed to be back by now, but his note said—"

"He didn't know when he'd be back." Frank's face creased in a leathery smile. "Or if he'd be back tonight at all."

*Oh, great.* "Let me guess. Our lady developer is good-looking, or at least built." Frank's smile widened. "So, Phil being Phil, he's off getting a little extra profit on his deal."

"One of them is, anyhow."

For the first time all day, Cassie laughed and meant it. Frank Yellowtail did that for people. He'd been the foreman at Twenty Mile for as long as she could remember, and his dry humor hadn't dulled with the years. Even these days, with jobs almost impossible to get here in reservation country.

So why was he planning to leave the ranch early?

When she asked, Frank's face closed up. Stepping onto the porch out of the rain, he took off his hat and just stared at her.

"What happened?" she asked. "Did Phil finally piss you off, or what?"

Frank shook his head, suddenly uncertain. She couldn't recall him *ever* looking that way. "Come on, spit it out. If Phil's done something, I'd better know. If it's something else . . ."

"Thought you'd remember. You were here often enough when it happened—just about branding time, usually. Every year.

He hesitated. "Only this year, there's no stock for it to happen to."

It was probably just the damp, but Cassie suddenly felt colder. She hadn't thought about the ranch's weird little secret in years—not since the 80s, anyhow, when that "harvesting" documentary had convinced her how bogus the whole cattle mutilation was. UFOs? Uh-huh, right.

Besides, what happened to cattle at Twenty Mile didn't look like the photos she'd seen in books.

Frank was right, though. Whatever it was did seem to happen every year at least once. At least it had when she was here, though her cousins had tried to keep her from finding out. And her uncle refused to let anyone call the vet when a carcass turned up.

"Oh, I remember, all right." She frowned. "But if Phil's sold off all the stock, then it couldn't . . ."

Something in Frank's eyes stopped her.

"Your cousin made a bad mistake," he said. "I tried to talk him out of it. Tried to get him to sell this place as a working ranch, but he wouldn't listen. The developer promised more money than any rancher could."

"And money's always been the big thing with Phil. I know."

Frank shook his head. "No, you don't. You don't know anything about what happens here every summer, and someone in your family should before it's too late."

He broke off abruptly, glancing up the road as though expecting Phil's car any second. Cassie looked, too, but all she saw was rain and darker clouds and thickening dusk. The lightning in the hills was getting closer.

Just the way it did every year, before the really bad night storms started. The ones that meant a missing cow or steer the next morning, and her uncle walking in with his "Don't Ask" face.

Cassie took a deep breath, hearing her own heart above the rain pounding the porch roof. "So tell me about it."

"Not here."

Given Phil's temper, it made a lot of sense. Cassie nodded. "I've got to drive up to Bear Lodge anyway, and I'm starved. Meet you at the Lazy B in an hour?"

Thanks to the slowest desk staff of any Motel 8 in the country, it took her nearly two hours to get to the cafe. Frank's battered green pickup was still in the parking lot, though, and his face as she walked in looked more worried than annoyed.

"Any problems on your way here?" he asked, between bites of rhubarb pie.

"I didn't meet Phil on the road out, if that's what you mean."

His expression said it wasn't, but the arrival of a waitress forestalled questions. Cassie ordered herself a cheeseburger, side salad, and iced tea, then peeled off her windbreaker and slid into the booth. One foot kicked something lumpy under the table.

"Sorry." Glancing down, she saw a worn Army surplus carryall. "What's in that?"

"Evidence. I packed it to show your cousin, back in January. He said he didn't have time."

Knowing Phil, that wasn't all he'd said. Her cousin had moved off the ranch right after college and never looked back. Anything or anyone that interfered with his plans for success in L.A. (where he allegedly worked for an investment firm) got shoved aside.

"Well, I do," she said, wondering how soon she'd regret this.

Frank had never talked much about his ancestry or his culture, but this whole scenario reeked of superstition. Old native curses, or the Crow equivalent. The folded leather packet he dug out of his carryall didn't help.

But when she untied the rawhide thong, she found a stack of Polaroid photos.

"I'd look at these *before* I started eating, if I were you."

It was good advice. Each picture showed a different carcass—some steers or bulls, some cows or heifers—cut up just the way she remembered. Unlike the well-publicized mutilations in Kansas and Minnesota in the 1970s, whatever got at Twenty Mile stock didn't limit itself to easily detachable extremities. Or even sex organs.

Instead, each animal had suffered a slightly different surgical fate. Some had their heads fully dissected with meticulous care, but nothing else touched. Some lay within a perfect circle of their own intestines. One cow had been found with her entire reproductive system laid out in some kind of pattern—one Cassie didn't recognize, though she was no stranger to comparative folklore.

"So what do you make of this one?" she asked, flipping through the remaining photos in search of similar designs.

The Crow foreman shrugged.

"I don't. Neither did my father, and *his* father was *Batce Baxbe* . . . what you'd call a medicine man. A man of power. Both of them lived in this area almost all their lives, and neither one ever saw anything else—even in a vision—that looked like that."

He glanced at the other Polaroids on the table. "Or that, either. Or *that*, though Grandfather fasted for weeks after it was found. He was afraid it meant something terrible, and wanted to know what."

Cassie picked up the black-and-white photo. It was one of the oldest, faded and badly stained. A label on the back read 20 MILE / JUNE 22 / 1959. 2? 3?

She was just about to turn it over when her dinner came.

Frank scooped up the Polaroids as the waitress set the food down. Cassie didn't ask for them back. She'd seen enough of the last to realize that "2? 3?" meant that the photographer wasn't sure how many cattle had been involved.

There *was* a very distinct pattern to it, though. One she'd rather consider without a cheeseburger in hand.

Turning her attention to salad instead, she ate in silence while Frank dug a black loose-leaf binder out of the carryall. It bulged with photocopies and typed pages, some of which threatened to fall out as he opened it.

"Most of this was my father's work. He interviewed as many of our elders as he could, looking for memories of this area before reservation times. That's around 1870."

"But Twenty Mile wasn't even a ranch then!" said Cassie. "There weren't any cattle to . . ."

"The land was still here. There were buffalo on it. And Crow horses, until the government shot them all in the twenties."

Frank paged past photocopies into yellowed typescript until he found one section marked with a paper clip. Reversing the binder, he pushed it across the table to her. "This is what I wanted to show your cousin—this and the photos, especially the bad ones." He indicated several lines highlighted in yellow. "I even marked up my father's transcript to help him understand."

*Too bad Phil only understands money.*

Still, curiosity started her reading. Back in the late 1940s, Frank's father had interviewed one Mary Iron Elk, who had a real imagination for an elderly Crow. Her description of a certain thunderstorm she'd seen as a small child camping with her family sent cold spiders down Cassie's spine. The camp had been on Twenty Mile land, of course, but that wasn't what made her read so carefully.

Too many details sounded familiar. How coyotes hadn't howled for several nights before the weather turned violent—or afterwards, either, until the strange storms passed. How Mary Iron Elk claimed that she could *feel* the thunder underfoot at the height of the tumult.

And, of course, what her family had found the next morning, less than a mile from where they'd slept.

Cassie looked up sharply from the page. "It happened to buffalo, too?"

"Buffalo and horses both. Buffalo, if they were available."

"You mean the biggest animals around?"

Frank's nod suggested another question, but she wasn't about to ask it yet. Not sitting here in the old familiar Lazy B talking about events even UFOlogists would dismiss.

Instead, she made herself start on her burger while she still had an appetite left.

She also read on, checking out other highlighted sections. Phrases like "*in the longest days.*" "*When the earth speaks to the sky.*" "*When the earth speaks to the sky, and the sky answers.*" And then, on another page even farther back, one phrase underlined in faded red pencil: "*The Ones Who Come.*"

She coughed as a bite caught halfway down. "Did you underline this, Frank?"

"My father did." He looked intensely uncomfortable, but Cassie waited until he went on. "It was something he heard several times, but only from the very oldest people he interviewed. Men so old they were living in visions."

"So he never was sure what it meant?"

"Something like that." Another silence, stretching until she flipped back to his own highlighting. "The 'longest days' are around the summer solstice, of course. 'When the earth speaks to the sky' . . . is that tremor that sometimes comes with the thunder," he said.

"Or before the thunder."

Frank looked at her with surprise and relief. "You've felt it?"

She nodded. It was another thing she'd learned not to mention at Twenty Mile—at first because her cousins laughed at her, later because her uncle didn't. She'd probably felt an aftershock from some West Coast quake, he said, and what was she doing up that late anyhow when she had chores in the morning?

"The sky answers in the lightning and thunder," she said. "That much makes sense—but how does the earth 'speak' in the first place? And why haven't more people noticed? Bear Lodge isn't that far away."

Frank looked grim and reached for the binder.

"My father wondered that, too. He spent a lot of time mapping individual incidents—where people saw and felt what as well as where carcasses were found—and he came up with this." He turned to a photocopied map of the Twenty Mile area. It was peppered with pencil marks but a single red pencil circle enclosed them all.

There was a blue ink *X* near the center of that circle. A little square had been drawn in pencil beside it, almost touching it.

Frank touched the square with a fingertip. "You know what that is, don't you?"

"The house." She frowned. "But there wasn't anything else there before it was built. I've seen old pictures. No rock formations, no trading posts, nothing." Her attention shifted to the *X*. "So what's that supposed to be?"

He didn't answer immediately. He just let her study the map for a while before he put it and the binder away.

"It's the epicenter, isn't it?" *Epicenter* felt like a good safe scientific word. Epicenters were only points—mathematical centers of events. They weren't really things in and of themselves.

But Frank shook his head. "It's more like an actual source. Or a focus. And it's underground—a long way down, but reachable." He hesitated. "I'll take you there tomorrow, if you want to see it."

His eyes met hers directly. "I think you should."

The slick red vinyl booths of the Lazy B seemed to close in around her, trapping her in a situation . . . no, a reality . . . she felt ill-prepared to cope with. Frank Yellowtail had never given her any reason to distrust him. Nor had he ever shown any sign of an overactive imagination, let alone the superstitious paranoia of the past several minutes.

Maybe it wasn't paranoia. Maybe it was early Alzheimer's. Frank wasn't young—and when he had been, he'd spent some wild years on the rodeo circuit. It could be another kind of brain damage from landing on his head too often.

Or maybe there *was* something under the earth of Twenty Mile. If Frank was right, it had been there a long time, killing buffalo and horses and cattle at a very specific time of year, in a gruesome and distinctive way.

And her cousin Phil hadn't even cared enough to hear Frank out.

"I don't know," she finally said. "What good could it do?"

The Crow foreman shrugged. "Maybe he'll listen to you. Or maybe he won't, but at least *you'll* know. And if it's ever your decision to make . . . about the land, I mean . . . maybe you'll make it differently."

More spiders skittered along her spine. Phil never listened to anybody.

And if she understood the rest of what Frank was saying, she didn't want to.

"I've got one more piece of evidence," he continued, when she didn't answer. "It's not something I can show you in here, though."

He lowered his voice. "Did you ever see one of the carcasses up close?"

"Yes."

"Then you'll know if I'm telling the truth."

Cassie nodded, suddenly repulsed by her own half-eaten cheeseburger on its greasy plate. Signaling for their checks, she paid them both and hurried out of the Lazy B.

Outside, the rain had finally stopped. The air was still damp and clammy, though, charged with the dark energy of storms to come. Cassie felt goose bumps starting on her arms. When Frank came out of the diner, she was glad to follow him to the island of security light where he'd parked his truck.

Unlocking the passenger door, he took another packet from his glove compartment. Its leather wrapping looked old and badly stained, but a few worn beads decorated its rawhide thong.

"This was my grandfather's," Frank said, handing it to her. "He kept it because he hoped it held power against The Ones Who Come. Before he died, he told my father he'd been wrong."

Cassie's throat tightened. "Is this your evidence?"

Frank nodded.

She made herself open the packet—and bit her lip as she saw what it held. One large furry ear, a buffalo's by the size of it, still attached to a neat circle of hide. No bloodstains. No signs of violence at all.

"Turn it over."

Her fingers were trembling too much. Frank finally did it for her, revealing the underside of the ear's attachment. Not tanned hide, or dried sinew and flesh, but tiny rust-red crystals glittering in the light.

She poked at the ear with a fingertip. It still felt soft and flexible, almost warm.

Absolutely fresh.

"Oh shit." She barely managed to hold on to the packet until Frank could take it from her. "This *is* from Twenty Mile, isn't it? But if it belonged to your grandfather, it must be . . ."

"Over a century old." He wrapped up the ear quickly and put it away again. "Are you going to be all right?"

*Depends.* She started taking deep breaths, trying to bring herself fully back to the present. Out of the memory coiled like a rattlesnake at the back of her mind. *Crystallized blood.* Just the way she'd seen it sparkle in a heifer's gaping belly one morning at dawn, when she'd been out riding fence before breakfast. Alone.

Her cousins had told her the rest later. How one of them, on a dare, had stolen a piece of intestine from a kill he'd found years ago. How he'd kept it in his closet for a good six months before their mother found it and made him throw it away. It hadn't rotted.

After that, their dad made them help him bury kills like that. Even coyotes and magpies wouldn't touch the meat.

"I think so," she finally managed. "I guess I just hadn't expected that kind of evidence." She hesitated, gathering her courage. "And what did you mean about your grandfather being wrong about 'power'?"

Frank stared at her. "It has to do with visions. Most whites don't believe in—"

"I don't know what I believe in right now."

"After that bad kill in 1959, Grandfather began fasting for a vision. He kept the ear by him as a focus. Some link to The Ones Who Come, so that his vision would help him understand them." Frank's expression hardened. "Fight them."

"And?"

"He dreamed . . . a great darkness. And strange stars in that darkness, though he could never say what made them strange. He only knew when he woke that The Ones Who Come couldn't be touched by this world's medicine. They had nothing to do with this world, or its spirits."

The black overhead was suddenly much too close. Cassie shivered in her windbreaker.

"You still haven't told me what The Ones Who Come *are.* And I don't know what this epicenter's got to do with them. Or the mutilations."

She glanced down, away from the sky. "But I'll come take a look at it with you tomorrow."

"Thank you." Frank put the carryall in his truck, shoving it far under the passenger seat. "Development or no development, what happens on that land isn't going to stop. Someone in your family needs to understand that, before . . ."

She didn't ask before what. She just nodded and told Frank to call her in the morning. Today was June 19, one day from the solstice.

And her gut said no coyotes sang tonight in the hills outside Twenty Mile.

The buffalo was a cow. Or it had been. Now it was sexless meat in the short prairie grass, its uterus wound into a fleshy flower blossoming from its open mouth. A long slit in the side revealed an artfully arranged cornucopia of organs glistening with dark crystals.

Only the animal's eyes marred the effect. Glazed with agony and panic, they stared up at the stars in dumb accusation.

Then it wasn't a buffalo staring up anymore, but a Hereford's red-and-white mask.

Then it wasn't anything bovine at all.

Just female.

Frank had told her to meet him at ten, but Cassie had been up since four, drinking bitter black coffee from the lobby to keep herself from slipping back into sleep. And dreams.

The Crow's face as he walked out of the bunkhouse said she hadn't been the only one.

"Are you ready to go?" He looked less than ready himself. "The entrance is only a few miles out, but this may take awhile. Time seems to . . . change, down there. Especially when Their coming is this close."

She wondered down *where*, but kept her mouth shut. Frank did the same as he started his battered pickup. He'd insisted on hiding her VW in the barn nearby, just in case Phil got back before they did. No sense making him more suspicious than he was probably going to be anyhow.

Unlike most June mornings here, humidity was practically gluing her to the seat. The sky was hazy rather than clear blue, with a few clouds already massing over the hills.

Her ears strained for echoes of thunder as they drove off-road through the brush, past most of the ranch's outbuildings into a no-man's-land between living space and grazing land. Even during her teen summers, no one had come here often. Now it felt even emptier than the rest of Twenty Mile—aside from one corrugated-metal shed that looked decades old.

"Okay," said Frank, stopping the truck beside it. "We're here."

While she fumbled with her seat belt, he dug two flashlights out of his carryall and handed her one. "I checked the batteries myself last night, but I've got extras if we need them. Sing out if your light starts to fade. The dark down there isn't friendly."

*Down where, damn it?*

Her answer came when he wrestled open the shed's sliding door. There was nothing inside but a hole—a long, slanting hole with handholds of scrap pipe driven into the earth. Frank switched on his flashlight and stuck it through his belt before starting his descent.

"It's not really that far down. It just feels that way because of the angle."

*Lovely.* Cassie gritted her teeth and started down behind him, wishing she'd brought gloves. Who knew what biting, stinging, generally disgusting critters might have moved in? She'd already been warned that the dark wasn't friendly.

"Not like that," said Frank, when she finally asked. They were standing at the bottom of the handholds now, with a tunnel—underground riverbed, maybe?—still slanting ahead of them. "Nothing much lives down here. Or ever has."

She glanced at the smooth walls: no cobwebs, no burrows. The silent air smelled of nothing but earth and time. Though the ceiling was too low for them to walk quite upright, Frank scuttled along at a brisk pace. Cassie's back and shoulders soon began to ache, but she didn't care. It took her mind off the fight-or-flight alarms pinging all over her nervous system for no good reason.

None except the realization that they were headed back towards the main house—and the blue *X* on Frank's map.

The epicenter.

When a sickly glow appeared up ahead, a part of her wasn't

even surprised. Gripping her flashlight tighter, she waited in the dimness while Frank moved on, scouting a cavern ahead for something she wasn't sure she wanted to ask about.

Whatever it was, he didn't find it. "Come on in," he called back to her. "I was right—their time is very close, but we're safe for now."

Stifling serious doubts, Cassie stepped inside and felt her breath catch. The cavern's interior looked almost slick, as if it had melted once . . . and that glow emanated from the wall to her right. Or rather, from something sticking out of it: a rough, curved object which might have been stone except for the shadowy colors flowing under its surface.

Colors like nothing in nature.

"What is it?" she breathed, staring. "It looks like part of a meteorite, except . . ."

"So far as we know, it *is* a meteorite. Or at least something that fell from the stars. Nobody my father spoke to even had an ancestor who'd seen it fall. It's so far down, I can't begin to guess at when that was."

Frank hesitated. "Most of the time, it doesn't look like this. It just looks like a big rock buried in the earth."

Cassie barely heard him. Staring at the meteorite—or whatever it was—she'd started noticing other things about it. Like a subliminal humming that ran directly through her bones. And the way those shadows writhed beneath the surface, as though they were cast by something deeper in the rock. Something with many long fine extensions that coiled and twisted in the color currents, reaching up ever closer as though . . .

"Get away from there!"

An arctic shock ran through Cassie as Frank grabbed her shoulder, pulling her away from the wall. By the time she caught her breath, he'd dragged her outside into the tunnel.

"You almost touched it," he said in a tight whisper. "It . . . They . . . wanted you to. You can't go back in there."

*Like I'd try it again in this lifetime!*

She took a few deep breaths to keep herself from heading right back down that tunnel as fast as she could go—away from whatever she'd nearly met and far away from Twenty

Mile. Just thinking what her relatives had been living above all these years made her queasy. How could they have ignored it? Maybe they didn't know about the meteorite (if it *was* a meteorite), but they'd known about the mutilations. And the silent coyotes, and the weird storms, and the tremors that came before the thunder.

"Because it's good land," Frank said, before the question was half out of her mouth. "Rich grazing land, and it always has been."

He hesitated. "A great chief said once that Crow country was good country because the Great Spirit 'had put it in exactly the right place.' When our people first came here and found . . . *that*, too, they tried to understand it. To make it a helper like Grandfather Sun or the Morning Star, and gain its medicine."

He turned his flashlight's beam back on the floor of the cave. At first, all Cassie saw was a scattering of beads and bright stones. Offerings to something the first Crow had tried to worship.

Then Frank's light found the dull ivory curve of ribs.

"One or two young men tried to seek visions here. They came down when they felt this place's power most strongly . . . the worst possible time."

He switched off the light again, but not quickly enough. Its beam caught the dark glitter of crystals streaking the bones. A second cold shock galvanized Cassie's spine.

"I want to leave. Now."

Frank didn't argue. As they hurried back down the tunnel, though, he kept up a steady stream of talk—warnings, memories, scraps of legend. Verbal force-feeding, she guessed. His last chance to tell her about Twenty Mile, because he had no intention of staying there any longer.

He didn't want her staying, either. "Whatever Phil says, get away before sunset. Before the thunder. Get him away with you if he'll go . . . but don't let him slow you down. This storm's going to be a bad one."

\* \* \*

Her watch showed well after four when Cassie returned to the house, though she didn't feel as though she'd been gone more than an hour. Phil still wasn't back. Digging a novel and a candy bar out of her glove compartment, she settled on the porch to wait, trying not to notice the bruised color of the sky. Or the wind's wet-earth smell as it rattled the old roof.

By the time Phil's rental car finally pulled into the drive, it was nearly six o'clock.

Her cousin wasn't alone, either. A redhead in a white suit sat beside him, leaning closer than just business would excuse. As she swung long tan legs out of the passenger side, Phil hurried to help her.

Then he glanced toward the porch and scowled. "Your stuff's in the living room, Cass. Just give me a minute, will you?"

She gave him five to get his California developer out of earshot. Then she yanked the sticking screen door open, praying for the thunder to hold off a little longer.

Phil emerged from the kitchen with a beer while she was rolling up the last of three worn Navajo rugs. Her cousin hadn't bothered to bundle them for her. Nor had he wrapped up the half-dozen Tiwa pots waiting beside them, though it was easy enough to find old newspapers and a liquor box.

Then the first tremor came, right through the floor and stronger than any she remembered. Cassie almost dropped one of her pots.

Phil didn't seem to notice. "Find everything all right?"

"I think so." She hesitated. "Did Frank talk to you about . . . ?"

"Frank Yellowtail's a crazy old man. A troublemaker." The false twilight hid his expression, but Cassie could still hear it. "Has he been bothering you with that damn notebook?"

"No, he's been *showing* me his father's notes. And all the Polaroids, and . . . and that buffalo ear. The one with the crystallized blood, just like all the kills around here have."

Her stomach tensed with sick fear, but she made herself keep talking.

"Did he tell you how long it's been happening? Centuries. Always at this time of year, always the biggest animals available—buffalo, then cattle. There aren't cattle here anymore. You sold them off and now what do you think is going to happen?"

Phil took a long pull on his beer and shrugged.

"That's really what this is all about, isn't it Cass? I sold what's mine to sell. You and your folks didn't get the cut you wanted, so now you want to screw things up. Scare off development so I can't make *my* money."

Another tremor came. Traveling up through her legs as she knelt on the floor, it reminded her hindbrain of thin strong tendrils that twisted in currents of color.

Tendrils like cold stinging knives. Like scalpels.

*And God, oh God, They didn't even kill first before They did it. They just paralyzed the meat and went right on doing whatever They wanted, whatever They'd come here to do. . . .*

She hadn't remembered her whole dream after all. Not until just this minute.

Scrambling to her feet, she started packing the wrapped pots into the box she'd found.

"I don't want your money. I just want you and that developer out of here, before something happens. There's nothing else bigger around here now, can't you understand?"

"Yeah, I understand." Her cousin took another swallow of beer. "Either you're lying out your ass, or Frank's got you *buffaloed* with his mystic Indian shit."

Cassie just stared. She could remember a younger Phil telling her about kills he'd helped bury, about his dad never letting anyone call the vet. Phil had seen a lot of things. He was sucking down that beer like mother's milk, but it wasn't enough. Right now maybe even the development money wasn't enough. . . .

"Phil? Is she still here?"

The redhead's voice came from somewhere up the stairs—the bedroom stairs—to Cassie's left. One glance at her cousin told her she'd be wasting breath from here on out.

There were things even evidence couldn't compete with.

"She's just leaving," Phil called back. "Won't be a minute."

Draining his beer, he set the can on the floor and finally

helped Cassie pack the last of the pots. Then he opened the front door while she struggled with the carton. "I'll bring out those rugs for you," he said. "No sense making two trips."

It was the nicest *get off my property* she'd ever heard. Cassie made herself thank him as she hurried her pots outside. By the time she'd gotten them safely stowed, all three rugs were waiting on the porch.

And the front door was locked.

A third tremor—followed by thunder and lightning much closer than before—sent her running for her car with the rugs. Shivering, she locked all four doors, shoved her key in the ignition, and got the hell out of Dodge.

Twenty minutes later, the rain began in earnest—not gradually, but as though something had split open in the sky. What she could see of that sky between laboring wipers was dark purple and twilight gray, punctuated by lightning that made her consider heading for a barrow pit on purpose.

*When the earth speaks to the sky, and the sky answers.*

It was answering so loudly and so often, she barely heard her cell phone under the seat. Cursing, Cassie pulled over onto the shoulder as quickly as she dared, hoping nobody rear-ended her in the process. Visibility was rapidly approaching zero.

"Hello?"

"This isn't funny, Cass. Why'd you do it?"

"Do what?" She frowned. Phil sounded half drunk, half seriously scared. "I only took what was mine and got out. What's your problem?"

"Car won't start. Looks like somebody tore out the coil wire. Plus slashed all four tires, just in case"—his voice broke up as thunder growled overhead—"called out to the bunkhouse, but Frank's not there. His truck's gone, too."

Cassie's throat clenched.

"He told me he was leaving this afternoon," she shouted back over the storm. "Don't know where he was headed, but I'm guessing Bear Lodge."

Her cousin's response nearly melted the phone. Hanging up, she sat staring out at the weather.

Frank had stranded Phil and the developer. She knew that beyond question—and worse, she knew why. Whatever The Ones Who Come were, he was mortally afraid of them. Of what might happen if They found nothing at Twenty Mile. How much farther out would the mutilations range? For all she knew, Frank might have relatives nearby, on the reservation or in Bear Lodge itself.

But Phil was a relative, too. She didn't have many left.

Breathing deeply to steady her hands, she pulled her VW back onto the road, then into a cautious U-turn. The rain was coming down faster than her wipers could handle, but she switched to high beams and drove anyway. It was early yet. Barely sundown.

When the rain turned to shimmering, twisting sheets ahead of her, she gripped the wheel harder and tried not to notice. Tried not to imagine twining shadows where there could be no shadows. Tried not to see the wet highway ahead as a slick black mirror.

Then her cell phone rang again, sending her fishtailing across the road before she managed to pull over. "Damn it, Phil! Do you know what you almost made me do?"

"This isn't Phil, Cassie." Frank's voice was a static-haunted whisper. "Did you get away from Twenty Mile?"

A sick sense of unreality washed over her. "Yeah, but I've got to go back. Phil's stranded—something happened to his car." *Or someone.* "I don't know how bad the storm is at the house, but he sounded—"

"Stay away from there. Just turn your car around and keep driving . . . please." His voice was scarcely audible, faint and old and tortured. "Do you think I wanted to do it? I had no choice!"

There were no words for that kind of necessity. And the rain was turning stranger now: She could almost see a *ropiness* to it in the distance, a hint of form inside those twisting sheets. Not shadows anymore, but solid presence. Presences. Tall knots of wind-whipped shadow and color and energy . . .

"Are you all right?" crackled Frank's voice. "Answer me, girl! Answer me and get out of there!"

She barely managed the first part. The second was worse: slewing around on that wet black highway without losing control and without checking her mirrors. Or her back windows. Without looking anywhere but straight ahead into the rain.

Into the lightning answering the tormented earth and what came out of it.

Numbing her mind to a gray blank, she aimed her car down the road toward Sheridan and simply drove, not looking closely at anything at all. Not hearing the thunder. A dozen meaningless signs flashed by.

Then the little box she'd thrown on her passenger seat started shrilling again. When it wouldn't stop after a very long time, she turned it on with one hand and pressed it to her ear.

After a moment, she shut it off again.

Quickly rolling down one window, she dropped it out into the rain and kept driving.

# ALL THE WORLD'S
# A STAGE

## *Brian Keene*

Downtown had gone to hell. Crumbling Victorian architecture bore mute witness to the cancer spiraling through its veins. The small-town innocence that dwelled here a decade before had fled, hounded by demons of the new millennium. Modern-day plagues such as drugs, homelessness, and crime contributed to the decline.

When Jim had been a boy, downtown had always held a certain allure for him. Now it seemed sinister, cloying. He still ventured through its decadent streets, but never that far.

And never at night. Especially since the disappearances had started.

They'd begun the previous winter. The throngs of homeless that normally crowded the streets vanished. The shelters were empty, the alleyways silent. Disease was mentioned. A serial killer or predatory gang was considered. But as winter drew on and the subway grates became easier to clear, the matter was dropped. Secretly, the city council was glad to see them gone. The general consensus was that they had shoved off for warmer climates, or possibly a bigger city.

When the coming of spring thawed the gutters and banished the snow, the "problem" remained behind. Seven more locals had vanished. Among them was a teenage couple, a prominent real estate developer, and a five-year-old girl named Kaitlin Roberts. Spurred on by these disappearances, the police department, city council, and the media got serious.

The little girl had been the worst. She and her mother had been walking downtown in broad daylight. Tugging free of her mother's hand, she had dashed off down an alleyway, excitedly shouting that she "wanted to see Micky Mouse," according to a passerby.

Two minutes later, a chilling shriek had tumbled from the alley's maw. The girl's mother was found drooling against the cool and musty bricks.

The girl was gone.

Kaitlin Roberts became the focus of one of the most intense searches in the state's history, but to no avail. Her angelic face had been flashed on every news broadcast and milk carton for months. The mother was briefly considered a suspect, but the fact that she was not catatonic stymied that line of thinking. Finally, perplexed law-enforcement personnel admitted they had no clues to Kaitlin's whereabouts and the media found new stories to try and new suspects to convict.

Despite the troubling atmosphere, downtown still called to Jim. He could spend hours in its dirty and decrepit womb, aimlessly browsing the bookstores and secondhand shops. It was his retreat from the rest of the world. Among the buildings of another era, he could be alone in the crowd.

In his favorite used bookstore, Jim found some Angus Griswold paperbacks that he'd been wanting. With his newfound treasures tucked into his backpack, he stepped outside and basked in the dazzling rays of the early-summer sun. A rare sense of tranquility enveloped him as he crossed the street . . .

. . . and stopped dead in his tracks.

Before him stood the old Majestic movie theater. It had closed down in 1985, the year Jim graduated high school, and time had taken an inevitable hold on the place. A faded FOR SALE sign hung askew in the filthy ticket window. Water stained the brickwork, eroding the outer walls. In place of a marquee that listed the current feature, graffiti now boldly exclaimed that VINNIE SUCKS THE BIG ONE and LAKIESHA IS A HO— NSB RULES! in Day-Glo letters. Rotted paper billboards advertised that the Misfits were appearing five years ago at a nightclub that had also closed down. A more current one advertised a band called Feo Amante, and that their new disc was available in alternative shops everywhere.

Jim wiped away a thick coat of dust and grime from the lobby window, and peered into the building. Although the afternoon sun shone brightly, the interior of the theater was obsidian.

He was overcome with a wave of nostalgia. It had been years since he'd noticed the abandoned relic. Its decayed condition saddened him. A childhood memory dimmed by time now came rushing back with crisp clarity. He was ten years old and his parents had let him go to the movies for the first time without adult supervision. He and his two friends, Doug and Ken, had seen their first horror movies that night: a double bill consisting of *Phantasm* and *Friday the 13th*.

He remembered cringing in the seats down front, munching popcorn with real, greasy butter. On the screen, Jason the maniac had taken care of the surplus teenage population of Crystal Lake and the flying metal balls had done battle with a hero his own age. For three kids whose only movie attendance up to that point had been cartoons and *Herbie Goes to Monte Carlo*, it was a glorious and horrible affair.

They had reveled in it.

In eighty-four, the gargantuan cinema complex had been built across town and within the year, the Majestic had closed its doors, standing lonely and vacant ever since.

Jim remembered the gorgeous crystal chandelier that had hung from the ceiling, and the huge screen, which had actually been partially made of real silver. He wondered if they were still there, trapped within this dilapidated husk, or if they had long since succumbed to the vandals and crack fiends that prowled the neighborhood by night.

An unpleasant odor drifted out from the theater's murky shadows. A damp smell of decay, but there was something more sinister underneath. The flesh on Jim's arms prickled, even as the warm sun beat down on him. Unsettled, he decided that it was time to leave.

He cut through the narrow alley that ran alongside the Majestic. At the other end, a mailman passed by lugging his bag of deliveries. At the sound of Jim's shuffling feet, he raised his head and nodded. Jim returned the greeting with a wave and the mailman walked on, whistling tunelessly as he passed from sight.

As Jim approached the other end, a terrified cry ripped the afternoon apart. Jim dashed around the corner and stumbled over the discarded mailbag. Letters had spilled like entrails onto the pavement.

There was no sign of the man.

Jim glanced around frantically. The towering brick facades loomed over him, staring back grimly. A rear stairway led from the back street down into the theater's basement. Jim ran over to investigate, considering the possibility that the mailman had fallen down the stairs. He peered into the gloom, but saw nothing. Disturbed, he looked away.

Behind him, at the bottom of the stairway, came a scuffling sound.

The disappearances of the last six months flashed through his mind. He knew that he should call the police, but he was afraid to leave the spot and search for a pay phone. What if the mailman was being mugged down there, or *raped*?

His senses screamed at him to leave, but he ignored them and started cautiously down the stairs. Placing a trembling hand on the cold, rusty handrail, he picked his way through the litter of debris. The passage was cluttered with moldy newspapers and magazines, crumpled cigarette packs, broken beer bottles, discarded condoms, and empty crack vials.

The same stench from the front of the building assailed him at the bottom. It was different now, mixed with the garbage and dried urine, but still powerful. The door at the bottom was barred and it was clear that nobody lay hidden in the trash.

Jim glanced around again and spotted the mailman's hat slumped against the wall. He stooped over to retrieve it, noticing something odd as he did. The concrete in front of the door was swept clean of debris, as if the door had opened and then shut.

He shivered. The dank air had grown colder and his breath formed wisps of cloud in front of his face. The sunlight failed to penetrate the murky stairwell. Jim tugged at the wooden barricade on the door, feeling it give slightly. Bracing his feet, he pulled harder, gasping in surprise as the door swung outward with a squealing protest from the hinges.

The barricade was a fake.

The darkness that poured from the doorway was a tangible thing. The reek hit Jim with full force. The distant sounds of a struggle drifted to him from within the confines of the basement. He fumbled out his lighter and held it aloft, but the feeble glow only made the darkness worse. The ebony air clung to the flame, trying to extinguish it.

Jim paused, letting his eyes adjust. There were no sounds now and the silence was deafening.

When his eyes grew accustomed to the absence of light, Jim crept to the far end of the cellar. The thick carpet of dust that blanketed the concrete had been recently disturbed. It looked as if something heavy had been dragged across the floor. He followed the trail to another stairway, this one leading up to the first floor.

Climbing the skeletal stairs, a scenario suddenly danced crazily through his mind. A crazed, chainsaw-wielding lunatic that made the theater his lair, watched him from the oppressive shadows. . . .

He paused in midstep. More likely a group of crackheads waited at the top to assault him. Still, he proceeded upward, driven by a mixture of curiosity and fear. His stomach heaved from the adrenaline that flooded it.

An icy blast of stale air slapped him as he pushed open the door that led into the lobby. The room was frigid! His breath hung suspended in the gloom.

The tattered red carpet was covered with mildew. Jim noticed a black stain, darker than the rest. He knelt, examining the reddish-brown crust, then drew his hand away in panic.

He knew what the stain was.

Suddenly, the lights inside the concession stand erupted into life. The dazzling fluorescent glow cast maniacal shadows across the lobby walls. Jim tumbled backward in surprise, his hand skidding through the fresh blotch.

The showcase was a fury of activity, as if the matinee were about to start. The popcorn and soda machines whirled into motion with a deep, mechanical hum. From his crouch, Jim peered into the glass showcase in revulsion. Where once had been candy bars and licorice, the display now teemed with maggots. Their bloated bodies wriggled blindly over one another in a coiled mass. Roaches exploded with tiny, wet sounds inside the popcorn machine. The soda fountain sputtered with a loud belch. Jim cried out in disgust as blood, darker than any cola, began to spurt from the nozzle. Scarlet rivulets ran down the side of the showcase, pooling onto the floor.

He would have run then, if not for the very human and extremely terrified scream from beyond the double doors that led into the theater. Rather than sprinting for the exit, he dashed toward the doors, rapping his knuckles on the thick mahogany as he flung them open.

Down front, past the long rows of moldy velvet seats, the movie screen blazed with a blinding, silvery light. A vast whirlpool engulfed the screen. The vortex was no celluloid image sent from the cameras above. It was all too real. He could feel the air rush past him as it was sucked towards it.

As Jim watched, absolutely transfixed, beams of light sprang forth from its center. A deep and sonorous humming began to reverberate throughout the Majestic. His scream was swallowed by the white noise coming from the screen.

At the base of the portal, the mailman struggled helplessly as six horribly misshapen dwarves dragged him towards it. Each creature stood about four feel tall and was cloaked in a filthy brown robe, their faces hidden within the folds of deep hoods. Even in his state of shock, the dwarves triggered a forgotten memory buried deep within Jim's mind. He was sure he had seen them somewhere before.

Frozen, he could only watch as the dazed postal worker was flung into the kaleidoscope screen . . .

. . . and vanished. The dwarves followed.

With a groan, the overhead speakers popped. Hissing static followed, then turned into the familiar theme from an old horror movie. Rapid-fire piano keys pounded frantically in his head, accompanied by sinister strings.

A chainsaw roared to life behind him. He whirled as two figures stalked toward him from the lobby doors.

The first glared with soulless black pits from beneath his hockey mask and revved the chainsaw to a concussive level.

The second was a normal-appearing man. Normal except for the fact that he seemed to consist of various shades of black and white. Devoid of any color, the man seemed to have just stepped from an old movie screen. He looked familiar to Jim. His gray hair was swept back over his head, his mustache well trimmed. His eyes were like mirrors.

"Hello, Jim," he spoke, in a brittle, clipped accent. Jim couldn't place it, but he'd heard it before. Many times in fact.

"This isn't real," Jim insisted.

"Everything is real when it's concrete and steel," the genteel, colorless construct responded, and took another step closer. Jim took a tentative half-step to the left, and the dungaree-wearing killer thrust at him with the chainsaw and closed the gap.

"Oh shit, this isn't fucking real," Jim sobbed again.

"All things are real," the black-and-white man said calmly. "Elvis is alive. There is a Santa Claus. God is an astronaut. Make yourself comfortable, Jim. You are our guest."

"How do you know my name?" Jim shouted over the buzz of the saw.

"I've known you since the night you were conceived. I watched your mother and father fondling each other in the front row. No respect for the talent on the screen."

The chainsaw was idling now and its wielder moved closer. Jim could smell the oil from its engine and feel the hot exhaust on his face.

"It's your choice, young master Jim," the actor said. "You can either pass through the gateway, or you can aid my friend here in making yet another dreadful sequel."

He performed a cursory bow and gestured toward the screen.

Jim backed up and the silver light engulfed him. It poured itself around his body like water, yet he could not feel it. Now he could see nothing but the light. The sounds of the chainsaw and the man's laughter faded.

There was a sensation of falling, but he couldn't be sure until he crashed into the ground with a bone-jarring thud. His breath escaped him in a violent whoosh. Gagging, he grasped at the surface, letting the soil flow through his fingers. The dirt was red. Afraid to look up, Jim closed his eyes again.

"Another fan," purred a sultry, feminine voice from behind him.

Jim opened his eyes and looked up into the face of a goddess. She stood before him, the ageless and eternal embodiment of sex. From blue-collar stiff to a U.S. president, all had adored her, an image that had only sharpened with time.

Despite his terror, Jim felt a stirring in his groin. She wore a flowing white gown that billowed seductively upward, blown by an unfelt gust of wind.

"Welcome," she whispered, reaching out for his hand.

He took it, and it was warm. She helped him to his feet.

The bottom fell out of Jim's world.

Spread out from one vast horizon to the other were endless rows of movie seating. The rust-colored landscape held no other features or structures. Just row upon endless row of seats. The missing residents of the town occupied the row directly in front of him. Slack-jawed and emaciated, their glassy eyes stared unblinking at the starless night sky.

She guided him to a seat between the mailman and Kaitlin Roberts. The postal worker still whimpered. The girl said nothing.

Gently, almost lovingly, the actress eased him into the chair. Her touch was a caress. The cushion squirmed beneath him. The armrests twisted, coiling around his wrists.

"I hope that you'll be comfortable," said Marilyn.

"I reckon he is," a masculine voice said from behind her. It held an unmistakable Western drawl.

His father's hero stepped before him, tipping his cowboy hat. Behind the Duke stood Bogart and Garbo. James Dean and John Belushi were partying to their left, while a bemused Phil Hartman and the Creature from the Black Lagoon observed. A fully animated duck in a sailor outfit quietly discussed Nietzsche with a black-helmeted villain from a popular series of space operas. A vibrant and colorful Bruce Lee sparred with a grainy black-and-white cowboy whose name Jim couldn't remember. The vampire from *Nosferatu* put the moves on Bette Davis, while Stan Laurel leaned sullenly on the hood of a Volkswagen that had been beloved by millions of children in the seventies.

More and more figures appeared, until they were swarming through the aisles. Every icon that had ever graced a movie screen, whether real or fictional, stood assembled before the captive audience.

"We get so lonely here," moaned a supermodel who had died in eighty-one of an overdose. A silent film star nodded in agreement.

The celluloid specters began to chant, voices rising into the void.

*"Watch us!"*

*"Love us!"*

*"WORSHIP US!"*

The endless sky peeled away, and images began to flicker across it.

The final curtain had risen. The show had begun.

# WHAT GOD HATH WROUGHT

## *Randy D. Ashburn*

". . . so, Cinderella and the handsome prince . . ." George Bauer paused to watch his son scramble upright in bed, his chubby pink face bobbing excitedly atop his Bugs Bunny pajamas.

"And they all live happy every after!" Timmy squealed.

George stopped himself from correcting the boy. A three-year-old's exuberance more than made up for a few grammatical slips—although his own father would never have buckled to such a flimsy excuse. Besides, the boy deserved a break or two after the way his mother had been treating him since . . .

A blond curl strayed into Timmy's eyes and George brushed it away, allowing his fingers to linger a bit longer than was absolutely necessary. "Good night, Timothy."

Timmy's small hand clutched at George's. "Daddy not go?"

George tried his best to look stern. "Big boys aren't afraid to sleep alone, son."

Timmy's eyes flashed green fire, and in that instant George couldn't believe how much he looked like his own father. "Timfy not scared sleep. Daddy not go. No *deevorss*."

The stone that had dangled over George's head for months finally dropped into his stomach. No matter how hard you try to spare them—assuming Margaritte *had* tried to spare Timmy—children always know.

"If Daddy go, make Timfy mad."

So *much* like his grandfather. "I'm not going anywhere, son.

That's why we came up here to the woods, so Daddy could fix things with Mommy."

"Good." Timmy scrunched onto his side and snuggled up to his pillow. "Ni-ni, Daddy."

George flipped off the light. Now, if only matters could be settled so easily with his wife.

*What God hath wrought, let no man tear asunder.* His father's voice erupted from somewhere deep inside and flowed over him like lava—thick and scalding. Dad would roll over in his grave if he knew any of his twelve kids was even *thinking* about divorce. Not that divorce court was part of the "happily ever after" life George had meticulously planned for himself, either.

He shook his head and silently blew Timmy a kiss in the darkness before pulling the door closed.

Margaritte leaned against the far wall of the living room, staring. "Finally get the little monster to sleep?"

George blinked away a flash of anger. Did she have any idea how casually cruel she could be?

She lurched away from the wall, her stagger making the ice in her glass jingle like the bells on a jester's cap. He didn't need to smell her breath to know what else was in the glass, ruining any hopes of fixing things tonight.

George went to the window and looked longingly at the calm, snow-silenced world outside. Rolling mounds of white stretched away into the blue darkness towards the deserted, tree-covered hills. The little frozen lake in front of their cottage was as smooth and gleaming as a mirror.

"Are you even listening to me?" Her lower lip had completely disappeared into her mouth—a sure sign that Hurricane Margaritte was about to blow through his life again.

He sat down and shoved the *USA Today* in front of his face like a shield.

"Oh, I see," Margaritte said. "Plenty of time for precious 'Timothy,' but not one minute to spare for your wife, huh?"

U.C. had won again. They looked like they could make it all the way to the Final Four. George smiled. A little March Madness might be exactly what he needed.

Margaritte opened her mouth wide and exhaled in a way that was probably meant to be a laugh. Her jaw hung slack for a long time, ripping a dark and ugly hole in a face that had once been attractive, refusing to snap shut until she tossed in more gin. The ice cubes jingled again, and George had a sudden vision of a crazy jester throwing gasoline into a furnace.

"You know—" she leaned forward as she sipped, making the pentagram pendant sway menacingly between her breasts—"if you keep all your emotions bottled up inside you like this, you're gonna explode someday."

*You keep enough bottles inside you for the both of us, dear.* "I have no idea what you're talking about, dear."

She slammed the empty glass onto the coffee table. "That's because you never talk to me at all anymore!" Every word was jabbed at him like a knife, and George watched with mild fascination as her face grew slightly redder with each sharp syllable.

Margaritte yanked up the glass and headed for the liquor cabinet. "A person can't just pretend he's got no feelings at all, dammit. You've gotta find a *con*structive outlet, or it's bound to find some *de*structive way to express itself."

George peeked above the paper and wondered if she realized that her clichéd little speech had gurgled along in perfect rhythm to the refilling of her glass. Yes, Hurricane Margaritte was definitely battering the shoreline.

George carefully straightened the edges of the paper before folding it in two. "Life's full of problems, dear. Like Father used to say, 'You just have to plow through.'"

Jagged laughter tumbled from her mouth, as lean and vicious as a pack of rabid Dobermans. "You never 'plow through' anything, George. You just dig a hole and wait for somebody to throw dirt on top of you!"

He closed his eyes.

"You can't just 'plow through' the fact that our marriage is dying . . ."

He ground his teeth together so hard that his ears rang.

". . . or that our daughter is already dead!"

George jumped to his feet as if she'd slapped him.

The shadow of Christie's smile swept across his mind. So beautiful. So much like her mother's; even in the way it could vanish in an angry instant. He could still hear the echoes of her wails through the long, sleepless nights—still hear the music of her cooing once he'd finally soothed the smile back onto her tiny face. He also still heard Margaritte droning on about how he'd taken too long, how she needed her rest for an important day of shopping, and how generally incompetent George was as he shuffled wearily back to bed.

He walked to the window and ran his fingertips along the frosted glass, letting the cold soak into his body, hoping it would somehow pull him back from that sweltering day last summer when Christie's cries had finally stopped for good.

". . . you listening to me?" Margaritte's hand was on his shoulder, so hot that it almost seemed to burn. He wondered for an instant what it would sound like if he slowly bent back each finger until it touched her wrist. Would there be a grinding crunch like dry twigs? Maybe nothing more than a series of short, sharp snaps like icicles brushed away from an overhang.

"Come on, Mr. 'Plow-Through,' tell me how you don't give a damn that Christie's six feet under the ground."

George could feel the slightest hint of a twitch at the corner of his mouth. Margaritte must have noticed it, too, because there was an ugly glimmer in her eyes. "Christina's in a better place now—"

"Crap!" she yelled.

"*You* would say that, what with your damned crystals and Ouija boards. What's the matter, is an idea like heaven too mundane for you?"

In the few seconds it took to realize he'd said that out loud, Margaritte just gaped silently. Then the bellowing began. He couldn't quite make out the exact words she hurled at him, but their meaning was clear enough from the fierce and primitive rhythm.

George fell into his own mind like a child down a well. The roar of her voice whorled somewhere very far away. He was vaguely aware of feeble blows on his back after he'd turned away, but her fists were nothing more than limp, gin-soaked dishrags.

It didn't matter. Nothing mattered now that there was no hope of turning back. He was a tiny spot of absolute calm in the center of raging chaos—the eye of Hurricane Margaritte.

Timmy's screams broke the spell.

George dashed towards his son and cradled his fragile little body to him. He glanced pleadingly at Margaritte, but her eyes held only contempt for them both.

Timmy pointed toward the door. "Want it stop!"

George's gaze followed his son's finger. He blinked twice, refusing to believe that all he could see through the big bay window was a swirling wall of white. The shaking glass boomed like a timpani, its roar so much like what had raged inside his head that at first he couldn't understand how Timmy could possibly hear it, too.

Margaritte's odd and angry stare only dared him to try to help her. Instead, he slipped Timmy under the massive butcher's block table just as a portrait of a nursing Madonna fell off the living room wall, impaling the Christ Child on the fireplace poker.

George hunched over Timmy while Margaritte cocked against the sink, one hand wrapped protectively around a crystal-clear bottle. She didn't even flinch when a dish slid out of the cabinet and shattered on the floor beside her. George pulled the boy farther beneath him, feeling shards of broken glass bounce harmlessly off his thick sweater. For hour-long seconds things shook from the walls, pelting his ears with staccato gunfire.

"It'll be okay," he mumbled over and over in a quaking voice. Margaritte shook her head and took a long, slow swallow of gin.

And then there was silence.

Margaritte was already at the bay window, so George went to the door and stepped outside. The cold tingled along his body, chilling his nerves into something similar to calm.

Stars glittered in the clear sky, and a fat moon tinged the wintry world with silver fire. But for ten feet around the cottage there was not a single flake of snow. Frozen blades of grass bent away from him, bowed by the wind, as if the cottage had been at the very center of the storm.

The eye of the hurricane.

George stood in the middle of a perfectly flat field that bubbled at the horizon with waves of heat. The summer sun was a bloated red fist, hanging so close to the ground that it seared the reedy grass grayish-brown.

A giant of a man laid on a narrow, black couch in front of him, his huge feet dangling over the edge. His stern jaw, the proper, melancholy frown, even the half-veiled disappointment lurking just behind the jade eyes were all achingly familiar.

"Dad?" George's voice was as thin as watered milk.

His father stood, slowly stretching higher and higher until his broad shoulders filled the sky. "Hotter than Hell today, hey, Georgie?"

Thick, sticky sweat seeped from George's pores like molasses.

Dad glanced at the sun, but did not squint. "Deadly little bastard, ain't it?"

George pushed an urge to apologize back down his lint-dry throat.

"What's the matter, boy, kitty snatch your tongue?"

George tried to answer, but when he opened his mouth, scalding sweat leaked in, choking off his words. He coughed and sputtered, struggling to draw a breath.

"Certainly made a mess for yourself this time, haven't you?" Dad's massive head shook unhurriedly from side to side. "No happy ending in the cards for you, huh, Georgie?"

George's eyes darted back and forth, scavenging for a way to answer without opening his mouth again. The bitter sweat clung to his tongue—not molasses like he'd thought at all, but oil. Cooking oil.

"Stings, doesn't it, boy? A slow burn is like that. A thousand tiny prickles from head to toe. Tiny but sharp, hey, Georgie? Sharper than serpents' teeth, I'd say."

George turned away from the brutal sun, and choked back a

scream. His feet were gone. Instead, boiling pinkish-gray puddles oozed across the blistered grass. He clutched his hands to
his chest, trying in vain to keep the melting fingers that hung
nearly to his knees from dripping into the goo. He clamped his
eyelids together, feeling the molten flesh of his forehead flow
over, sealing them shut.

"For the love of God, boy, open your eyes!" His father's
voice boomed like a whirlwind. "This isn't a fairy tale, Georgie.
Stop avoiding the Truth."

He would have screamed that he had no idea what the
"Truth" was, but his mouth had melted away. He was nothing
but a bubbling smear at his father's feet—no more than a
child's ice cream cone abandoned to an August afternoon.

"Poor Georgie. Your inside never did match your outside,
did it?" His father's voice became almost tender. "You know
the Truth, son, I know you do. And you know what you have
to do about it, too. *Just open your eyes!*"

Somehow, George's fingers were there again, solid as knife
blades. He had no idea where they'd come from, but he was
certain his father did. Dads always know.

His newfound talons dug at the muck that was once his
face. When he finally ripped the eyelids apart he was whole
again—yet he still couldn't see. Tarry darkness clung to him,
close and stifling like the inside of an oven.

Ghostly light flitted ahead. George burrowed his fists into
his eyes, and slowly, the dancing forms became solid shapes.
Familiar shapes. He was back home, in the second-floor guest
room. Only, it wasn't a guest room yet. It was still Christie's
room.

"Suffer not a witch to live." He spun towards a voice that
sounded so much like Margaritte's—but it was too high, too
soft.

Christie lay in her crib, giggling as she banged together
brightly colored blocks. George reached for her, but stopped
when he saw that the fluorescent orange, green, and yellow
letters at his baby's feet spelled a word.

MURDER.

\*     \*     \*

George shot upright in bed, his body drenched in sweat.

When he saw that he was still in the cottage, he drew a deep breath and swung his feet onto the floor. It was firm and solid, the way reality should be. Soothing shivers raced up his legs as he curled his toes in the deep carpet.

Already, the details of the nightmare were vanishing. Like smoke, the harder he tried to grab it, the more it dissolved, leaving behind only stench and stains.

George slipped into his dark gray robe, cinched it tight around his waist, and marched to the window. There was snow outside, just as there should be. But within the eerily perfect circle around the cottage there was only bare, frozen ground.

It wasn't *all* a dream, then. George swallowed hard. The fairy-tale existence he'd longed for came from Disney, not the Brothers Grimm.

With no hope of getting back to sleep, George wandered out of the bedroom. Margaritte sat at the kitchen table, concentrating on a game of solitaire in the dim glow of a candle. One hand dragged cards from the deck while the other loitered beside the reflection of the jittery little flame in a half-filled glass.

"Can't sleep either?" he asked.

Margaritte jumped at the sound of his voice, and for just an instant, it seemed that she didn't realize who he was. In that sliver of a second, she'd almost looked like the woman he'd married all those years ago—soft, unguarded, capable of anything—even love. The candlelight flickered once, twice, on the face of his bride. But with the third glimmer, recognition fell over her face like a veil, and along with it came the heavy toll of years and alcohol.

"What's the matter?" The sharp snap of a card thrown onto the table accented the even sharper tone of her voice. "Too late past my bedtime?"

*Too late for both of us, I'm afraid.* "Sorry. I didn't come out here to start a fight."

She raised an eyebrow and snorted mirthlessly.

George watched as she carefully laid out one card after another. There was something buzzing at the back of his head, something from that crazy dream. Maybe it'd been some kind of sign. Maybe Dad just wanted him to open his eyes to what was going on so that he could save the marriage.

"Margaritte?"

She looked up at him, and the weight of her gaze forced his eyes down to the table. He could feel words that he'd locked away for a very long time scratching at the back of his throat. Maybe there *was* still a hope for them. Maybe . . .

Then his eyes fell on the tiny portrait of a sickle-swinging skeleton staring up from the butcher-block table, and hope became as elusive as his nightmare—just stench and stains.

"Tarot cards?"

She kept dealing.

"I thought you said you gave away all that witch crap after . . . you know . . . Christina and all."

The buzzing at the back of his head swelled into a human voice. An all-too-familiar voice. *No happy ending in the cards for you, huh, Georgie?*

Margaritte frowned around a mouthful of gin.

George took a deep breath and tried to make his voice as firm and unquestionable as his father's had always been. "You know how I feel about that sort of thing in the house. What if Timothy saw?"

"What makes you think he hasn't?" Margarite huddled the tarot cards together and slipped them into an ornate little box. "He *is* my son, too, you know. I have just as much right to teach him my traditions as you have to drag him off to mass every Sunday so he can pretend to eat the flesh and blood of your god!"

"Don't blaspheme."

Margaritte thrust her middle finger into the air and stormed out of the kitchen.

Timmy knew about his mother's . . . "religion"? In the flickering gloom, the world grew smaller, rushing in on him until there was no room left to breathe. His face felt hot and bloated. Tiny beads of sweat crawled out from under his receding hairline like ants.

*Hotter than Hell today, hey, Georgie?*

Reality tilted to let the nightmare slide in. His hand shot out against the wall to keep his balance. Numb fingers stumbled onto a switch and desperately flipped it on.

Margaritte hissed like a scalded cat. "Turn off that god-damned light!"

George stared at her, unable to speak.

*What's the matter, boy, kitty snatch your tongue?*

He squeezed his eyelids together as tight as he could, trying to stop the twitching under his left eye. But it was no use. An angry little beetle was burrowing into his cheekbone. Or digging its way out.

He felt Margaritte's humid breath on his face—a sticky, stinging cloud of booze. "Can't you hear either?"

*For the love of God, boy, open your eyes!*

Her face was just inches from his own, spasms of rage twisting it like melted wax. The embers that had long smoldered in her dark eyes were fully ablaze. Her hand slowly rose, the fingers curled into a claw. What little reason remained in George told him that she was reaching for the light switch, but for the second time that night he thought that she looked capable of anything—anything at all.

*Stop avoiding the Truth.*

"Is it light-time yet?" Timmy's drowsy voice was barely a whisper as he stood in the doorway, rubbing his eyes.

"Sorry, son. Let's get you back to bed, and Mommy and Daddy will try to keep it—"

"Timfy watch TV?"

Margaritte stalked towards the child. "You know what a little hellion you are when you don't get enough sleep."

"Want TV."

"I said, get your ass back in bed. *Now!*"

George glanced at his feet, ashamed to look his son in the eye and admit that he couldn't protect him. It wasn't supposed to be like this.

*This isn't a fairy tale, Georgie.*

Of course not. In fairy tales the *step*mother was always the wicked witch.

". . . not sleepy!"

"You'll do what I say or else, you little . . ."

George's head throbbed from the noises inside and out, as Margaritte heaped one insult after another onto their little boy, each word bristling with rusty fishhooks. No one was safe from her razor tongue; even little Christie . . .

A thought flashed across his mind—a thought so horrible that he refused to let it linger even a second, unable to look at all its grotesque implications.

*Just open your eyes!*

Timmy was screaming back at her now, both of them crimson with rage. George turned to the fireplace, studying the gray stones mortared neatly one on top of the other. Was it insane to envy stones? Calm. Cool. Orderly. Nothing like the chaos swirling behind him.

Why, if his mother had ever done this, his father would have . . . well, he didn't want to think about what his father would have done. But he should've expected this from Margaritte. After all, the witches he'd read about *ate* little children, didn't they?

*You know the Truth, son.*

What else would witches do to children? Or even babies? Say, a baby she was left all alone with on a sweltering summer day? A day so hot that the house had probably felt like an oven. The kind of oven a witch lures babies into. Babies whose crying takes her away from sleep and shopping. A baby she never wanted in the first place. A baby whose colicky wails could be silenced so easily.

*You know the Truth, son, I know you do. And you know what you have to do about it, too.*

Timmy's jaw was firm, and his green eyes blazed as furiously as his grandfather's ever had. "Mommy mean. Make Timfy mad!"

Margaritte took one step towards him, her fist clenched high above her head.

*MURDER.*

"Timfy punish."

"Timothy Matthew Bauer, if you try it, I swear I'll—"

If she finished that sentence, George never heard it. It was drowned out by the sharp slap of flesh against flesh. The universe collapsed into nothing but the sight of his little boy's face twisting into a grimace, his small hand fluttering towards his cheek like a mangled butterfly, brushing the angry red mark tattooed there by Margaritte's fist.

*Suffer not a witch to live.*

George didn't remember crossing the room. He didn't remember his fingers squeezing tight about the chilly metal of the fireplace poker. But he was keenly aware of the exact instant that the sharp end of the poker pierced Margaritte's left eye with a soft, wet pop. She jerked once, blood blossoming from the wound, flowing into her mouth, choking off a scream. Her hands clutched at the cold, gray rod, but George twisted deeper. The muscles of his forearms knotted painfully until he finally heard the whispered scrape of metal against the back of her skull. She went suddenly stiff, then limp—extinguished like a candle.

"Daddy?" Timmy looked up at him, the red bruise blanching white.

*Certainly have made a mess for yourself this time, haven't you?*

George swept Timmy up in his bloody hands and rushed out of the cottage. The snow nipped at his bare feet with a thousand tiny fangs. He ran. He stopped. He ran the other way, only to stop again after slamming into the hard reality that there was no escape.

George Bauer sat down in the snow, and didn't move again for a very long time.

"Cold, Daddy. Cold."

George wrapped his robe around the boy and held him close, rocking back and forth. Blood was smeared across Timmy's perfect three-year-old face. Blood from his father's hands.

Timmy shivered and hunched down farther into the dark gray robe. "Please, Daddy, stay Timfy. Now Mommy sleep, no yell."

George's hands tingled painfully. They'd be as numb as his feet soon, though.

"Sleep?" George nuzzled his chin against the tiny blond

head. Snow blew into George's face, sticking to the tears and . . . other fluids splattered there. "Sleep."

Timmy forced a smile through chattering teeth. "Mommy told me how Chrissy sleep."

Nothing could fight its way past the fist that'd been shoved down George's throat.

"Chrissy sleep." Timmy snuggled closer. "Her bad. Make Mommy yell. Chrissy punish."

George leaned against the snow that had drifted halfway up his back. "Did . . . did Mommy tell you she . . . made Christina go to sleep?"

"Mommy no make Chrissy sleep!" The boy grinned. "Timfy make Chrissy sleep. Chrissy make Mommy yell. Timfy punish Chrissy."

George blinked twice.

"Mommy bad. Daddy punish Mommy."

The wind howled insanely.

"Now Daddy no go. No *deevorss*. Daddy stay family."

"Th-there is no family anymore," was the best George could manage to squeeze between his dry lips.

"No worry, Daddy. Mommy teached Timfy lots of things when Daddy at work. Know how to make wind blow hard, know sleep, know wake up, too!"

Even over the wind, George heard the cottage door creak open, but he refused to turn around. He couldn't bear to see a metal rod sprouting from the hole where Margaritte's eye used to be.

Instead, he ran—just like he'd always run before.

"No, Daddy!"

*Poor Georgie. Your inside never did match your outside, did it?*

He turned towards his son, trying hard not to see the figure that lurched behind the boy, its chaotic jerking looking for all the world like a marionette whose strings were held by a child.

"Daddy no go!"

"Timothy . . ."

"No *deevorss*!"

"Timmy . . ."

"Daddy bad. Daddy sleep, too."

Snow crunched beneath him as George sank slowly to his knees. His vision melted away until all he could see through the blinding whiteness was the smiling face of his beautiful little boy.

"Us all stay together for always, just like book, Daddy." Timmy's fading voice squealed merrily from a million miles away. "And they all live happy every after!"

# WE'RE *ALL* BOZOS ON *THIS* BUS!

## *Peter Crowther*

*um sie kein Ort, noch weniger eine Zeit.*
(Around them no space, and even less time.)
—Goethe, *Faust* Part II, Scene of the Mothers

Frank shuffled around in his seat and looked out the window.

Gray buildings were passing by in a thin haze of drizzle, town houses scrunched up like sentries, standing gable to gable in blocks of eight or ten, interspersed with seemingly endless gray streets stretching off at ninety degrees into some indeterminate distance, the sidewalks filled with people trudging along, leaning forward, coat collars pulled up, and umbrellas held aloft to protect them from the rain. The color of the afternoon was wonderful . . . a kind of purple glow to everything, with the storm clouds gathering over to the east, far out at sea but heading landward as fast as they could.

The promise of a real storm held dominion over everything.

Frank had no idea where they were—only that it was somewhere between his homeground in The Bronx and the relatively sleepy Connecticut coastal town of Bridgeport, where Frank's new foster parents were taking him for what they had said would be a kind of early Thanksgiving, but it was really a late summer break. Whether it turned out to be much of a break—which Frank doubted having seen the condition of the bus and his new parents, who hardly seemed like partygoers—it was certainly late. The fact was that tomorrow would be November . . . only seven weeks or so until Christmas and here they were, traveling without any sense of urgency, puttering along a series of small roads through the equally small towns that littered the Connecticut hinterland instead of hammering up I-95. It was like driving through one of those calendars they'd had in the orphanage, pictures of smiley-faced people, cute kids, and nice pets, all painted by some guy called Rock-something-or-other—like the PI on the old shows they seemed to repeat on TV all the damned time.

But Frank knew that life wasn't like that.

Frank was looking forward to Christmas this year. It would be his first for many years spent away from the orphanage and he felt he'd earned it. After all, he had worked very hard to achieve it. Just thinking about how hard made Frank's cheeks hot. He'd been sure he'd blown it when the couple came around to the orphanage, Frank standing in line with Sammy Leifrickson and wall-eyed Richard Thomas—*never trust a guy with two first names instead of a first and a last*, Frank's real father had told him in one of the all-too-rare sessions of communication that did not entail physical combat—while the geeks from upstate checked them over.

Frank had had the place pretty much under control since he'd been moved there, after his father had jacknifed the Dodge and his rusty old trailer right across the central reservation coming out of Philly where he and his mother had been for a weekend with Uncle Ray and Aunt Jean. Jean was Frank's mother's sister, but when the authorities told her about the accident, Jean suddenly discovered she just didn't have the room in her trailer.

But Frank didn't care.

Frank didn't care diddly.

It had been clean in the orphanage and he had had decent food at regular times . . . something he never had back at home. And best of all, he had been able to get his own way.

It hadn't always been easy, at least not at first, but the other kids soon came around to Frank's way of thinking—once he'd taken the time to explain all the consequences in detail. Bunch of losers, every one of them. Oh, there had been a couple who fancied themselves as hardmen but they weren't, not when Frank took them to one side and told them the facts of life the way his father had told *him* . . . in a soft voice that was more like a hiss, with his hand clamped around their nuts and a big wide grin on his face. The message was simple—either they were with him, or they were against him; part of the solution or part of the problem. That was the way Frank's daddy had told Frank, too, breathing liquor smells all over him and resting his hand just a little too long on Frank's knee . . . when he'd done squeezing Frank's balls until Frank figured they were about to burst.

There were just the four of them in the age range the geeks had requested and Frank had been worried that Little Jack Mendala, a Macauley Culkin lookalike—the way Culkin had looked in the *Home Alone* movies, before Hollywood took him by *his* nuts and squeezed all the childhood out of him early—with an engaging lisp and big curly eyelashes, would walk away with the prize. But then Litle Jack took a tumble down the main stairs, hit pretty near every step on the way down, messed his face up good, and cracked a couple of ribs. Little Jack spent the next couple of days down at the hospital, had to miss the visit from the prospective "parents." Frank's cheesy smiles had won the day, though, even though he had felt that the geeks—particularly Mister Geek—had seen the shadows behind those smiles . . . seen them for what they really were: a damned determined last-ditch attempt to get the hell out of the orphanage and start living it up in comfort.

*Call me Joe, Frank,* Mister Geek had said in a voice that sounded like the preachers' on Channel 11. *I'm betting we could be real good friends* . . . and Mrs. Geek (*This here's Elaine*, the man had said with a big smile) had done that thing with her head that made it pull back so's her chin ran all the way down into the folds of her neck, lifting her shoulders as she beamed a big dumbass smile at Frank like he was sitting in a baby carriage dribbling onto his blankets. *He's so sweet,* Elaine the Geek had trilled and then, with what looked like a knowing wink to Frank, *I think he's the one, honey,* to which Joe Geek had nodded enthusiastically. *I think he is too,* he'd said, smiling. *I think he is, too.*

Frank looked up and noticed that the man in one of the seats in front of him—he presumed it was a man—sitting against the aisle, had put a handkerchief on his head for some reason; maybe it was because of the sun, Frank thought glancing back at the window and the dismally overcast day outside. Then again, maybe it wasn't. Maybe the guy had a piece of shrapnel lodged in his brain and the cloth helped to shield him from local radio broadcasts.

He looked back at the pointed white corner of material hanging down over the back of the seat in front of his foster mother, watching it bob and waft to the motion of the bus. Frank frowned and shuffled the pile of comic books on his lap in an attempt to pull himself up to get a better view. He reached forward and gently took hold of the headrest but something touched his left hand—something cold and wet—and he heard a growl. He pulled his hands away quickly and dropped back into his seat.

A dog. The assholes in front of him had a dog in their seats, for crissakes. He tried to remember if he'd seen the occupants of those seats get onto the bus but he couldn't. The truth was that Frank couldn't remember any of the other passengers when they'd got on the bus in New Rochelle. He had been far too busy choosing comic books from the swirling rack in the bus depot to pay attention to the queue of people waiting for the bus and even busier looking through the books once he was on and in his seat.

Thinking back, Frank suddenly recalled his new foster parents exchanging greetings with a lot of the other passengers. He hadn't seen these exchanges as such, being immersed in the swirling comic book racks, but he had heard them, even though they were quiet. Maybe a lot of these same people went to Bridgeport every year at this time, which was how his new foster parents seemed to know them all. And maybe it was just that they were so very friendly they were just passing the time of day with fellow travelers.

But he didn't recall anyone having an animal with them.

It seemed funny because Frank didn't think they allowed animals on the bus. He sniffed at the slimy patch on his hand and screwed up his nose. It smelled like . . . like shit—and it *looked* like shit, too. Brown and almost rusty. Maybe it wasn't

the dog's nose he'd touched after all. Maybe it was— He
imagined a smiley-faced dog in the seat in front, sitting with
its backside up in the air and a spacey expression on its face,
like the guy with the melting head on the Robert Crumb poster
his father had kept in the TV room . . . the dog smiling as this
hand—*Frank's* hand, ladies and gentlemen!—came over the
seat back and inserted a finger up its ass.

Frank pulled a face and rubbed his hand against his trousers
until he thought it was dry.

He looked over at his foster mother, Elaine Geek—it wasn't
really Geek; their name was Finderswitch—sitting next to him
in the aisle seat. She was asleep. Her mouth had dropped open
slightly and there was a thin drool of saliva perched in the corner, threatening to drop onto her coat. The saliva looked red,
though it was probably just from her lipstick.

Another growl from the seat in front made him turn back,
just as he had thought he had seen his foster mother watching
him through slit eyes (and even worse, just as he had been
about to stick his tongue out at her or give her a resounding
bird with his right and), and he stared in fascination as the
back of the seat resting against his knees seemed to belly out-
wards.

There was no way it was a dog. Probably just the man's
wife—the wife of the man with the handkerchief on his head—
turning in her sleep. Snoring. That must be what the growl
was. And the wet against his hand must have been the
woman's mouth. And it must be her bad teeth that had caused
the smell.

Jesus, this was a bus full of losers, like geriatrics going out
to the coast for the day

*Hey, what's that big pool of water out there, huh?*

*That's the fucking Atlantic, Methuselah . . . and this here's a
two-fingered jab in the old eye sockets, ya old fart*

to maybe buy an ice cream and a hot dog, like they did in
the old days, back when they were alive.

Frank settled back in his seat and frowned, staring at the
flap of white material. Come to think of it, that was a funny-
looking handkerchief. It seemed bigger than the checkered one

in his own pocket, and it had moon shapes and planet shapes
on its corner. Maybe it had them on all the corners—Frank
couldn't see from where he was sitting.

He yawned and looked out the window again.

More gray streets. There must have been a circus in town,
whatever the town was, because he saw a clown walking along
the pavement alongside him. His seat seemed to have lowered
itself because his face now barely reached the rim of the window where the upholstery stopped. And the clown must be on
a bicycle of some kind because he was keeping perfect pace
with the bus, like he was guiding it or something. The clown
turned to face him and smiled. Frank smiled back. Then the
clown seemed to stop dead, slapped the bus side like he was
letting it through a customs barrier . . . and the view cleared to
just more gray streets. And more rain.

Frank's new foster father said that it always seemed to rain
when they went to Bridgeport. Every year the same, rain rain
rain. But at least Frank had his comic books. He didn't mind
the rain.

He looked down at the one on top—*Preacher.* The cover
showed the intrepid Irish vampire, Cassidy, holding up a glass
of blood like he was toasting Frank right off the page. Great
stuff. Frank didn't think his new foster parents knew what
kind of stuff they put into the comic books these days—they
probably thought it was just costumed superhero shtick—and
he made sure he kept his pile to himself.

Frank's foster mother moaned in her sleep and he turned to
watch her face. Whatever she was saying sounded like gibber-
ish. Maybe she was talking in her own language. Frank's foster
father had said she was from someplace called Vladivostok—
Frank had never heard of it. Sounded more like some weird
kind of superglue than a town.

She was frowning, the little saddle of skin at the bridge of
her nose all puckered up like a soft knuckle. But Frank was
sure she was watching him, her eyes glinting between the
lashes, a thin shaft of white. White? Shouldn't there be a pupil
or something showing? Frank leaned forward so that his face
was almost touching hers and blew softly. She did not re-

spond. As he reached up slowly with his hand and gently touched his foster mother's right eyelid

*and this here's a two-fingered jab in the old eye sockets, ya old fart*

it flipped up and showed only an expanse of whiteness.

Someone coughed behind him and Frank realized that his face was now actually over the gap between his own headrest and that of Mrs. Geek, exposed to the man sitting behind his foster mother and next to his foster father, Joe Geek . . . Joe sitting in the window seat behind Frank. But when he glanced through the gap, Frank saw that the man, a very small man it seemed, was also asleep. Sound asleep, like Frank's foster mother . . . which was why her pupils had rolled up out of sight. She must be dreaming.

Frank watched the man. He was so asleep that even the fly on his face didn't seem to be bothering him at all. As Frank watched, the man's mouth slipped slightly open, his chin already resting on the collar of his jacket, and the fly slowly crawled towards the opening.

Frank considered saying something to the man

*hey, asshole, there's a fly in your mouth*

or at least making a noise, like a cough or something. Like the noise that the man had made, must have made in his sleep. But, instead, he just stared as the fly ambled across the man's upper lip, turned southwards and then stopped, as though checking out the terrain below. Maybe the man could feel the fly, because the corner of his mouth was moving, turning into a snarl. Frank was about to move his head back when he saw that the mouth was not moving because of the man but rather because of something inside it trying to get out.

A fine pink tip, like a worm's tail, snaked out of the corner of the man's mouth, twirled around as though it was testing the breeze—*smelling* the breeze, Frank thought with more than a frisson of discomfort—and then it pulled back out of sight. His tongue, Frank realized. It was the man's tongue, coming out to moisten the area of his lip that the fly had irritated. And, sure enough, the fly took to the air in a circular

motion until it achieved a height above the seats and then
moved off towards the back of the bus. Frank watched it go.

As the fly disappeared from sight, Frank's vision dropped
down and he saw that two heads were craning above the seats,
one about three or four rows back on his side and the other another two rows farther back on the other side of the bus. The
head on his side was that of an old man, and it was topped by
a thick and wiry thatch of white hair shaped into a cone. The
man must have been twiddling his hair, Frank thought. There
was no way that a human head could be that conical shape,
like a knight's helmet. The man seemed to be having trouble
seeing, his eyes all white as though they had rolled back in
their sockets. This man must be dreaming, too.

Frank knew somebody at the orphanage who could do that,
roll his eyes up out of sight—Frank didn't like to see it. It
made the boy look like the crazy woman in the old William
Castle movie they'd shown on the Sci-Fi Channel, the one with
Vincent Price. He didn't like it at all here, either. When the
man's head dropped from sight, Frank was relieved.

The other head was that of a young man with a long scar
down the side of his face. The matron in the orphanage always
told them not to stare at people with any kind of disfigurement
but Frank just couldn't resist staring at this. And the man
wasn't looking at Frank—instead he seemed to be sniffing the
air, like he could smell something cooking—so it didn't matter
anyway.

Frank pulled his face back against his own headrest but kept
enough of it in the gap between the two seats so that he could
continue to watch. Bus journeys got so boring.

The scar ran the full length of the man's face, from his tem-
ple down to his chin, pulling across just below the mouth. It
looked as though it had been done recently. Maybe the man
had been in a fight. Frank curled his knees up on his seat and
felt some of his comic books slide onto the floor. He reached
out and grabbed the pile—he had been bought a lot of comic
books, he suddenly realized . . . far more than he'd expected:
For some reason, that bothered him suddenly, though he
couldn't figure out why—and pulled them across to his left

side where he jammed them between his hip and the armrest's metal support. Then he shuffled forward and down, arching his back, until he was kneeling on the floor. Amazingly, his foster mother never moved, even though Frank knocked her knee a couple of times.

On the floor of the bus it was a different world.

The light was more muted—but then it was very gloomy outside—and the constant *shush*ing of the bus's tires on the wet road had disappeared. But there was another sound down here.

Placing his face against the plush upholstery he had been sitting on minutes earlier, Frank rummaged around beneath his seat with his right hand in an attempt to retrieve his comic books. He thought they would have just piled up in the footwell but nothing was ever that simple: The books had slid—with the bus's motion, he supposed—completely out of sight. And the gap was far too narrow for him to be able easily to get his head right down to see.

He felt around without success.

And as he felt around, he heard whispering and a shuffling sound, like clothes moving.

And then, something took hold of his hand.

It was another hand, cold and small—Frank could tell it was small by the way the hand held only the ends of his fingers—and once it had taken hold of him, the hand didn't move.

Frank instinctively tried to pull back but the hand's grip was tight—very tight for a child's hand, for what else could it be? It had to be a young child that had got down on the floor while its parents were probably asleep and was busy now adventuring and exploring. Frank glanced down at the dusty floor and the flattened cigarette ends and grimaced. Somebody wasn't going to be too pleased when they saw the state of the child after crawling around in that.

For that matter, where *were* the parents? Only Frank's father and the man with the pointed tongue were sitting in those seats and that meant that the child—possibly even a baby or a toddler, though wouldn't it be making more noise than it was doing if that were the case?—had crawled from its own seat and under his foster father's. But why wasn't Joe Geek saying something? It must be a very careful toddler to be able to negotiate itself along without disturbing anybody.

Frank shuffled around and managed to get his head down next to his foster mother's legs. He saw that her stockings were torn and her leg—he couldn't tell which one because they seemed to be entwined somehow—looked as though it had been grazed on something.

Forcing his attention away from her legs, Frank laid his left shoulder on the bus's floor and stared into the gloom beneath the seats.

At first, he couldn't make out much of anything, just a vague lumpy shape that seemed to fill the entire recess. He blinked a couple of times and then waited, the way he always waited when he was alone in his bed trying to adjust his eyes to the darkness, when the orphanage lights had been turned off for the night, watching it take shape and substance all around him.

Then he heard a hiss.

Shit! It *was* a dog. But the fucking thing wasn't in the seats in front of him—at least it wasn't anymore: Now it had moved behind him. It must have gone along the aisle when he wasn't watching. But a dog with *hands*? Tiny hands that held on to Frank's own hands? Didn't make sense.

Now the shape was beginning to take more definition.

Its eyes came first. Sharp, glinting eyes that seemed to glow. Then a bulbous face, all jowly and flabby, with folds of skin hanging on either side of the mouth—at least, Frank presumed that slit was a mouth: Actually, it more resembled a hole in the ground, dug into the soil, and fashioned into a kind of semi-roundness. He didn't like the look of it. Then, when the hole got bigger and wider, he decided he wanted to put some space between it and him.

Unfortunately, at the very same instant, the dog-thing decided it wanted to reduce the gap and it shuffled towards him. Frank tried to ignore the fact that the thing didn't seem to have any legs

*so how's it getting along?*

*heh . . . just fine*

on the side of its body (which, incidentally, Frank couldn't see: Only the head was visible) and he tried to push himself back out from beneath the lip of the seat. But his right shoulder had got caught on one of the staples that held the upholstery to the seat frame, and the more he struggled, the tighter caught he became.

He shrugged his body upwards to free his left arm from beneath his body and nudged Mrs. Geek's legs hard. The legs shook for a moment and then there was a loud thud in the aisle. Frank moved his head in a little to see what it was, ignoring the snuffling-panting coming from the dog-thing which, he was pleased to note, didn't seem to be making much progress.

Just for a second, Frank could make out a face looking at him from the aisle, frowning at him between Mrs. Geek's ankles and the metal upright supports of her seat, and then it was gone . . . kind of pulled up into the air. He thought the face was a woman's face but he couldn't be sure. And what the hell was a woman doing lying out there in the aisle?

Maybe she was looking for her dog—Frank wanted to call out to her . . .

*hey, lady, look no further—the mutt's right here*

to call out to anybody who would listen to him, to get him free from the damned seat. And then he was free, like his prayers had been answered.

Frank pulled and pushed himself back out of the foot well and onto his knees. Then he managed to stand up, shuffling his legs around, lifting first one foot and then the other, not giving the dog-thing enough time or space to grab hold (he didn't like to think about what it might grab hold with . . . seeing as how he hadn't been able to see any legs, let alone any tiny child-like hands: But then it was mighty dark under there).

When he glanced at his foster mother, Frank saw that she had turned her head away from him. Hey, she had turned her head so far it was almost facing backwards on her neck, nestled in the high frilly collar of her blouse. Frank frowned. There was a cigarette butt in her hair.

The bus gave a jerking movement and Frank pitched to the

side against the window. They were going over wooden slats—
maybe a bridge. He looked outside and saw that it was now
getting pretty dark. Shouldn't they be turning on the bus lights
round about now? He grabbed hold of the window side of the
seat in front to steady himself and leaned closer to the window.

All he could see were bushes and a couple of wooden supports every few seconds. He leaned closer to the window and
looked up: The supports were holding some kind of wooden
roof—it must be a covered bridge. Boy, you didn't see too
many of those in New Rochelle.

As they passed between the final supports, the bus took a
sharp turn to the right, joggling all the way. Jesus Christ, what
kind of a road *was* this? Tree branches were clawing at the
windows, raking wooden knuckles across the glass. And now
it looked really dark out there . . . now that they seemed to be
actually moving between the trees. Frank tried to squint down
to see the road but all he could see was grass, thick grass, and
a few rocks here and there. Boy, this guy had taken the mother
and father of all wrong turns.

"No, he hasn't, Frank," a deep voice whispered behind him.

When Frank turned around, the man was there . . . the little
man sitting behind Frank's new foster mother. He was perched
on his seat with his arms stretched out and his hands—dirty
hands, with what looked like soil stuffed under the fingernails—holding on to Mrs. Geek's seat. Frank couldn't help but
notice that the man didn't have any legs: He was just perched
there on the seat like the little fat egg-shaped character in the
old nursery rhyme.

"We're here now, Frank," Joe Geek said.

Frank turned around to the window and looked out into
what seemed to be a small glade surrounded by trees. In the
fading light, he could make out a series of tall stones—like the
ones that the fat guy in the *Asterisk* books carried around all
the time—set out in a kind of circle. And in the middle of the
circle was a large stone slab laid flat on a whole bunch of
smaller stones.

"Where's here?" Frank asked.

There was a loud snort from behind him and when he turned

around, he saw that his foster mother was sitting up in her seat, her shoulders going up and down. Jesus, the old crone was laughing—what the hell was she laughing at, for crissakes? Must be something over on the other side of the bus, because her head was still turned that way—it was turned at a funny angle too . . . must be kind of uncomfortable. Maybe she'd slept wrong or something, got a crick in her neck. Frank wanted to reach out and take the cigarette butt from her hair but it looked kind of funny up there, so he decided to leave it and let someone else point it out. Might give some of the other old farts something to chuckle about.

Though, truth to tell, they sounded like they'd already found something funny. Laughter rang out from all corners of the bus . . . some of it belly laughter and some of it chuckles, some of it suppressed laughter, like the kind Frank used to do when he farted in the little church back at the orphanage. Frank was a great farter—he could do it pretty much any time he wanted, just like some kids could do that swallowing air trick that made them burp to order.

"The end of the road," the legless man said from the seat behind, and somebody clapped their hands a couple of times.

When Frank looked around at him, he saw that the man was now holding a knife and fork . . . and he'd jammed a napkin into his shirt collar—one just like the handkerchief that the guy in front had been wearing on his head . . . all moons and stars and that kind of shit. The man jiggled his head side to side and rubbed his knife and fork together, like he was sharpening them.

"Okay folks," a loud voice boomed from the front of the bus. "Time to get off and chow down."

More laughter.

Frank craned his head in time to see the bus driver walking down the aisle, carrying a big bunch of chains. He was wearing dark glasses . . . dark glasses for crissakes, in *this* light!

At his side, Mrs. Geek had lifted her head right off her neck and was busy turning it around so that it faced Frank. A long sticky thing—that surely was too long for a tongue—appeared from somewhere out on the aisle and wrapped itself around the cigarette butt in Frank's foster mother's hair, and then disappeared. Her eyes rolled up in time to see the thing grab the butt and she burst into more hysterics.

Frank backed against the side of the bus, dislodging his comic books and scattering them on the floor. When he looked down he saw a long bandaged torso—like a cross between a worm and one of those butterfly pupae things he'd seen on the *National Geographic* channel one time—shake itself clear of the books. Boy, it sure did have a big mouth, Frank thought. Sharp-looking teeth, too. And it was going straight for his foot.

A thin, high-pitched whine had started from somewhere nearby . . . and Frank had a good idea it was him.

The man in the seat in front of Frank got to his feet and, without turning around, arched his back and flipped his arms up to rest on the seat back right next to Frank's face. Without even realizing he was doing it, Frank lifted the corner of the handkerchief and saw a gaping hole just below the man's hairline. The hole made a retching sound and a thin stream of viscous brown goo ran out onto the seat.

"Welcome to our Thanksgiving," Mrs. Geek said as the bus driver wrapped the chains around Frank's neck, like a wonderful metal necklace. Everyone started laughing but Frank didn't see anything particularly funny.

Mrs. Geek took hold of Frank's crotch and twisted his balls around in their sac, feeling them pushing themselves together and chuckling.

But Frank wasn't taking much notice. The pain in his balls wasn't anywhere near as bad as the pain in his foot.

He opened his mouth wide and threw back his head to scream . . . and the many-eyed thing hanging from the ceiling squirted something into his mouth from its underbelly . . . something that tasted hot and sweet.

"He *is* the one!" Mrs. Geek was saying. She had unzipped Frank's trousers. She sounded as though she were almost crying.

Frank let his head roll forward, swallowing some of the gunk in his mouth while he made to spit the rest out but there was nothing much there to spit. He felt it rolling down his throat, warming everything on the way down. He felt a rising giddiness and, opening his eyes, started to laugh. The thing on the bus roof scurried across towards the front and dropped out of sight.

A tall man in the aisle behind Mrs. Geek was stretching himself, and a pair of wide leathery black wings unfurled from his back. " Oh," the man groaned, "that feels good."

Frank shook his head, the gunk warming his stomach and sending out waves of pure pleasure the length of his body. Hell, he couldn't care about anything and he laughed to show it. "Hey, neat!" he said, pointing to the winged man, his voice sounding strangely thick and drunken.

Others were standing up, some of them craning to get a look at what was happening to Frank and others just pulling off the clothes they had been wearing and slipping into robe things, most of them black or deep blue, and covered in the moons and stars. Looked like most of them needed a good wash . . . some of the dirt even seemed to have congealed into scales.

"I think I'd like to try him out before we eat," Mrs. Geek was saying, her voice soft and almost whisperlike. Somehow, somebody had slipped a tall black hat onto her head, a tall black hat covered in moons and stars and stuff like the hand-kerchief and the legless man's napkin, and dented towards the point, making it lean outward drunkenly.

And boy, where did all those warts on her face come from . . . ? Sprouting what looked like tufts of crabgrass.

Frank was finding it difficult shuffling down on the floor between the seats—particularly with all the chains around his neck and the thing that seemed to have replaced one of his feet . . . which, incidentally, seemed to have gone completely numb (he could already feel a gnawing sensation on the shin of that same leg, and moving upwards)—but he did the best that he could and, anyway, he seemed to be getting a lot of help.

Somebody shouted—somebody with a deep voice that clipped all the words—"Geh hi ou on stone!" *What a bozo*, Frank thought as Mrs. Geek lowered herself towards him.

"We're *all* bozos on *this* bus," she whispered into his ear. Then she started to move, slowly at first.

Frank hoped this wouldn't take long. He was getting hungry. And . . . he needed to go clean himself up. His backside felt a little on the warm-and-wet side. But as Mrs. Geek speeded up, the mess in his pants didn't seem quite so important. Thankfully, the laughter and the applause drowned out his own fervent and repeated approval and he fell into some kind of sleep.

A little later, refreshed by the open air and the knives and the hypnotic sound of chanting, Frank woke up.

He felt very cold, as though the wind were blowing right into his stomach . . . blowing across his insides like they'd been laid out on the stone—but that was ridiculous, of course. He tried to lift a hand to cover himself but his hands were tied somehow. The stone was hard beneath him.

Candles were burning everywhere.

All the passengers on the bus were facing away from him, singing some kind of song. A lot of them had on those wing-harnesses—Frank still thought those were neat, particularly as you just could not see the straps, no matter which angle you looked from—and most of them wore pointed hats. Craning his head, Frank could see that a lot of the trees in the direction that the passengers were facing seemed to have been pushed aside somehow . . . like a bulldozer or something had driven through. Maybe the land was marked for redevelopment . . . though he wondered what they would do with the stones if that happened.

As the song grew still louder, Frank heard a lot of noise—wood snapping, leaves rustling, branches falling to the woodland floor. Sounded like a bulldozer was coming back, though he couldn't hear an engine.

Pretty soon, he knew, the party—all the singing, and the dancing, and the eating (Frank guessed there'd be a lot of eating)—would begin proper. He could hardly wait. Boy, was he ever hungry.

# THE WHIRLING MAN

## *David Niall Wilson*

The little man spun, whirling forward and back, trapped in the center of the rubber band between Mason's fingers. The two little handles could be pulled farther apart—tightening the twist, speeding the motion. Just as the molded plastic features would come into focus, materializing from a red blur, Mason's wrist would flex and the dance began again.

His apartment dripped with a thick coat of suggestive shadow. The small shaft of moonlight slicing beneath his drawn shade pooled in the contours of a discarded food wrapper. Down the hall the soft glow of a single lamp shone from the crack beneath the bathroom door.

On the wall, the slightest shiver of shadow reflected from the whirling man, its efforts to gain recognition competing with the plastic man's chances of escape in a battle of futility.

Mason's mind was a million miles away. Another time, another life, rooms with sunlight and garbage that made its home in cans, not strewn across the horizontal surfaces like a rotting carpet. A world with sound and color, voices and faces whose names he knew from more than the evening news or a stolen magazine.

The words wouldn't let him go. Jesse's face haunted each corner of his mind and prevented him from escape. Her lips moved—were always moving—but her voices were myriad, blending and warping to those of others and back.

"It's not you," she whispered, "it's me."

Mason yanked violently on the rubber bands, spinning the whirly man into a frenzy.

"Your brother needed the money for grad school, son," she explained patiently, in his father's stolen voice, eyes dead and not really watching him at all. "Maybe next semester we can get you in . . . but he does so well. . . . Bud down at the garage is looking for someone. . . ."

The room spun, the little man danced, and Mason could feel the paper tearing, again, and again could see the words *art* and *school* splitting down the center. The two halves floated beside Jesse's haunted half-smile, held in mirror sets of Mason's own hands and torn, multiplying and tearing again until his mind rained confetti and he jerked the whirly man into another helpless jig.

In the shadows to his left, the one ordered space in his personal chaos, were the notebooks and the sketch pads that chronicled his life. Each was different—either the size or the color, the binding or the paper. They were lined up like a demented, too-thin regiment—one notebook for each sketch pad. Words and form. Life.

Mason's mind flickered into the present and he glanced down at the pad sprawled in his lap. He could just make out the carefully etched text. Uniform. What had his father said so often?

"Each thing has a form. Each form has a perfect state. Each time you re-create the form, you redefine the thing."

His father had been full of shit, but the words still haunted Mason. He couldn't form a letter, or a complete word, without painstakingly comparing them to those that had come before. The words were his life, and he couldn't bear the thought that as he wrote them, he was re-creating himself. He didn't want to re-create the insanity, only to explore it, and record it. Exactly as he lived it. Exactly as it happened.

The notebooks he remembered best were those filled with pain.

"We build a world of walls that surrounds us," he'd written. "They keep us happy, safe, and oblivious. Pain ignores the walls and rearranges life to suit its own ends. Nothing is ever as it seems."

Jesse was the latest notebook. Deep purple in color, bound in steel coils that spiraled out to sharp ends. Mason had filled every line with her, the magic, the heat—each scent and sound. Each moment. His fingers had stroked those spiral bindings and the coils had clenched his heart with each caress. The metal was smooth and cool, like her skin. Like the lying surface of her eyes, rippling with a love and compassion that faded—like a screen of smoke—to ice and boredom.

In the end, that is what Mason had symbolized, her boredom. Jesse bounced from man to man, occasionally to another woman, time and again. Nothing captivated her. She found someone with real passion, with a vision that drove them, and she latched on, leeched the "high," and moved on when the thrill faded.

Mason had been a three-month binge on the thrill scale. She had loved it when he drew her—preened as he posed her to paint, laughed and blushed at his showing of the work, more of her revealed to the world in those lines and angles and colors than even a nude walk on the beach could have shown—all in his art. All from his passion and gift—curse—of insight.

If only he'd stopped while she was still smiling. If only the art didn't mean more to him than the rest of life combined. If only he hadn't seen through her.

The painting stood in the corner, draped with dark cotton and coated in dust. He'd had offers for it—solid offers—but he could no more sell the painting than forget the expression of shock and betrayal that had washed across Jesse's face when he'd unveiled it.

The image was as clear in his mind as the first moment he'd lived it. Jesse was a tall woman, slender and sharp angled. Where some women had soft curves formed of circles and smooth skin, Jesse had classic, sculptured beauty so sharp it could cut. That is how he had painted her, in the end. Line upon line forming angles and honed edges, eyes bright like diamonds. Tubes extended from her heart, thousands of snaking, tangled tubes, whirling toward the edges of the canvas in a spiral and at the end of each, a face. A person known, or yet to be known.

There were tiny colored droplets beaded along the lengths of the tube, sliding through the centers and back toward her heart, but never would that imperfect vessel fill. There was a drain at its base.

Jesse's head was flung back, those diamond-chip eyes beseeching—someone, something—above. Her hand, long, slender fingers curled back, as if to stroke the base of her breast, or to unbutton an unseen blouse, held the plug to that drain, a self-assured, self-induced lack of fulfillment echoing through the chambers of her heart.

At the lower corner of the painting, Mason himself hung suspended from a deep, forest-green tube.

There were twists in the tube. Twin, winding clots in the artery attempting to drain his soul, held thus by wooden handles. Each handle was held in a hand, and those hands Mason was intimately familiar with. Each line, each hair, vein, and knuckle, had been copied with the same, exacting precision as the words in his notebooks—as each letter mirrored the last. Mason had wanted her to see them, the same hands that had teased her hair and cupped her breasts, crawled hungrily over her flesh—those same hands were what had saved him.

The painted image of Mason was a blur. Whirling up and down, backward and forward. The tube was caught mid-twist, trapped in the moment of his painting the image at the point where nothing could flow between the ends of it. Cutting her off.

That painting was the one he'd saved for last—the end of the exhibit. There had been others at the showing, others who appeared in the painting. Tall, lean Lydia with her metal sculptures and metal-piercing jewelry and cold, gun-metal eyes. Lydia, who'd done Jesse in cold steel.

Robert, the poet, whose career had nose-dived after Jesse had twisted his gift for angst and despair into a sappy string of words defining unrequited passion. Only the devastation she'd left in her wake had saved Robert. Robert's tube was pale yellow, his features drawn and taut.

There were others, some who had sprung to life only in
Mason's mind's eye—potential. Still more hovered, like Patrick.
Patrick was a concert violinist. His hair was feathered back like
something from an Armani commercial, and his style matched
it. He watched Jesse constantly. Mason could see the man undressing her with his serpent eyes, tongue lashing the corners of
a too-dry, too-thin smile.

Patrick wasn't undressing her to linger over what Jesse's
body might offer. He was undressing her to rebuild her in the
image of his perfect fashion accessory, and more and more
Jesse's glance had begun to shift to the rings, and the gold
chains, the expensive suits, where others wore Levi's. More
and more she had looked elsewhere when Mason talked, her
enthusiasm slipping away.

The painting had a home for Patrick, too, in the intricate
framework that surrounded Jesse's form. His tube was blue—
blue blood—blue for the pain he caused as he tried to draw on
Mason's green and Robert's yellow to encase Jesse's heart and
display it on his shelf. He could not. She was his failure—his
perfect prize denied, and he would never match here with any
other. Fashion was his passion, what was that song?

The words faded again and Mason drew the handles in his
hand apart once more, sending the small figure dancing.

He glanced down the hall. The bar stood against the wall
outside his kitchen. There were colored bottles lined across the
top. Mason didn't buy his drinks for their taste, or out of habit.
He had a rainbow of liqueurs, whiskeys, mixes, and gin. He
could see none of the colors in the dark, but he knew them.
Each stood in its place. He had arranged them the day after
that last show. The colors matched those in the painting. The
bottles were full, stoppered and safe, and Jesse would not be
dropping by to drain them. Not anymore.

She'd stood in front of that painting for what had seemed an
eternity. Mason had pulled aside the covering and stood back
to watch.

The others had crowded around to see, but as they caught
full sight of the piece, and of Jesse's face, they'd given her
space, backing to a safe distance. Not too far. Everyone

wanted to see. Those who found themselves in the frame had glanced at Mason, astonished. Some miracle allowed them all that long moment without the taint of anger. The anger had come later.

Jesse had stood, and stared, and then she'd just been gone. One quick spin, like the whirling man, only she'd jumped off her rubber band at half-twist and launched herself at the door, scattering those who'd crowded too close, and who flowed into the gap she'd left without even glancing at her back.

Mason caught one kaleidoscopic flash of light from Jesse's eyes as she spun. Colors whirled in those depths, captured colors, and for just a moment he could see the tubes, see the flowing creativity, the heat and the joy, the pain and the maniacal laughter. A hot pulse of— something—flowed between them in that instant. Green and snaking. Mason's wrists had flexed and the world spun away. He'd staggered, nearly falling, and when he snapped his eyelids open once again, Jesse was just gone.

Mason had left Gwen and "her boys" to close the show. He'd covered the painting, ignoring the cries to leave it—and the offers to take it—ignoring everything but the words and the images and the pain. The muscles of his heart whirled inward, spinning tight and releasing, sending him stumbling into the night, the canvas in a death-grip clutch against his chest.

Now the painting was just another shadow in a dark landscape, shrouded and cataloged. Mason had put the image in the front of the purple sketchbook in black and white, carefully recreating each line—the colored droplets chrome-bright in their stark lack of pigmentation. This time there had been no room for distraction. Jesse's voice haunted him, and his father's voice haunted him through Jesse's image. The words and pictures he had so carefully locked away in the notebooks leaked at the edges, threatening to spill over and infect those he was recording. The letters fought him, *g* warping to *q* and back—the *l*'s crossing themselves into *t*'s.

Still, in the end, Mason had finished the sketches, and the

words. The Jesse he'd first met. The Jesse he'd manufactured in his mind. The Jesse from late-night drunken stories of her childhood. Nude, alive, sleeping. Every aspect that had joined them, one to the other. Every angle that crossed had been penciled in and recorded. The pages were bound in the spiral metal loop that so signified Mason's life.

The whirling man spun and suddenly, it was too much. Too fine a mirror of his own soul. Mason violently flung the toy against the wall. Still spinning, it crashed loudly against the windowsill and clattered to the floor. For a long moment, that sound echoed unchallenged, then, with a tired squeak, Mason rolled forward, closing the notebook carefully and leaning to place it on the shelf beside his chair.

There were no lights burning, but Mason knew the well-worn track between chair and bed too well to trip. Oblivion beckoned. Beneath the window, the whirling man lay in a tangled, twisted heap of plastic limbs across the remnant of weeks of fast-food wrappers and soft drink cans. Maybe months. The days had been blurring for so long it hardly mattered.

He knew he'd have to call out eventually to find out if he was poor yet. He'd made a lot of money on that final show, more money than he'd ever expected to see in his life, but he knew it wouldn't last forever. Some things had to be faced— time was one.

He passed the doorway to his studio and paused. As he scuffed to a halt, dust rose from the polished, wooden boards of the floor to nearly choke him. Too long. He couldn't remember the last time he'd felt he could paint. In the center of that room his easel stood, blank canvas facing the window beyond, so light that never shone through too-dark shades would illuminate its surface and guide him from synapse to shadow, angles and deep shades of gray. Everything was gray since Jesse had stormed out of the show, despite the array of colored tubes that haunted his mind.

In the hall stood a small table—more a desk—that held his phone and had once held his mail—when he still checked to see if he had any. Momentarily, his mind hung on this. How long would the postman continue to pile mail in a box before it was all carted away and returned to sender? How much mail might be waiting for him outside his door?

To the left of the phone, where the mail had once lain in careful piles, was a wooden case. This case had been specially ordered, made to Mason's specifications. The wood wasn't important, nor was the carefully tooled latch, though it had cost more than it was worth. Mason lifted the lid and peered inside.

Lined from one side to the other, separated by thin slivers of wood, were the straws. Green, blue, red, and yellow, every color of the rainbow and then some. Each was carefully categorized by color, circumference, and length. Each had come into the house with a meal, sometimes four drinks with one burger, or a pizza with five sodas.

It had taken a long time to find the colors, to learn which restaurant served what with their drinks. Each straw had been cleaned and stored, and as the patterns had emerged, Mason had woven them carefully, making certain he had equal numbers. Tubes. He couldn't get them out of his mind.

With a soft click he let the lid close and turned slowly toward his room. No time. Too sleepy to put them together carefully, and he didn't want to turn on a light. Without the light, the colors blended and leaked. Like the words in the notebooks, reforming and blending, changing what he knew to be the past and confusing what he knew to be reality.

With a quick lurch, he stumbled into his room and turned to sit on the edge of his bed. He was facing the window, and the shadows played light and dark games on his ceiling. Spinning. Neon lights below flashed, strobing against the white backdrop of his ceiling, shadows from the power lines outside the window dancing. Whirling.

The little plastic man whirled before his mind's eye, trapped, spinning, not releasing its energy down the rubber bands, but unable to reach out. Unable to use that energy itself. Trapped.

Jesse had trapped him. Bound and whirling, he sat and stared into the night, guts clenched tighter than any rubber band and head pounding in time with his pulse. He couldn't paint. He'd kept her from stealing that from him. That had been the essence of his painting, of *her* painting. That was the essence of the whirling man. She had gone away unfulfilled, but she had left him stagnant, filled to overflowing with images and pain and unable to draw the least bit of inspiration from any of it. He'd kept her from stealing it, but what good was that if he couldn't release it? Who had won, in the end?

Lying back across his rumpled bed, Mason clutched the sheets close to his chest, not bothering to undress. Even as his head met the stack of sweat-stained pillows, he was drifting away. He had been up far too long, too many hours of nothing but going over and over and over the words and the images, staring at the tiny plastic man whirling his life away in effigy. The straws and the bottles, and always that painting, hunched in the corner, watching him with eyes that didn't exist, and never closed.

The walls melted to darkness, then unfolded like heavy velvet curtains. Mason sat up, though some inner sense of balance and propriety told him he had not. The room had elongated, the ceiling had dropped lower, and the window was an endless row of slats, striping his world in black and neon-strobed yellow from the streetlights beyond.

Shadows flickered beyond the door to his room, as well, but they were ill-defined. He couldn't tell if someone were there, or if something flapped in an impossible breeze. There should have been no light to cast the shadows, and yet they danced.

As if in counterpoint to the impossible motion, a murmur of voices slipped in and out, around and about the bed, confusing his senses. Mason thought he recognized some of them, though it was hard to tell. They were too low and indistinct to make out, and each confused the other. Each slid over the walls and blended with the shadows, and with a gasp, Mason saw that each shadow had taken on a hue of its own, dim at first, like a halo around the perimeter of darkness, then brighter.

Yellow. Pale yellow, snaking and thrashing and held tight by some unseen pressure at its base. Red, bright and running, loud and breathy—so bright that the sound almost worked its way free into words. Almost. There was blue, and silver, violet and beige. An insane rainbow to shame sixty-four color crayons with its complexity. Whirling.

The bed shifted, and Mason tried to roll to one side. His limbs were too heavy, veins running with lead, and his eyes were stuck open, held as if with superglue beneath each lid. He tried to lean back, but the bed folded neatly in the center, mattress re-creating itself in the form of a chair with rests for his arm and a rounded pillow at the nape of his neck to hold him stiff and upright.

He should have been able to stand. His feet brushed the floor, but when he tried to lean forward, needle-sharp bindings bit into his throat and shoulders, knees and thighs, and he shrunk back with a small cry. He felt tickling trickles along his skin. Blood? Insects? Fingernails?

A sudden flash of memory blinded him, and Jesse was there, long, crimson nails caressing the underside of his chin, pressing into his throat, sliding back through his hair as her lips pressed closer. At those moments, she always whispered to him questions, endless questions about the art, the colors, what he was feeling, and how he would work the two together. Like a leech. She wanted to know the paintings before they *were* paintings. She wanted it for her own, even though she knew that if he could give it to her—if he could make her see it, deep within her soul—it wouldn't matter. The paintings were not hers, never would be hers.

Mason's vision cleared, or shifted. The bed that was a chair now had spun toward the door, and he could make out the shadows beyond more clearly. Long, slender shadows, like the antennae or feelers of some giant crustacean, shivering along the walls. They glinted with light, translucent. Each left a glimmering light dancing in its wake against the wall . . . each was a different color.

Sweat oozed through every pore in Mason's skin. His hair matted itself to his brow, but he couldn't lift a finger to straighten it, nor to flick away the trickles of blood and sweat teasing his wrists, and his nose, sliding around the curve of his lip and down to dangle maddeningly from the tip of his chin.

The chair flattened at his back. Not like the mattress, not exactly. Taut. It was taut like the skin of drum—like the skin of his face as he tried to work the droplets of sweat free, quivering with the effort. His arms stretched, legs widened and extended to toe-curl against the backdrop. The canvas. Sweat trickled deep forest green down his cheeks and arms.

The shadows drew closer, swirling. At first they brushed against the wall, whispering sandpaper touches just loud enough to keep the voices in the back of his mind from reaching coherency. Then the tendrils of color began to cross, and re-cross, the rainbow-hued blending, twisted and untwisted, very slowly. It was mesmerizing, and Mason felt something deep within his chest growing tight, drawing outward. He fought it, fought to twist his head to the side, but he could not. The canvas behind him grew tighter, and the colors whirled faster. He could not close his eyes.

His heart clenched so tightly it felt as if it would burst. Mason gritted his teeth, shivering wildly, but before he could brace against the pain, it released, and he felt his head dip forward. Fast. The floor rose to his dropping gaze and passed, inches only, his hair brushing the solid wood of the floor and up in back—over and again.

He whipped around, faster and faster, skin stretching and twisting, grinding into his bones. He wanted to scream, but he could not. The only sounds were the voices. Soft, sibilant voices. Hungry voices. Then he stopped. Just for an instant. Long enough to see. Long enough for the world to coalesce into a single solid image.

Long enough to see the endless lengths of straws, joined end to end, groping through the doorway and across the floor toward his feet. If he could have moved his eyelids, they would have shot wider, just as he whipped backward, away and down, and up again. Whirling.

The last sound Mason heard was the clink of colored glass. He didn't know how he knew, but each color had a distinct tone. A voice. Each cold empty bottle cried out to be filled.

The tubes slide nearer with each passing breath. Joined and separate. Each in its place.

"Each thing in its place," his father whispered.

"What do you feel?" Jesse crooned in his ear, her voice like the passing horn of a vehicle on a long, lonely stretch of road. Passing too quickly, high-to-low-to-high. "What do you feel, just when you first . . . touch?"

He whipped back and the tubes, cut to sharp tips, drove into veins, deep, following his motion and wrapping around him.

Mason clenched his heart, but the colors flowed. He felt them, draining slowly, then more quickly, then more slowly. Pulsing. He whirled, back and forth, heard the soft, chuckling laughter as the handles were pulled. Tighter, released, and tighter still.

Then it was gone.

Mason woke to the scents of old sweat and fresh coffee. The blinds had been rolled up to allow far too much sunlight access to his room. He found the drumbeats of music just loud enough on his stereo to make out and not loud enough to hear. He heard the clink of glass—or cups.

Rolling to a sitting position, he crossed his legs, and wrapped his arms tightly around his chest.

Footsteps approached softly, and in the periphery of his vision, he could just make out their shadow.

Jesse entered the room on cat-feet, sleek and smiling. Her hair was brushed back just so, tied with a deep green ribbon, and in her hands she carried a tray. Mason didn't ask where the tray had come from, where she'd found coffee in a home where only the remnant of last week's fast food should remain. The tray held two cups, steaming.

It also held a notebook. A brand-new, spiral-bound green notebook, and a pen. Wrapped tightly around the pen, rubber bands twisted so tightly they should have snapped, rode the tiny plastic man.

Already the letters were forming in his mind. He could see them, lined up like soldiers, even and ordered. Words and images—images and words.

He could see the gleam in Jesse's eyes.

His father's voice whispered through her breath as she leaned closer to his ear. "Each time, you redefine."

Her lips brushed softly at his skin.

"What do you feel?"

# ASIAN GOTHIC

## *Shikhar Dixit*

### 1. The Tracks

The railroad tracks that ran behind our house were where I first became thoroughly acquainted with death. I had a ritual on my off days from school—after eating breakfast, I would go downstairs, outside, and stumble down the rocky hill. I would hit rocks across the tracks with a scrawny stick, or test my balance walking on the rails. Decembers in North India are bitter cold, and though the sun smiles down on you all through winter, its brightness is utterly ineffectual at the task of casting warmth.

Patna's population of homeless found it comfortable, for some odd reason, to camp out across the tracks and drink cheap scotch. When a train announced its imminent approach by shaking the earth, they moved away long enough for it to blast by, then resumed their seats on the chill rails.

Sometimes, though, they fell asleep.

Coming down to the edge of the tracks, I was already slamming rocks into orbit. In my mind, I occupied the center of attention in a national cricket match. My feet grew numb, my face stung from the breeze. I wore only a plain, white kurta. The cuffs of my pants and shirt flapped violently. Selecting a series of larger rocks, I set to hitting them as straight and as far as I could. The stick was tough—once upon a time a tree branch. I selected the biggest rock I could see, lifted it, and

turned it over until a grimace of terror glared up at me. The
mouth stretched wider than seemed possible under lidless eye
sockets, only one of which remained occupied.

A few years later, my father insisted—despite my lack of
the memory—that I would not put it down, even as he and my
mother came running down the incline, summoned by my
screams. The transient's body was long gone, probably miles
down the tracks by then.

Over the following years, my brother and I were to discover
three others; our sisters never played by the tracks. It's odd
only now, as I look back, that this was not a great fear in our
lives. This was routine.

## 2. The Sun Palace

My mother and father moved to Patna in 1942. My father
had gotten a job for Tata Oil Mills. He worked in the capacity
of sales rep at the local distribution center. This was how my
parents started their life together—a promising one. At first
they only rented one bedroom and living room on the spacious
second floor of Suraj Mahal; the kitchen area and bathrooms
were communal. As my mother gave birth, first to my elder
brother, Sandeep, then my older sisters Rachita and Shreya,
they rented more of the second floor, eventually buying all
eleven rooms. They sublet three of these to a family I never
knew, the Avasthis, and two smaller, attached ones to the
Adityal family, whom I fairly grew up with. I came into the
world in 1947, on a rare December night when, strangely, a
harsh rain slapped the concrete balcony in what I imagine was
a staccato patter, increasing the already unbearable cold. The
water tank above the latrines must have echoed faux gunfire
during the deluge.

So I entered the world, the first home I ever knew, Suraj
Mahal, whose name means, ironically, "The Sun Palace." The
hands of our midwife caught me, swaddled me in a fresh blanket, and delivered me into the proud, strong cradle of my father's arms.

A year later, out came my younger sister, Ankita, and a year after that, our clan was completed by Reema's winsome cries. But only my birth was accompanied by a rainstorm, and as I was to learn later, something else far more aberrant.

At three years old, I was energetic, always on the run from my parents and older siblings, and only when they needed me to run off and play, inconveniently underfoot. I remember none of this, but I've been told stories of how I would race out of Sandeep's and my bedroom, grasp the ornate, wooden railing of the front-facing balcony, and begin squeezing myself through the bars. My father would come careering around the corner, snatch me up, and deliver two quick slaps to my bottom. I would cry for about five minutes, then happily wander about my games. They watched me constantly, and I could not leave the rooms unaccompanied by Sandeep.

I behaved in this manner for the next two years, wild, free of the burdens of school, and despite the birth of my baby sister, far more demanding of my mother's time, for Ankita was always a quiet and manageable child.

Of my fifth year, I remember only two things unaided by my family's stories. I remember walking down Station Road with Sandeep, Rachita, and Shreya, towards school, my meal box swinging easily in my right hand, stuffed as it was with *daal*, *bhaat*, *aloo*, and moist, cold *chapati*. We wore our uniforms, black trousers (skirts for my sisters) with white dress shirts, and black shoes, our school's crest embroidered onto our sleeves. Station Road was full of children, lines of them laughing, screaming excitedly. There were so many people that I felt only delight at the prospect of my impending education; I had not known there could be so many people in the world. It was a happy, blustery hot morning, with the sky a bottomless cerulean—crisper than any in my memory before that. The sun poking its head from the east cast long, cool shadows across the asphalt, the shadows of bulbous, black and white autos parked here and there along the sides of the street. I don't recall how the rest of that day actually went.

My other recollection is of sliding from my bed one night, an urgent call of nature hurrying me out into the hallway and towards the latrines. Just in front of the row of two baths and two latrines, a rectangular opening in the roof allowed a clear view of the water tank atop them. An old, dark-skinned woman—skin so dark that I could only think of it as *kali*, utterly black—stood atop the tank, cleaning. It seemed too late—with the crescent moon hanging above, gilding a rectangular patch of concrete at my feet—to be cleaning anything. I rushed into the latrine and let a stream of urine slap the cold stone basin in the grimy floor. The door creaked open slightly behind me. As I stepped out, I happened to glance up at the tank, curious as to why this cleaning woman should be working so late. My mother and father were not tyrannical people; they treated our servants as friends. In India, all the middle-class had servants; it was not an indication of status among the rich. Even the "untouchable" class, *bhanghi*, were not regarded as they once had been, for these were the forties. But I was only five, and the simple truth was this—that while I was not then aware of class structure, I knew my parents would never assign such a dangerous task so late in the night.

When I looked up again, I found only the golden tint of moonlight glimmering off the curved surface of the tank.

### 3. The Monsoon

My seventh June opened with the heaviest monsoon season I could recall. The State of Bihar, as far north as it was, took the brunt of the storms as they drifted down from the Himalayas. Patna was a well-planned city, accustomed to hundreds of years of flooding, and fairly flat at its high elevation. Most of the rain rolled out of our city and flowed south, joining the Ganges where the rest of Everest's thawed snow raced towards the Indian Ocean. Our summers were spent playing games inside the house and staring wistfully at the muddied landscape, the railroad tracks virtually invisible behind the wall of torrential assault.

This season was far more brutal, however, and gusts reaching fifty kilometers per hour turned the pelting droplets into horizontal projectiles. We were forced to hide in our rooms as the open hallways were made unpleasantly wet. I played gin rummy with Shreya, while Sandeep lay on the floor, toiling away at the flank-view of a tank with pencil and newsprint. His eraser continually ripped and wore gouges through the drawing, and within an hour, he surrendered with a disgusted grunt. My father had stayed home. The visibility was too poor for travel. I could hear laughter from across the hall, where Rachita played with my younger sisters. Shreya, Sandeep, and I considered ourselves above such nonsense. We were "grown up" now, and uninterested in the pursuits of children. Rachita, on the other hand, I'd been certain would one day become a schoolteacher.

As the day wore on, my mother and father sent Shreya, Sandeep, and I across the hall. They insisted that Reema and Ankita take an evening nap with them. It was a custom for children and adults, not those of us who considered ourselves in-between. We slapped our way across the wet floor and found ourselves drenched even before we had reached the other bedrooms. I spotted Sigit Adityal, standing before the latrines, glaring up at the opening in the roof. I couldn't imagine how he was able to breathe while that cloudburst battered his face. Then we were inside, drying ourselves off, shamelessly stripping off our clothes as only young siblings could.

As we sat laughing, playing more cards, the power flickered off. Sandeep lit an oil lamp and stood it on the corner table. Shreya made a lame attempt at a ghost story that would not have been scary had the punch line not been accompanied by an ear-shattering scream. I was the first one out into the hallway, and as such, I could never be really sure of what I saw. Vishi Adityal stood before the back railing, biting her knuckles. I could not see Sigit anywhere. Something wavered above the latrines, indistinct, like a smudged pane of glass. Then my siblings were past me, gazing over the railing.

I kept trying to reconcile what I'd seen, but before I was quite aware of what was happening, my father angrily dragged me indoors. Sirens cut the steady thrum of the deluge in half. When my mother went out to comfort Vishi, covering her in a thick blanket, I caught the flicker of red light suspended in streaking spherules of rain. The puddles in the hall seemed painted in blood, but I realized before my father slammed the door, that this was the reflected light of the ambulance's beacon.

When my father locked eyes with me, I saw something there—secret knowledge? Complicity? I could not label it exactly, but a warning to me seemed buried within. "Do not let your sisters attend the latrines alone, do you understand? You are their brother and you must protect them at all times." I pondered his strange words to me for the rest of the night. The next morning, when I asked my mother what he'd meant, she shrugged. She honestly didn't seem to understand.

That was the thing about her. My mother never understood any of it—the fear, the paranoia, the superstitious admonitions. She was a practical woman, my mother.

The months that followed were fearful and quiet. We all slept during the long rains, and on the few days when the sunlight broke through, we would gleefully erupt from our isolation and run about the town all day. At night, we had taken to going to the latrine in groups. It reached the point where there were two pilgrimages nightly, first around midnight, and then again around three A.M. I always kept an eye on my sisters, but occasionally, Shreya or Rachita would grow abruptly brave and skeptical—in imitation of our mother, no doubt—and sneak out alone.

We never spoke again of Sigit Adityal or his strange plummet to the concrete below. Sometimes, I would wander outside, to the very spot where he impacted, and imagine that I could see the design his splattered mind had painted, but there was nothing to see. The rains had washed it away after it happened.

## 4. The Empty Rooms

So there I had stood in the company of death, but still we had not been formally introduced. I never saw what remained of Sigit Adityal, nor did I view any other calamity of the flesh until I was twelve—on the cusp of adolescence—when I mistook a human head for a large stone. And once grasped in my hands, I could not put it down. That is what my father told me.

Another time, during my twelfth year, I came in late from playing. My friends were hooligans. I will not lie about that. They would scare away the vagabonds on the tracks with lengths of chain, or steal cigarettes from the tobacconist down Station Road. For me to pretend otherwise would have been a grand insult to my father, who somehow always knew these things.

So I stepped into my room two hours after sundown, and there sat my father, drunk. He was not the pleasant, swaying, loudmouthed drunk we so enjoyed playing with during *Diwali*, that lovable patriarch who would carry us about on his shoulders and playfully wrestle with us until we each grabbed a wrist, an elbow, a hand, and dragged him to the ground with us. This was quiescent darkness. Pinpoints of light jabbed out at me from beneath sleek, heavy lids. The rank odor of scotch reached across the room and froze me in the doorway. He sat very still on my bed. Sandeep was nowhere in evidence, and I felt certain my father had sent him to sleep in our sisters' room. I immediately began crying. "S-sorry. I-I didn't d-do anything." While this was not precisely true (I had shoplifted a cricket ball under the impelling gazes of my older hooligan friends), it turned out to be irrelevant. He waved my weepy protests aside, as if these were all misdemeanors—and they were just that, paltry children's games that paled in contrast to the weight my father carried upon his soul.

I was on the brink of confessing every crime I'd ever committed when he said, "She is dead now seventy years, and still, she is not tired of falling."

Pretending ignorance is a pointless gesture around my father. I only nodded, and to my incomprehensible disconsolation, he smiled. It was the weariest expression I'd ever seen on my father's face. My throat bloated with sorrow; I ran into his arms. He held me tight, then, and sang to me until I appeared to drift off. He was aware however, that I was wide-awake. Caressing my head, then, he told me the story of my birth night.

*They were a vibrant, artistic family named the Avasthis. A man, a woman, a boy, and a girl—their names are not important. They were always happy. A type of family that has become rarer with the passage of years, they were truly altruists and artists, lovers of life and, as my father called them, bourgeois philanthropes. When my mother grew ill during her pregnancy with Shreya, Ashla Avasthi stayed night and day with her, feeding her teaspoonfuls of water or turmeric and honey. She also delivered Rachita, swaddled her in soft towels and delegated shifts to our family during which someone would sit with the newborn and carefully observe her. Anand Avasthi drove my nervous wreck of a father to and from work for the seventy-two-hour period of emergency. They brought my family through the crisis, and through careful, personal attention, lovingly delivered Shreya, and later Rachita in the same manner.*

I knew then, as my father described them to me, that the many paintings and sketches that decorated our apartments were provided by the Avasthis. They were, my father said, the ultimate affirmation of life.

Every one of them perished on the night of my birth.

*My mother was a champion carrier by then, and she went about performing her daily chores, even as her water broke. Calmly retiring to bed, she awaited Ashla's arrival. As the contractions grew closer, my father summoned Sinha, the midwife of his supervisor's daughter.*

*December is not a time for rain in India, but much like the monsoon that accompanied Sigit's fall, there was horizontal rain blasting through our hallway. I was delivered safely and without urgency, and only after my father had held me for half an hour, he went to pound on the Avasthis' doors. They had explanations to provide, as our family had become so dependent upon them at birthing time.*

Here, as I lay across my father's lap, he described to me the burden he'd carried with him for twelve years.

*There were three heads, each carefully arranged—the stump of each neck centered with obsessive care on its own ceramic plate—and positioned such that their wide eyes glared directly at my father as he stepped into the kitchen. Each sat in a halo of blood. Like gravy, the blood had been pooled so that it barely touched the plates's ornamental rim.*

*The rest of them was stacked neatly in the back of the children's bedroom—mother, father, and son—bodies like bags of flour. The daughter, an introverted adolescent of fifteen, was named Purnina. She was nowhere to be seen.*

"Girls of that age are powerful, and disturbed. You and Sandeep, you have responsibilities you *must* take seriously . . . especially here in Suraj Mahal. No more running with your hooligan friends, do you understand?"

I'd opened my eyes and nodded then. It was the most solemn vow I would ever take, and utterly useless as it turned out. There was nothing that could be prevented.

*Purnina was found in one of the latrines, her wrists opened so deep that the knife she used was still embedded in her left arm, her right hand curled tightly around it— so tight with rigor that the knife was cremated with the rest of her. There was no doubt among the Patna Police that it was the same knife that had been used on the rest of the Avasthis.*

Realization struck me. My siblings and I had always assumed the three rooms cross from the Adityals were storage. They remained locked, so we never wandered in, nor did we want to. Had it always had this air, that I would not want to go inside even if it occurred to me that I could? My father admitted, when I asked him, that all three rooms were completely empty. "Another family tried to live there," he said, "and they left with my blessings after only two weeks. The woman miscarried three nights before they left. They told me that the midwife I had sent for had seemed unstable. How could I recommend someone like that? they asked.

"Of course, I never sent for any midwife. I do not know who delivered their dead child to them."

"Why have you told me all this?" I asked.

I thought, *I am only twelve. How can you tell me a story like this?* I was not angry or scared, however. I was proud, for my father had confided a great secret in me. Of all my family, he had shared the truth with me. He did not answer me. Instead, he said, "Next time you think you see something on the water tank, look at its feet. Otherwise, do not ever deign to look at it again. And soon, I will obtain a transfer at work and we will move somewhere else."

He'd silently left my room sometime during the night, after I had drifted off to sleep. When I awoke in the early-morning hours, the hallway floor was still damp, but streams of moonlight hovered in desolate puddles just outside the canopy. I shuffled bleary eyed to the latrine, alone, for I was a man of the house and not one of my sisters. Nothing hovered over the water tank. I longed to see her visage, to understand how a vision in the night could make a teenage girl murder her entire family, or make a sane man jump to the concrete.

I conducted my business and imagined the head from the railroad tracks—that it might be afloat in the hole in the floor beneath me, tasting my urine as the amber tides slapped its bloated features.

I ran from the latrine, back to my room, suddenly—and sensibly—afraid of the things I had seen, heard, and thought, on this day of my twelfth year in Suraj Mahal.

## 5. The Head

I found two more heads upon the tracks. One, thrown nearly fifty meters up the hill from the tracks, was incomplete below its left eye. Tangles of fibers and chipped bone dangled from the neck and jagged break in its cheek. It did not look human, and so, seemed far less disturbing than the first. Sandeep, of course, called the police himself, and everything was squared away in good measure.

When I found the third, just days after my seventeenth birthday, I was a sturdy man of five feet, ten inches. Wiry muscles wound about my arms and legs, and my pectorals bulged like stone from my chest. I had been working the past few summers at the railyard, loading and unloading supplies, bringing home my keep. It felt good to work my body, to feel like a force in a world of forces—one not easily taunted or pressured by the hooligan friends he'd abandoned years ago.

I hadn't seen the figure atop the tank in several years, though I initially spent every night making frequent visits to the latrines. My mother accused me of having an ailment of the bladder and kidneys. One did not argue with her about health matters. I had to be officially cleared by a multitude of doctors before she would let the matter drop. Through all this, my father watched me knowingly—and disapprovingly. I stopped obsessively stalking the spirit roughly when I developed an interest in the opposite sex. By the time I found the third head, I no longer believed any of it had happened—but I still escorted my frightened sisters to the toilets in the dead of night. It was a duty hammered into me early on. Besides, it seemed, at least, that my sisters believed it.

I was not at the tracks for play, but to confront a pack of drifters who screamed during the night—throwing about bottles and laughing at odd hours—waking my younger sisters, who slept fitfully. Sandeep, Shreya, and Rachita had gone off to college in Bombay, and my father relied on me to deal with these matters.

When the screams awoke me, I naturally thought those same drifters were at it again. I hurriedly pulled on my kurta, stepped into my slippers, and went downstairs and out into the night. Moonless, and trapped under a thick cover of clouds, the sky offered no illumination. I knew the way still, so I did not bother with a lantern. To me, fear and surprise were useful tools in scaring off ruffians and bums. I grabbed only a cricket bat, swinging it about in rehearsal.

A man stood upon the tracks, occluded by the substantial

darkness. I yelled for him to leave, told him that sensible, hardworking people made their homes here. This was not a place for celebration. I advanced on him, hulking as menacingly as I could, swinging the bat in swift, sure strokes before me. If he decided to attack me, I could send his skull into orbit, bounce it off the Soviet Sputnik. I beheld his emerald eyes—eyes that suggested an ancestry in northern-most India. Perhaps Kashmir. I groped for the right words as, wide-eyed (*in terror?*), he glanced over my shoulder and rushed towards me. . . .

I cannot accurately relate what happened after that display; I can only express the final result . . . that I stood upon the tracks, alone, in the company of *a disembodied head*, which I held close. No corpse lay within my visual range, and *the cricket bat was nowhere in evidence*, even after several harried minutes of searching.

My kurta seemed stained with darkness—coated by its inky presence—and the cloth adhered to my skin with a moist, warm cling.

I looked down upon his face, touched finally, after all these years, by terror.

I raised my hand to my face, letting the head drop to the tracks once more. I could see no way around the facts. Stripping off my clothes right there upon the tracks, I climbed the hill to my house and immediately went to the latrines. A cold bucket of water remained from the previous morning's draw upon the tank. Taking a rag, I cleaned the blood from my body (and hair!) with rough, painful strokes, until, to my eyes, I appeared clean. Crimson water whirlpooled into the drain, and with strategically directed spills of water from the bucket, I erased any evidence of it. Then I crept to my room, which I alone occupied now, and put on fresh clothes.

I called the police.

They never questioned me. The bloody kurta upon the tracks was accepted as belonging to the decapitated head, never mind that the body was gone, apparently unclothed—never mind that, for some reason, the trains did not even pass through that night. No one ever asked me any questions.

After all, he was only a vagrant.

And what of his eyes? Those emerald eyes, that had beheld the back of my house in such terror. Where had they gone? How did I come to be holding this man's head, all other evidence that he had existed gone, only empty, black eye sockets remaining in his face?

Upon waking the following morning, I found Ankita out on the railing—*walking* upon the railing, her bare feet struggling to maintain a grasp on the wood. I stood absolutely still once I noticed her. "Ankita," I whispered, so low that she could not have heard me. I was terrified of scaring her off the railing.

She crossed back and forth like a tightrope walker, her hands extended to the sides. She only glared ahead of her. She wavered momentarily and my heart nearly ground to a halt. As she regained her balance, I felt overcome by a numbing uncertainty. I had felt like the man of the house for some time now; now I felt like a child.

Raising her head, she looked through the opening above the latrines. Following her gaze, I saw nothing—only the glint of early-morning light against the water tank's cool metal.

Forcing myself to take action, I began to creep towards her. She took no notice of my approach, didn't even seem to know I was there. I closed the distance, pace by anguished pace, until only a meter or so separated my rescuing arms from her frail, precariously poised body.

I stepped closer still, until I could put my arms around her, and did so, pulling her into an embrace and sweeping her off the railing. I held her tightly, shivering, crying. The terror I felt . . . I wanted to move, then—with or without my family— away from this hell where the very air seemed to continuously conspire against us.

As we broke fast later that morning, I related the incidents of the previous night and this morning—leaving out the mysterious disappearance of the vagrant's body and the bloodying of my kurta—to my father. I asked him, then, point-blank, in the presence of my mother and two sisters, "Who is she? Who was she and what does she want?"

"She was nobody—just the foreman's wife. She fell from

the roof, above the latrines, before Suraj Mahal was completed. Why was Ankita outside alone? Why were you not with her?"

"She did not wake me. I only happened out into the hallway so that I could uses the latrines." The revelation that Ankita had not even tried to awaken me thoroughly shook my father. A familiar terror twisted his expression again. Things were out of control.

That evening, he came to my room. "We are leaving tomorrow. I thought, if we were vigilant and good, if we prayed daily to Shiva, this thing could not hurt us. Tonight Ankita and Reema will sleep with us. You will leave your door open so that any noise will wake you. Tomorrow, we will leave for Bombay."

"Where will we stay?"

"With Chachi. I will find us a good place quickly. For you, it will be a short walk from home to university when you begin in the autumn. And we can have Sandeep, Shreya, and Rachita back with us to help out."

I merely nodded, suddenly filled with a blossoming hope I could not recall feeling in ages. The skies had finally cleared— the monsoon of years had blown over.

The next day both Ankita and Reema were dead, and my hopes dead with them. I had failed as their older brother, as the man of the house.


## 6. The Life

They had sleepwalked, of course, both of them slipping from my parents' bed so stealthily that my mother and father remained oblivious as Ankita and Reema went outside and climbed upon the rail. Even *I* managed to sleep through all this, so dead-tired was I from the previous days' events.

We moved to Bombay several weeks later—after the cremations had been completed, and Suraj Mahal properly sold. I never asked my father about the new tenants. I didn't want to know.

By degrees, life regained a measure of normalcy in Bombay. The streets were noisy every night, and the daytime world occupied by a bustling race for success. Bombay was a busy city, and this suited me fine. Our toilet was indoors, a regular bathroom of sorts, and our water supply was piped in directly from the water treatment plant.

I did well in college and graduated with honors in chemistry. There, at university, I met the woman who would be my wife. Sarala Gupta—a fine, lovely, and very intelligent girl from a wealthy family—swept *me* off *my* feet, and despite my middle-class status, was handed to me with a suitably manageable dowry. I graduated to a higher caste by this marriage. I was now a Brahmin. Worldly, respectable, and imminently beyond the sway of superstitious belief. With our degrees in hand, we left India.

We flourished, bred, and worked. The American dream embraced us. Our son grew up bilingual and quiet. Our daughter turned rebellious and wild. I made fragrances for Colgate-Palmolive. Sarala designed software—primarily computer games. Our level of wealth tripled. Quadrupled.

Rahkihs, our son, attended Harvard and walked away with a law degree. Our daughter, Sheila, attended Rutgers University as a visual arts major. She dropped out. She disappointed us. She fought us every step of the way.

She fled to reside with her maternal grandparents. I had forgotten where they came from; I had failed to realize that life for me was a spiral of coincidence designed to constrict the very souls from my loved ones. They were wealthy, after all. The Guptas owned many properties. It wasn't until my only daughter, my precious, lovely, vibrant wild daughter, whose face was the very replica of my sister Ankita's—it was not until after she was dead that I knew the name of the family that occupied Suraj Mahal after my family.


## 7. The House

This thing had stalked me around the world.

But it also resided *in* me. I could never reconcile it, any of it. Long after Rahkihs had made his way in the world, raking it in through the subtle art of personal-injury litigation, his mother, my wife—to whom I had failed to be very much of a husband after our daughter died—died herself.

I found her slumped on the floor of our living room, emaciated as she had become, her eyes thrown wide with the final shock of her death. Her hands lay trapped beneath her, stiff and clenched into tight fists. I felt nothing, for my destiny was death. This was why I stayed away from my mother and father, my brother and remaining sisters . . . my son.

There was a crumpled note trapped in her rigor-locked hands. It was not delivered to me until after she had been taken to the morgue. The doctors said that her brain had filled with blood when a vessel ruptured near the front of it.

No writing adorned the small page, only a drawing. A simplistic cylinder with a pointed roof, a squiggly star upon its side to signify moonlight.

After the cremation, I accompanied the ashes back to my homeland. I was fifty-seven, yet appeared seventy, and as I watched my reflection in the plane's window, a flicker of movement cut the air behind me. Just a blur really. I was close to home by then.

I took a connection from Bombay straight to Patna.

At the house—furnished differently now, with fully functional western toilets occupying the rooms that were once the Avasthis' apartments—I mourned with her parents. They mourned for their lost daughter. I cried for myself.

The latrines had been converted into a large storage closet. The tank was still atop it, a rusted hulk badly in need of removal. Although the rest of Suraj Mahal seemed renovated and modernized, the tank remained as it was, ravaged by nature, but untouched by time.

During my days in Patna, I asked around. No one remembered anything about the foreman or his wife. Neighbors as old as the street itself, older than my father, swore that the house had always been there, before Patna became a thriving metropolis. My life seemed covered by layer upon layer of lies. Angry, I called Bombay. My family's phone had been disconnected. A series of calls led me to the revelation that my mother had passed on years before. My brother's whereabouts were a complete mystery. The Guptas hadn't maintained any more contact than I had.

My older sisters . . . well, I had grown tired of searching, because I knew deep down inside that they were gone, one way or the other. I wondered about my father . . . not where he was—I was indifferent to that—but who he had been. The man who had told me that story long ago, stroking my forehead as I lay upon his lap—what else had he seen? What else had he *done*?

One night I walked out into the hall. I glared up at the tank atop the shed.

There she was, wiping down the tank, finally allowing me the glimpse I'd awaited so long. Her feet were twisted around, so that her toes pointed behind her. She turned and looked upon me. Beyond the apparent madness in her eyes, beyond the wretched condition of her mashed, fractured face and the cut bisecting her body at the neck, her eyes told me a story of madness and death. I cannot share this story with you, for its logic cannot be explained—it has to be arrived at through years of wretched loss and suffering. It has to be cultivated in the blood of hapless vagrants and unwary daughters.

I'll only tell you this. Young daughters do not kill their loved ones. It is wearied, soulless fathers who see the strange logic in such a solution. Only such a man might have allowed his daughters to slip from their bed in the middle of the night and plummet to the hard floor of oblivion. Only such a man might have done whatever he could to complicate the delivery of yet another crying, hungry mouth into the world.

# HELL CAME DOWN

## *Tim Lebbon*

I went looking for him where it was dry and parched, where the skeletons of cattle decorated the outskirts of town like grotesque, bleached baubles, where children lay on pavements and breathed shallowly, painfully as their mothers tried to squeeze a drop of moisture from sagging breasts, where the sun had leached all color and the facades of buildings presented a uniform paleness, where streambeds were crazy paving punctuated here and there with dead weeds, where people wandered in a haze to and from the watering hole that was little less than mud now, mud that could be squeezed for a few precious drops, sometimes, if they were lucky. A place where death was sometimes a release, and cadavers were never put to waste. Dead fathers gave their children a source of sustenance for a day or two. They would have wanted it that way.

I knew Lucien would be here. Where better to find a rain-maker?

Heads turned my way as I entered the town. The dying people heard the slosh of water in my canteen, a sound that doubtless haunted their dreams, waking and sleeping. Some looked pleadingly, others scheming. They saw the rifle across my shoulders and perhaps thought better of it, but even without that I would not have been concerned. I had other ways of protecting myself.

I looked for signs of his presence. It was no use asking be-

cause they all thought he was trying to help them: Lucien
bringing down rain onto parched lands, urging the clouds to
form and the droplets to condense, conjuring life back into a
dead place and a dying people. They thought this even though
he had yet to bring a storm . . . of rain, at least. In Birmingham, a shower of frogs had emerged from the clear blue skies
and splattered across the ground around him. I had not seen it
happen, but I had heard others talk of it. In Bristol, dogs and
cats, clogging the remaining streams and watering holes with
rancid bodies crawling with fleas and God knew what else.
Some of the cats had two tails. Some of the dogs were new
breeds.

Still, they worshiped him.

The man shrugged, looking as embarrassed as a man slowly
dying of thirst and hunger could. "A frog." He had eaten it, his
expression made that clear. Its blood, its mucus, its fluids . . .
moisture of a kind.

"I need to find him," I said. "He's making all this worse."

"No, he's making it better!"

"Then where are the rains?" I roared, standing and advanc-
ing on the man, angry and desperate and so willing to cause
pain . . . though I had caused enough already. The trail of Lucien's devastation across the land displayed that so well. "Show
me how he's helped!"

"He said . . . he said that if I talked—"

"I'll give you water!"

"No, I can't, he said—"

I grabbed him by the shirt, lifted him and pressed him
against an old poster for Chelsea buns. "Tell me where he is!"

"The Courthouse. Last I heard he . . . he was . . ." The baker
gagged, his eyes turned up in his head, he bit straight through
the end of his own tongue.

I dropped him. I didn't want to be covered in his mess.

The young man who looked so old slipped to the dusty tiled
floor of his shop, twitching and twisting himself into unnatural
shapes, arms and legs entwining as whatever was inside sought
escape. His eyes bulged, as did his stomach. He screeched, a
high keening sound that scared the few remaining birds outside

into flight, and set a rabid dog growling somewhere in the distance. His hands clawed. I backed away. His nails scored into his throat and chest as he ripped at himself.

I was standing outside on the pavement when his stomach ruptured and a sickly grey mess spilled across the floor, steaming precious fluids to condense and dry on the walls of his shop. He twitched one more time, then was still.

Lucien was covering his tracks well, but not well enough. Perhaps, despite all his powers, he was not expecting me.

I had to find the Courts.

I was not a bad teacher. It was Lucien who was a poor pupil. My real mistake was in not seeing that, and this is why I had to pursue him across the country, closing in day by day, until that time I confronted him in the old Courts in Usk.

He had come to me as a boy and begged to be shown the weird ways, and even then he displayed some level of barely restrained potency that made me seem an amateur. I took him in. He had fled his family years before, his peculiar gift effectively ostracizing him, even from them. He had worshiped, venerated, and heeded me, absorbing what I taught, listening when I warned. He was a strong young man haunted by what his mind contained. And that should have been my first warning: It haunted him, but did not control him. He fought it. He fought his gift from God.

I should have killed him there and then.

I walked along the town's main street, trying to smile at one or two people but seeing only pain and fear sent back at me. The heat had been so great for so long that some of the buildings were crumbling, their brick- and stonework destroyed from within, heated and expanded and cracked to ruin. On the left, an old antiques store had lost its window and surround. The sign still hung above, letters faded and forgotten, but all it housed now was a mountain of yellowed books. A fire waiting to happen. And indeed, farther along the street there was a charred gap in the row of shops, a place where fire had come and taken its due. A few roof members had survived, protruding from the black mass of stone and concrete, thinned out by the flames. There was something else lying there as well, in among the wreckage. It glinted white, but only because carrion creatures had picked its cooked bones clean. Carrion creatures and, perhaps, carrion humans as well.

I reached an intersection of two roads. There was a banner strung across the street from years ago, a bitter in-joke that the townsfolk seemed still to be playing upon themselves. It read: USK IN BLOOM. They had been gardeners, flower growers, feeding into the ground the water which they so craved now.

It had not rained for over a year. The country was in ruin.

I saw a bank, a restaurant, a clothes shop, all totally redundant now that famine and disease was grinding the last dregs of humanity into the soil. Some people still tried to keep a hold on what they had once been, and I was sure I saw the shadowy movement of someone behind the bank's counter. Perhaps even now they counted useless millions and slipped out with a secret note here, a note there, slowly accumulating a fortune as worthless as the dry riverbed, or the underground water pipes that had cracked in the heat and given their final precious drops to the dry earth.

"You!" someone shouted. "Hey, you!"

I could not locate the caller at first, so I closed my eyes and found them in my mind. Above and behind. I turned and looked up at an open window. There was a woman leaning out, naked and filthy, hair knotted and skin cracked beneath the dirt. Dried blood clotted around her joints. Her eyes were wild, at least the one I could see, squinting at me along the length of a shotgun.

"The water. Throw it up."

"You really think it will save you?"

"You think I give a fuck? It's for my baby." She was mad with thirst and hunger, I could tell that much at least, but her aim never wavered: my head. I could see right into the barrels.

I closed my eyes again and moved up to her, felt into the gun, saw that it was loaded. No bluffing, then. She really meant it.

I opened my eyes and leaned slowly against the wall beside me. I made certain that my hands stayed at my sides. There was no way I could reach my rifle in time. Besides, there were other ways of stopping her.

"Don't make me kill you," I said quietly.

She laughed. "Your head will be all over the road before you even touch that gun. Now throw up the canteen and you can go on. I mean it. I won't kill you."

"I know you won't," I said, "but the water will kill your baby. It's black water."

"He's drunk dirty water before."

"Never black."

I closed my eyes one more time and moved back up there, fingering my way into her mind this time, desperate not to see what was inside there but more desperate not to have to kill her. I knew how risky this was. I could spend precious seconds convincing her, or I could just slip in and throw a switch, kill her painlessly and without a sound, drop her to the floor and go on my way. I had killed before, many times. I would do so again, soon, when I found Lucien. But it was ironic that now, with my own head framed by a shotgun's line of fire, one more life seemed so precious among a billion dead.

She was mad. There were visions in there that terrified me, perverted truths that lied even to themselves, a fragrant paranoia that stank of neglect and pain and decades of abuse, stemming from long before the drought and famine, rooted in a past so dark that even the black water would taste sweet in comparison. I closed my mind to these places and tried to pass through, feeling the soapy touch of terror attempting to drag me from my path and lose me in the depths, places where direction was lost and simply being was all there was, being awed, being feared, being trapped.

At last I found the center of her, the place where all sanity had been driven and where, even now, madness was eating away at its edges like an eternally patient caterpillar chewing at the boundaries of the mightiest forest. She had been a good woman once, a mother and a wife and a librarian, fighting a difficult past by revelling in a content present, little suspecting what the future held.

Then I showed her the black water.

"Get that fucking shit away from me!" she screeched, seeing instantly, not giving me a chance to withdraw before panicking.

I pulled out and went back to myself, opened my eyes, stunned by her quick reaction and suddenly knowing my mistake. She may be mad, yes, but she was desperate as well. She had a child to save when her own life was already wasted.

I had time to slip inches down the wall before she pulled the trigger.

Most of the shot struck the brickwork directly where my head had been a second before. Shattered brick rained down on my head and shoulders, and I felt something plucking at my forehead and right eye, something that felt cold but quickly turned hot, white hot, burning its way into my head and down through my neck. I screamed, fell to the ground, and put my hands to my face. The ruin of my eye was leaking from its socket. My good eye was blinded by pain. The blood and fluid was thick and slimy like a broken, raw egg.

Any normal man would have died or curled up with the pain. I stood, unslung the rifle from my pack, and opened up at the window. I tried to probe at the woman but the pain was too great. I could not detach properly, and besides, I had the feeling she had fled. The sight returned slowly to my left eye, fading in from a bright white to a semblance of what was around me, and I emptied the clip at the window and those either side of it. Glass smashed, stonework spat out powdered eruptions, a bullet ricocheted along the street and starred the windscreen of an abandoned car.

Then I turned and ran. In my blinding agony I ran without direction. I automatically replaced the magazine in the rifle, but no one seemed keen to stop or tackle me. I must have presented a fearsome sight, a big man with bloodied face, ragged eye socket, water canteen, and rifle, sprinting along streets where nowadays people could barely crawl.

I ran for five minutes. My blood pumped, my heart thumped, I bled out the pain. By the time I stopped, my eye had ceased bleeding and was already scabbing over. The pain had reduced to a bright throb, flashing into my head as if my eye was still there and I was looking directly at the sun. I slumped against a garden wall, unhooked the canteen and took a swig of the black water.

It tasted awful, but it invigorated me, giving sustenance and strength and power of mind and will with one swig.

And I suddenly realized the truth. Things had come to a head without me even instigating it. I had to catch Lucien now, within the next few minutes, because he would have heard the shooting, and if he'd learned anything good from me it was an aggressive instinct for self-preservation. Wherever he was, whatever he was doing, he would be readying to leave. If I lost track of him now it would take me weeks, or even months to find him again, wounded as I was. Weeks or months may be far too late for this place. I may not even have days.

In Devon, I had found a whole village killed by the scorpions Lucien had brought down from the sky when he was trying to conjure rain. When I arrived, the air was still tainted with his pain, his guilt, his growing madness. He was trying, trying again, striving to get it right, but wherever he went, things were getting worse, the manifestations matching his increasing frustration. There were over five hundred bodies in that place. They were swollen and bloated and burst from the effects of the scorpions' poison. Some of the creatures had been as big as my hand. Many had possessed a sting at both ends.

It could only get worse.

I pushed myself from the wall and went to the nearest house showing signs of habitation. I probed inside, saw that they had no weapons of threat to me, smashed on the door until it gave way. There was no time for niceties.

A little girl scampered into a room to my left. Her father stepped into the corridor, a short-bladed knife in his hand and a look of resigned terror in his eyes. He was ready to die for her. He looked about set to die anyway, all the signs of hunger and thirst evident on his face. It was obvious that he had been giving all the food and drink he could scrounge or steal to his daughter.

I grabbed him, shoved him against the wall, knocked the knife aside.

"I'll let you live if you tell me where the old Courts are in the next three seconds."

"Your . . . your eye."

"One."

I was choking him. He could barely talk.

"Two."

"I . . . I . . ."

"Three."

"Show you . . . I'll show you. . . ."

I let him slide down until his feet touched carpet, then I let go. He looked down at the knife on the floor but obviously thought better of it. Rubbing at his bruised neck, he glanced into the room at his daughter, tried to smile at her. She cried at his grimace.

"That way," he said, pointing out the front door and to my right. "Two streets along, then turn left. Iron railings. But I don't know what you want with the Courts . . . they're haunted."

"I know," I said, and although I was lying—I didn't know whether they were haunted or not—I was sure they soon would be. I turned to leave. "Sorry," I muttered. I felt the man's stare, felt him beginning to crumple. His daughter ran to him and he was trying to hide his tears, but he was nearing the end of a life of weakness and loss, hopelessness and shame.

Sometimes I saw far too much to bear.

Lucien was still there.

As I neared the Courts, I saw signs. Cracked paving slabs at first, whatever falling things that had caused their destruction long since vanished. A row of houses with shattered slates, the holes in the roofs adorned with wispy material, flickering like spiderwebs in the subtle breeze. It could have been roof lining, or dusty webs snagged on the broken timbers, or skin. Then living things: a beetle with two heads, scurrying along the gutter on twelve legs; a butterfly spiraling in lazy, pointless circles, its wings a death mask with bleeding eyes; and a hummingbird, probing at withered flowers in its useless quest for sustenance. Alien animals to these shores, perhaps even alien to this world.

Especially the rat. It was as big as a tomcat, and as it ran across the road I saw traces of bloodied ginger fur around its jaws. A tomcat's match as well, evidently. It had a horn protruding from the center of its forehead, serving no purpose other than to give it a hateful appearance.

I turned away and jogged along the street. Each footfall provoked a spike of pain in my head from my destroyed eye socket, but I welcomed it. It told me that I was still alive. The chaos Lucien had caused was my fault, and if half-blindness and constant pain was all the punishment I would receive for such a heinous mistake, then it was light indeed, for I was as guilty as sin.

The Courts were large and imposing. Columns graced the entrance, leaded windows on either side stared out like grey dead eyes, iron railings contained the building within its gardens, once lush, but now brown and dry and dead. There was an old fountain in the front courtyard with a body curved around its central spout. Perhaps whoever had crawled here to die had believed that, if a miracle did occur and water flowed again, they would be revived. Most of the flesh had been chewed away. A denim jacket covered the ribcage. Rings, a silver necklace, and a glittering anklet all touched bone.

I probed inside, carefully so that Lucien would not sense me. He was powerful, but mad with it, a twisted genius. If I was careful he would not notice me.

I gasped. There were things in there . . . I had felt ghosts before but never like this, never in such profusion. And the strangest thing was, they were all new, all recently dead, all inhabiting the same place in this doomed town.

Here, an old woman wandering in a circle, in and out of this world, seeking her husband both here and elsewhere. *Have you seen my Gerald?* she asked. *He's a farmer. . . .*

A young girl, too, barely into her teens, crawling around the ceilings inside as if too afraid to touch the ground. Her mouth was open in a permanent scream. Her skin was raised in grotesque humps, each of them capped with a poison-filled pustule. *The ants, the ants, the ants, the ants . . .*

A man and a woman, husband and wife, twisted together

and merged where something had gored them to death. *I love you . . . love . . . love you . . .* their voices entwined madly, neither of them realizing that they had no reason to haunt.

Lucien's dead, I knew, those who had perished because of his failed efforts, killed by creatures they knew or monsters they did not.

I probed further, trying to ignore the anguish and the pain and the resentment that only the dead can truly feel. I sensed old ghosts, too, ground back into the shadowy realms of this place by the new, fresh anger of the recently dead. And then I found him: Lucien, sitting at a table in the old library, reading from a book written in Latin, able to understand if he so desired but merely skimming the pages, relishing the peace to muster his energies.

I realized how late I had left all this. He was going to try again in minutes, try one more time to put things right where he had done so much wrong. I opened my good eye and glanced at the sky. Thunderheads were forming from nowhere as his energies converged, darkening the sky and bringing yet another false promise of rain. Guilt should have driven me after him sooner, but pride had held me back. The two had torn me apart. They were still tearing, deep inside, sparring with accusatory feelings and a dreadful home truth: That I had created a monster.

*You.*

He had sensed my furtive probings. I withdrew quickly and ran to the front doors, unslinging the rifle. So damn clumsy of me! If he hadn't found me I could have slipped into his mind, distracted him, shot him through a window, then torn him apart inside as he lay there bleeding. I did not want to do it. I hated to have to kill him. But like all mistakes, if I let him live, I knew he would only come back to haunt me again. And there really was no other way to stop him.

I kicked open the doors and ran into the lobby, already lifting the rifle, ready to fire as soon as I burst into the library.

Surprise had gone, but I had speed and strength . . .

. . . which I knew, instantaneously, to be outforced.

He slammed me back against a wall without touching me.

The rifle tumbled from my hands and disappeared beneath a bench in the lobby. The ghosts screamed and I tried to shut them from my mind, but I felt Lucien's fingers in there, rooting around and opening up all the routes to my self, letting in his victims, giving him respite as they poured their rage into me.

I screamed. My wounds bled again.

He emerged from the library. "You," he said, standing before me.

"Lucien, you have to stop!"

"The world is dying! And what have you done to help it? Nothing."

"You'll kill it yourself," I shouted, barely hearing myself above the screams of the dead.

"I'm giving it life," he said. "I'm bringing a storm. A flood. Can't you feel it brewing? Can't you feel the electricity in the air, the hairs on your arms standing on end, your teeth tingling? A storm to wash away the bad and bring goodness once again."

Somehow, I formed words around all the pains in my head, forcing them out, not knowing whether they made sense or not. "Lucien . . . help me help you. I made a mistake with you, I admit it—"

"Admit this, old man! That you're proud and arrogant, and you cannot . . . for . . . a . . . second believe that I've taught myself more."

He pressed me harder against the wall and I felt my lungs compressing, my heart being forced flat, blood pounding in my ears and pouring from my eye.

"Your dead are screaming at me!" I tried to shout, not even knowing if my voice was working anymore. "How many more are you going to make?"

The noise stopped. I fell to the floor. I hugged myself, trying to make sure all my parts were still there.

"Look at me," he said.

I looked up. There was the Lucien I had known, a thin, short man with long hair and a face to match, down-turned eyes that gave him a begging-puppy look, clothes that never seemed to fit. Someone who had never seemed able to leave the angst of his teens behind. Someone with so much power, but who looked so weak.

"I'm a good man," he whispered. "You told me that. I'm here to bring good. I'm going to bring rain and end the famine, because I'm the rainmaker. You told me that, too."

I went to say that he was wrong—that I had been wrong— but my voice did not work.

It had gone dark, an instant dusk. "The storm's beginning," he said. Then he turned his back on me and went outside.

I heard it from where I lay, unable to move, paralyzed by fear and defeat. Lucien roared. I imagined him standing out there with his arms outstretched, his palms facing skyward as he invoked what he thought would be a downpour to save this blighted land. I sensed the ghosts in the building cowering from the fury he imparted, hiding themselves away, the dead fearing something far worse than death.

I tried to stand. I could not. Perhaps it was failure, because I knew even then that I could not stop him. He was right. I was arrogant. I had not for a second believed that he could face me and win.

For a time, I thought he had prevailed. There was a glass atrium in the Courthouse's lobby, and for a long few seconds something pattered wetly onto the frosted-glass canopy above me. I lay on my back and so wished that he had succeeded, but then I knew that was not the case. Rain did not crack glass. Rain did not leave bloody smears behind. Most of all, rain did not scurry away after it had landed, searching for dark places in which to hide.

*No.* I felt Lucien say in my mind. He must have seen something horrible coming down. I resisted the temptation to say I'd told him so; it was too much effort, and I had no energy left.

*No . . .*

Something massive hit the ground outside. The lobby windows blew in, letting in a terrible stench of rot and insides turned out.

*Oh no,* Lucien said again. *I'm sorry. . . .* Perhaps he was even talking to me.

Other things began to fall, bigger and smaller, growling or roaring when they hit. Many of their calls halted instantly, but some went on. Some survived.

I sensed Lucien extinguished like an ant beneath the foot of a giant.

His death should have stopped it. It did not. The storm went on all night.

Lucien was right. He did cause a flood.

I managed to crawl to a place of safety while that long night brought chaos down to earth. I remained hidden in the basement of the old Courts for two days, recuperating and using my battered powers to hide myself when anything came inside to investigate. Once, I heard a creature on two feet drag something across the mosaic-tile floor above me. It grunted, chewed, spat. Sniffed the air. Held still.

I closed my eyes and had to use all my energy to turn it away from me. Its mind was revolting. And victorious.

When I left the Courts, I fled the town as quickly as I could, shielding myself from view with simple but energy-consuming invisibility. The flood was diminishing, but only because the things that had fallen that night were spreading out. I saw a tiger strolling carelessly along the main street; a bulging black mass hanging from a telegraph pole, dropping spiders as big as my head to the ground; something that looked like an alligator but had wings; and a wolf and a bear hunting together. I saw carcasses stripped clean, and the living results of Lucien's final storm were well fed.

The town was obliterated. Every building was damaged, most completely shattered, and as for the inhabitants . . . a limb here, a blood-smeared pavement there. Most of the things that had come down, I knew, were carnivorous. Lucien's final, desperate, anguished attempts had made them so.

I've been hiding in the hills for several weeks, hiding like a criminal . . . and I suppose I am. I trained the person that ended the world, after all.

Sometimes I sense Lucien, a wandering ghost whose powers are ineffectual now that he has moved far, far on. But he still cries, and I cry with him. He was an innocent. I'm the one to blame.

When the things that fell that night finally find me, it will be only what I deserve.

# Classic Science Fiction & Fantasy

**2001: A SPACE ODYSSEY** by Arthur C. Clarke
Based on the screenplay written with Stanley Kubrick, this novel represents a milestone in the genre. Now with a special introduction by the author.
0-451-45799-4

**ROBOT VISIONS** by Isaac Asimov
Here are 36 magnificent stories and essays about Asimov's most beloved creations—Robots. This collection includes some of his best known and best loved robot stories.
0-451-45064-7

**THE FOREST HOUSE** by Marion Zimmer Bradley
The stunning prequel to *The Mists of Avalon*, this is the story of Druidic priestesses who guard their ancient rites from the encroaching might of Imperial Rome.
0-451-45424-3

**BORED OF THE RINGS** by *The Harvard Lampoon*
This hilarious spoof lambastes all the favorite characters from Tolkien's fantasy trilogy. An instant cult classic, this is a must read for anyone who has ever wished to wander the green hills of the shire. This is a must-read for fans and detractors alike.
0-451-45261-5

To order call: 1-800-788-6262